LETTERS FROM VICTOR

LETTERS From VICTOR

Inspired by a true story

NADINE THEISS

Paperback ISBN: 979-8-9907745-4-4
eBook ISBN: 979-8-9907745-5-1

Edited by HEA Author Services
Formatting and interior design by Joanne Martin
Cover design by GetCovers

This is a work of fiction *inspired by a true story*. While the events that form the foundation of this narrative were drawn from real-life correspondence, the characters, dialogue, and plotlines are fictionalized. Any names, characters, places, or incidents that resemble actual persons, living or dead, or real events are purely coincidental or used fictitiously.

Published by Saffron Ink, LLC
Summerville, South Carolina

Library of Congress Control Number: 2025910706

To the ones who whispered,
'There has to be more than this.'
Who dreamed in silence.
Who chased a life they weren't supposed to crave.
This story is your mirror. Your rebellion.
Your permission to break free.

———

For J and D—
You lit the match.
The flame lives on in these pages.

THE SOUNDTRACK

"Unforgettable" – Nat King Cole
"Dream a Little Dream of Me" – Louis Armstrong and the All Stars
"Orange Colored Sky" – Nat King Cole
"I Don't Want to Set the World on Fire" – The Ink Spots
"Moonlight Becomes You" – Bing Crosby
"Bewitched, Bothered, and Bewildered" – Doris Day
"All of Me" – Billie Holiday
"Blue Velvet" – Tony Bennett
"I Get Ideas" – Tony Martin
"I'll Be Seeing You" – Bing Crosby
"They Can't Take That Away From Me" – Ella Fitzgerald & Louis Armstrong
"Come Away With Me" – Norah Jones

AUTHOR'S NOTE

Letters From Victor is a noir romance intended for mature audiences. It contains explicit sexual content and graphic violence, including on-page depictions of murder and execution. These elements are integral to the story and are presented unapologetically. Please be aware that some content may be potentially triggering. I encourage you to proceed with caution and take care of your well-being as you read.

This story was inspired by a true one.

Years ago, I was entrusted with a stack of love letters—written in the early 1950s by a man utterly, hopelessly in love with a woman he was never supposed to have. I never saw her replies, but his devotion burned through every page. The longing. The reverence. The way he spoke to her, as if she were light and salvation and everything in between. With the family's blessing, I set out to honor that kind of love the best way I know how: by writing it down.

But while the original story lit the match, what follows is entirely my own creation. This is not a biography. It's not a factual account. It's a work of fiction, *full stop*. I've invented characters, imagined events, and reshaped timelines to serve the heart of the story. Any resemblance to real people beyond the original inspiration is purely coincidental.

That said... the letters you'll find woven through these pages? *They're real.* Adapted, yes—but drawn from the source. So if you find yourself wondering whether people really wrote like that... they did.

For the dreamers, the rule-breakers, the ones who burn for more—
This story was always meant for you.

Enjoy the journey,
Nadine

PROLOGUE

Frank Jr.
June 2012

There are two ways to leave a hospital: the front door and the back door.

Today I walked out the front.

Mom left by the back.

Or however the deceased are removed.

There's something creepy about dead people's houses. I'd been in Mom's house earlier that morning—when she was still alive. But now that she was dead, everything felt different. Suffocating.

The deafening silence was broken only by the creak of the floorboards and the soft thud of my tennis shoes as I climbed the wooden stairs. Even though the house was empty, it seemed as though Mom's eyes watched me from every photo on the walls.

Artistic black-and-white portraits of her from the 1940s and '50s lined the hallway. My stepdad had been a photographer in his free time, and Mom had always been his favorite subject. She was a bombshell—as odd as it is for a son to say.

I stopped in front of Mom's closed bedroom door, my hand hovering over the knob. As a kid, I was never allowed in their bedroom. Even now, at sixty-four and with them both dead, it still felt wrong to go inside.

I took a deep breath and turned the knob. The door creaked open to reveal the forbidden sanctuary of my parents' private lives. The room was dark, the curtains drawn. I flipped on the lights, illuminating the space that had been off-limits for so long.

Mom's vanity sat in the corner, her hairbrush still strewn with tangled strands of golden hair. Even at eighty-six, she refused to go gray—always a blonde, right to the end. Her perfume bottles were neatly arranged, the scent of Chanel No. 5 lingering like a ghost in the air. I ran my fingers along the edge of the vanity, picking up a thin layer of dust. It seemed wrong that dust could settle so quickly.

I made my way to the vast walk-in closet and opened the door to a rainbow of dresses, suits, and shoes. Mom had always been sharp when it came to clothes. Her closet was a museum of fashion from the last sixty years, and several pieces were even her own designs. I ran my fingers along the silky fabrics, the beading, the embroidery. Each dress was a work of art. It was hard to believe that the woman who had worn these dresses was gone, her body lying cold and lifeless on a slab.

I was supposed to pick out a dress to take to the funeral home—something that would show off her beauty one last time. But as I pushed hangers aside, something on the top shelf caught my eye—a small wooden chest tucked behind a stack of hatboxes. It was ornately carved, the patterns intricate and worn smooth by time. I didn't recognize it.

Curiosity edged out grief, and I pulled it down, my heart ticking faster. The lid didn't budge—it was locked. A quick scan of the closet turned up nothing useful. No key. Just dust and silence. Reaching into my pocket, I flipped open my multi-tool and used the tiniest screwdriver to loosen the latch. A few careful turns, and the plate came free. The box creaked open.

A stack of yellowed letters tied with a faded red ribbon lay nestled atop a bed of old photographs and mementos. I carefully untied the ribbon, the delicate fabric nearly shredding in my hands. The letters were written on onion-skin paper, the ink slightly smudged but still legible. I unfolded the first one—the paper crackling with age—and began to read. The handwriting was elegant, bold, and confident. I recognized it instantly as my stepfather's.

My darling Barbara,

I haven't slept. Every time I close my eyes, I see you there—your smile in the candlelight, the way you reached for my hand when you thought no one was watching.

You have an uncanny way of undoing me without even trying.

I don't know where this path leads, only that I'm already too far along to turn back.

Say you feel the same.

—V

A flush crept up my neck as I read the intimate lines. I should have stopped reading—I knew that. But the box felt like a doorway I'd already stepped through. There was no unseeing what I'd seen. No unreading those words.

I set the letter back in the box, closed the lid, and carried it downstairs. It felt heavier than it should have—like the weight of decades had settled into the wood.

The dining room was still and sunlit, the long table gleaming like it had for every Thanksgiving, every birthday, every ordinary Wednesday night. I sat at the head of the table and gently unpacked the box's contents—letters, photographs, scraps of a life I thought I knew.

One by one, I began sorting the letters, arranging them by date. The earliest was from January 1951. I would have been two years old.

I stepped back and looked at the letters spread across the table—an entire life scattered in ink across paper, each note whispering a piece of a story I had never been told.

A forbidden love. A life stitched together with secrets, seduction, and scandal.

And the gut-punch realization that I hadn't known my mother at all.

1

BARBARA

December 1950

"When did you buy a new dress?" Frank eyed the black satin garment I'd carefully laid across the bed. It was trimmed with a wide leopard-print collar and had a matching belt.

"I made it," I answered, pinning a blond curl into place. The bedroom smelled of powdery pomade and perfume. I put the finishing touches on my updo, the faint sheen of hairdressing cream smoothing the last of the flyaways.

Frank raised his eyebrows and let out a small huff before crossing over to the mirror in the corner of the room.

As I applied my rouge and deep red lipstick, I caught Frank's reflection in the vanity mirror, fumbling with his bowtie. The soft glow of the bedroom lamp illuminated the lines of worry etched into his forehead.

"Let me help you with that," I offered, crossing the room and taking the silk fabric in my hands. As I deftly tied the bow, I felt the tense coil of muscle at his neck and caught the faint hitch in his breathing. "Are you sure we should go out tonight? Maybe we should stay in, save a little money," I ventured, straightening his bowtie.

Frank sighed heavily. "We have to go, Barb. This dinner with Mr. Cardello could mean big things for my career. We need this." He slipped on his suit jacket.

"I was thinking," I began, smoothing his lapels. "Maybe I could look for a job. Just something part-time to help out until things get better. I could always go back to modeling…"

"Out of the question, Barbara." Frank's tone was stern as he took hold of my hands, his eyes narrowing. "We've discussed this before. Your place is here, taking care of our home and Frank Junior. I won't have my wife parading herself around like some common showgirl."

A flare of indignation rose within me, but I bit back the sharp retort that danced on the tip of my tongue. Instead, I plastered on a smile and nodded—the perfect picture of a dutiful wife.

"Of course, dear. You're right. I just thought I could contribute…"

"You contribute plenty by being a good wife and mother. That's all I ask of you, Barb." Frank pressed a perfunctory kiss to my cheek before turning toward the door. "Now come on, get dressed. We don't want to be late."

He pulled a pair of brown leather loafers out of the wardrobe and buffed them with a worn, dingy cloth.

As I stepped into my black satin dress, the fabric cool and slippery against my skin, I couldn't shake the sense of unease that had settled in the pit of my stomach. I smoothed the fabric over my hips and reached behind to zip up the back. The leopard-print collar tickled the nape of my neck.

"Frank, darling," I called out, my voice echoing in the stillness of the bedroom. "Tell me more about this Mr. Cardello. You've done business with him before, haven't you?"

I turned to admire my reflection in the full-length mirror, the dress hugging my curves in all the right places. For a moment, I felt a flicker of my former life of films and photo shoots.

"Victor Cardello? He's a businessman. Runs a huge real estate firm. He's got his hands in just about every property deal in Los Angeles." Frank stepped into his shoes and tucked a pale blue pocket square into his jacket.

I clasped a double strand of pearls at the nape of my neck and shivered as the chill kissed my skin. "How do you know him again?"

Frank paused, his hand resting on the knob of the bedroom door. "I've insured a few of his properties. High-end stuff, Barb. Hotels, office buildings, that sort of thing." He glanced over his shoulder at me, a hint of pride flickering in his eyes. "He's a big fish, and if I can reel him in, it could mean a promotion, a raise…"

"I see," I murmured, slipping into a pair of black patent leather pumps. The shoes pinched my toes, but I ignored the discomfort. Pain was beauty. "What's he like?" I asked, curious about the man who held such sway over our evening plans and potentially Frank's career. "You've never mentioned him before."

Frank shrugged, turning to face me. "He's a businessman, through and through. Charming but ruthless. Knows how to get what he wants." He took a step closer, his gaze sweeping over me. "You look beautiful. Just remember, tonight is all about impressing Mr. Cardello. Let me do the talking, okay?"

I nodded, a tight smile on my lips. "Well then," I said, straightening my shoulders and lifting my chin, "we'd best not keep him waiting." I brushed past Frank, my heels clicking on the hardwood floor as I made my way down the hall.

2

VICTOR

The purring engine of my jet-black Rolls-Royce Silver Wraith announced my arrival as I pulled up to Dorothy's house. Her neighborhood was a picture of post-war suburbia with manicured lawns and white picket fences—a far cry from the gritty streets of downtown Los Angeles where I made my fortune.

As I stepped out of the car, I adjusted my black pinstriped suit, ensuring every crease was immaculate. I nodded to my driver, Gino, before walking up the path to the front door and ringing the bell. The chime reverberated through the house. I reached into my coat pocket and fished out my wedding ring. As I slid it onto my finger, I flexed my hand a few times to ease the foreign discomfort. After a moment, the door opened, and my wife, Dorothy, emerged from the house, her dark hair perfectly coiffed and her red lips pursed in a tight smile. She wore an emerald dress that hugged her waist and flared out over her hips, a string of pearls adorning her elegant neck.

"Victor," she greeted me coolly as she pulled the front door closed. She brushed past me on her way to the car. I nodded in acknowledgment and followed, opening the car door for her.

Dorothy slid into the backseat, careful not to wrinkle her dress. I joined her, the scent of her floral perfume mingling with the rich leather interior.

As Gino pulled away from the curb, I studied my wife's profile, her face sporadically illuminated by the passing streetlights.

Without looking at me, Dorothy asked, "Who is it we're meeting tonight?"

"Frank Evans," I answered.

"And what does Frank do?" Dorothy's monotone didn't match her questions.

"Insurance," I replied, watching the play of emotions on her face—or rather, the lack thereof.

"An insurance man?" Dorothy arched a perfectly sculpted eyebrow. "I thought you preferred to associate with people with more…influence."

I chuckled, the sound low and humorless. "Frank may not be the most exciting dinner companion, but he has his uses. His firm insures some of my most valuable properties. It pays to keep him happy." I adjusted my tie. "Besides, Frank is… impressionable. With the right persuasion, he could be a valuable asset to our business."

Dorothy let out a small, humorless laugh. "*Our* business? Since when do I have any say in your affairs, Victor?"

I clenched my jaw, biting back a sharp retort. "This dinner is important, Dotty," I said, my voice low and measured.

She finally turned to look at me, her dark eyes cold. "Play the sweet, charming wife. I know the drill."

I ignored her jab, instead focusing on the glittering lights of the city as we drove through the heart of downtown. Staring out the window as our drive passed in icy silence, my mind drifted to the dinner ahead and the potential opportunities it presented.

As Gino pulled up to the restaurant, I noticed Frank Evans and his wife already waiting outside. Frank looked every bit the unremarkable insurance salesman in his ill-fitting suit and nervous smile. But his wife caught my eye. She was a vision in an elegant black dress, her blonde hair catching the light like a halo. The neckline of her dress accentuated deliciously ample breasts. She was tall, slender, and carried herself with stunning poise.

I exited the car and walked around to open Dorothy's door, offering her my hand. She took it reluctantly, her skin cool against mine. We approached the other couple and plastered on fake smiles.

"Frank, good to see you," I said, shaking his hand and clapping his arm. "Do introduce me to your vision of a wife."

Frank cleared his throat nervously. "Mr. Cardello, this is my wife, Barbara."

Barbara extended her hand gracefully. "A pleasure to meet you both." Her voice was like honey—smooth and alluring—with a soft, airy quality, like a film star.

I took her hand, bowing my head to place a chaste kiss on her soft skin. "The pleasure is all mine, Mrs. Evans. I must say, you look absolutely stunning this evening."

Barbara's cheeks flushed a delicate pink as she withdrew her hand. "Thank you, Mr. Cardello. You're too kind." Her blue eyes sparkled.

"Please, call me Victor."

Dorothy cleared her throat. I stepped back and ushered her forward.

"This is my wife, Dorothy. Dorothy, this is Frank and Barbara Evans."

Dorothy surveyed our dinner companions with a cool, appraising gaze. "Shall we head inside? I'm famished." Her tone was clipped, impatient.

"Of course, darling," I replied smoothly, offering her my arm. She took it, her grip a little too tight to be friendly.

As we entered the restaurant, I couldn't help but steal another glance at Barbara. She moved with a graceful elegance, her black dress shimmering beneath the chandeliers. There was something captivating about her—a vivacious spark of life.

The maître d' led us to a private table in the back, away from the prying eyes of the other diners. I pulled out a chair for Dorothy, and she sat down without so much as a glance in my direction. Frank, however, did not do the same for Barbara.

As we settled in, a waiter appeared with a bottle of champagne. I nodded my approval, and he began to pour the bubbling liquid into our glasses.

"To new friendships and prosperous partnerships," I toasted, raising my glass. The others followed suit, and a pure note rang out as the crystal flutes clinked together.

I took a sip of the chilled champagne, the effervescent bubbles dancing on my tongue. As the conversation began to flow, I found my eyes repeatedly drawn to Barbara. She listened attentively to Frank's mundane anecdotes about the insurance business, nodding and smiling at all the right moments. But there was a distant look in her eyes—a restlessness lurking beneath her polished exterior.

Dorothy, on the other hand, remained aloof and disengaged, her gaze flickering around the room. She sipped her champagne with a detached air, her red lips leaving a faint imprint on the glass.

An awkward hush settled over the table, so I seized the opportunity to steer the conversation in a more interesting direction. "Tell me, Barbara," I began, leaning forward. "You look so familiar, but I can't place it. Have we met before?"

"No, I don't believe so." Barbara smiled demurely, a hint of mischief in her eyes. "Though I did some modeling and acting before I married Frank. Perhaps you saw one of my advertisements or films."

I raised an eyebrow, intrigued. "An actress, you say? I can certainly picture that. You have a face made for the camera."

Frank chuckled nervously. "Yes, well, Barbara's put that life behind her now that we've settled down." He reached over and patted her hand.

Barbara's smile tightened. She gently pulled her hand away under the pretense of reaching for her champagne glass. "It does feel like another lifetime," she agreed, taking a delicate sip. Her eyes met mine over the rim of her glass, and I swore I saw a flicker of wistfulness in their blue depths.

3

BARBARA

Amber light glinted off the ice in Victor's bourbon. The cubes spun around each other, stirred by his strong but oddly supple fingers wrapped around the glass. He tossed back the rest of his drink in one swift motion. The glass clinked against the table as he lifted a cigarette to his lips with his other hand. Eyes closed, he took a long drag, the ember flaring orange at the tip. Then he leaned back and flicked the cigarette with his index finger, gray ash falling into an ornately carved white marble ashtray.

"Barb?"

Startled, I glanced to my right. Frank looked at me expectantly, his eyebrows slightly raised. "Sorry," I replied, shaking my head. I smiled sweetly at him. "I was lost in thought."

"Dorothy was asking about Frank Junior," Frank summarized, placing a hand on the back of my chair.

"Oh, of course." I shifted my gaze across the table to Dorothy, Victor's wife. She was a brunette with a heart-shaped face. Her green dress was a shade small and hugged her bust a little too tightly. "Frankie is two now. He eats everything in sight and is outgrowing whatever I put him in." I paused, desperately searching my memory of our earlier conversation for their daughter's name. "And Margaret?"

Dorothy beamed. "She's becoming quite the young lady. She's in the third grade now, and I don't know what I'm going to do with myself."

The five-piece band across the dining room started another song. Our waiter, tuxedoed with white gloves, approached the table. Frank ordered something for the two of us, along with another drink, and I excused myself to the ladies' room.

Once there, I let out a long breath through pursed lips. The ladies' room was empty, save for me, and quiet, save for the muted music and ambient chatter filtering in from the dining room. I leaned back against the black-and-cream brocade wallpaper, closed my eyes, and let out another long, controlled breath.

The door squeaked quietly, and I jerked my body upright and my eyes open as Dorothy entered, her drab brown pumps unsteady on the high-pile crimson carpet. "You all right, Barbara?"

I smiled. "Yes, just needed to freshen up a little."

Dorothy plopped her clutch on the counter and pushed at the bobby pins in her hair. She made eye contact with my reflection in the mirror. "You know every man in this place can't keep their eyes off you."

"Hardly."

"It's true. You're blonde with one hell of a figure. How on earth did you manage to get your waistline back after the baby? Margaret's eight, and I'm still trying to find mine." She dabbed her forehead and nose with pressed powder.

"I guess I'm just lucky."

"I'll say!" She clicked her compact closed and tossed it back into her clutch. "There's bound to be a lot of jealous wives every time you walk by." She surveyed me in the mirror before digging out a lipstick tube from her bag.

I walked over to the sink to stand beside her. Even in heels, her head only came up to my shoulder. I smoothed my black dress and adjusted the leopard-print belt and matching wide lapel. "I'm sure I have no idea what you're talking about."

She leaned in close to the mirror to apply her grapefruit-colored lipstick.

I stared at my reflection, meeting Dorothy's gaze in the mirror, as a woman's rendition of Bing Crosby filtered through the closed restroom door. The air between us crackled with tension. I knew what she was implying, but I refused to acknowledge it.

I smiled tightly. "We should probably head back. The boys will be wondering where we are."

Dorothy smacked her lips and dropped the lipstick back into her clutch with a clatter. "Of course. We wouldn't want to keep them waiting." Her tone was saccharine, but her eyes were hard, calculating.

I led the way out of the ladies' room, feeling Dorothy's stare boring into my back. As we wove through the tables, I was acutely aware of the appreciative glances from the men we passed. I held my head high, ignoring the whispers and the envious looks from their dates.

4
VICTOR

Barbara glided across the dining room floor with a natural grace, the satin of her black dress shimmering and shifting over her lithe figure. The fabric clung to the soft curve of her backside, drawing admiring glances from the men she passed. My stomach tightened at the thought of lesser men's eyes on her.

Frank nursed his martini, fidgeting with the olive spear. He didn't even give Barbara a second glance as she walked away.

I cleared my throat and turned to Dorothy. "Why don't you go powder your nose, darling? Keep Barbara company."

Dorothy's eyes narrowed slightly at the dismissal, her gaze flicking between me and Frank. With a curt nod, she rose from her seat, smoothing her emerald dress. "Of course. If you'll excuse me, gentlemen." Her heels clicked on the parquet floor as she followed Barbara's path to the ladies' room.

I waited until Dorothy disappeared from view before leaning back in my chair. The waiter delivered a fresh bourbon, and I picked it up, swirling the amber liquid in my glass. The ice cubes clinked against its sides. I took a long, slow sip before setting the drink back down on the table and shifting my gaze to Frank.

"Frank, old boy, now that the wives are gone, what did you really want to talk about?"

Frank fidgeted with his napkin, his gaze darting around the room before finally settling on me. He leaned forward, his voice low and laced with desperation. "Listen, Victor, I've got a problem."

I raised an eyebrow as I took another sip of bourbon. The rich, smoky flavor coated my tongue and burned a smooth path down my throat. "Oh? Do tell."

Frank glanced over his shoulder as if checking to make sure no one was eavesdropping. The clink of silverware against china and the gentle murmur of conversation filled the air as waiters scurried between the tables and the kitchen. Seemingly satisfied that we wouldn't be overheard, he turned back to me, his brow furrowed.

"It's the money I owe you," he said, his words tumbling out in a rush. "I'm having a hard time coming up with it. Business has been slow, and with the new baby…" He trailed off.

"Your boy is two, Frank. That's hardly new."

Frank ran a hand through his thick, curly hair, a sheen of sweat glistening on his forehead under the warm glow of the chandeliers. "I know, I know. It's just…expenses keep piling up, and Barbara has expensive tastes." He let out a shaky laugh. The sound grated on my nerves. "You know how women are."

I leaned forward, resting my elbows on the pristine white tablecloth, and lit another cigarette. The smoke masked the scent of Frank's cheap cologne mingling with the aroma of sizzling steaks and buttery lobster wafting from the kitchen. "Believe me, I'm well aware of the costs of maintaining a certain lifestyle, Frank." I took a long drag, the acrid smoke dancing a tingling path across my tongue and throat. "But a debt is a debt. I expect to be paid what I'm owed."

Frank swallowed hard. "Absolutely. And I will pay you back. I just…"

"You just what?"

"I was hoping you could push a few properties my way. The extra commissions would really help."

I leaned back in my chair, taking another drag of my cigarette as I considered Frank's request. I exhaled, the smoke curling lazily from my lips as my eyes never left his face. Frank squirmed under my gaze, his fingers tapping nervously against the stem of his martini glass.

"I'll see what I can do," I said finally, flicking the ash from my cigarette into the marble tray. "But I can't make any promises. The market's been tight lately."

Frank's shoulders sagged with relief. "Thank you, Victor. I appreciate it. Truly." He took a large gulp of his martini. The olive bobbed in the clear liquid. "Barbara even suggested getting a job, but what kind of man would I be if I allowed that? The war is long over, thank God. Women don't need to work now."

I leaned back in my chair, studying Frank through the curling tendrils of cigarette smoke. "Barbara wants to work, you say?" I kept my tone casual, but my mind was racing with possibilities. "The girls certainly showed us they were capable during the war."

Frank's eyes widened, his brow furrowing in confusion. "What do you mean? I can't have my wife working. What would people think?"

I waved a dismissive hand, the smoke from my cigarette trailing behind. "People will think what they want, regardless. But you have a bigger problem."

"And what's that?"

"That dame is a looker. If I were you, I'd be doing everything in my power to keep her happy. But I'd be more than a little nervous about letting her out of my sight. Letting her go to work around a bunch of fellas with wandering eyes, if you catch my drift."

I took another long drag on my cigarette, the nicotine buzz sharpening my focus. Frank's eyes darted around nervously, unable to meet my steady gaze. The band played a slow, sultry number, the singer's husky voice crooning about lost love and regret.

"Listen, Frank," I said, leaning forward and refocusing on him. The leather of my chair creaked. "I think I might have a solution to benefit us both."

Frank's eyes snapped to mine, a mix of hope and trepidation swimming in their depths. "What do you mean?"

I stubbed out my cigarette, the smoldering ember hissing as it met the cold marble of the ashtray. "You need money. I need a new secretary. Someone with class and sophistication to handle delicate matters. Someone who can be…discreet."

I watched the confusion play across Frank's face. His lips parted to speak, then closed again. He took another sip of his martini, the ice clinking against the glass. The sounds of the restaurant faded into the background as I awaited his reaction.

"You…you want Barbara to work for you?" Frank finally stammered.

I sat back in my chair, the rich leather cradling my shoulders. "Think about it, Frank. It's the perfect solution. Barbara gets the excitement and purpose she craves. You get the extra income to pay me back. Along with a few more properties to insure. I get a beautiful, intelligent woman to class up my office. And I keep her safe from prying eyes. Everybody wins."

5

BARBARA

January 1951

Frank silently fiddled with the brim of his hat on his lap as I parked our car in front of his office building.

"Barb, are you sure about starting this new job? If it's about the money—"

I cut him off. "Yes. And it's not just about the money, Frank."

He heaved a sigh as he turned to face me, his eyes filled with concern and resignation. "I know you've been restless, Barb. I just… I worry about you, about us, about Frank Junior. This job, it's going to change things."

"It's only three days a week. And Edith is happy to keep Frankie."

Frank sighed again. "Your sister really does love the boy."

I kept my eyes forward, focusing on the morning sun glinting off the hood of our Plymouth, avoiding the disappointment and worry etched across his features.

"And your mother doesn't approve of you working for some rich businessman downtown when you've got Frank Junior and me to look after at home." Frank's voice was strained.

I closed my eyes and let out a slow breath through pursed lips before I turned in the driver's seat to look at him. "Mother has something to say about everything. And besides, this job was your idea in the first place. You set this up with your pal, Victor. Remember?"

Frank shrank back against the window. "I know, I know. And I thought it was a good idea. At the time."

I softened my tone. "Please, Frank. Just let me try. I need this."

Frank met my gaze and held it for a long moment before he nodded. A small, sad smile tugged at the corners of his mouth. "All right." He reached over and squeezed my gloved hand. "I love you."

"I love you too, Frank." I leaned in and pressed a soft kiss to his cheek, inhaling the familiar scent of his aftershave. "I'll see you tonight."

With a final nod, Frank opened the passenger door and stepped out onto the sidewalk. He straightened his tie and donned his hat before striding into the towering office building, quickly becoming lost in the morning crowd of suited businessmen.

I pulled away from the curb and merged into the busy Los Angeles morning traffic. The January sun hung low in the sky, its weak rays doing little to combat the winter chill that seeped through the thin material of my gloves as I gripped the steering wheel. I flexed my fingers and sat a little taller. This was the start of something, whether I was ready or not.

———

I followed behind the receptionist, Mrs. Miller, a stout brunette with gray-streaked hair pulled up in a tight bun. Her heels clicked sharply against the polished marble floor as she led me down a long, wood-paneled hallway. Framed photographs of racing cars spanning back a few decades adorned the walls.

We stopped in front of a large oak door that bore a gleaming brass nameplate reading "Victor Cardello" in bold typeface. To the right of the door sat a cluttered but well-appointed desk, complete with a sleek black typewriter and a vase of fresh flowers.

"This will be your workstation, Mrs. Evans."

I nodded, taking in my new domain. Mrs. Miller's lips pressed into a thin line as she surveyed the cluttered surface of the desk.

"I apologize for the state of things, Mrs. Evans. Mr. Cardello's previous secretary left rather abruptly, and we haven't had a chance to tidy up."

"It's no trouble at all, Mrs. Miller. I'm happy to take care of it." I offered her a reassuring smile, already mentally sorting through the disarray.

I removed my gloves and settled into the plush leather chair as Mrs. Miller rattled off a list of instructions—filing systems, phone etiquette, coffee preferences. I nodded along, trying to absorb every detail while my eyes kept darting to the imposing oak door.

After what felt like an eternity, Mrs. Miller finally departed with a curt nod, leaving me alone in the quiet anteroom. I began to sift through the jumble of papers, organizing them into neat stacks.

I just about had everything sorted and filed when a shadow suddenly blocked my light. I looked up to see Victor Cardello perched on the edge of my desk. Startled, I jumped.

"Mr. Cardello," I stammered. "I'm so sorry. I didn't hear you come in."

He smiled, his dark eyes twinkling with amusement. "Please, call me Victor." His voice was smooth and rich, like aged whiskey poured slow and neat. "I see you've already worked your magic on this disaster of a desk."

I felt a flush creep up my neck as I straightened the last stack of papers. "Just trying to make myself useful, Mr. Card—Victor." His name felt foreign yet thrilling on my tongue.

Victor picked up a crystal paperweight, turning it over in his large, well-manicured hands. "I knew you'd be the perfect addition to my team the moment I met you." He set the paperweight down with a soft clink. "You have a keen eye for detail, Mrs. Evans."

"Barbara," I corrected him, surprised by my boldness. "And thank you."

His dark hair was slicked back, and his pencil mustache was impeccably groomed. He wore a finely tailored charcoal suit that accentuated his broad shoulders and lean waist.

Victor's gaze lingered on me for a moment before he gestured toward the heavy oak door. "Come, Barbara. Let me show you around my office."

I hesitated, glancing at the organized stacks of paperwork on my desk. "I really should finish getting everything in order out here."

"Nonsense." Victor chuckled, his eyes crinkling at the corners. "That can wait. I insist."

Reluctantly, I rose from my chair and followed him into his spacious office. The room was adorned with rich mahogany paneling and plush burgundy carpets. A large window overlooked the bustling city streets below. The morning sunlight filtered through the slats of the Venetian blinds, casting striped shadows across the room.

A large mahogany desk dominated the center of the office, its surface nearly bare save for a few neatly arranged pens, a silver photo frame, and a leather-bound calendar diary.

Victor crossed to his desk and retrieved the diary. He held it out to me, his fingers brushing the gold-edged pages. The cover was embossed with an intricate design, the ridges and whorls catching the light as I turned it over.

"I'll need you to manage my schedule—ensure I'm where I

need to be when I need to be there," Victor explained, his voice low and close to my ear.

"Of course, Mr. Cardello, but—"

"Victor," he corrected.

I nodded. "Victor… But as I mentioned during my interview, I'm only available to work in the office three days per week."

A slow smile spread across Victor's face, his dark eyes glinting with amusement. "What a fortunate coincidence. Those are the only three days I frequent the office myself."

I shrugged and nodded. "Unconventional, but clearly, it works for you."

Victor perched on the edge of his desk and studied me for a moment. "Conventional is the absolute last thing I want to be."

My breath caught in my throat as Victor's intense gaze caught and held mine. I was drawn to him like a moth to a flame, unable to look away despite the warning bells sounding in the back of my mind. Clearing my throat, I managed to break eye contact and focused on the diary in my hands, flipping through the gold-edged pages.

"Well then, shall we go over your upcoming appointments for the week?" I asked, my voice strained, even to my ears.

He nodded, and I flipped open the diary to the current week. Victor's elegant script filled the pages—names, times, and places penned in black ink.

"I don't see anything for today, but you have a meeting at ten-thirty tomorrow morning," I remarked, glancing up at him. "Someone named Kowalski."

Victor nodded and consulted his gold wristwatch. "Yes. A good learning opportunity for you, I think."

"For me?"

Victor nodded again. "I'd like you to assist me in that meeting. Nothing complicated. Coffee, take notes, that sort of thing."

"Do I need to prepare anything?"

"No, Mr. Kowalski is coming to me with an offer. All we need to do is listen. And hear what he's not saying. You up for it?"

I smiled. "Sure."

"And one more thing, Barbara."

My stomach twitched as I blinked and looked up at him. "Yes?"

"Block my schedule from noon to two today."

"Of course." My stomach calmed, and I exhaled a small sigh. "Any reason you'd like me to notate?" I smoothed the front of my pale blue dress.

He smiled, a slow, indulgent grin creeping across his face. "I'm taking you out to lunch."

6

VICTOR

I opened the passenger door of my car and gestured for Barbara to slide into the luxurious leather seat.

She hesitated for a moment, her eyes wide. "This is yours?"

I grinned, rocking back on my heels. She ran a gloved hand over the sleek lines of the chassis. The pale cream paint stood out from every other black and dark green car in the garage. "It's an Aston Martin."

"I've never heard of that."

I nodded. "Not surprised. It's an import. Cars are one of my…indulgences."

Her eyes flickered with uncertainty before she gathered her skirt and slipped into the car. I couldn't help but appreciate the graceful way her hips swayed, accentuating every curve of her body.

As I rounded the front of the vehicle and slid behind the wheel, her perfume enveloped me—a soft, floral aroma with just a hint of spice. It was refreshing—so different from the cloying, heavy fragrances favored by the women who usually found their way into my orbit.

"Do you have many?" she asked, neatly folding her gloved hands in her lap and crossing her ankles. Such a lady.

"Cars?"

"No. Indulgences."

I glanced at her, expecting her to avert her eyes down to her lap in a coy play, but her piercing blue eyes met me head-on. I held her gaze for a long moment, the corners of my mouth curling into a smile. "A few."

The engine roared to life as I turned the key in the ignition, then settled into a low, idle purr. As I eased out of the parking garage, I felt Barbara's eyes on me. Since she arrived this morning, she'd been studying me with a wary curiosity.

"And what about you, Barbara? What are your indulgences?" I asked, glancing over at her as I merged into traffic.

She blinked, clearly caught off guard. "Oh, I don't know. I suppose I don't have any."

"Come now." I chuckled. "Everyone has something they enjoy. Something that makes them feel alive."

Barbara shifted to face the window, her body—and eyes—turned away from me. "I'm not sure I've ever let myself have any."

"Pity."

I stopped at a red light, the pause giving me a chance to study Barbara more thoroughly. The midday sun illuminated her profile, her delicate features bathed in a golden glow. A strand of blonde hair had escaped from her neat chignon. I had the sudden urge to reach out and tuck it behind her ear, to feel the softness of her skin beneath my fingertips.

Clearing my throat, I focused my attention back on the road as the light turned green. "Well, perhaps it's time you start."

"Start what?"

"Indulging yourself. Allowing yourself to experience things that bring you joy, that make you feel alive."

She let out a soft, humorless laugh. "I'm not sure Frank would approve."

The mention of her husband's name sent a flicker of irritation through me. I raised an eyebrow. "And why does that matter?"

Barbara shifted in her seat, the leather creaking beneath her. She stared out the windshield, her eyes following the flow of traffic. "It's not that simple, Victor. I have responsibilities, obligations. To my husband, to my son."

I drummed my fingers on the steering wheel, considering her words. "And what about your obligations to yourself, Barbara? Don't you deserve to pursue your own happiness?"

I glanced at her as she turned to look at me again, her eyes wide and searching. "I...I'm not sure I know how to do that anymore. Or if I ever did."

I shifted gears and accelerated around a slow-moving truck. The Aston Martin responded beautifully, the engine growling with power. "Let me help you rediscover it then."

"Victor, I'm married. Happily married." But there was a momentary waver.

"Relax. I'm not asking you to run away. Just let me help you indulge in a hobby." I parked the car in front of Perino's and turned off the engine.

After a long moment, she looked up at me, her eyes sparkling with determination. "All right. On one condition."

I raised an eyebrow, intrigued. "And what might that be?"

"That we keep this...arrangement...strictly professional. I'm your secretary, nothing more. I won't do anything to jeopardize my marriage or my family." Her voice was firm, unwavering.

I couldn't help but admire her resolve, even as a part of me bristled at the limitation she was placing on our interactions. "Deal." I stepped out of the car and walked around the back to open her door for her. She slipped a gloved hand into mine as I helped her out of the car. "Have you ever been to Perino's before?"

She looked up at the bright white building façade, her hand shielding her eyes from the sun. "Can't say that I have."

"Then you're in for a real treat."

As we stepped through the heavy wooden doors into Perino's, the maître d' greeted me with a deferential bow.

"Mr. Cardello, welcome back!"

"Always a pleasure, Joseph."

"Your usual table?"

I nodded, lightly placing my hand on the small of Barbara's back as Joseph led us through the elegant dining room. The warmth of her skin radiated through the thin fabric of her dress, and a slight tremor ran through her at my touch.

Joseph pulled out a chair for Barbara at a secluded table in the back corner. The stark white linen tablecloth gleamed under the soft glow of the chandeliers. I waited for her to be seated before taking my chair across from her.

"Champagne?" Joseph asked me as he draped Barbara's napkin across her lap.

"Please," I answered.

"At lunch?" Barbara asked after Joseph left.

I shrugged. "Indulgence, remember?"

Barbara glanced around the opulent dining room, taking in the gold-and-crystal chandeliers, the gleaming white tiled floor, and the gold-leaf embellished walls. She looked like a deer caught in the headlights, her eyes wide and uncertain.

"I'm not sure I belong here," she murmured, her fingers nervously smoothing the linen napkin in her lap. "I'm quite underdressed."

I leaned forward, resting my elbows on the table. "Nonsense. You're stunning, and you belong anywhere you want to be, Barbara."

She met my gaze, a tentative smile tugging at the corners of her mouth. "It's just...all of this"—she gestured around the room—"is so different from what I'm used to." She paused as she glanced down at the table. "At least, it is now."

Joseph returned with a bottle of champagne nestled in a silver ice bucket. He popped the cork with a practiced twist and poured two glasses.

I watched Barbara take a small sip of the champagne, her eyes fluttering closed for a moment. When she opened them again, there was a spark of something new—a glimmer of excitement.

"And what were you used to before?" I asked, taking a sip of my champagne. The bubbles danced on my tongue, crisp and effervescent.

Barbara traced the delicate stem of her glass with her fingers as she considered my question. "A different life," she said softly. "One filled with dreams and ambitions that seem quite foolish now."

"Says who?"

"Frank. My mother. Society, apparently."

I took another sip. "They don't matter," I said with a wave of my hand. "Did you want to keep doing films? Or 'lensing,' as they say?"

Barbara smiled. "You have a good memory." Her expression turned wistful. "Maybe. I enjoyed acting. The modeling too, but..."

"But what?"

She glanced up at me through her eyelashes, considering. "I really wanted to be a designer. I love clothes and fashion. And so much is changing right now. I actually design and make a lot of my own outfits." Her eyes sparkled as she spoke, but she paused, and that light dimmed. "But it's not sensible for a wife and mother."

I shook my head, a spark of anger igniting in my chest. The very idea that Barbara's dreams and ambitions were somehow less important or less valid because she was a wife and mother infuriated me.

I leaned forward, holding her gaze. "Barbara, listen to me. Your dreams matter. Your passions matter. Being a wife and mother doesn't negate that. If anything, it should fuel it. What kind of example do you want to set for your son? That he should settle? Give up on what makes his soul sing?"

Barbara blinked, clearly taken aback by my intensity. She opened her mouth as if to speak, then closed it again, her brows furrowed in thought. "I've never thought of it that way before," she admitted softly, her fingers twisting the napkin in her lap.

Joseph returned, interrupting the charged atmosphere with a polite clearing of his throat. "May I take your order?"

I watched Barbara, her eyes darting to the menu she hadn't touched. She seemed lost—adrift in the sea of options she wasn't accustomed to navigating alone. Her gaze flicked back to me.

"Would you care for some recommendations?" I offered, my voice low and soothing.

Barbara hesitated and then nodded appreciatively. "Yes, please. I…I'm not quite sure what to choose."

I turned to Joseph. "What would you recommend for the lady?"

Joseph bowed his head slightly. "May I suggest the *piccata di vitello, signora.* It's a tender veal dish, lightly breaded and sautéed in a buttery lemon and caper sauce. An authentic Italian classic that's both delicate and flavorful."

"That sounds delicious, thank you," she said with a nod.

I held up my hand. "Are you sure? You only heard one recommendation."

She nodded quickly, sliding her menu toward Joseph. "Yes, it sounds lovely. Delicious, in fact."

I studied her for a moment before I let it go. "The spaghetti bolognese for me, please, Joseph."

"Absolutely, Mr. Cardello," Joseph said with a curt nod before rushing away.

As he departed, I turned my attention back to Barbara. "Why do you find it so difficult to order your own meal?"

Her cheeks flushed a soft rose. "I'm not sure I know what you mean."

"Sure you do. When the four of us went to dinner last month, you let Frank order for you. I don't think you even picked up the menu."

"You really do have a good memory," she mused with her head cocked to the side.

"And you're dodging the question," I pressed.

Eventually, Barbara sighed and admitted, "Frank likes to order for both of us when we go out. I suppose I let him because it makes him feel…important." She took another sip of champagne, taking a moment before continuing, "It's just easier that way. No fuss, no arguments."

I leaned back in my chair, studying her thoughtfully. "But what about what *you* want?"

Barbara's eyes met mine, a quiet determination flickering in their depths. "You served in the war, didn't you?"

"I did."

"Then you'll understand choosing your battles. Sometimes, it's better to keep the peace than to fight for what you want."

I laughed softly. "Then you don't understand much about being a soldier. Not that I'd expect you to. There is no option to 'choose your battles.' Your battles are chosen for you by people you'll never meet. People who don't give a damn what happens to you because they'll never see those battles."

She held my gaze—a thousand questions swimming just beneath the surface—but said nothing. After a moment, she took a delicate sip of her champagne, the bubbles in the glass twinkling like stars under the light.

"I'm sorry. Of course, you're right," she conceded softly. "I've never thought about it like that before. That was stupid of me."

"No harm done."

"What I was trying to say is that I've just been…comfortable, I suppose. It's easier to go along with what's expected of me rather than fight for what I truly want. Don't rock the boat, as it were."

I leaned forward, captivated by the melancholy in her voice. "But that's not who you really are, is it, Barbara? I see the fire in your eyes, the spirit that refuses to be contained. I think it's high time you let that part of yourself shine. Before that beautiful light is snuffed out completely."

Barbara's cheeks flushed a deeper shade of pink, but she didn't look away. "You...you truly see that in me?" she asked, her voice small and vulnerable.

"I do," I replied, my gaze steady. I reached across the table, lightly brushing the back of her hand with my fingertips.

She looked down at the contact but didn't pull away.

"So, you want to be a designer?" I smiled, letting it warm my voice. "Fabulous." I took her hand fully into mine and grazed my thumb over her knuckles. "What would it take to make that real?"

7
BARBARA

The aroma of beef and onions filled the kitchen as I stirred the stroganoff, mesmerized by the sporadic bubbles that bloomed and popped as the creamy sauce simmered.

Frankie giggled as he sat near my feet, banging his wooden spoon against the linoleum floor. I glanced down at him, his cherubic face a reminder of the love that kept me tethered to this life. But even as I smiled at my son, I couldn't shake the restlessness that had taken root in my heart.

Frank was slouched in the sage-green armchair in the living room with his legs crossed in a figure-four, his eyes glued to the evening paper. The ice cubes clinked in his glass as he took another sip of whiskey, the golden liquid refracting the light from the overhead fixture. The newspaper rustled as he turned the page. In the background, a radio announcer droned on—a somber news report about the ongoing tensions in Korea.

Frank hadn't said a word to me since we got home, and he'd barely spoken to me when I picked him up from work. He said he'd had a rough day, but it felt like a block.

I longed for him to look up, to see me. But he didn't.

I stirred the stroganoff, then pulled the skillet off the heat to rest. My thoughts drifted back to lunch at Perino's. To the way Victor looked at me with those piercing dark eyes, like he could see straight into my soul. The way his words danced around me, enticing and unsettling.

The memory sent a flutter through me, followed quickly by a sharp pang of guilt. I shouldn't be thinking about another man like this, especially not my employer and my husband's business associate. But there was something about him that drew me in. The way he spoke of dreams and possibilities—his smooth-as-silk words had awakened a yearning buried deep inside me.

I busied myself with setting the table, the clink of silverware against china plates cutting through the stillness. I plated dinner for Frank and me and cut up the noodles and beef strips into a toddler-friendly size for Frankie.

I absently twisted my wedding band around my finger as I stared at the plates, no longer seeing them. Instead, I saw the curve of Victor's lips as he smiled at me across the table, the way he gestured with understated confidence as he described his vision, the heat of his hand holding mine…

The sudden swell of music from the radio snapped me back to the present. I blinked, my surroundings coming back into focus—the yellow floral wallpaper, the hum of the refrigerator, Frankie's babbling.

"Dinner's ready," I called out as I picked Frankie up from the floor, settling him on my hip and taking him to the table.

Frank grunted in response, folding the newspaper and tossing it onto the coffee table. He switched off the radio and lumbered into the dining room, the floorboards creaking under his heavy steps. As he settled into his chair, his gaze flitted over the meal before him, never quite meeting my eyes. "Stroganoff again?" he muttered, picking up his fork.

A flare of irritation burst to life in my chest at his uncharitable tone, but I tamped it down and forced a smile. "I thought it would be nice to have something hearty after a long day," I said mildly, sliding Frankie into his high chair.

Frank shoveled a forkful of noodles into his mouth. I watched him chew, his jaw working mechanically. The silence stretched between us, thick and heavy, broken only by the clink of utensils against plates and Frankie's occasional babbling.

"How was your day, darling?" I asked.

"Fine," Frank said flatly, not looking up from his plate. He stabbed at a stack of noodles and beef strips with his fork and shoved the bite into his mouth, his teeth clicking against the fork.

I waited for him to say more, but he just kept eating, his eyes fixed on his food. I suppressed a sigh and turned my attention to Frankie, cutting his beef into smaller bites.

"My day was lovely. Thank you for asking..." The words slipped out before I could stop them, laced with a bitterness I hadn't intended. Frank's fork paused halfway to his mouth, his eyes finally meeting mine. For a brief moment, I saw a flicker of surprise in their blue depths, quickly replaced by a harsh glare and a set jaw.

"What's that supposed to mean?" he asked, his voice low and tight.

I immediately regretted my petty jab, but the frustration that had been simmering all evening bubbled over. "Nothing. It's just...you didn't even ask about my first day at work."

Frank set his fork down with a clatter and leaned back in his chair. "I thought we agreed you would just help out for a bit. Not make a career out of it."

"It's hardly a career, Frank. It's a temporary secretarial position." I tried to keep my tone light, but an edge crept in anyway. "I don't understand why you're so opposed to me working. It's only part-time, and the extra money will really help."

Frank's lips pressed into a thin line. "It's not about the money, Barbara. It's about you being out there, exposed to all kinds of unsavory characters. I don't like it."

My fingers tightened around my fork, the metal biting into

my palm. "Victor has been nothing but professional and respectful. He's a successful businessman, not some shady criminal."

"Oh, so it's *Victor* now, is it?" Frank's eyes narrowed, his voice taking on a mocking tone. "Getting awfully chummy with the boss on your first day."

Heat rose in my cheeks, a mix of anger and something else I didn't want to acknowledge. I held Frank's gaze, refusing to look away. "Don't be absurd," I said, my voice tight. "Mr. Cardello is my employer, nothing more. I'm simply trying to do my job well."

Frank scoffed, shaking his head. "Yeah, I bet he'd love for you to 'do your job well.'" His words dripped with insinuation. My stomach churned.

I set my fork down, my appetite gone. "That's enough, Frank. I won't sit here and listen to you insult me." I stood up abruptly, my chair scraping against the hardwood floor.

Frankie began to whimper, startled by the irritated voices and my sudden movement. I scooped him up and hugged him close to my chest as I turned to leave the room.

"Where do you think you're going?" Frank demanded.

I paused in the doorway, my back to Frank. "I'm going to put our son to bed," I said, trembling slightly. I didn't wait for his response, striding down the hallway to Frankie's nursery.

The pale blue walls and soft yellow curtains did little to calm me as I changed Frankie into his pajamas, my hands still shaky as I fumbled with the tiny buttons. He was quiet as he looked up at me with curious eyes, almost as if he could sense my disquiet. Maybe he could.

I sighed as I picked him up and settled into the wooden rocking chair. Holding Frankie close, the gentle creaking thrummed through my body as I rocked back and forth. He nestled his face against my chest and sighed deeply.

A lullaby—the same one my sister, Edith, used to sing to me when I was a little girl—danced gently on my lips. When I had nightmares, she—not Mother—had always been the one to soothe and comfort me back to sleep. The melody wrapped around us like a warm blanket, and Frankie's breathing deepened and slowed as he drifted off to sleep. I envied his peaceful slumber, wishing I could escape into dreams as easily. But my thoughts were tangled tonight.

As I rocked Frankie, my mind drifted back to my lunch with Victor. The way he had looked at me—really looked at me—as if he could see straight into my soul. The way he spoke about my potential, about the things I could do if I just had the chance. It was intoxicating, that feeling of being seen and understood.

But then there was Frank's reaction, the suspicion and jealousy simmering beneath his words. The way he had insinuated that Victor only wanted me for…for what? My looks? My body? The very idea made me feel dirty, tainted.

I glanced down at Frankie—his face relaxed in sleep, his tiny hand clutching my blouse—and a fierce love surged through me. This was my life now. This was what I had chosen when I married Frank. A husband, a child, a home to keep. It was what I should want, what any good wife and mother would want.

The sharp slam of the front door shattered the quiet of the nursery like a gunshot. I flinched, my arms instinctively tightening around Frankie's sleeping form. He stirred, his rosebud lips puckering in a sleepy pout, but he didn't wake.

I held my breath as the heavy tread of Frank's footsteps stomped down the porch steps. The crunch of gravel signaled his path to the driveway, and then the all-too-familiar rumble of the Plymouth's engine roared to life.

He was leaving. Again. Off to some watering hole to drown his sorrows and nurse his wounded ego in cheap whiskey and the sympathetic ear of whatever barfly would listen. Leaving me alone with a toddler, a sink full of dishes, and a swirling mind.

As the rumble of the car's engine faded into the night, I let out a shaky breath. Silence settled around me like a shroud, broken only by the soft ticking of the nursery clock and Frankie's gentle sighs.

I carefully stood up from the rocking chair, my legs stiff from sitting. I placed a soft kiss on Frankie's mop of messy, straw-colored hair before lowering him into his crib. He barely stirred as I tucked his favorite blue blanket around him, his little fingers clutching the satin edge.

I paused, watching the steady rise and fall of his chest, marveling at the perfect innocence of his sleeping face. What I wouldn't give to have that kind of peace, that blissful oblivion.

With one last glance at Frankie's slumbering form, I quietly closed the nursery door. The hallway stretched before me, the floral wallpaper muted in the dim light. My shoes scuffed softly against the hardwood until I reached the dining room.

The remains of our aborted dinner still littered the table—half-eaten plates of stroganoff congealing, Frankie's highchair tray splattered with smears of gravy and stray peas. A wave of weariness washed over me at the sight, but I couldn't just leave it. Mechanically, I cleared the table, scraped the wasted food into the garbage pail, and stacked the dishes to be washed.

As I filled the sink with hot, soapy water, my mind drifted yet again—back to lunch, back to Victor. The way his eyes had sparkled with mischief and promise as we talked. The way his fingers brushed against mine. The way he held my hand. And I had let him.

The warmth of his touch still lingered on my skin—imagined, maybe, but no less vivid. I could still feel the slight roughness of his fingertips and the gentle pressure of his palm against mine. It was a simple gesture, but it had sent a jolt through me like an electric current.

I shook away the thought as I plunged my hands into bright yellow dish gloves. I scrubbed at the dishes as if I could scour away the confusing feelings swirling inside me, along with the crusted food remnants. The hot water scalded my hands through the rubber gloves, but I welcomed the discomfort. It grounded me, kept me tethered to the present moment instead of floating away on forbidden currents.

The sharp trill of the telephone pierced through the quiet house. I jumped, sloshing sudsy water down my apron. Cursing under my breath, I quickly removed my gloves and hurried to the phone table in the entry hall, my heart pounding in my chest.

I lifted the heavy black receiver to my ear, the bakelite cool against my skin. "Hello?" I said, trying to keep my voice steady.

"Babs? It's Edie." My older sister's warm, rich voice flowed through the earpiece, instantly soothing some of the tension in my shoulders. She was the only one who could get away with calling me Babs. "I wanted to check on you. You seemed a bit… off when you picked up Frankie this afternoon."

I sighed, leaning against the wall and twirling the phone cord around my finger. "I'm fine, Edie. Just tired." Even as the words left my lips, I heard how flat they sounded.

There was a hollow pause on the other end of the line. I pictured Edith's expression—her brow furrowed, her lips pursed in that way she had when she was trying to decide whether to push me or let me be.

"Babs…" she said finally, her voice gentle but firm. "I know you better than that. What's going on? Is it Frank?"

I closed my eyes, my throat tightening. Part of me wanted to spill everything, to let the words come tumbling out in a cathartic rush. But another part of me—the mayor's daughter, the well-brought-up girl trained to keep up appearances, smile, nod, and pretend everything was just swell—held back.

"Frank and I just had a little disagreement, that's all," I said, trying to inject a lightness into my voice that I didn't feel. "You know how he gets sometimes."

Edith was quiet for a moment, aside from her soft, even breathing on the other end of the line. "Just answer 'yes' or 'no.' Is he in the room with you?"

"Relax, there's no need. He's gone out. Probably to the bar."

"Is this about your new job?" she asked finally.

I felt a flutter of surprise. "How did you…?"

"Oh, Babs." She sighed. "I could see the excitement on your face when you dropped off Frankie this morning. And this afternoon, you were lit up like a Christmas tree. And then you got that look—the one you get when you're bracing for a fight. So I figured Frank doesn't approve."

I swallowed hard, my fingers tightening around the phone. Edith knew me too well and could read me like an open book, even through the crackle of the phone line. "You're right. Frank doesn't like the idea of me working," I admitted. "Especially not for someone like Victor Cardello."

"Someone like Victor Cardello?" she repeated, a hint of curiosity in her tone. "What do you mean by that?"

I hesitated, unsure how to put into words the confusing mix of emotions that Victor stirred in me. "Nothing particularly. I just think Frank is…intimidated."

She was quiet for a moment, and I could almost hear the gears turning in her head. "Intimidated?" Edith asked, her voice taking on a playful lilt. "Well, well. This man must be quite the charmer to get Frank all riled up."

I felt a blush creep up my neck, grateful that Edith couldn't see me through the phone. "It's not like that," I insisted, but the lack of conviction in my voice was painfully clear. "Mr. Cardello is just…different. He's sophisticated and worldly, and he talks about things like art and literature and travel and dreams and passions. Things that Frank doesn't understand or care about."

"But you do," Edith said softly. It wasn't a question.

I closed my eyes, leaning my forehead against the cool wallpaper. "I…I don't know, Edie. I thought I had put all those silly dreams behind me when I married Frank. But now—"

"Babs," she cut me off, her voice gentle but firm. "I know you love Frank. And I know you love being a mother to Frankie. But that doesn't mean you have to give up everything else that makes you who you are. You're a smart, talented, passionate woman. You deserve to have dreams and ambitions of your own."

I pressed my lips together and looked up at the ceiling.

"You're too young to remember what life was like for women before the war. I, alas, am not. We clawed our way out of the kitchen, and I'll be damned if we're going to be shoved back in."

"Mother would disagree with you," I countered.

"She's from a different generation. And a politician's wife through and through. Everything is about appearance for her. Always has been. Doesn't make it right."

I sighed, twirling the phone cord tighter around my finger until it bit into my skin. "I know. But sometimes I wonder if she's right. If I should just be content with what I have. Frank is a good man, and Frankie is my world. Maybe I'm being selfish wanting more."

"Nonsense," Edith countered. "You're not selfish for wanting to use your brain and your talents. And if Frank can't see that, well, that's his problem, not yours."

Her words sent a surge of warmth through me, easing some of the tightness in my chest. "Thanks, Edie." I sighed. "I don't know what I'd do without you."

"You'd muddle through somehow," she chirped, and I could hear the smile in her voice. "But luckily, you don't have to."

8

VICTOR

I descended the creaky wooden stairs into the damp, musty basement. My footsteps echoed off the bare walls. A single naked bulb flickered overhead, casting eerie shadows. Joey Rizzo stood waiting, hat in hand, shifting from foot to foot. Beads of sweat dotted his brow despite the chill.

"Mr. Cardello, I'm real sorry. It's just…some of these shop owners are barely scraping by as it is. A few are threatening to go to the cops if I keep leaning on 'em."

I stepped closer until I towered over Joey's wiry frame. He shrank back but had nowhere to go, trapped between me and the rough brick wall. I reached out slowly and straightened his rumpled collar, letting my hand linger near his throat.

"I don't recall asking you about the shop owners." I glanced over my shoulder at my lieutenant. "Phil, did I ask Joey here about any shop owners?"

Phil folded his thick arms across his broad chest, straining his jacket seams at the shoulders. "No, sir. You did not."

"I did not," I echoed, smoothing Joey's lapel before sliding my hands into my pockets. "In fact, I didn't ask you anything. I never said a word about the protection money. But you did. And it's short."

A bead of sweat rolled down his temple, trembling on his jaw before dropping onto his collar. His eyes darted to Phil, then back to me, searching for a shred of mercy. But I had none to spare for dishonesty.

"Well, Mr. Cardello, sir, it's just that...I mean..." Joey stammered, tripping over his words as he fumbled for an explanation.

I let the silence stretch between us, the tension thickening with each passing second. Joey's breathing grew more ragged. His hands shook as he clutched his hat like a lifeline. I savored his discomfort, letting him marinate in his own deceit.

"You know, Joey," I mused, keeping my voice mild even as my words carried an undercurrent of steel, "I've always prided myself on being a fair man. I give people a chance to prove themselves, to show their loyalty. And when they do, I reward that loyalty. Generously."

I let that hang in the air for a long moment, watching Joey squirm. His Adam's apple bobbed as he swallowed hard.

I leaned in closer, my eyes boring into his. "But when someone betrays that trust, when they think they can pull the wool over my eyes..." I trailed off, letting the implication sink in.

Joey's face paled. His lips trembled as he tried to form words. "I...I would never, Mr. Cardello. You know I'm loyal. Always have been."

"That's twice you've lied to me."

Joey opened his mouth, closed it, and opened it again. No words came out. Just a dry, clicking sound as he tried to swallow past the lump of fear in his throat.

I savored his every twitch, every bead of sweat that rolled down his face. He knew he was caught, knew there was no lie he could spin that would save him now. But still, he tried.

"Mr. Cardello, I swear, I didn't...I wouldn't..." His voice cracked, desperation seeping into every word.

"Let's cut to the chase, Joey," I finally said, my voice low and measured. "We both know the real reason the protection money is light. And it has nothing to do with anyone threatening to go to the cops. They all know better."

Joey's eyes widened, his face going even paler. "I...I don't know what you mean, Mr. Cardello," he finally managed. "I would never—"

"Steal from me?" I finished for him, my voice deceptively soft. "Skim a little off the top, thinking I wouldn't notice? That I wouldn't find out?"

Joey shook his head frantically, his hat tumbling forgotten to the floor. "No, no, I swear it! I've always been loyal to you, Mr. Cardello. I would never betray you like that!"

I sighed. "That's three lies."

"Four, sir," Phil corrected.

I stepped back, letting Joey's own terror do my work for me. His breaths came in short, panicked gasps as his eyes darted around the dank basement, looking for an escape that didn't exist.

"Mr. Cardello, please," he begged, his voice cracking. "I...I can explain. Times have been lean. I just needed a little extra cash. I was gonna pay it back, I swear!"

"Then you should have asked."

"I...what?" Joey stared at me, confusion replacing the fear in his eyes. "I don't understand. You...you would've loaned me money?"

I almost smiled at that. Almost.

Instead, I stepped closer, watching the fear rush back into Joey's face. "You're a smart man, Joey. Or at least, I thought you were. If you needed money, you should've come to me. I take care of my own."

"I...I didn't think...I was afraid..." Joey stammered, his voice trailing off into the damp air.

"Afraid of what? That I'd say no?" I cocked my head, studying him. "Or afraid I'd say yes, and then you'd owe me?"

Joey's silence was answer enough. I let out a long, slow breath, shaking my head. "You disappoint me, Joey. I had such high hopes for you." I turned to Phil, silent and imposing in the shadows. "Phil, do you remember when your mother was sick a few years back? How she needed those expensive cancer treatments?"

Phil nodded, his eyes never leaving Joey's trembling form. "I remember, Boss. I was at my wits' end, not knowing how to pay for it all. The hospital bills were piling up, and I was working every hour I could, but it still wasn't enough."

I smiled, but there was no warmth in it. "And what did I do, Phil? When you came to me and asked for my help?"

Phil's voice was steady, filled with a quiet reverence. "You paid for everything, Boss."

I turned back to Joey, letting the weight of Phil's words sink in. Joey's eyes were wide, his skin ashen under the flickering light.

"You see, Joey," I said softly, "when one of my own needs help, I provide it. No questions asked. That's what loyalty means to me. It's a two-way street. I take care of my people, and they give me honesty and respect."

Joey fell to his knees, his hands clasped in front of him. Tears streamed down his face, leaving glistening trails on his pallid cheeks.

"Mr. Cardello, I'm sorry. I'm so sorry," he babbled, his words tumbling out in a rush. "I made a mistake, a terrible mistake. I see that now. I was weak and stupid, and I let my fear get the best of me. But I swear to you on my mother's grave, it will never happen again."

I crouched down, putting myself at eye level with him. "Considering that your mother's alive and well, that's not much of a promise." I patted his shoulder as I stood, looming over him. "And you're right."

He looked up at me, confusion and desperation splashed across his face.

"It will never happen again."

I straightened my suit jacket and adjusted my cufflinks with deliberate, almost leisurely motions. A sad smile played at the corners of my mouth as I pulled a cigarette from my silver case and lit it with a steady hand. Drawing on the cigarette, the sweet, acrid clouds filled my chest, and I savored the brief moment of respite.

I turned to Phil and gave him a quick, silent nod. His expression didn't change, but there was a flicker of understanding in his eyes. Without a word, I clapped his shoulder and crossed to the stairs.

Phil's heavy footfalls and Joey's desperate pleas faded into the background, drowned out by the steady drip of water from a leaky pipe overhead and the creaking of wooden stair treads underfoot.

9

BARBARA

Tract housing blueprints and property maps lay spread across the conference table. The developer, a balding man in his fifties, sat back in his chair, hands steepled under his chin as he watched Victor pore over the plans.

"As you can see, Mr. Cardello," the developer said, his voice gritty from decades of smoking, "these new neighborhoods will be a goldmine. With the post-war boom, people are clamoring for a slice of the American dream. A house, a yard, a place to raise their kids away from the grime of the city."

Victor nodded, his expression unreadable as he traced a finger along the proposed streets and cul-de-sacs.

"I don't doubt that, Mr. Kowalski. Though I'd like to know what you specifically mean by 'grime.'"

Mr. Kowalski shifted in his seat, a thin sheen of sweat glistening on his upper lip. "Oh, you know," he said with a dismissive wave of his hand. "The crowding, the pollution, the crime. People want a fresh start, a place where they can breathe easy."

His eyes darted away from Victor's as his stubby fingers clawed to loosen his tie and his jaw clenched a bit too tightly.

"As long as that's all you mean," Victor said, his voice low and even. "I own a lot of properties in the city. I would hate to think you consider them grimy." He drained the last of his coffee and glanced at me.

I rose from my chair and smoothed the front of my dress. I retrieved the coffeepot from the sideboard and glided around the table to Victor's side. The scent of fresh coffee mingled with Victor's crisp cologne as I leaned in. Steam curled invitingly from the dark liquid as I tipped the carafe, pouring until his cup was full. Victor gave me an almost imperceptible nod of thanks, his eyes never leaving Mr. Kowalski's face.

As I moved to refill Mr. Kowalski's cup, I felt his gaze crawling over my figure, eyes lingering a bit too long in places they shouldn't. I kept my expression neutral, focusing on my task even as discomfort prickled under my skin.

"Cream and sugar?" I asked politely, holding the sterling silver creamer poised over his cup.

Mr. Kowalski's thin lips curled into a smirk. "Yes, doll face. And in my coffee too." He winked and shifted his gaze down to my bust.

Victor stood. "He doesn't need any, Mrs. Evans." He walked around the table, straightening his tie.

"Well, actually…some cream would be nice."

I looked at Victor for direction, and he shook his head. I pulled back the creamer.

Victor perched on the edge of the conference table next to the developer. "I suggest you apologize to the lady," Victor said, his voice eerily calm. Too calm.

"Come again?"

Victor shot his hand out, his fingers clamping down on Mr. Kowalski's wrist with a viselike grip. The developer let out a yelp of surprise and pain, his eyes wide as saucers. I jumped back, my heart pounding against my ribs.

"Apologize to the lady."

Mr. Kowalski's face reddened, his jowls quivering as he stammered an apology. "I…I'm sorry, Mrs. Evans. That was…

inappropriate of me." Sweat beaded on his forehead, and his eyes darted nervously between Victor's impassive face and his own trapped wrist.

Victor held him a moment longer, letting the lesson sink in before releasing his grip. He patted Mr. Kowalski's shoulder, the gesture somehow more threatening than comforting. "I'm glad we understand each other."

Mr. Kowalski nodded frantically, cradling his wrist to his chest. He looked like he wanted nothing more than to bolt from the room, property maps be damned.

"Now, about these developments," Victor continued, as if nothing untoward had happened. He tapped the map to draw the developer's attention back to the matter at hand. "I think we can make this work, but there will need to be some changes."

Mr. Kowalski swallowed hard. His eyes darted to the map and then back to Victor's face. "Changes? What kind of changes?"

Victor traced a finger along one of the proposed streets. "For starters, we'll need to ensure adequate infrastructure to support these new neighborhoods. Roads, sewers, utilities. All of that costs money." He glanced at the developer, one eyebrow raised. "Money that will need to come from somewhere."

Mr. Kowalski nodded eagerly, seeing a chance to redeem himself. "Of course, of course. We've budgeted for all of that. It's built into the cost of each lot."

Victor smiled, but it didn't reach his eyes. "I'm sure it is."

I settled back into my chair, pen poised over my notepad, as I watched the interplay between the two men. The air in the room was thick with tension, and the ticking of the clock practically echoed in the silence.

Victor returned to his high-back leather chair at the head of the table, steepling his fingers under his chin as he studied the map. "Infrastructure is only part of the equation, Mr. Kowalski. We also need to consider the long-term viability of these neighborhoods. The kinds of amenities that will attract buyers away from Lakewood and the other cheaper developments. We need to keep property values high."

Mr. Kowalski nodded, dabbing at his forehead with a monogrammed handkerchief. "Absolutely. We've planned for parks, schools, and shopping centers. Everything a growing family could want."

Victor leaned back, crossing one ankle over his knee as he lit a cigarette. He took a long, slow drag, letting the smoke curl lazily from his lips as he studied the plans. The silence stretched, broken only by the distant clatter of typewriters.

"You've done your homework, Mr. Kowalski," Victor said at last, tapping ash into a cut crystal tray. "And I'd like to help you. I really would."

"But…"

Victor took another long pull from his cigarette, the tip flaring bright in the cool white light of the conference room. He exhaled slowly, the smoke drifting toward the drop ceiling.

"But," he continued, his voice smooth as silk, "I have concerns about the margins on this project. The cost of materials, labor, permits…it all adds up quickly. And with the market being what it is, there's no guarantee we'll see your projected returns. We may be in a boom now, but a boom only lasts so long."

He leaned forward, bracing his elbows on the polished mahogany table. The cufflinks at his wrists glinted—twin points of gold against the stark white of his shirt peeking out from his charcoal pinstriped suit jacket.

"If I'm going to put my money, my name, and my reputation behind this, I need to know it's worth the risk. I need to see the numbers line up in a way that makes sense. I'm not running a charity here."

A thrill ran through me as I watched Victor work, admiring the initial subtlety of his approach that culminated in a sharp punch.

Mr. Kowalski shifted uneasily in his seat and licked his lips nervously, his eyes darting between the papers and Victor's impassive face.

"I understand your concerns, Mr. Cardello," he said, his voice wavering slightly. "But I assure you, we've done extensive market research. These neighborhoods will practically sell themselves. The demand is there, and with the right marketing strategy, we'll make a healthy profit."

Victor leaned back in his chair, fixing the developer with a penetrating stare.

"I don't doubt your research, Mr. Kowalski. I'm sure your bean counters and number crunchers did a fine job." He stubbed out his cigarette and stood. "Come back to me with a twenty percent increase in my margin, and we'll talk."

Mr. Kowalski blinked, his mouth opening and closing like a fish gasping for air. "Twenty percent? But that's…that's not possible." He fumbled with his tie. "The margins are already razor-thin as it is. If we increase your cut by that much, there won't be enough left over to cover our costs, let alone turn a profit."

My pen flew over the paper as I recorded Victor's concerns and demands in my notes.

Victor shrugged, the motion fluid and effortless beneath the fine wool of his suit jacket. "Then I suppose we don't have a deal." He turned to me, his dark eyes glinting in the fluorescent light. "Mrs. Evans, would you be so kind as to show Mr. Kowalski out?"

I closed my notebook and stood. "Of course, Mr. Cardello."

Mr. Kowalski lurched to his feet, desperation etched into his face. "Wait, wait," he pleaded, holding up his hands, palms out. "Please, Mr. Cardello, let's not be hasty. I'm sure we can come to an arrangement that benefits us both."

Victor paused, his hand resting on the back of his chair. He cocked his head. "I'm listening."

Mr. Kowalski swallowed hard, his Adam's apple bobbing above his too-tight collar. "What if…what if we sweeten the pot a bit? Offer some additional incentives to make the deal more attractive?"

Victor's eyebrows lifted a fraction. "Go on."

The developer leaned forward, his voice low as if sharing a secret. "Picture this: not just tract houses and parks and schools, but an integrated commercial center. A drive-in theater, diners, a centralized shopping complex, and more."

Victor sat back down, and I took my seat beside him and reopened my notebook.

"I know it's a bit daring, but I really think this is where we're heading. One-stop shopping. Why travel all over the city when you can get everything in your neighborhood?"

"And commercial properties keep paying out," Victor added.

"Exactly! Houses pay once, and then they're done. But businesses…" He waved his hand as he let his sentence trail off.

Victor nodded. "Come back to me with an updated proposal that meets my increased margin, and we'll talk again."

The men stood, and Mr. Kowalski rolled up his plans and papers and tucked them under his arm. Victor reached out to shake his hand.

"Mrs. Evans will show you out." Victor didn't let go of the man's hand. "And I trust you will show her every ounce of respect she's entitled to." His voice was low and dangerous. "I certainly wouldn't want any more…unpleasantness."

I rose from my chair, smoothing the front of my tailored dress. "Right this way, Mr. Kowalski," I said with a polite smile, gesturing toward the door.

He followed me into the hallway, where the scent of lemon polish and cigarette smoke hung in the air. I walked a half-step ahead, the click of my heels punctuating the tense silence.

As we waited for the elevator, Mr. Kowalski shifted his weight from foot to foot, clutching his rolled-up plans to his chest like a shield. He shot me a sidelong glance.

"Your boss is a real shark, isn't he?" he muttered, dabbing at his forehead with his handkerchief.

"I'm sure I don't know what you mean," I answered demurely, my expression carefully masked.

The elevator doors slid open, and he got in.

I smiled sweetly. "Thank you for your visit."

The doors slid closed, and I let out a sigh.

"How badly did that one sweat?" Mrs. Miller piped up from behind the reception desk as she checked her pink nail polish for chips.

I walked over to her, the scent of her perfume—something floral and powdery—enveloping me as I approached. She glanced up from her nails, her glassy green eyes sparkling with mirth.

"Oh, he was practically drowning," I said, leaning against the polished wood of her desk. "I thought I was going to have to mop up after him."

She let out a tinkling laugh, her pink-painted lips curving into a knowing smile.

I sighed, glancing back toward the conference room. "Are all the meetings so…intense?" I asked.

"These big-shot developers think they can waltz in here and charm their way into a deal." She shook her head. "But Mr. Cardello is on top for a reason."

"Yeah, I'm gathering that."

The telephone rang, and she reached for the receiver, giving me a polite smile and nod.

I tucked my notebook under my arm and returned to my desk. My mind replayed the meeting—the way Victor commanded the room, the sharpness of his gaze, and the subtle danger that laced his every word. There was something thrilling about being in his presence, like standing on the edge of a cliff, the simultaneous pull of fear and exhilaration.

The door to Victor's office was open, and I peeked my head inside. "Would you like me to type up my notes?"

"Eventually, yes," he answered, leaning back in his leather chair. "But I'd like to hear your take first."

"My take?"

"Yes." He motioned to the empty twin chairs in front of his desk.

I tentatively entered the room and sat on the edge of one of the chairs, the cushion stiff beneath me. I smoothed my skirt over my knees and crossed my ankles.

"Well," I began, choosing my words carefully, "I think the project is a good idea. There is a lot of expansion into the suburbs right now, and it makes sense to jump on that bandwagon."

Victor nodded, his dark eyes fixed on mine. "But?"

I hesitated, biting my lower lip. "It's not my place."

A smile played at the corners of his mouth. "I insist. I want to know what you think."

I let out a controlled breath. "To be perfectly honest, I don't like the guy."

Victor leaned forward and rested his elbows on the desk. "Go on," he encouraged, his dark eyes glinting with interest.

I shifted in my seat, the leather creaking softly beneath me. "He just seems…slimy. The way he wouldn't stand on the merits of his own proposal. At the first sign of challenge, he changed his tune to tell you exactly what he thought you wanted to hear." I didn't say it aloud, but I mentally added the unsavory way he looked at me. I shook my head, a shudder of revulsion running through me at the memory. "I don't trust him."

Victor's smile widened, transforming his face from handsome to devastatingly so. "You have good instincts, Barbara. I don't trust him either."

My heart fluttered at his praise as a warm flush crept up my neck. "Thank you, sir."

"Victor," he corrected.

"Victor." I nodded. "But if you don't trust him, why are you considering doing business with him?"

He leaned further across the table. "I'm not."

I blinked, confusion crossing my features. "But…the meeting, the negotiations…"

Victor laughed, the sound sonorous and rich. "It's all part of the game, Barbara. Let him think he has a chance. Let him sweat and squirm. Most importantly, let him do all the legwork."

I tilted my head, trying to wrap my mind around his strategy. "So you're letting him think there's a deal on the table even though you have no intention of following through?"

Victor leaned back in his chair. "Precisely. Let him run around —gather data, crunch numbers, sweeten the pot. He'll bring me a much better proposal, thinking it's his last shot to win me over."

I couldn't help but smile, impressed by Victor's shrewdness. "And then you'll turn him down flat."

"Precisely." Victor's eyes glinted with satisfaction. "And in the meantime, I'll have all the information I need to move forward with the project on my own terms. If I decide it's worth pursuing at all."

"And do you think it is?"

He studied me carefully. "I'm far more interested in what *you* think."

"I can't imagine why."

"You don't see yourself clearly at all, do you? You have a keen mind and a sharp eye. And you're no bootlicker. You don't tell me what you think I want to hear."

My cheeks warmed at his praise, my heart fluttering in my chest.

His dark eyes bored into mine, as if he could see straight into my soul. "So tell me, do you think this suburban development is worth pursuing?"

I took a deep breath while I assembled my thoughts. "I think it's certainly worth considering."

"Less diplomatic this time, please."

I met Victor's penetrating gaze and decided to be fully candid. "Yes, I think it's a smart move. The demand is clearly there. People are eager to escape the city, put down roots, start families. And they'll pay handsomely for the privilege." I leaned forward slightly, warming to the subject. "But if you want them to pay, it can't just be rows of carbon-copy houses. It needs to be a community, a lifestyle. The commercial center was a good idea—one-stop shopping, entertainment, dining. Make it easy. Make it convenient. Make it attractive."

Victor nodded, a glimmer of approval in his eyes. "Go on."

I sat up straighter. "And the location matters. Not just proximity to the city, but the land itself. Rolling hills, nice views, good schools nearby. You're not just selling houses. You're selling a dream. A fresh start for growing families. An escape after the insanity of the past two decades."

A slow smile spread across his face, his eyes alight. "I knew I was right about you."

"Sir?" I asked, a bit thrown by his reaction.

"Victor," he corrected again. "And I mean that you have a gift, Barbara. You see what so many of these pompous stuffed shirts miss. And I think you just wrote our marketing campaign."

Warmth spread from my chest to my cheeks. It was a novel sensation, having my ideas not only heard but celebrated. Sought after, even. Frank always nodded absently when I shared my thoughts, his attention more focused on the newspaper or radio. But Victor—he listened, truly listened. And better still, he seemed to genuinely value what I had to say.

"I'm flattered you think so," I said, ducking my head slightly to hide my smile.

When I peeked up, Victor's dark eyes glinted with something I couldn't quite name. Approval, certainly, but there was a heat there too. An intensity that made me feel seen in a way I never had before. It was thrilling and terrifying in equal measure.

I held Victor's gaze for a long, charged moment. My heart pounded against my ribs, and my skin tingled with awareness of his presence. I should've looked away, broken the moment—it was dangerous to let the connection linger. But I found myself powerless to break the spell.

"I have business across town this afternoon," he said, finally cutting the silence, his voice smooth as scotch. "But before I go, I have something for you."

He reached into his desk drawer and pulled out a package wrapped in crisp brown paper tied with a simple string. He held it out to me, his expression inscrutable.

"What's this?" I asked, hesitating before taking the parcel from his outstretched hand. The paper was smooth and cool beneath my fingertips.

"Call it a hunch," he said enigmatically as he leaned back in his chair and casually crossed his legs. "Open it."

Curiosity piqued, I carefully untied the string and unfolded the paper to reveal a red leather-bound sketchbook and a set of pencils.

"I don't understand," I murmured, running my fingers reverently over the sketchbook's supple cover. "Why are you giving me this?"

Victor's gaze was steady on mine, unwavering in its intensity. "I seem to recall a conversation we had over lunch yesterday. Something about a certain young lady's ambition for fashion design."

My breath caught in my throat, my fingers stilling on the buttery-soft leather. He remembered. Amid all his weighty responsibilities and the gravity of his position, he had not only listened to my wistful musings, but he had heard me. Truly heard me in a way no one else ever had.

"Victor, I…" My voice faltered, threatening to crack under the swell of emotion rising in my chest. "I don't know what to say." Gratitude, disbelief, and something more profound—more primal—swirled within me.

He stood and buttoned his suit jacket. "You don't need to say anything." His voice was soft and intimate. "Just promise me you'll use it."

I swallowed hard past the lump in my throat, my fingers curling around the sketchbook like a lifeline. "I will," I managed. "I promise."

His lips curved into a smile, warm and genuine. It transformed his face, softening the hard edges, and I saw a hint of what he must have looked like as a roguish and mischievous boy. "Good." He glanced at his watch, a flash of gold against his tanned wrist. "I'm afraid I have to run. But I'm going to take you on a tour of some of our properties and prospects tomorrow."

I stood as he approached me. The air tingled with electricity that intensified the closer he came.

"It'll give you a better grasp of the business." Victor paused before me, standing close enough that heat radiated from his body to mine. The spicy, woodsy scent of his cologne made my head swim pleasantly. My heart thudded against my breastbone as I tilted my head back to meet his gaze, my lips parting slightly.

His gaze dipped briefly to my mouth before flicking back up, dark and intense. "Be ready at nine sharp," he murmured, his voice a low rumble I felt in my bones.

"I will."

His dark eyes searched mine for a long moment. I stood frozen. I almost thought he would lean in to kiss me.

Then, with a slight nod, he stepped around me and strode toward the door, leaving me bereft and off-kilter in his wake.

10

VICTOR

"Divorce? Good God, man! You can't be serious." Lawrence quickly shut his office door and pulled the shade over the frosted glass. He eyed me with concern and disbelief.

"Look, I just want to know what it will take. Hypothetically, of course."

He removed his gold-rimmed glasses and pinched the bridge of his nose. "Are you asking me as your lawyer or as your friend?"

"Both."

Lawrence crossed to a small sideboard and poured two fingers of whiskey into a pair of plain lowball glasses. He handed me one, and I took a long sip, savoring the smooth burn as it slid down my throat. Lawrence settled into the leather armchair across from me and slipped his glasses back on. He sighed heavily and finally spoke. "Victor, as your lawyer, I must advise against this course of action. The social and legal repercussions would be…significant."

The whiskey warmed my chest. "It's 1951, Larry. Times have changed."

"Not enough." He took a long drink. "If you do this, every

aspect of your life will be fair game for investigation." He shot me a knowing look. "Do you really want to open yourself up to that kind of scrutiny?"

Damn. He made a good point. "That's fair." I paused. "And if I'm asking you as my friend?"

"As your friend…" Lawrence blew out a shaky breath. "I'm sorry you're unhappy."

"What would it take?"

"For starters, you need to decide if you'll sue Dotty for the divorce or let her sue you. Essentially, figure out which one of you will take the blame. And on what grounds."

"I don't care about a black mark. I'll take the blame." I reached into my breast pocket for my cigarette case.

Lawrence held up a hand, gesturing to the case. "Please don't smoke in here. My lungs got burned up pretty bad in France, and I don't care to hack out what's left of them this afternoon."

"Of course," I responded, shaking my head as I returned the case to my pocket. "Force of habit. It completely slipped my mind." I threw back the whiskey instead. "Anyway, I can take the blame."

"You could, but then Dotty would have to be the one to file for divorce. And I don't think she'd do that. I certainly wouldn't, were I in her shoes. When we drafted up your separation agreement three years ago, Dotty got a damn good deal—generous income, the Pasadena house, a new car every year." He ticked the items off on his fingers. "She'd be a fool to give that up without a fight. Unless something's changed between you two that I don't know about."

I shook my head again. "No, nothing's changed."

"It's a good deal. Separate lives, no public scandal. All the freedom of a divorce without the stain of one. Why stir up trouble?"

I nodded slowly, swirling the amber liquid in my glass. "I know it's not ideal, and it won't be easy. But there has to be a way."

He leaned back in his leather chair, the springs creaking softly. Lacing his fingers together, he appraised me over the rims of his glasses. "Then you file for divorce, but you need grounds. In your case, you've really only got two options. You could claim mental cruelty, but that's a tough sell. The courts tend to favor the wife in these matters. Adultery is your other option, but you'll need hard proof—photographs, hotel receipts, love letters, that sort of thing. And even then, it's no sure thing."

"What about separation?"

"You're thinking of desertion. And living in separate households doesn't cut it."

I stood and paced the width of the modest office a few times before turning back to him. "People get divorced all the time. There's got to be a way."

Lawrence was quiet as he sized me up. "What's really going on here? Why do you suddenly want to go down this road?"

"What do you mean? Dotty and I have been on the rocks for a long time. You know that."

He nodded and sighed. "Who is she?"

I pressed my lips together. "Who is who?"

He stood, walked over to me, and clapped me on both shoulders. "Victor, look at me. I'm not one of your employees or your lackeys. And I'm certainly not your mother."

"No, you're my friend."

He dropped his arms to his side. "Yes, I am. And we've been through a lot. We shed blood together, and that means something."

My mind flashed back to deafening mortar fire that shook the ground, blinding bursts of white-hot light in the pitch of night, and the snaps and whistles of gunshots.

"So who is she, Victor?"

11

BARBARA

The clock on the nightstand ticked softly, its hands inching toward midnight. The house was still, the silence broken only by the occasional creak of the floorboards settling. I was sitting in bed with my back resting against the headboard, gliding my fingers over the supple leather cover of the sketchbook Victor had given me. My gold wedding band caught the light from the bedside lamp.

I glanced over at the empty half of the bed next to me. The pale blue coverlet and cream sheet were neatly turned down, waiting for Frank to climb in eventually. I'd lost track of how many times I'd gone to bed alone, only to be awoken hours later by Frank stumbling in, reeking of cheap whiskey and cigar smoke, words slurred, eyes unfocused. There was a time when his absence filled me with a sense of longing—a desperate ache for his presence, his warmth, his touch. But now I savored the solitude. It was the only time I was free.

The thick pages whispered against each other as I thumbed through the blank sketchbook. A loose sheet of paper folded into quarters fluttered onto the bedspread. I unfolded the note, smoothing it open against my lap. The message was brief, written in a bold, angular script that I instantly recognized as Victor's.

It's time to let your light shine.

My heart fluttered in my chest as I traced my fingertip over the ink, feeling the gentle indentations left by the pen. I imagined Victor bent over his massive mahogany desk, pen in hand, deliberately choosing each word. A thrill raced through me at the intimacy of it, as if he had reached out across the distance between us to whisper in my ear.

Conflicting emotions warred within me—guilt, desire, confusion, yearning, intrigue. I knew I shouldn't indulge these feelings for Victor. And yet…some reckless part of me didn't want to stop. When I was with him, I felt alive, seen, understood, encouraged. Like I was finally waking up from a long, monochromatic dream.

I carefully refolded Victor's note and tucked it inside the sketchbook before setting it in my nightstand drawer. The drawer's latch clicked softly as I shut it away. My secret.

As if on cue, the front door opened and closed, followed by the thud of Frank's footsteps in the foyer. I quickly switched off the bedside lamp, plunging the room into darkness. Burrowing beneath the covers, I closed my eyes and steadied my breathing, feigning sleep. The bedroom door groaned as it swung open. Frank lumbered in and bumped against the dresser. Rustling fabric cut through the quiet night as he shed his clothing on the floor on his way to the en suite bathroom.

A few minutes later, he emerged and mumbled something unintelligible as the mattress dipped under his weight.

Frank's hot, moist breath slithered across the back of my neck as he nuzzled against my hair. The sour burn of whiskey churned my stomach. His sweaty palm dragged over my waist and grabbed at my hip. My skin prickled, and I suppressed the urge to recoil from his touch.

"Hey, baby, you still up?" His words bled together.

I kept my eyes screwed shut and tried to ignore the sandpaper rasp of his unshaven cheek abrading my shoulder. His thick, clumsy fingers pawed at the delicate lace trim of my nightgown. I clenched my jaw and lay rigid, forcing my breathing to stay even, willing him to stop. Frank sloppily kissed my neck, his lips wet and slack against my skin.

"C'mon, Barb, I know you're awake," he slurred, tugging at my shoulder, trying to roll me toward him. The stale stench of alcohol and cigar smoke clung to him like a noxious cloud.

I squeezed my eyes tighter and didn't respond, feigning the deepest of sleep as my heart thudded wildly against my ribs. After a few more insistent pulls at my arm, Frank finally gave up with an exasperated sigh. The mattress bounced and swayed as he flopped onto his back.

His heavy, uneven breaths soon gave way to the stuttering snores of drunken slumber. I exhaled slowly and unclenched my muscles as the tension gradually drained away. Blinking into the inky darkness, I listened to the soft ticking of the clock marking the languid passage of time.

My mind churned, unable to quiet the restless yearning that had taken root inside me. Despite my best efforts, my thoughts kept wandering back to Victor like a compass needle irresistibly drawn north. My skin tingled from the phantom touch of his strong hands. I adored how his eyes crinkled at the corners when he smiled at me, making me feel like the only woman in the world. The hypnotic timbre of his voice resonated through my bones. He had awakened something inside me—a part of myself I didn't even know existed until now.

Sleep eventually came for me, and when it did, it swept me away to a dream world where Victor was waiting for me. In the hazy logic of the dreamscape, I found myself standing on the porch of a weathered beach cottage, its white clapboard siding bleached by the sun and crusted with salt spray. The rhythmic crash of waves against the shore and the lonely cry of seagulls echoed in the distance.

Victor emerged from the cottage, and my breath hitched at the sight of him. He wore a loose white linen shirt, unbuttoned at the collar, and faded blue trousers rolled at the ankles. The ocean breeze ruffled his thick, dark hair. His eyes, mysterious and alluring, fixed on me with an intensity that made my knees weak.

"I've been waiting for you," he said, his velvety voice wrapping around me like an embrace. He extended his hand, palm up, long fingers beckoning.

I placed my hand in his, thrilled by the feel of his warm, rough skin. Electricity surged through me at the contact. Victor drew me to him, and I went willingly, powerless to resist his magnetic pull. He wrapped his arms around me and held me flush against the solid planes of his body. I melted into him, yielding to his strength, craving more.

Victor's knuckles skimmed along my jaw, igniting sparks in their wake. He tipped my chin up with a single finger, his eyes, deep and dark as obsidian, bored into mine. The rest of the world fell away until there was only Victor, only this moment suspended in time.

"Barbara," he whispered, his breath a feather-soft caress against my lips. He leaned down, his movements achingly slow, and brushed his nose along the slope of my cheek. My heart raced, and my ears grew hot. Victor's lips hovered a hairsbreadth from mine, not quite touching, letting the anticipation build until I thought I might shatter from the sheer wanting of it.

Just as Victor's lips were about to meet mine, a distant rumble of thunder jolted me. My eyes flew open, and I was back in my bedroom, staring at the ceiling. Rain pattered against the window, and lightning flashed in the distance.

Damn it.

12

VICTOR

Despite the overnight thunderstorms, the next morning dawned clear and bright. The sun danced off the sleek midnight-blue hood of my Jaguar MK V as I navigated the winding streets of northwest Los Angeles. Barbara sat poised beside me, her golden hair delicately pinned back into soft curls that grazed her shoulders. She wore a pale yellow dress that set off her luminous skin and traced the graceful lines of her neck and bust. I tried to keep my eyes on the road, but my focus kept straying, drawn to the flush on her cheeks and those rose-petal lips.

A pair of cat-eye sunglasses shielded her eyes, but I could feel her watching me, studying my profile. As the city's congestion and towering buildings fell behind us, giving way to the rolling hills and fragrant orange groves of the San Fernando Valley, I finally broke the silence.

"Tell me something—how does a girl like you end up married to a guy like Frank?" I kept my tone light, but I was genuinely curious. From my dealings with the man and the little Barbara had shared, Frank had all the charm of a bowl of cold oatmeal.

She sighed, twisting her delicate fingers together on her lap.

"It's not a very exciting story, I'm afraid. I was at the Hollywood Club, rubbing elbows with the sailors on shore leave. One of my films had just released, and the producer sent the cast out to 'mingle for morale,' as he called it. Frank came into the club that evening with a group of his Navy pals."

I nodded, encouraging her to continue.

She sighed. "I was twenty, and I fell in love with a uniform."

"And then what happened?" I prodded gently, sensing there was more to the story.

Barbara turned toward the window, watching the passing scenery. Groves of orange trees stretched as far as the eye could see, their waxy green leaves shimmering under the brilliant blue sky.

"Frank got his discharge papers, and I turned twenty-one," she said softly, still gazing out the window. "We got married because that's what you did. It's what my family expected. Find a man, settle down, start a family." She laughed, but there was no mirth in it.

I glanced at her. Melancholy had settled over her delicate features—her brow furrowed, her lips turned down at the corners. My chest tightened. I wanted to pull over, take her in my arms, and kiss away that sadness—until all she felt was pleasure and the only name on her lips was mine. I tightened my grip on the steering wheel, knuckles blanching.

"Frank's a fool," I said, my voice low and rough with restrained emotion.

Barbara turned sharply toward me, lips parted in surprise. I met her gaze unflinchingly, willing her to see my sincerity.

"He's a damn fool if he can't see what he has in you."

I looked back at the road and shifted gears as we rounded a bend, the Jaguar hugging the curves like a lover's caress. The engine hummed, the only sound besides our breathing and my pulse pounding in my ears. I swallowed hard and laid my cards on the table.

"There's a fire inside you, Barbara. I see it. You're not content to just be some man's pretty little trophy. Nor should you be."

Barbara didn't say anything. Even through the dark lenses of her sunglasses, I felt her gaze cutting into me.

I pulled the car off to the side of the road and shifted into park. Silence stretched between us, thick and charged, the air crackling with tension. Slowly, she removed her sunglasses and folded them with deliberate care. When her eyes met mine again, they glistened with unshed tears.

"Why are you saying these things to me, Victor?" Her voice wavered, but there was an undercurrent of steel beneath her words.

I held her gaze steadily, unblinking. "Because it's the truth. And I think you know it too, even if you're afraid to admit it to yourself."

A single tear escaped, tracing a glistening path down her cheek. I ached to reach out and brush it away, to feel the satin smoothness of her skin. But she beat me to it, dashing the tear away with a flick of her fingertips. She took a deep, shuddering breath and squared her shoulders, composing herself.

When she spoke again, her voice was steady. "I'm not afraid. I'm...confused."

"By what?"

"By you. By the way you make me feel."

My pulse kicked hard. I turned toward her, my knee grazing hers. "Tell me how I make you feel, Barbara."

Her tongue skimmed over her lips, and heat unfurled low in my abdomen as I tracked the movement.

"You make me feel...alive. Awake. Like I'm finally seeing the world in color after a lifetime of black and white."

I reached for her then, unable to hold myself back a moment longer. I cradled her face in my hands, my thumbs sweeping over the delicate arches of her cheekbones. Barbara's eyes fluttered shut as she leaned into my touch, nuzzling her cheek against my palm. Her skin was like warm silk, impossibly soft.

The sweet floral scent of her perfume clouded my head, making me dizzy with longing.

"Look at me, Barbara."

Her lashes lifted, and her gaze locked with mine. Those wide, luminous eyes were deep enough to drown in, flecked with bits of gold that sparkled in the sunlight slanting through the windshield. In their shimmering depths, I saw longing and trepidation—desire tangled with uncertainty. I wanted to erase every doubt, to show her with my words and my body how precious and extraordinary she was.

I had no reason or ability to resist. I leaned in slowly, giving her time to pull away. But she didn't. Instead, she parted her lips on a soft sigh. That was all the invitation I needed. I closed the remaining distance between us and brushed my lips against hers, gently at first—a barely there whisper of a touch—her mouth soft and pliant beneath mine.

I traced the seam of her lips with my tongue—tasting, savoring. Barbara's lips yielded under the gentle pressure of my mouth. I lingered in the velvet slide of her lips against mine, the heat of her breath mingling with my own. My hands slid into her silken hair, angling her head to deepen the kiss.

A soft moan rose in her throat, and the sound hit me low and deep. Her fingers skimmed over my shoulders, slid up the back of my neck, and tangled in my hair. I groaned against her mouth as her nails lightly scraped my scalp, sending shivers cascading down my spine.

Blood roared in my ears, and my heart hammered in my chest as our kisses turned more urgent, more consuming. The world fell away until there was only Barbara—her ragged breathing, her intoxicating scent.

Barbara let out a soft sound, caught between a gasp and a word. She tensed and pulled away abruptly, her fingertips pressed firmly to her lips. She turned her face toward the passenger window, but not before I caught a glimpse of the confusion and desire warring in her eyes. Slowly, I let my hands slip from her hair, already aching to have the silk of it between my fingers again.

Silence stretched between us, broken only by our ragged breathing and the distant trill of a bird. Barbara fixed her gaze out the window, but I could see her reflection in the glass. A becoming flush painted her cheeks, her lips parted and glistening.

"Why did you stop the car?" Her voice was slightly breathless, but it sounded like she was aiming for casual. She missed.

I bit back a smile, admiring her attempt to steer us back to safer ground. I dragged a hand over my mouth and drew a deep breath as I fought for composure.

"To show you this." I gestured out the windshield at the expanse of undeveloped land stretching before us—rolling hills dotted with towering oak trees and swaying grasses that shimmered gold in the sunlight. "This is where I'm going to build my new suburban development."

Barbara shifted in her seat, her wide eyes drinking in the view. "It's beautiful, Victor. Like something out of a painting."

"I've been buying up the land, and I think the time is right for this project." Excitement thrummed through me as I pictured the future—this rugged stretch of wilderness transformed into a thriving, lucrative community.

I hopped out of the car, circled to open Barbara's door, and offered my hand. Her slender fingers slid into my palm, and a jolt of electricity crackled up my arm. I savored the delicate weight of her hand in mine as I helped her from the car, steadying her when the stiletto heel of her shoe sank into the soft earth. I held on to her a moment longer than strictly necessary before reluctantly letting go, then guided her to the edge of a grassy bluff overlooking the valley. The land rippled out in gentle swells of winter green and gold, dotted with sprawling oaks that cast dappled shadows on the undulating ground.

"Just imagine it," I said, sweeping my arm out in a broad arc.

"Streets lined with sycamore trees winding through the hills. Gracious ranch-style homes with wide picture windows to flood the rooms with California sunlight. And best of all, everything in one location—schools, shopping, dining, entertainment, the cinema, you name it."

Barbara listened intently as I painted the picture, her eyes sparkling. "It sounds like a little slice of paradise," she said, her voice soft with wonder.

I nodded, warmed by her understanding and appreciation of my vision. "Exactly. And you're the reason I'm making it happen, Barbara."

She turned to me, her brows furrowed in confusion. "Me? Whatever do you mean?"

I held her gaze, willing her to see the depth of my sincerity. "Your passion, your drive, it's infectious. You've inspired me to stop dragging my feet and make this a reality. Before someone else does."

Barbara shook her head. "Victor, that's very generous of you, but I've only worked for you for three days."

I stepped closer. "And what an incredible three days they've been."

Before she could respond, I guided Barbara back to the Jaguar, my hand resting lightly on her back. As we settled into the supple caramel leather seats, I turned to her with a mischievous grin. "I have one more property I want to show you today, if you're game."

Barbara smiled, intrigue flashing in her eyes. "I'm game."

13

BARBARA

The Pacific Coast Highway was a symphony of nature's beauty, each curve revealing a new vista of majestic cliffs plunging into the azure water. Sunlight painted golden brushstrokes across the rugged landscape, casting a warm glow over everything it touched. As we wound westward toward Malibu, I couldn't resist turning my face toward the heavens, letting the sun's warm caress kiss my skin through the car's windshield. The drive would be spectacular in the summer with the top down.

As we rounded a bend, a striking modernist structure came into view—all clean lines and walls of glass perched on a bluff overlooking the Pacific. Victor steered the car onto a crushed-shell driveway and killed the engine. In the sudden hush, the mournful cries of seagulls circling overhead and the undulating crashes of waves on the beach wrapped around us as the ocean breathed. Victor came around and opened my door, offering his hand, his touch warm and solid.

The salty tang of the ocean danced on the breeze. I shielded my eyes from the sun as I took in the magnificent structure. Bright ribbons of light reflected off the vast glass panes. "It's stunning," I mused. "Whose is it?"

Victor rocked back on his heels as he looked up at the house. "It's mine."

I blinked in surprise, my gaze darting back to Victor. "Yours? I had no idea you owned a beach house."

He flashed me a roguish grin. "It's not something I advertise. This is my private retreat—a place to escape the hustle of the city." He gestured toward the front door. "Would you like the grand tour?"

Before I could respond, Victor's hand settled at the small of my back, guiding me up the path. Even through my dress, my skin tingled at his touch. We ascended a few steps onto a spacious deck that wrapped around to the ocean-facing side of the house. Victor unlocked the door and ushered me inside.

The interior was just as striking as the exterior—wide open spaces, gleaming hardwood floors, and walls of glass framing the endless Pacific. I stepped further into the space, my heels clicking against the polished wood. A massive stone fireplace anchored one wall, its earthy tones echoing the natural warmth of the space. The soaring ceilings and minimalist decor evoked a feeling of tranquility and spaciousness. Sleek, low-slung furniture in soft neutrals complemented the million-dollar ocean view rather than competing with it.

Victor stepped beside me, his posture loose and easy, his hands tucked into his pockets. "So, what do you think?"

"It's incredible." Awe crept into my voice as I took it all in. "The way the light moves through the space, the airiness of it all. It feels…freeing, somehow."

He smiled. "That's precisely the idea. A place to shed the weight of the world and be at peace."

I moved toward the windows, drawn to the vast Pacific stretching endlessly to the horizon. The water sparkled like a blanket of diamonds under the golden sun. Frothy white-capped waves curled and crashed rhythmically against the rocky shore.

I was keenly aware of Victor's presence behind me. My skin

prickled, every nerve ending attuned to his nearness and the heat of his body. I swallowed hard, forcing the flutter in my stomach to settle, and kept my eyes trained on the vista, though I could see his reflection in the glass.

"Is Mrs. Cardello home?" I smoothed an invisible crease from my dress.

Victor's reflection shifted slightly, amusement flickering across his features. "No, Mrs. Cardello isn't here. She prefers our home in Pasadena." He paused, seeming to choose his next words carefully. "We've kept separate residences for some time now. It suits us both."

Heat crept up my neck at the implication. Excitement and shame churned low in my stomach. I fixed my gaze on the ocean, watching a seabird coast on a wind current, its wings outstretched. Silence pooled between us, charged with unspoken words.

Victor cleared his throat. "Would you like to see the rest of the house?"

Relieved for the shift in conversation, I turned to face him with a smooth smile. "Please. Lead the way."

He showed me the sleek, modern kitchen—crisp white appliances in clean, rounded lines. From there, Victor led me down a hallway lined with framed black-and-white photographs. I paused before a striking image—an abandoned gas station, its paint-chipped sign fading into the barren desert beneath an endless sky. The composition was masterful, the play of light and shadow evoking a sense of lonely desolation.

"Did you take these?" I asked, moving to another—the weathered remains of a sagging, dilapidated barn, captured in exquisite detail.

"I did," Victor confirmed, stepping beside me. "Photography is a passion of mine. Has been since I was a boy."

I glanced at him, seeing him in a new light. "You have a remarkable eye." I moved to the next photo—a child with twin braids down her back, weaving a straw basket. Her dress was ragged at the edges, patched in places, yet she looked content. "The textures, the tones, the emotion you draw from them—it's moving."

Victor dipped his head slightly in a rare show of humility. "Thank you, Barbara. It means a great deal to me to hear you say that." He eyed me silently for a moment, then took a sharp breath and moved closer. "If you like my work, I'd like to show you something."

We walked in silence down the hallway, stopping at the last door. Victor hesitated, resting his hand on the brass knob. "This" —he eased the door open and stood back, gesturing for me to enter—"is my sanctuary."

The room felt worlds apart from the rest of the house— intimate, dimly lit, wrapped in rich textures and dark wood. Heavy black velvet drapes covered an entire wall. A pristine white backdrop stood against the opposite wall, flanked by tripods and lighting rigs in an organized chaos.

Victor entered the studio with quiet reverence, his fingers laced together in front of him. He moved to a table along the back wall and lifted a large leather portfolio.

"Other than what I have framed, these are some of my favorite works." He opened the portfolio with care, turning it to face me. Inside lay a series of striking black-and-white photographs, each matted and boldly signed *VC*.

I drew closer, spellbound. A lonely dock reaching out into a misty harbor, an empty park bench framed by bare trees, a little girl in a window gazing out at the rain—all were imbued with a haunting beauty. Victor's mastery of composition, light, and shadow made the ordinary hauntingly beautiful.

"What do you think?" Victor asked, his voice low.

"Victor, these are exquisite." My fingers hovered over the photographs, instinctively careful not to touch. "I can feel your passion in every detail." I looked up and met his gaze, my heartbeat quickening.

Victor moved closer, his eyes never leaving mine. "There is one thing missing, though." He reached out, his fingers gently brushing back a lock of my hair. "A subject worthy of immortalizing."

My lips parted, but no words came. His touch left a trail of fire on my skin.

Victor tilted his head, studying my features. "Let me photograph you, Barbara. Please," he said, his voice low, his eyes burning.

My chest tightened as I stared at him. Every instinct told me to say no, to flee this room and put as much distance between us as I could. But there was something in his gaze that pinned me in place.

Slowly, I nodded.

Victor's eyes lit up, and a smile curved his lips. He gave my hand a light squeeze and led me to a simple wooden stool in front of the backdrop. He glided around the space—flipping on lights, adjusting rigs, loading a fresh roll of film in his camera.

I perched there, frozen, heart racing. What was I doing? This was madness.

"Just be yourself," he said gently as he adjusted the lights. "You're no novice at this."

I drew in a slow breath, willing myself to relax as Victor studied me through the lens with an artist's eye, taking in every detail. The bright lights illuminated my face, and I felt exposed, vulnerable. Victor moved silently, angling and filtering the lights just so until the glow was soft and diffused.

"There," he murmured, more to himself than to me. He crouched down, eyes sharp behind the viewfinder. I held still, watching him. His strong, elegant hands delicately manipulated the focus ring. A stray lock of dark hair fell across his forehead, and he swept it back absently, consumed by his craft.

My pulse thrummed as his eyes met mine again over the top of the camera. "Don't look at the lens. Look at me," Victor commanded. His voice was low, intimate. Click. Our gazes locked, and the rest of the world fell away. Click. It was just the two of us suspended in this moment. Click.

I shifted on the stool, suddenly self-conscious under Victor's lens. What had come over me, agreeing to this private photoshoot? I was a married woman, yet here I sat, allowing another man to photograph me.

"You're a natural, Barbara." Click. "Perfect," Victor said as he changed his angle.

I swallowed hard, warring with myself. I should have cut this off, should have left. But the way Victor saw me—truly saw me—was addictive. I blossomed under his attention.

Victor lowered the camera and stepped toward me, his eyes intense. "Let me try something different," he said quietly. Reaching out, he gently brushed my chin and tilted my face toward the light.

I shivered at his touch, my pulse racing. His fingers traced my jawline, lingering a beat too long before dropping away. He pulled a heavy black drop cloth from a table and pinned it over the white background. He picked the camera up again and adjusted the zoom and focus.

"Stunning." Click. He stepped onto a low stool and stood over me. "Look at me." Click, click. He stepped down and moved to my side. "Now turn your head—look at me over your shoulder."

I followed his commands without hesitation.

"Just like that." His voice was husky. Click. Victor let out a long—almost unsteady—breath as he set the camera on the table.

"Are we done?" I asked.

He chuckled. "For today."

I sucked in a deep, fortifying breath through my teeth as Victor stepped closer. His eyes trailed over me, making my skin tingle.

"You have a rare beauty, Barbara," he murmured. "Inside and out. I knew it the first moment I saw you."

Heat bloomed on my cheeks under the weight of his gaze. "Victor, I…"

His fingers brushed my chin, lifting it gently. Our eyes locked, and an electric current passed between us. Slowly, giving me time to pull away, Victor lowered his head until his lips met mine in a soft, tentative kiss.

At his touch, a flame ignited within me. My hands reached up of their own accord, fingers tangling in his dark hair, drawing him closer as I returned his kiss. I stood, pushing myself up into him. Victor's strong arms encircled me, pulling me flush against his broad chest. All thoughts of propriety vanished; there was only this man and the fire raging between us. His kiss deepened, full of pent-up longing and desire. I clung to him, dizzy with the taste and feel of him.

He slid his hands down my back, gripped my hips, and lifted me onto the edge of the table. He stepped between my knees, his body pinning me in place as he trailed hot, open-mouthed kisses along my throat. I wrapped my legs around his waist, pulling him against me, arching into him.

"Barbara," he murmured, his voice rough with want. "You are exquisite."

His praise sent a thrill through me. I felt beautiful, desired—seen in a way I hadn't been for so long. I threaded my fingers through his dark hair and urged his lips back to mine.

He obliged, a smile breaking through his kisses. His hands caressed my thighs, rucking up my dress. I shivered and gasped at the sensation of his palms against my bare skin.

At the sound of my sharp inhale, Victor broke the kiss and pulled his hands out from under my dress, his breathing ragged. He pressed his forehead to mine as he gripped the table's edge.

"Tell me to stop, Barbara," he whispered. "Tell me this is madness and you never want to see me again."

But the words wouldn't come. "I can't," I finally murmured.

Victor's dark eyes searched mine, seeking answers I wasn't sure I had. "You can't do this? Or you can't ask me to stop?"

"I can't...ask you to stop." My voice quivered under the weight of my confession. "I don't want you to stop."

He exhaled a ragged breath, knuckles white beside my hips. "Neither do I."

14

VICTOR

Barbara was a vision—her half-lidded eyes, the flush of her cheeks, the rising swell of her breasts with each heavy breath. I scooped her up and laid her on the thick, plush carpet beneath the intense studio lights. Her dark eyelashes fluttered as she looked up at me, her golden hair fanned out around her.

Bracing my weight on my forearms, I hovered over her and kissed her deeply, hungrily—pent-up longing exploding to the surface. She responded in kind, her hands gripping my shoulders, nails digging in. I trailed kisses down her neck as she arched into me, soft gasps escaping her lips. I ran my hands over the delicious, supple curves of her body. As I glided over her breasts, she let out a soft moan. I slipped one hand under her skirt and slid up her thigh to graze the strip of tender exposed skin—warm and smooth as satin—above the band of her nylons. She let out a soft whimper.

But it was when I cupped the warm silk of her panties that she truly surrendered to me, her delicious heat radiating beneath my fingertips, melting any resistance I had left in me.

I claimed her mouth again, nipping and sucking on her lower lip, eliciting a series of soft pants and moans as I stroked my fingers back and forth over the thin fabric. She was so wet. Practically dripping. Ready.

I pressed her thighs apart with my knees and fingered the band of her undergarments. My groin ached, pulsing hard against my trousers. I wanted nothing more than to give in to desire and have my way with her, to completely ravish her.

But a small voice of reason broke through the haze of lust. As much as I craved Barbara, I couldn't exploit her vulnerability. She deserved more than a sordid tryst on the floor of my studio.

It took every ounce of willpower I had, but I pulled my hands away, chest heaving, as I pushed up to my knees.

She grasped at my shirt as I moved away. "Don't go…"

I smiled gently as I took her hands and helped her sit up. She looked so unguarded, so desirable with her disheveled hair and swollen lips. "I'm not going anywhere. But this can't happen. Not like this." I tucked an errant blonde curl behind her ear.

Confusion and hurt flashed across her face. "Why?" she whispered. "Don't you want me?"

"Oh, God, yes." I groaned as I cupped her face in my hands. "I want you more than I've ever wanted anyone. Ever." I pressed an urgent kiss to her soft lips. "But not like this."

"I'm sorry," she said, her voice small. Tears welled in her eyes. "You must think I'm—"

"No, no, my darling." I tilted her chin up to meet my gaze. "Don't apologize." I wiped away twin streams of tears from her cheeks. "Not to me. Not ever."

Sitting beside her, I pulled her into an embrace, and she melted against me, her head nestled perfectly under my chin. I held her close, breathing in the sweet floral scent of her flaxen hair.

"You're not a conquest, Barbara. You're not some cheap broad, and I won't treat you like one." I kissed her hair. "You're a lady, and you deserve far better than a few frantic moments on the floor." I tipped her head back so she'd look up at me. Her blue eyes shone like the ocean. "When we come together, I want to worship every inch of you slowly, tenderly. To give you the pleasure you've been denied for so long." I leaned down to kiss her lips. "To treat you like the goddess you are."

———

Barbara sipped from a bottle of soda pop, her lips wrapped delicately around the striped straw. Golden afternoon sunlight streamed in through the passenger window, gilding her profile. Damn, she was a vision.

"Your turn," she said, breaking the silence.

"My turn for what?" I kept my hands firm on the wheel.

"Well, you asked me about Frank on the drive out here. It's only fair that you tell me about your wife on our way back."

I tensed. Dorothy was the last thing I wanted to talk about. "What do you want to know?" I asked carefully.

"How did you meet? When did you get married?" She hesitated. "What went wrong?"

I pressed my back into the leather seat, silent as I downshifted into a curve on the highway.

"You don't have to tell me, not if you don't want to," she said gently.

I exhaled slowly, eyes fixed on the road. "No, it's all right. Dorothy and I... Things haven't been right for a long time." I paused, gathering my thoughts. "We met in college at USC. I was finishing up a degree in business, and she was studying English. She was pretty, sweet—easy on the eyes, and easy company." I let out a long breath. "I had just graduated when the war broke out. I answered the call and joined up, and we got married in a hurry like so many young couples did in those days. Looking back, it was madness, but it made sense at the time."

"Then what happened?"

"The war changed everything. When I got back, I was a different man. I'd seen and done things I hoped never to speak of again. Dorothy didn't understand. She wanted her college sweetheart back." I shook my head. "But that man was long gone."

"And then Margaret came along."

I winced internally and glanced at Barbara. "You have a good memory."

She smiled but said nothing.

"Dotty got pregnant almost right away, and Margaret was born while I was overseas. She was two—almost three—when I finally met her." I smiled sadly as memories of holding my daughter for the first time washed over me. "Margaret was my one bright thing in those dark post-war days. I adored her from the moment I laid eyes on her. She was the only innocent, pure thing left in my world." I gripped the wheel tighter. "Dotty and I quickly realized we had nothing in common anymore. The sweet, carefree girl I had married was gone—replaced by a bitter, resentful woman. And I..."

Barbara placed her hand gently on my arm. "You don't have to say any more, Victor. I think I understand."

I looked over at her—this angelic blonde in my passenger seat. "You're easy to talk to, you know that?"

She smiled, dipping her head, as if that would hide the flush in her cheeks from me.

"I threw myself into work," I continued. "The hours were long and relentless. I wasn't around much. Dorothy resented me for it, accused me of abandoning her and Margaret all over again." I rolled my shoulders as if that could shake off the weight. "And I'm man enough to admit there was some truth to that."

We crested a hill, and there it was—the vast Pacific, unfurling before us in shades of slate and sapphire, shimmering under the late afternoon sun. I was quiet for a moment, drinking in the sight. This view never failed to soothe me.

"It's beautiful," Barbara said softly.

"It is," I agreed. "This is my favorite drive. Clears my head."

We drove in easy silence. Barbara seemed content to let me keep company with my thoughts.

"Dorothy and I keep up appearances," I said after a while. "But we lead separate lives. She has the house in Pasadena, and I keep an apartment downtown near the office."

"And a beach house, apparently."

I grinned. "An indulgence."

Barbara furrowed her brow, looking troubled. "What about your daughter?"

"Margaret stays with her mother mostly. I get to see her on holidays and such, but Dorothy keeps her from me more often than not." I paused, uncertain how much more to divulge.

Something about this woman inexplicably loosened my tongue and melted my guard like butter under a hot blade. A part of me wanted to tell her everything—the dark secrets, the ruthless deeds, the steep sacrifices I made for power. But the larger, wiser part of me held back. She was still innocent in so many ways—still beautifully sheltered from the grittier truths of the world she lived in. I wouldn't be the one to tarnish that. Not yet, anyway.

"It's complicated," I finally said. "My work keeps me busy, and Dorothy and I have never seen eye to eye on things. She thinks I'm a bad influence." I gave a rueful chuckle. "She may be right about that."

Barbara gazed thoughtfully out at the ocean as we continued down the coastal highway. My words were clearly troubling to her, though she was too polite to pry further.

"Don't fret about it, doll," I said gently. "It's ancient history now."

She turned to me, concern shadowing her blue eyes. "I just hate to be a homewrecker."

A hearty laugh rumbled from my chest. I reached over, grabbed her hand, and kissed the inside of her wrist. "First of all, you have absolutely nothing to worry about on that score. My home is already well and truly broken. But the concern should be mine, not yours." I pressed another kiss to her silky skin and inhaled the soft trace of her floral perfume. "I don't want to ruin your life." I placed her hand back in her lap with a sigh. "I just..."

"You just what?"

It took me a moment to find the words. "I just wish I'd met you first."

Barbara turned toward the passenger window, silent for a beat. "Do you really mean that?"

I glanced over briefly. Her gaze lingered on the horizon, but a quiet, vulnerable hope in her voice hit me square in the chest.

"Of course I do," I said gently. "From the moment we met, I felt something—a spark—that I've never known with anyone else."

I kept my eyes on the road, but I could feel her gaze slide over to me, lingering. "Do you say this to all your girls?" she asked, her tone breezy but just a beat too slow to sell it.

I let out a heavy sigh as I steered through an intersection. This was not an easy subject for me. "I'm not going to lie. I've had other women over the years," I admitted. "But they were just dalliances—a good time and nothing more. Maybe some flowers or jewelry as a parting gift, but it never went further than that." I paused to gather my thoughts. "I know men say this sort of thing when chasing a beautiful young woman—which, of course, you are. But if all I wanted was to take you to bed, I would have done it."

Barbara was quiet. I snuck a glance at her lovely profile, simultaneously fearing and longing for her reaction.

"Why are you telling me all this?" she asked, so softly I almost didn't hear her.

"Because you deserve the truth." I reached over and took her hand in mine. "With you, everything's different. I'm different. When we're together, I don't feel like I have to put on a mask or pretend. It's...liberating."

"I feel the same way," she said in a hushed voice. "When I'm with you, it's like I can finally breathe. I don't have to keep up the act or pretend to be someone I'm not." She let out a soft, nervous laugh. "It's crazy, isn't it? We barely know each other." I heard the faint rustle of fabric against leather as she shifted beside me. "But it's true. At home, I feel like I'm playing a part, being the perfect wife. I'd like to say that Frank tries, but he doesn't. He just wants the perfect wife, the storybook life. He doesn't understand me. Doesn't even see me." Her voice caught. "Not like you do."

"I *do* see you, and you're extraordinary." I turned into the office parking garage. "Where are you parked?"

"Second level, by the stairs."

I maneuvered the Jaguar around the curves and up the ramp.

As we crested the second level, she pointed to a black sedan. "The Plymouth."

I pulled into the empty spot beside it and shifted the car into park. Barbara stared at her hands folded neatly in her lap, uncertainty clouding her delicate features.

"What are we doing, Victor?" she asked softly. "This is madness."

I gripped the wheel hard and pulled in a slow breath. She was right, of course. This whole situation was reckless, dangerous even. But I'll be damned if I was going to walk away now.

"I know." My words came out rough and low. "Believe me, I know we're playing with fire, but that doesn't change a thing. I can't stay away from you, Barbara. I don't want to." I drew in breath to speak but cut myself off.

She tilted her head, eyes narrow as she studied me. "What were you going to say?"

I let out a nervous laugh. "Nothing gets past you, does it?"

She didn't answer.

"I was going to ask you to take the rest of the week and weekend to think long and hard about it. About us. And let me know your answer when I see you on Monday."

"Monday?"

"Well, you only work Monday through Wednesday. And it's Wednesday, Barbara. So, yes, Monday."

"Do I still have a job with you?"

"Of course you do, doll." I chuckled, trying to lighten the tense mood. "You're one of the best secretaries I've ever had, and I won't deprive myself of that talent just because we…"

Barbara blushed a deeper shade of pink, but her eyes sparkled with mirth. "I'll see you Monday then." She reached for the door handle, but I stopped her with a touch. She hesitated and turned back to me, uncertainty and longing flickering across her face.

"Wait," I said softly. "Before you go, there's something I need to say."

Barbara's eyes searched mine. "What is it?"

I steadied myself. "I know this is dangerous. If we pursue it, there will be consequences—for both of us." I reached up and tenderly brushed my thumb across her cheek. My heart thundered. "You deserve so much more than the life you have. You deserve passion, adventure, love. I want to give that to you, Barbara."

She drew in a sharp breath, tilting her face down as she struggled for composure. When she finally lifted her gaze to meet mine, her eyes were luminous, glistening like a film starlet's.

"Victor, I…I don't know what to say," she began haltingly. "A part of me wants to throw caution to the wind and run away with you right now."

My God, she even sounded like a starlet.

"But the rational part of me knows that would be reckless. And then there's little Frankie. I can't do anything to hurt him."

I took her hand, giving it a slow, reassuring squeeze. "I understand. I would never ask you to do anything to hurt your son. Take the time you need to think things through." I pressed a gentle kiss to her hand. "You're worth the wait."

Barbara nodded, blinking as a few tears slipped free. She quickly dashed them away. "Thank you, Victor." She leaned in and brushed the faintest kiss against my cheek. Even that whisper of contact sent a charge through me. "I'll see you Monday," she whispered. Then she slipped out of the car before I could respond.

15
BARBARA

Afternoon sunlight streamed through the lace curtains as I tidied the living room, gathering Frankie's toys and straightening the embroidered pillows. My fingers trembled as I placed the toys into a wicker basket, my thoughts drifting. What would it be like to surrender to Victor? To feel alive and free, swept up in the breathless grip of a clandestine romance?

The echo of his touch lingered on my skin. The ghost of his kiss danced on my lips. My stomach fluttered.

A sharp rap at the front door jarred me from my reverie. I steadied my nerves and smoothed my dress and hair as I went to see who it was. A smartly dressed private courier stood on the front porch, a single cream-colored envelope in hand.

"May I help you?"

He checked the envelope. "I have a letter for Mrs. Barbara Evans."

"I'm Mrs. Evans."

"Sign here, ma'am," he said, offering me a clipboard and pen. I signed my name, and he handed me the letter.

"Thank you."

He tipped his navy-blue cap. "Have a nice day." He tucked

the clipboard into his satchel, mounted his bicycle, and pedaled off.

I glanced up and down the street. Other than Mrs. Tucker walking her two Pomeranians, it was empty and quiet. I went back inside and shut the door.

The envelope bore my name, typed neatly, with no return address. My hands trembled as I turned the envelope over and sank onto the sofa. Who could it be from? And why had it been delivered by courier instead of through the mail?

I carefully opened the envelope and unfolded the letter inside. The stationery matched the envelope—thick, luxurious, and unmistakably expensive. Victor's bold, elegant script flowed down the page.

January 18, 1951
Thursday
10 p.m.

Hello, my darling—

Thursday night, and I'm "working." At any rate, I'm here at the office, and the best thing I could possibly do is tell you how dear you are to me. It's quiet here, and I'm all alone and so very lonesome for you, sweetheart. I know you won't mind if I take this opportunity to tell you, in my own inadequate manner, how much I adore you. I'm always so full of big ideas about the things I want to tell you. Then I find myself face to face with you, and I lose my powers of communication. Might as well be without a voice.

I find myself daydreaming of you constantly—you and your beautiful eyes. The whole day has been a maze of little things I remember about you—how you look when you're about to be kissed, how your hand touches mine and the tingle that engulfs me so completely, how your lips form my name so beautifully, darling.

It feels like we've loved each other always, and yet I know it's not true because we've hardly loved each other at all. Just scratched the surface. And yet there is so much waiting for us—so many wonderful things in store—that the minutes and days until I see you again drag by at a snail's pace. The ache inside is an almost unbearable thing. And when I do see you again, it will be as if the entire world has been magically lit up.

How can I tell you how very much you mean to me? How can I project for you the picture of complete devotion I have in my head? If you only knew—and dearest, I think you do—that my complete program from here on out is built around you. My one constant desire is that you will allow me to take care of you, to respect, to cherish and adore you until there is no more time. Make my life full again, sweetheart.

There's really no reason to cram all the volumes

of things I feel I must say to you into one little note. I hope we've got a long time together, so I'll ration them out—whispered more appropriately into that wonderfully soft ear of yours while you're snuggled in my arms.

But until then, my darling, until you're all mine, until I hold you tight again...

—V

A rush of exhilaration flooded through me. Victor's boldness was thrilling, even as it filled me with trepidation. I knew this was reckless. But the thought of being in his arms again overpowered all apprehension.

I read the letter again and again, savoring every delicious, forbidden word. His passion leapt off the page and set my heart racing. I traced my fingers over his bold script, imagining his strong hands penning each line, pouring out his desire for me. Those same hands that had glided up my thighs beneath my dress. A fiery ache pulsed between my legs. My head swam, light and hazy, like I was two bourbons deep.

Frankie's babbles cut through the fog. "Mama!" he called from his room down the hall.

I took a deep breath to calm the swirling tempest inside. "I'll be right there, sweetie," I answered back as I rose to my feet. I carefully folded the letter, slipped it back into the envelope, and tucked it into my brassiere.

Frankie stood tall in his crib, gripping the railing, when I opened the door.

"Awake already, my love?"

He bounced on chubby legs, his cheeks still flushed from sleep. "Up! Up!" he chirped, reaching for me.

I lifted him into my arms, his warm little body pressed against my chest, the letter hidden between us. He wrapped his arms around my neck and nuzzled close, the scent of baby powder floating around him.

I carried Frankie to the changing table and laid him down. As I changed his diaper, my thoughts drifted once more to Victor, to the intoxicating promise of passion and fulfillment.

Frankie giggled and kicked his legs, snapping me back to the present. I tickled his round belly and cooed as he squealed with delight. "Are you hungry, sweet pea?" I asked as I carried him to the kitchen. "Let's get you a snack, and then you can play until Daddy gets home."

I settled Frankie into his high chair with crackers and a sliced banana to keep him busy. As he babbled happily to himself, I set about preparing dinner, my thoughts still consumed by Victor's letter. I moved through the motions of peeling potatoes and chopping vegetables in a daze, my mind replaying every word, every promise.

Frankie's cheeks were covered with smeared banana by the time he was finished. "Silly goose," I chided gently as I wiped his face with a clean washcloth. His bright blue eyes shone up at me. My precious boy. I set him up on a blanket in the living room with a basket of toys while I got back to work.

I slipped a Nat King Cole record on the turntable and placed the needle. After a few scratchy seconds, a lush instrumental intro swelled through the living room. Closing my eyes, I smiled, humming along with the tune.

I turned to folding the laundry I had taken off the line earlier, letting the rhythm settle my thoughts. I focused on the warm, clean scent of the sun-dried linens, the soft, worn cotton of Frank's undershirts, Frankie's pajamas, and his tiny socks.

The last wisps of daylight bled into an indigo sky. There was something winsome about a winter twilight—a quiet, simple, understated beauty. With a sigh, I drew the curtains closed and went to the kitchen to slide the meatloaf into the oven. I wiped my hands on my apron and glanced at the clock. Frank would be home soon, and I needed to pull myself together before he arrived.

I switched on a few lamps to dispel the encroaching shadows and returned to the living room. Frankie was still absorbed in building a tower with his wooden blocks, his little brow furrowed in concentration. I settled onto the sofa and picked up my mending basket, hoping the routine task would steady my nerves.

As I stitched a split seam in one of Frank's work shirts, the front door clicked and swung open, followed by Frank's heavy footfall in the foyer.

I took a steadying breath and schooled my expression into a warm smile as I set aside my sewing and stood. "Welcome home, darling," I greeted him sweetly, crossing the room to take his coat and hat. The wool was damp from the misty evening fog, cool beneath my fingertips. "How was your day?"

Frank loosened his tie and ran a hand through his hair, the curls mussed from hours beneath his hat. "Brutal," he muttered. "That new accounts manager, Anderson, is a real piece of work —breathing down everyone's necks over every damn detail." Frank's shoulders were slumped, his face drawn with fatigue.

I made a sympathetic noise as I hung his coat and hat on the rack by the door. Frank exhaled heavily as he trudged toward the sideboard in the living room.

Frankie's face lit up as he spotted his father. "Dada!" he squealed, scrambling to his feet.

Frank gave him an absent pat on the head as he passed by on his way to pour himself a generous three fingers of bourbon into a cut crystal tumbler. The amber liquid sloshed against the sides as he raised it to his lips and took a long swallow. He closed his eyes for a moment, then grimaced at the burn.

"What's for dinner?" he asked, setting down his glass.

"Meatloaf."

He grunted. "Good. I like that." His gaze swept over the tidy living room and the folded laundry stacked neatly on the end table. "Looks like you finally got caught up on the housework today."

I bristled at his tone but smoothed my expression as I turned away. "I did have a productive day, yes," I replied evenly, moving to the kitchen to check on the meatloaf. The savory aroma of onions and herbs wafted out as I opened the oven door. "Dinner will be ready in about twenty minutes."

The music cut off abruptly, replaced by the crisp click of the radio dial. The evening news broadcast played as Frank settled into his armchair with a weary groan. I set the table with our everyday dishes—plain white porcelain edged with a thin blue stripe. The clinking of the plates and cutlery punctuated the droning voice of the newscaster. Steam curled toward the ceiling as I lifted the meatloaf and casserole dishes out of the oven and set them onto trivets on the cream-colored countertop.

I stepped into the doorway to call them to dinner but paused, watching the scene unfold. Frankie toddled over to Frank, his chubby hands outstretched. "Play, Dada?" he asked hopefully, holding up a red wooden fire truck.

Frank barely looked at him. "Not now, kiddo. Daddy's tired." He took another swig of his bourbon and rested his head against the back of the armchair, eyes closed.

Frankie's bottom lip quivered, but he didn't cry. He was already learning to swallow his disappointment. My heart ached for him.

"Spill it, Babs."

The gilt-rimmed china plate slipped from my soapy fingers, but I caught it before it crashed onto my mother's kitchen counter. I looked up at Edith and cleared my throat. "Spill what exactly?"

She nudged me with her hip as she picked up another plate

from the sink and wiped it with a blue-and-white checkered dish towel. "You're twenty million miles away and sighing like a schoolgirl fawning over Cary Grant." She shot me a knowing look. "I know you. Something's clearly on your mind, so spill it."

I set my towel aside and leaned against the marble counter, my hands pressing into the cool stone. "You're right," I admitted with a sigh. "There is something I need to talk to you about. But not here."

I glanced through the kitchen doorway toward the living room where Mother, Frank, my brother Bill, and his wife, Janette, sat around a square table playing bridge. Frankie lay curled on the sofa, fast asleep. Mother insisted the staff have Sundays off—one of her grand magnanimous gestures—but that meant Edith and I were left to manage the aftermath of family dinners ourselves.

"Can we step outside for a bit?" I asked.

Edith arched an eyebrow but nodded. She draped the damp checkered cloth over the faucet. "Lead the way."

I wiped my hands on my apron, untied it, and hung it on the hook by the pantry. Edith followed me through the kitchen door onto the back porch.

"Are the dishes done, girls?" Mother hollered at us.

"We'll finish them in a minute," Edith called over her shoulder and closed the door behind us before Mother could protest. "Ugh! I'm forty, but she still treats me like a child."

The Sunday afternoon air was crisp and mild. A cool breeze whispered through the hedges, carrying the faintest trace of salt from the distant ocean. Edith lit a cigarette, took a long drag, and sank gracefully into a wrought iron chair. She tipped her chin toward the chair opposite her.

"All right, it's just us now. What's going on?"

"Well…" I started as I sat down. "I'm not sure how to begin."

Edith tapped the dead ashes off her cigarette. "Let's start with how utterly mussed you looked when you picked up

Frankie on Wednesday. I hope you cleaned up your appearance before Frank got any ideas."

I let out a shaky laugh. "I did, but I'm not sure he would have noticed regardless."

Edith narrowed her eyes and leaned in, her cigarette poised between two elegant fingers. "Does this have something to do with your swanky new boss? What's his name—Victor?"

My stomach flipped at the sound of his name on her lips. I swallowed hard and nodded.

"I knew it." Edith took another slow drag, the cigarette's ember flaring bright orange against the fading light. "So, what exactly happened between you two? And don't you dare hold back on me. You know I don't give a fig about propriety and all that jazz. My only concern is for you, your happiness, and your well-being."

I hesitated, my fingers twisting in my lap. The ghost of Victor's touch lingered on my skin. "He wants to be with me."

"Be with you…? As in take you to bed? Take you to the movies? Share your seat on the streetcar?"

"Edie, I'm serious." I sighed and looked out across the lawn, the last golden rays of sun dappling the grass through the nearly bare branches of a line of oak trees. "Victor wrote me a letter," I said quietly. "Had it delivered by private courier on Friday. He said…more than I ever expected. How much he adores me, how he yearns for me constantly, how he wants to take care of me and cherish me. How he feels we're meant to be together…" I took a deep breath and let it out slowly, my gaze fixed on my lap. "He wants…everything with me. Not just an affair. A future." I lifted my eyes to meet Edith's. "He says he's in love with me."

Edith's eyebrows shot up. She stubbed out her cigarette in the ashtray and leaned back in her chair, crossing her arms over her chest. "Well, I'll be damned. That's quite the declaration." She tilted her head, studying me. "And how do you feel about him?"

I bit my lip, my heart fluttering like a trapped hummingbird.

"I'm drawn to him in a way I've never experienced before. When I'm with him, I feel...alive. Seen. Understood. Desired." I shook my head, a rueful smile tugging at my lips.

"Are you sure he's not just looking to get you between the sheets?" She held up her hands. "Not that there's anything wrong with a good jaunt."

"Edie!" I hissed.

"What? You think I don't know how to have a good time?"

I shook my head again, more firmly this time. "It's more than that, Edie. So much more. The way he looks at me, talks to me, touches me... It's like he sees right through me. Like he knows me better than I know myself." I took a shaky breath. "And God help me, but I want him too. So much it frightens me."

Edith whistled low. "Sounds like you've got it bad, Babs." She leaned forward, her expression sobering. "But you know this is playing with fire, right? You're a married woman with a child. Are things so terrible that you'd throw it all away for this Victor fellow?"

"Yes," I answered quietly, my eyes widening at the admission. "Heavens, I haven't said it out loud before." My shoulders slumped as I sank further into my chair. "I'm suffocating, Edie. Trapped. I've known it for some time, but it's taken this to make me admit it to myself. If the war taught us anything, it's that life is too short to be miserable. I have a chance at some happiness. And I'm going to take it."

16

VICTOR

"Good morning, Myrtle," I said, leaning against Mrs. Miller's reception desk, startling her from a note she'd been writing. She quickly smoothed her gray-streaked dark hair.

"Oh! Good morning, Mr. Cardello. You're in early for a Monday."

"Wanted to get a head start on the day. How are the grandkids?"

She beamed. "Oh, they're wonderful. Growing up too fast, of course."

I snuck a glance down the hallway. "Is Mrs. Evans in yet?"

"Oh yes, and hard at work. She's a keeper."

I dipped my head and smiled. "Yes, I believe she is." I glanced around the reception area. "Anything going on this morning?"

"Mr. Kowalski's office called earlier. He wants another meeting. I told him I'd check with you."

I shook my head. "I want to see his updated proposal first. If I'm happy, we'll schedule a follow-up meeting."

She nodded. "Very good. I'll take care of it."

"Thanks, Myrtle. You're a gem." I patted her hand and flashed her a smile.

She blushed and adjusted the collar of her blouse.

I strode down the hall, my pulse kicking up with each step, anticipation curling in my chest.

As I rounded the corner, there she was—bathed in morning sunlight, a vision as she sat typing. Her delicate fingers flew across the keys, and waves of golden hair spilled over her shoulders. The sight of Barbara stole my breath, just as it had the first time I saw her.

I paused, taking her in—the graceful line of her neck as she bent over her work, the rosy flush of her cheeks, the way she nibbled on her bottom lip when she concentrated. She wore a navy-blue dress with a fitted bodice that accentuated her breasts. A simple string of pearls adorned her neck, drawing my eyes to the creamy skin below.

Every little detail held me spellbound. In that moment, I fell for her all over again.

Barbara glanced up as if sensing my presence. Her cornflower-blue eyes met mine, widening slightly as a blush bloomed across her cheeks.

"Good morning." Her voice was professional, but her lips betrayed her with a secret smile.

"Good morning, Barbara," I replied, my voice low and warm. "You're looking especially lovely today."

Her blush deepened, and she dipped her head shyly. "Thank you."

I put my hands up. "Don't let me distract you when you're hard at work. I just had to admire the view." I winked at her before moving toward my office door.

"Oh, it's no problem. I'm just finishing up my notes from the Kowalski meeting last week. I hate to let a project go unfinished."

"That works out well. Mrs. Miller said Kowalski's office wants another meeting. She's going to have them send over his updated proposal before we agree to anything. When it comes in, go over it and note anything that stands out."

"Will do."

"What's on my schedule today?"

She flipped open my leather-bound calendar. "Nothing scheduled."

"Good." I grinned and opened the door to my office. "Finish up what you're working on while I get myself situated. Then come see me."

She grinned and went back to her typewriter.

I settled into my leather chair, the supple material creaking as I leaned back and surveyed my desk. Stacks of papers and files sat in precise order—a holdover from the Army. I skimmed a handwritten chart from Phil detailing our business owners and collections for the month. The columns were coded, but the meaning was clear enough. Things were already picking up after the unfortunate Joey Rizzo complication had been handled. I was tucking the file away when a soft knock sounded at the door.

"Come in," I called, knowing full well who it was.

Barbara stepped inside, a steaming cup of coffee in hand. The rich aroma drifted toward me, warm and inviting. She moved toward my desk, her hips swaying just so, and set the cup down on a coaster.

"One black coffee," she announced with a smile, her voice melodic. "Just how you like it. I thought you might need a cup to start your day."

Warmth bloomed in my chest. "You remembered how I take it."

"Not exactly a complicated order." She glanced down, nibbling her bottom lip before looking at me again. "And after your...eloquent declarations, I'd say a cup of coffee is the least I can do."

I chuckled as I leaned back in my chair. "You got my letter, I take it."

Barbara nodded, a shy smile playing on her lips. "I did. It was…quite something."

I stood and crossed the room to close the office door. Then I turned to her, stepping close enough to catch the intoxicating floral notes of her perfume. "I meant every word," I said softly, trailing my fingers along her jaw.

Barbara's eyes fluttered closed as she leaned into my touch. "Victor…" she breathed.

I silenced her with a long, gentle kiss. She sighed as I pulled back.

"Don't leave me in suspense, my dear. Will you make me a happy man?"

Barbara gazed up at me, her blue eyes shining with anticipation and desire. "Yes," she whispered, a delicate tremble in her voice. "Yes, I'll be yours, Victor. Completely."

A rush of elation surged through me. I claimed her lips in a searing kiss, pouring all my longing and devotion into it. Barbara melted against me, gliding her hands up my chest to wind her arms around my neck. I wrapped my arms around her waist, pulling her flush against me. Her soft curves molding to my hard planes set my blood on fire.

I deepened the kiss, my tongue sweeping into her mouth to dance with hers. She tasted of coffee and strawberries. A soft moan escaped her, and I swallowed the sound greedily. My hands wandered the length of her back as I trailed kisses along her jaw and down the slender column of her throat, reveling in her silken skin and the fluttering pulse beneath my lips.

"My darling," I breathed against her neck. "My sweet, perfect angel. I'm going to worship every inch of you. I'll treat you like the goddess you are."

I drew back to gaze into Barbara's eyes, darkened with desire. "I want to make love to you properly, to spend hours exploring and savoring you." I stroked her cheek with the backs of my fingers. "I need to finish up a few things here. But then will you let me take you to my downtown apartment? It's not far." I traced the plump curve of her bottom lip. "Please."

Barbara nodded, her cheeks tinged a delicate pink. "Yes," she whispered. "Sounds heavenly."

"Good girl," I purred, my mouth brushing her neck before I caught her earlobe between my teeth, eliciting a shiver. "But first, I need a taste. A little preview to whet both our appetites for later."

In one smooth motion, I grasped Barbara's hips and lifted her onto the edge of my desk. She gasped in surprise as I pushed up her skirt to reveal the lacy tops of her stockings. I nudged her knees apart and stepped between her thighs, my hands gliding up the silky smoothness to toy with the garters. Barbara's breath hitched as I caressed the sensitive skin of her inner thighs. Heat radiated through the thin fabric of her panties.

Pushing her skirt higher, I revealed the creamy expanse of her thighs. Anticipation coiled tight in my gut. I hooked my fingers in the delicate fabric of her panties and slowly dragged them down her legs, baring her most intimate parts to my hungry gaze.

I paused for a moment to admire the breathtaking sight before me—Barbara spread open on my desk. Slowly, reverently, I parted her with a single finger. Silky, scorching, drenched. She shuddered and bit back a whimper at my touch. I circled her swollen clit, slick and throbbing.

Barbara's hips twitched, and she pulled back as she gasped.

"Spread your legs wider for me, angel," I instructed, my voice a low rumble. "And remember, quiet now. Wouldn't want Mrs. Miller coming to investigate."

Barbara bit her lip and nodded, her cheeks flushed a deep rose.

I circled her swollen clit with the pad of my thumb, applying the lightest pressure. She shuddered and bit back a moan, gripping the edge of the desk, her knuckles white.

"That's it," I purred. "Just relax and let me make you feel good."

I slipped a single finger inside her and groaned at the exquisite velvet grip—she was so incredibly tight. I pumped slowly, curling to stroke that spongy spot along her front wall.

"Oh God!" Barbara keened before clapping a hand over her mouth. I smirked up at her.

"How many times have I asked you to call me Victor?"

Barbara let out a breathy laugh that quickly became a gasp as I added a second finger, stretching her deliciously. I set a steady rhythm, pumping and curling, building her need slowly, stoking the fire I had started. My thumb circled her clit in tandem with my thrusts.

Barbara writhed on the desk, sending papers scattering across the floor. Her head lolled back, eyes fluttering closed, lips parted on a silent cry of ecstasy. The cords of her neck strained as she fought to stay quiet. A light sheen glistened on her flushed skin.

"That's it, angel," I encouraged in a heated whisper, easing her to lie back on the desk. "Keep those beautiful legs wide open for me."

I drank in the glorious sight of Barbara splayed out before me —golden hair fanned across the dark wood of my desk, cheeks flushed the same delicate pink as her parted lips. Her chest heaved with each panting breath, the swell of her breasts straining against the confines of her dress. The flutter of her long lashes against her cheeks as her eyes squeezed shut in exquisite abandon.

Slowly, I withdrew my fingers, relishing her whimper of protest at the loss. I lowered my head, eyes locked on Barbara's as I placed a soft kiss on her inner thigh. She shivered, watching me, hooded eyes dark with desire, bottom lip caught between her teeth. Slowly, reverently, I trailed open-mouthed kisses along her silken skin, inhaling her intoxicating scent—sweet and musky, the essence of aroused woman.

With a long, slow lick, I parted her. Exquisite.

The moment my tongue touched her swollen clit, Barbara jolted and muffled a cry with her fist. I gripped her thighs, holding her open as I lapped at her, savoring her tangy musk on my tongue.

"Victor!" she gasped, her fingernails digging into the edge of the desk. "Oh God…oh!"

I pulled back. "When we're back at my place, I want you to scream until the walls come down. But here"—I slid my middle finger in deep, coaxing a soft whimper—"you've got to stay silent." I curled it deliberately, drawing another shaky breath from her. "Can you do that for me, angel?"

She pressed her lips together and nodded.

"Good girl." I held Barbara's hips steady as I devoured her, my tongue swirling and flicking in all the places that made her respond so beautifully. Barbara writhed beneath me, her thighs quivering and taut as bowstrings. I slid a second finger inside her, curling and stroking in tandem with the movements of my tongue.

Her breathing grew ragged, interspersed with muffled whimpers and gasps. I could feel her begin to flutter around my fingers. She was close, so deliciously close. I wanted to draw it out, to push her to the very precipice and keep her suspended there until she shattered.

I gentled my touch, slowing the thrust of my fingers to a torturous pace, moving my tongue against her in featherlight flicks. Barbara whined in frustration, her hips churning as she sought more friction.

With a wicked grin, I increased the pressure and speed of my fingers and tongue, driving her relentlessly toward the edge. Barbara's body bowed off the desk, hands scrabbling for purchase on the smooth wood.

"Let go for me," I coaxed between licks. "I've got you."

A few more firm strokes of my fingers and flicks of my tongue sent her soaring. Barbara's hand flew to her mouth to muffle her moans as she came apart, clenching hard around my fingers as waves of ecstasy crashed over her. I worked her through it, drawing out her pleasure until she collapsed back onto the desk, limp and sated.

I sucked at her gently as she caught her breath, savoring the proof of her surrender on my tongue. Finally, I withdrew my fingers with a satisfied hum.

"That was just the beginning, my darling."

17

BARBARA

I couldn't get inside Victor's apartment fast enough. Before he had even closed the door behind us, I kicked off my heels and was peeling him out of his suit jacket. Fire rushed through my veins, embers stoked into a raging inferno. Every nerve tingled with electric anticipation.

Victor backed me against the wall, his lips claiming mine in a frenzied kiss that left me breathless. I fumbled with the buttons of his shirt, desperate to feel his heated skin against mine.

Victor chuckled, a low rumble in his chest, as he captured my wrists and pinned them above my head against the wall. His body pressed into mine, hard planes and coiled power. I whimpered at the exquisite pressure, aching for more.

"Impatient, aren't we?" he purred, nuzzling my neck. He grazed my racing pulse with his teeth before soothing the sting with his tongue. "I like that."

"Victor, please," I breathed, straining against his grip. "I need you."

"Oh, I know, angel." He slid his free hand down my side, the heat of his fingers searing through the fabric of my dress. He gripped my hip and ground against me, drawing a low moan from my throat. "I can feel how much you need me," he growled. "How badly you want me inside you, filling you up."

I shuddered and rolled my hips, seeking more delicious friction. "Yes," I gasped. "Please, Victor..."

He captured my lips in another scorching kiss before pulling back, his dark eyes glinting with lust. "I'm going to take my time with you, Barbara," he promised in a low, rough voice. "I'm going to worship every inch of your exquisite body until you're trembling and begging for release." He released my wrists and stepped back, drinking in the sight of me with unconcealed hunger. "Strip for me," he commanded. "Slowly."

A shiver raced down my spine at his authoritative tone. I met the heat in his expression and reached behind my neck to unclasp my dress, sliding the zipper down in a whisper. The garment slithered off my shoulders and pooled at my feet, leaving me in my brassiere, panties, garter belt, and stockings.

Victor's eyes darkened further, pupils blown wide with lust. "Keep going."

I held his heated gaze as I reached back to unclasp my brassiere. The lacy garment fell away, baring my breasts to the cool air—and to him. I hooked my thumbs in the sides of my panties and eased them down my hips in one slow, unbroken motion. I unhooked my garters and slowly slid my stockings down my legs, bending at the waist, taking my time, putting on a show for him. Finally, I unclipped my garter belt and let it drop to join the pile of discarded clothing on the floor.

I stood before Victor—bare, exposed, chest heaving. His eyes raked over my body, taking in every dip and curve. The raw hunger in his expression sent a fresh wave of desire crashing through me. He looked like he wanted to devour me. And God help me, I wanted to be devoured. I was a willing offering, and he was every inch the predator.

"Perfection," he murmured reverently, closing the distance between us. He skimmed his palms up my sides, leaving trails of fire in their wake. His fingers traced the curve of my waist, the swell of my breasts, the slope of my neck. Every brush of skin on skin sent electric sparks racing through me. I shivered under his worshipful touch, my body singing with anticipation.

Victor threaded his hands into my hair and tilted my head back for a deep, consuming kiss that left me dizzy and aching. I clung to his shoulders, the fabric of his shirt and vest bunching under my fingertips.

"Too many clothes," I mumbled against his lips, tugging impatiently at his collar.

Victor chuckled, a dark, sinful sound. "So eager, angel." He pressed his hips into me, rock-hard beneath his trousers. Without my shoes, he was a touch taller than me, and our bodies lined up like they were made for each other.

In one smooth motion, he swept me up into his arms. I let out a surprised gasp, automatically winding my arms around his neck for balance as he carried me down the hall to the bedroom.

Victor laid me on the plush comforter. Slowly, deliberately, he unbuttoned his vest and shrugged out of it before tossing it over the back of a chair. He loosened his tie and pulled it free, letting it snake to the floor. Eyes locked on mine, he unbuttoned his shirt.

I swiped my tongue across my bottom lip at the sight of him —broad shoulders, chiseled chest dusted with dark hair, the defined V of his hips disappearing into his trousers. My fingers itched to touch him, to map the ridges and planes of his body. But I stayed still, transfixed by the erotic spectacle of Victor undressing for me. Returning the favor, as it were.

He toed off his shoes and socks and unfastened his belt and trousers, letting them fall to the floor. Finally, he undid the top two buttons on his shorts and slid them down his muscular thighs, revealing his impressive erection. Anticipation coiled tight in my belly at the sight of him hard and ready.

Victor crawled onto the bed, settling his hips between my thighs. Heat radiated off his body, stoking the flames within me. He braced himself on his forearms, caging me in with his body. I traced the sharp line of his jaw, the roughness of his stubble prickling my fingertips.

Victor turned his head to press a kiss to my palm. "You are so beautiful," he murmured, his lips brushing against my palm. "A goddess in the flesh."

His words sent a shiver racing down my spine. No one had ever looked at me the way Victor did—like I was the most precious, most desirable creature on earth. Like he would move heaven and earth just to be with me.

Slowly, reverently, he trailed open-mouthed kisses down the column of my throat, across my collarbone, over the swell of my breasts. He lavished attention on each peaked nipple, swirling his tongue and grazing with his teeth. Liquid heat pooled low in my belly as he mapped my body with his lips and hands, igniting every nerve.

His lips blazed a trail down my stomach, his tongue circling my navel in a slow tease before continuing lower. I shuddered in anticipation as he nudged my thighs further apart, his breath hot against my skin.

"Victor, please…" I panted, writhing restlessly on the bed.

He looked up at me, a wicked smirk tugging at his lips. "Please what, angel? Tell me what you need."

I flushed, equal parts aroused and embarrassed by his command. I'd never been vocal during lovemaking before, much less ever been asked what I wanted.

Ghosting his fingers along the sensitive skin of my inner thighs, he danced just shy of where I needed him most. His silence demanded mine to break first. My face burned, but the ache between my legs overpowered any lingering shyness.

"Can you…"

"Can I what, darling?"

I bit down on my lower lip. "Can you…do what you…" I couldn't bring myself to say the words.

He chuckled softly. "Let me help. Do you want me to use my fingers or my mouth?"

"Both." The word flew from my lips. My cheeks flamed.

Victor raised his eyebrows. "Greedy," he chided with a sinful grin. "As my lady commands." Slowly, teasingly, he lowered his head.

The first long, slow lick of his hot tongue ripped a low moan from my throat. My hips bucked off the bed at the exquisite sensation. Victor pinned me down with a strong forearm across my pelvis as he licked and sucked. I fisted my hands in the comforter, head thrashing on the pillow as he drove me to dizzying heights.

Victor slid first one, then two long fingers inside me, pumping in tandem with the movements of his agile tongue. I keened and writhed beneath him.

He pulled back long enough to speak. "Don't hold back. We're not in my office anymore."

I let out a ragged moan as Victor's fingers curled inside me, stroking that place that made my toes go numb. His tongue was hot and insistent. The sensations were almost too much to bear. Tension coiled inside me like a spring.

"Oh God, Victor!" I cried out, arching off the bed. "Don't stop, please don't stop!"

He growled against me, the vibrations sending sparks skittering across my skin. "That's it, angel," he encouraged between licks. "Let me hear you."

Spurred on, I let myself go, moaning and gasping freely as he worked me higher and higher. My thighs trembled and toes curled. I was on the precipice, ready to snap.

"Victor, I…" I panted, barely able to form words. My voice was foreign to my ears, high, breathy, and desperate.

He hummed against me and redoubled his efforts, lashing his tongue in tight relentless circles as his fingers stroked and curled. The vibrations combined with the pressure catapulted me into ecstasy.

It hit like a freight train, stealing my breath and setting me alight with rapture. I shattered, clamping down on Victor's fingers in rhythmic pulses as waves of sensation radiated out to the tips of my fingers and toes. A symphony of gasps, moans, and cries spilled from my lips, bouncing off the bedroom walls. I thrashed on the bed, fingers digging into the comforter, back bowing until only my shoulders and hips touched the mattress. He worked me through the aftershocks, his touch gentling as I floated down from the pinnacle.

Victor pressed a final soft kiss to my inner thigh before crawling back up my body. I reached for him, wanting to feel his solid weight anchoring me. I was trembling, my nerves still sparking and sizzling in the aftermath of the most intense pleasure I'd ever experienced.

He gathered me into his arms and held me close, brushing my damp hair away from my face. "You are so incredibly divine when you let go like that," he murmured, his lips grazing my temple. "The way you look when you come apart for me… You're fire and silk, and I'm a ruined man."

His heated words and the awe in his voice sent a thrill racing through me. I felt powerful, desired, cherished. Adored. I never wanted the feeling to end.

I tilted my head to gaze up at him, still catching my breath. Victor's eyes were dark and hooded, pupils wide with arousal. His hard, hot length pressed insistently against my hip. I shifted, hooking a leg over his waist to draw him closer.

"I want to make you feel good too." I slid my hand down his chest and abdomen to wrap around his thick shaft. "Let me…"

Victor groaned, his hips flexing into my touch. But he caught my wrist, stopping my exploration. "Not this time, angel," he said, his voice low and rough. "Right now, this is all about you." He chuckled. "But not to worry, I'm enjoying myself immensely."

His dark eyes roamed over my body like a physical caress, igniting flames under my skin wherever his gaze lingered. He traced a finger down the center of my chest, circling each nipple before continuing lower. I squirmed beneath his touch, still sensitive from before.

"Are you ready for more, my darling?" He skimmed his fingertips along the crease of my thigh.

"Yes," I breathed, arching into his touch.

He settled his weight on top of me, skin to skin, heartbeat to heartbeat. He was hot and hard, nudging against me. But he made no move to take things further, seemingly content to let the anticipation build until I was mad with wanting.

"Victor," I moaned. "Please…"

"You'll have to be more specific. Tell me exactly what you want." His voice was a low, seductive rumble that I felt all the way to my bones.

"I want you."

He pressed his hips against mine. "You want me to what?"

The heat of his body seared into mine everywhere we touched, igniting a raging inferno within me.

"I want you inside me," My voice shook. "I need to feel you, all of you. Please, Victor."

His lips curved in a slow, sensual smile. "I love hearing you beg for me," he purred. "Keep going."

I swallowed hard, desire and desperation overriding any lingering timidity. The words tumbled out in a rush. "I ache for you," I confessed, my fingers digging into his arms. "I've never wanted anything or anyone the way I want you." My face flushed at my boldness, but I was too far gone to care. I needed him like I needed air. "Please, Victor. Make me yours."

His voice was gravel and heat. "Spread your legs for me, angel," he commanded.

I did as I was told, opening myself completely to him.

"Wider."

My hips ached, but I obeyed happily.

He pressed his tip against me, teasing me with the promise of fulfillment. "Shall I tell you what I want?"

I nodded.

"I want to claim you completely," Victor growled. "To make you mine in every way possible. I want to bury myself inside you until you can't tell where I end and you begin."

He rocked his hips, teasing me without entering. My body trembled with need.

"I want to hear you scream my name as I make you shatter over and over again," he continued, every word steeped in passion and possession. "To feel you fall apart around me, to know that I'm the only one who can give you this kind of pleasure."

A shudder of anticipation raced through me. I arched my hips. "Please, Victor."

"So beautiful," he murmured, "and all mine." His voice was low, commanding—dangerous in the way that thrilled me. "Say it, Barbara. Say you're mine."

"I'm yours." The words spilled out, raw and certain. "Only yours, Victor."

With a low groan, he slowly pushed inside me, stretching and filling me exquisitely. I gasped at the delicious burn, digging my fingers into his shoulders as I adjusted to his impressive size. Victor stilled once he was fully seated, giving me time to acclimate.

"God, you feel incredible," he rasped, his voice tight with the effort of restraint.

Victor began to move, slowly at first, with long, deep strokes that made me gasp and shudder. Each thrust sent sparks of pleasure radiating through my body as I met him thrust for thrust.

"That's it, angel." His voice dropped to a low rumble against my ear. "Take all of me."

He gradually increased his pace, his hips snapping forward with more force. The room filled with the sounds of our mingled gasps and moans, skin on skin. Victor kissed his way to my neck, sucking and nipping as he drove into me relentlessly.

"You're mine," he growled against my throat. "Say it again."

"I'm yours," I gasped, arching into him. "Only yours, Victor. Always."

He slammed his hips forward, and I screamed, unable to hold back. I was lost in a haze of sensation—the delicious friction of him moving inside me, the weight of his body pressing me into the mattress, the heat of his skin against mine. Every nerve sang. Victor's pace grew more frenzied, his thrusts deeper and harder. I wrapped my legs around his waist, pulling him impossibly closer.

"Oh God, Victor!" I cried out. "Don't stop, please don't stop!"

He groaned, digging his fingers into my flesh as he pounded into me. "Never," he growled. "I'll never stop. You're mine now, Barbara. Mine to worship, mine to cherish."

The coil of tension in my core wound tighter and tighter with each thrust. I was teetering on the edge, so close to shattering completely. Victor adjusted his angle to grind his pelvis against me with each stroke. Every muscle in my body tensed until, at last, without control, I exploded.

"Victor!" I cried out as ecstasy crashed over me in waves. My body clenched around him rhythmically as heat poured through me. I clung to him desperately, raking my nails down his back as I shuddered and convulsed beneath him.

Victor groaned, his hips stuttering as my bliss triggered his. With a final powerful thrust, he buried himself deep inside me and found his release. His entire body shuddered, and he buried his face in the crook of my neck as he gasped my name like a prayer.

We lay tangled together, our skin warm and dewy, hearts pounding as we caught our breath. Victor's weight anchored me to the mattress, keeping me grounded even as I floated in a blissful haze. The tips of my fingers and toes tingled like radio static.

After a long moment, he lifted his head to gaze at me. His dark eyes met mine, filled with warmth and tenderness. He brushed a strand of hair from my forehead, his touch featherlight. "Are you all right, my darling?" he murmured.

I nodded, still breathless. "More than all right," I whispered, a languid smile curving my lips. "That was…incredible."

He chuckled softly and pressed a tender kiss to my forehead. "You're incredible," he said, his voice thick with reverence.

Victor eased out of me, then gathered me into his arms. I nestled against his chest, relishing the solid warmth of his body and the steady thump of his heartbeat beneath my ear. He traced lazy patterns along my spine as we basked in the afterglow.

"I meant what I said before," Victor said, his lips brushing my temple. "You're mine now, Barbara. Completely and utterly mine."

His possessive words sent a thrill through me. I tilted my head back to meet his intense gaze. "And you're mine," I replied softly but firmly. "I don't want anyone but you, Victor."

A slow, satisfied smile spread across his face. He cupped my cheek in his large hand, stroking my cheekbone with his thumb. "My beautiful, perfect angel," he murmured. "I'll give you everything you've ever dreamed of and more. I'll cherish you, protect you, worship you." His eyes blazed with conviction. "You'll never want for anything again."

18

VICTOR

"I have something for you."

Barbara shifted to sit up from lounging on the sofa, dressed only in my button-down shirt.

I waved her back down. "Don't move an inch. You're stunning like that, my dear."

I retrieved a slim black folio from the kitchen table and carried it to her, savoring the flicker of anticipation in her eyes. She traced the edge with her delicate fingers before carefully opening it. A soft gasp escaped her lips as she beheld the black-and-white photograph nestled inside.

The image captured Barbara in profile, her head tilted back, eyes closed in quiet rapture. Shadows and light played across the elegant curve of her neck, the swell of her breasts beneath the bodice of her dress. Every detail was crystalline—the sweep of her eyelashes, the fullness of her parted lips, her luscious hair spilling over one shoulder in silken waves of light and shade.

"Victor, it's…" She exhaled, her voice trailing off as she gazed at the photo.

I settled beside her on the sofa, drinking in the sight of her long legs stretched out, my shirt riding up to reveal a tantalizing glimpse of thigh.

"Beautiful," I finished for her, tracing my finger along the elegant line of her neck in the photograph. "Just like the subject."

Barbara's cheeks flushed a becoming pink as she gazed at the image.

"I have the rest back at the beach house. It was hard to pick a favorite. You're so photogenic, my darling. But in this one"—I traced my fingers over the photograph—"you're so…natural, raw, unguarded."

Barbara's eyes shone with quiet wonder as she studied the photograph. "I can hardly believe that's me," she murmured. "I look so…free."

Cupping her cheek, I turned her face toward mine. "That's exactly how I see you. Radiant. Vibrant. Utterly captivating." I brushed my thumb across her bottom lip.

She set the folio aside and shifted onto my lap, the hem of my shirt riding up to bare the smooth curves of her thighs. My hands automatically settled on her hips as she wound her arms around my neck.

"Thank you," she breathed, her blue eyes shining. "Not just for the photograph, but for everything. For making me…" Barbara's voice faded as she held my gaze, emotion brimming in her eyes. I could see the words she couldn't quite bring herself to say reflected in those sapphire depths—*for making me feel alive, for showing me who I truly am, for loving me as I am.*

I pulled her closer, sliding one hand up her back to tangle in her silken hair. "You don't need to thank me, my darling," I said softly. "Loving you, cherishing you, showing you your true self —it's as natural and necessary to me as breathing."

Barbara's lips met mine in a tender kiss that quickly deepened, igniting the ever-present spark between us. She rocked her hips, grinding against my rapidly hardening length. I groaned into her mouth and gripped her thighs.

"Insatiable minx," I growled playfully.

Barbara's eyes sparkled with mischief as she slowly unbuttoned my shirt that she was wearing, revealing tantalizing glimpses of creamy skin. "Can you blame me?" she purred, rolling her hips again. "You make me feel things I've never felt before."

I slid my hands up to grip her waist. "You're playing with fire, angel," I warned, my voice low and rough with desire.

She leaned in close, her lips brushing the shell of my ear. "Then burn me," she whispered.

Heat surged, sharp and sudden. I stood, hauling her up with me in one swift motion. She squealed in delight, wrapping her legs around my waist as I carried her back to the bedroom. I tossed her onto the bed and tore off the last of my clothes before climbing in after her.

The sight of her stole my breath—golden hair fanned out on the pillow, blue eyes dark with desire, lips flushed from our kisses. My angel. My goddess. Mine.

I trailed heated kisses down her neck. "Careful, sweetheart. I'm tempted to tie you to my bed and never let you go."

Barbara arched into me, her breath catching as I nipped at her collarbone. "Is that a threat or a promise?"

I chuckled darkly, skimming my fingers down her sides. "Both."

I slid my hands under the shirt she still wore, pushing it up to reveal more of her creamy skin. Barbara lifted her arms, allowing me to pull the garment off completely. I tossed it aside, relishing the sight of her bare beneath me.

"Stunning," I murmured, roaming my gaze over her lithe form, tracing the curve of her waist, the swell of her breasts. "I'll never tire of looking at you."

I reached for my discarded necktie, the silk cool and smooth against my fingers. Barbara's eyes widened as she watched me, her chest rising and falling with quick, shallow breaths.

"Do you trust me, angel?" I asked softly, running the tie through my hands.

She nodded without hesitation. "Completely."

"If anything feels uncomfortable or you want to stop, just say the word," I instructed. "I want you to feel safe and cherished always."

Barbara gave me a tender smile. "I know. I trust you, Victor."

My heart swelled with emotion at the faith and love shining in her eyes. Gently, I lifted her hands above her head, kissing each delicate wrist before looping the tie around them. With a simple knot, I secured her hands to a slat in the wooden headboard, leaving enough slack for her comfort.

"Now what shall I do with you?" I trailed my fingers down her arms, savoring the shiver that ran through her body at my touch. The sight of her, vulnerable beneath me, sent a fresh wave of arousal coursing through me.

She tugged experimentally at the silk tie, but it didn't give. "Whatever you want," she breathed, her voice husky with need.

"Careful what you wish for."

I lavished attention on her breasts, alternating between gentle kisses and playful nips. Barbara arched into my touch, soft gasps and whimpers escaping her lips as I teased and tormented her sensitive flesh.

Leisurely, reverently, I worshipped every inch of her body with my hands and mouth. I savored her gasps and moans, the way she writhed beneath me, desperate for more. By the time I settled my hips between her thighs, she was trembling with need.

"Look at me," I commanded softly.

Barbara's eyes fluttered open.

I held her gaze as I sank into her, savoring the exquisite sensation of her enveloping me. The way her eyes widened with awe was delicious. A low moan escaped her lips as I filled her.

"So perfect," I breathed, stilling to let her adjust. "Like you were made just for me."

I set a maddeningly deliberate pace, drawing almost all the way out before sinking back in with long, deep strokes. I savored every sensation as I moved within Barbara—the silken heat gripping me, the subtle fluttering inside her, the way her body yielded and welcomed me deeper each time. Each languid thrust sent waves of pleasure through me, stoking the fire in my veins to a roaring inferno.

Her breasts swayed enticingly with our movements, peaked nipples begging for attention. I lowered my head to lavish them with kisses and gentle nips, drinking in her gasps of pleasure.

"Do you feel how perfectly we fit together?" I whispered against her flushed skin. "Like two halves of a whole finally united."

Barbara wrapped her legs around my waist, urging me closer, deeper. But I maintained my leisurely pace, reveling in the slow burn of desire building between us. I wanted to draw out her pleasure, to keep her suspended in ecstasy for as long as possible.

The subtle shifts of her hips, the quickening of her breath, the soft whimpers escaping her parted lips—every reaction fueled my desire. I wanted to memorize every detail, to burn this moment into my mind forever.

"You're so responsive," I murmured, trailing kisses along her jaw. "So wonderfully sensitive. I could spend hours exploring every inch of you, learning all the ways to make you tremble and moan."

I picked up the pace. The change in rhythm drew a sharp gasp from her lips. Her fingers curled around the silk tie binding her wrists as her cries of pleasure grew louder, echoing off the walls. The sound was intoxicating—raw and unrestrained. I reveled in knowing I was the one drawing those sounds from her, that I alone could bring her such ecstasy.

"That's it, doll." I nipped at her earlobe. "Let me hear how good I make you feel."

Heat radiated between us, our skin slick with perspiration. The air was thick with the scent of sex and Barbara's soft floral perfume. I breathed her in deeply. The slap of skin on skin filled the room, punctuated by our mingled gasps and groans. Barbara's body yielded to me, taking me deeper with each thrust. The exquisite friction of her gripping around me threatened to undo me entirely.

"God, you feel incredible."

Barbara keened, her back arching off the bed.

"Can you take it harder?"

"Yes," she panted. "Harder. Please."

I obliged gladly. I pulled out and pushed her legs back until her feet touched the headboard. The sight of Barbara splayed out before me made my groin pulse and ache.

I thrust back into her with renewed vigor, the new angle allowing me to penetrate even deeper. The headboard rattled against the wall with the power of each stroke. A guttural moan tore from my throat at the exquisite sensation of being inside Barbara. She cried out, her head thrown back in ecstasy, utterly magnificent in her abandon. I gripped her hips, my fingers digging into her soft flesh as I pounded into her relentlessly.

"You're close, aren't you?" I purred, my voice thick with desire. "I can feel it. You're gripping me so tight."

I shifted my angle, and a sharp cry erupted from Barbara's delectable lips. She fluttered and clenched around me, signaling her impending release. Her breathless cries grew more urgent, her body trembling beneath me. I redoubled my efforts, determined to send her soaring over the edge.

"That's it, angel. Let go for me. I want to feel you come undone."

With every thrust, she tightened around me.

God, this was ecstasy.

Barbara's body went taut as a bowstring, every muscle tensing as she teetered on the precipice of surrender.

"Victor!" she cried out, her voice raw and desperate. She squeezed her eyes shut. "Oh God—"

"Look at me," I commanded. "I want to see your eyes when I make you feel heaven."

Her eyes flew open, locking on mine with an intensity that stole my breath. In that moment of perfect connection, I saw everything—her vulnerability, her trust, her unbridled passion. It was the most erotic, most beautiful sight I'd ever beheld.

With a keening wail, Barbara shattered. Her back arched off the bed, pressing her breasts against my chest as aftershocks rippled through her lithe frame. She pulsed around me, gripping and releasing in an exquisite rhythm, the sumptuous friction threatening to pull me under with her. But I held back, determined to prolong her bliss.

"That's it, my angel." I maintained my relentless pace. "Let me feel every quiver, every pulse. You're so beautiful when you come apart for me."

The way she came undone was mesmerizing—head thrown back, exposing the elegant column of her throat, lips open with cries of pleasure. Her sapphire eyes locked on mine, dark and hazy with euphoria. I drank in every detail, committing the moment to memory.

As her body relaxed, I fought to maintain control, my body trembling with the effort of holding back my release. I wanted to savor every exquisite sensation, to draw out our union for as long as I could. But the sight of her flushed and sated beneath me, her silken heat still pulsing around me, nearly wrecked me.

"You're so perfect, angel," I murmured, my voice rough with barely restrained passion. "I could spend eternity buried inside you, and it would never be enough."

I resumed my thrusts, slower now but no less intense. Barbara whimpered, oversensitive in the aftermath. I felt the familiar tightening at the base of my spine, pleasure coiling in my core.

In that moment, I knew with bone-deep certainty that I would do anything—give up everything—to keep her by my side.

"You're mine." I pressed my forehead to hers. "Tell me you're mine, angel."

"I'm yours."

She squeezed around me, and I let go.

With a guttural groan, I buried myself deep inside her. The dam burst, and wave after wave of release crashed over me as I stiffened and exploded within her. My hips jerked erratically, and I drove into her one final time as I emptied myself completely.

I collapsed onto Barbara, burying my face in the crook of her neck as I caught my breath. Her skin was flushed and damp, her pulse racing against my lips. I pressed tender kisses along her throat, savoring the lingering taste of salt on her skin.

After a moment, I eased away and reached for her wrists. I untied them slowly, massaging the delicate skin where the silk had left faint marks, gently kissing each pulse point.

Barbara let out a soft, contented sigh as I gathered her close, her body melting into mine. I ran my fingers through her tousled golden hair, relishing the silky texture against my skin. After a while, she tilted her head back to gaze up at me, her blue eyes soft with emotion.

"That was..." she began, her voice trailing off.

"Incredible? Mind-blowing? Earth-shattering?" I supplied with a playful smirk.

She laughed softly, the tinkling sound like music to my ears. "All of the above," she murmured, pressing a tender kiss to my chest. "I've never felt anything like that before."

Pride and satisfaction swelled within me. I tightened my arms around her.

"I never knew it could be like this." Her voice was soft with wonder. "So intense, so...all-consuming."

I inhaled the sweet, powdery scent of her hair. "This is how it's meant to be, darling. Two souls merging, bodies and hearts in perfect harmony." I skimmed my hand down her back, savoring the satiny texture of her skin. "You deserve nothing less than complete devotion and pleasure beyond your wildest dreams."

Her lips curled into a slow, satisfied smile. "You certainly deliver on both counts."

"As do you."

A shaft of late afternoon sunlight slanted through the curtains, casting a golden glow over Barbara's skin as she lay nestled in my arms. Dust motes danced in the air, suspended in time—like us. I could have stayed there forever.

Barbara shifted slightly, her gaze drifting to the clock on the nightstand. She tensed, a slight furrow creasing between her brows.

"What is it, angel?" I brushed a strand of hair from her forehead.

She sighed, looking at me with regret and resignation. "I need to leave soon. Frank's shift ends at five, and I have the car."

"It's 1951. A lady like you should have her own car."

Barbara sighed softly, a wistful smile playing on her lips. "Perhaps one day." She gently pressed her palm to my chest. "But it wouldn't change the fact that I still have to go."

I tightened my arms around her, reluctant to let her leave our intimate cocoon. "Stay a little longer," I murmured, nuzzling her hair. "I'm not ready to give you up just yet."

"I wish I could stay forever," she whispered. "But you know I can't."

Reality crept in, slow and unwelcome, like dusk stealing the last light of day. I cupped her cheek, stroking her soft skin with my thumb. "Maybe not today. But one day, my darling, I hope you stay and never leave. Let me give you the life you deserve." I gazed into her eyes, willing her to see the depth of my conviction. "I promise you, Barbara. I'll move heaven and earth to make it happen. Whatever it takes."

She said nothing in response, but her understated nod and smile were assent enough.

With a soft sigh, she disentangled herself from my arms and sat up, the sheet pooling around her waist. I drank in the sight of her bare back, golden hair tumbling over her shoulders.

Her tone was wistful, but her words were as neat and necessary as a pressed shirt. "I should get dressed."

19
BARBARA

"What's with the scarf?" Frank asked as he glanced at me from the passenger seat of our Plymouth.

I adjusted the silk scarf covering my hair, smoothing it into place. "Oh, I went to visit some of Mr. Cardello's properties. My hair got messed up." Technically, neither of those statements was untrue.

"What properties?" he pressed.

"A few apartment buildings downtown, some hotels, a department store or two, and a future residential site." Again, not a lie. I glanced at him sideways. "It was pretty windy."

I turned my attention back to the road, my fingers tightening on the steering wheel. The silence stretched between us, thick with tension. From the corner of my eye, I caught Frank's jaw flexing as he stared out the windshield.

"I don't like it," he finally said, his voice tight. "You running all over town with that man. It's not proper."

I took a deep breath, willing myself to remain calm. "It's part of my job, Frank."

"You're a part-time secretary, Barbara. Your job is to type letters and answer phones," Frank retorted, his voice rising.

"Not to go traipsing around the city with your boss like some… some…"

"Some what?" I challenged, my temper flaring.

Frank's jaw tightened. "You know what I mean," he muttered.

I clenched the steering wheel so hard, my knuckles turned white. "No, Frank, I don't know what you mean. Why don't you enlighten me?"

"People will get the wrong idea," he said quietly, eyes fixed on the road ahead. "The war is long over. You don't need to be out there being Rosie the Riveter."

I bit back a sharp retort, taking a deep breath to steady myself. "Mr. Cardello values my input," I said carefully. "He's teaching me about the business. It's an opportunity to learn and grow."

Frank scoffed. "Learn and grow? What on earth for?"

His words stung, rekindling the familiar ache of unfulfillment.

"This job… It gives me a sense of purpose. Is that so wrong?"

Frank sighed heavily, rubbing a hand over his face. "I just don't understand why you need more, Barb."

"Why does it bother you that I want something for myself, Frank? I'm still your wife."

"Then act like it!" he snapped. "A proper wife doesn't spend more time with her boss than her own husband. A proper wife is home when her family needs her."

I bit back every fiery retort that bloomed on my tongue. It wasn't worth it.

I pulled into our driveway and shifted the car into park.

Frank glanced up, then turned to me, brow furrowed. "Aren't we going to Edith's place to pick up Frank Junior?"

"*I* am," I answered. "I just figured I'd give you a head start on your whiskey." My tone was ice.

Frank's face flushed red. "What's that supposed to mean?"

"It means I know you'll head straight for the liquor cabinet the moment we walk through that door. So why don't you get a head start while I pick up our son?"

Frank's jaw clenched as he glared at me. "You're out of line, Barbara," he growled.

"Am I?" I shot back, my composure finally cracking. "It's the truth, isn't it?"

We stared at each other in tense silence, neither willing to back down. Then, Frank shoved the car door open and got out, slamming it behind him hard enough to make the whole vehicle shake. I watched him stomp to the house and fumble with his keys before disappearing inside.

He shut the front door so violently, the windowpanes rattled. Tears stung my eyes, but I blinked them back. I wouldn't cry. Not over this. Not over him.

Not when I had someone far better.

———

"Where did you stash Frank?" Edith glanced over my shoulder at my empty car in her driveway.

"I left him at home."

She smirked, giving me a once-over. "So…"

"So what?"

"Don't play coy with me. How did it go?"

I hesitated, glancing around Edith's front porch. "Let's go inside."

Edith nodded and ushered me in, closing the door behind us. She led me to the living room where Frankie was playing with wooden blocks on a lime-green-and-yellow crocheted rug.

"Hi, sweetie," I cooed, bending down to ruffle his soft blond hair.

He beamed up at me, proudly showing off the tower he had built. "Look, Mama!"

"That's wonderful, sweetheart." I kissed his forehead. "My little architect."

He smashed the tower with a firetruck. His eyes lit up at the destruction, and he set about stacking the blocks anew.

Edith settled onto the sofa, patting the spot beside her. "All right, spill. I want all the juicy details."

I sank down next to her with a heavy sigh, a dreamy smile tugging at my lips as memories of the past hours washed over me. "He's everything I imagined," I said, soft and reminiscent. "Passionate, tender, and utterly sure of himself. When I'm with him, Edith…it's like he sees straight into my soul. Like he knows every secret desire I've ever had. He's unlocked a part of me that I didn't even know existed."

"He's that good, huh?"

"Earth-shattering."

Edith raised an eyebrow, her expression a mix of skepticism and concern. "And you're sure this is what you want? To risk everything for a fling?"

I bit my lip, the reality of her question sinking in. "It's not just a fling, Edith."

"Then what?"

I looked away, my eyes wandering to the framed photographs on Edith's mantel—pictures of her and her late husband, of our family, of her adventures in exotic locales. "I don't know," I admitted quietly. "But when I'm with him, it feels real. It feels like…love."

She sighed, uncrossed her arms, and leaned forward, her expression softening. "I just don't want to see you get hurt, sis. Remember when you thought marrying Frank was the solution to everything? That it would make you happy and fulfilled?" She held up her hands before I could retort. "You made the twenty-one-year-old marriage just like I did. Anything to get out of Mother's shadow. Believe me, I get it. But you rushed into that, and look where you are." She paused and looked at me poignantly. "And now you're rushing into this with Victor."

"It's different," I insisted.

"I'm sure it is."

Edith's telephone rang. "Hold that thought," she said over her shoulder as she stood and walked to the kitchen. "Hello?"

I turned my attention back to Frankie, watching him drive his wooden cars around the rug like a racetrack.

Edith returned to the living room, stretching the phone cord as she walked. "Barbara, it's Frank."

I stepped forward, but she cut me off with a raised hand.

"He wants to know if you're still here," she whispered, cupping her palm over the mouthpiece.

"Tell him—" I started, then caught myself. "Tell him yes."

Edith shrugged and uncovered the mouthpiece. "She's still here, Frank."

I turned to leave, but Edith motioned for me to stay. She winked at me. I froze.

"And she and Frankie are staying for dinner."

"Edie," I whispered urgently, but she waved me off.

"Frank," she said, her voice thick with syrupy sweetness. "You're a big, strong man. You can handle dinner on your own for one night. Surely you can make a sandwich without Barbara's help."

"Edith!" I hissed.

She turned her back to me, stretching the phone cord as far as it would go. "Oh, come now, Frank. It's not that hard. A bit of bread, some ham, maybe a slice of cheese."

My heart pounded, and my ears burned hot. I was in for it now.

I strained to hear Frank's response, but his voice was a muffled growl through the receiver. Edith listened, her lips curling into a feline grin—the kind that spelled trouble. She was enjoying this far too much.

"Of course," she said, cutting him off. "I'll make sure she gets home safely. Bye now." She hung up the phone while he was still talking and turned to me, hands on her hips.

"Are you insane?" I spat. "He's going to be livid!"

"Let him be," Edith said, unperturbed. "You need some time

away from him to think clearly." She walked past me and into the living room, where she picked up a stuffed elephant and handed it to Frankie. "Besides, I miss my baby sister. We hardly get any real time together now that you're such a career woman."

I stood in the doorway to the kitchen, arms crossed tightly over my chest. "Edith, I can't—"

"You can," she interrupted, returning to the kitchen. "Sit. I'll make spaghetti."

"Edith—"

"Sit," she commanded, pulling a pot from a cupboard. "Frank will cool off."

I hesitated, then nodded and settled into a chair at the kitchen table. Edith opened her icebox and rummaged through it, pulling out vegetables and a package of ground beef.

"So," she said, setting the items on the counter, "you never finished telling me about your day with Victor."

I shrugged, feigning nonchalance. "It was wonderful."

"Details, darling. I live vicariously through you now." She chopped an onion with swift, practiced strokes.

I sighed, knowing she wouldn't let it go. "We skipped out of work mid-morning and went to his downtown apartment."

Edith's eyes gleamed with mischief as she set the pot on the burner. "Straight to the den of sin. Bold move." She opened a cupboard and took out a box of spaghetti.

"He owns the whole top floor," I said, the memory washing over me. "The view is breathtaking." My words were laden with the awe I had felt standing in Victor's arms, the world seeming small and conquerable from such heights.

"And conveniently, no neighbors to share walls with…" She winked.

I bit back a smile, unable to suppress the warmth spreading through me.

"And how is he in his natural habitat?"

"He's very…assertive," I said, shivers rippling down my

spine at the memory of his hands on me and that commanding voice. "He knows exactly what he wants and takes it. He's intense, and it's irresistible."

Edith smirked. "And you like being taken, do you? Like a damsel in one of those cheap romance novels?"

I blushed, heat rising from my chest to my cheeks, but I didn't answer. How could I explain the thrill and sheer electric rush of surrendering to someone so powerful without sounding like one of those silly heroines?

She raised an eyebrow, her lips curving into a knowing smile. "There's nothing wrong with a bit of rough passion, Babs. Sometimes a girl just needs to be ravished." She tossed the spaghetti into the pot of boiling water.

"Oh God, I needed it," I said, the confession slipping out before I could stop it.

"I bet." She gave me a sideways glance, but there was no malice in her tone—only the supportive understanding of an older sister who had been through it all and seen far more of life than me.

"He has this way of commanding me. No one's ever talked to me like that before. And no one's made me feel the way he does. I didn't even know I could feel like that. It's…exhilarating," I finished, my voice trailing off as I was flooded with memories of Victor's touch, his voice, the raw conviction behind every word and glance.

Edith leaned against the counter, crossing her arms over her chest. "It sounds like you've already made up your mind," she said, her voice more serious now. "That you're all in with him."

I looked down at my hands, twisting them in my lap. "It's not that simple. Frank—"

"Ugh, Frank," Edith interrupted, rolling her eyes. "Let's not muddy the waters by talking about Frank. Besides, it doesn't take a genius to recognize that your marriage is not what you need right now. That it's *never* been what you needed."

I opened my mouth to protest, but she held up a hand to stop me. "I'm not saying you should leave him, Barbara. At least, not right now. I'm just saying you need to be honest with yourself about what you want. About what will make you happy."

Silence settled over us, heavy and contemplative. Edith turned back to the stove, stirring the spaghetti with a wooden spoon. The aroma of sautéed onions and ground beef filled the warm kitchen.

"I just don't want to see you make the same mistakes I did," Edith said softly, almost to herself. "We're cut from the same cloth, you and I. Ambitious, restless. You need to find a way to balance it all."

I bit my lip, the weight of her words sinking in. "Did you regret it? Marrying Bob?"

She shrugged, not meeting my eyes. "We all have our regrets." A pause. Then she turned, holding the wooden spoon like a scepter. "But this isn't about me. It's about you. So, what's the plan? Will you keep sneaking around, hoping Frank doesn't find out? Or will you make a choice?"

I didn't have an answer for her. The thought of choosing—of committing to one path and forsaking the other—was paralyzing.

Edith studied me for a moment, her expression unreadable. "And to answer your question, yes."

"Yes, what?"

"Yes, I regretted marrying Bob." She exhaled through pursed lips. "It feels a little unfair to say it out loud, but it's true. And if I can't tell you, who can I tell?"

"Then why did you marry him?"

She gave a short, mirthless laugh. "Because it was easier than listening to Mother and Father harp on about my 'future' every time I walked into the room." She stirred the sauce with unnecessary force. "They were worried about my 'reputation.' You were probably too young to remember, but I ran wild back in the twenties." She smiled wistfully.

I did remember—at least, vaguely—the gaudy strings of

beads, the scandalous short hair, the bright red lipstick. As a child, I'd idolized Edith's fearless spirit. I suppose I still did.

"They thought marriage would settle me down."

"So they pushed you into it?" I asked.

Edith shook her head. "Didn't take much pushing." She sighed, the sharpness in her voice giving way to reflection. "Bob was one of my running buddies. He checked every box for them—well-off, respectable, steady as a metronome." She hesitated, tapping the wooden spoon against the edge of the pot. "And, of course, Bob had his own reasons for needing to marry."

I frowned. "What do you mean?"

Edith arched an eyebrow. "Come now, Barbara. The only time Bob ever touched lace was when he was picking out curtains."

It took a moment to register her meaning. "Are you saying Bob was…"

"Gay as springtime," she said with a flourish of the wooden spoon, as if she were revealing the climax of an old vaudeville joke.

I stared at her, stunned. "So your whole marriage was just…a convenience?"

She nodded. "We played our parts and kept up appearances. It worked. He had his freedom, and so did I. It wasn't an unhappy marriage—we were good friends."

"And when he died…"

For the first time, Edith hesitated. "When he died, I mourned a friend. But not a husband."

"I never knew, Edie…"

She waved me off. "Of course you didn't. You were what, five when I married Bob? There's a lot I've never told you, Babs." She stirred the sauce absently before looking back at me, her expression suddenly fierce. "But do you see why I'm telling you this now? Life is short. Shorter than we ever think it's going to be. You're still young, but I'm staring middle age in the face. Don't waste time living a life that isn't what you want it to be."

The oven timer dinged, and Edith pulled out a pan of garlic

bread, the crust crackling as it hit the cool air. She set it on the counter and wiped her hands on her apron.

Then, switching gears, she grabbed three mismatched plates from the cupboard. "Come on, let's eat. And while we do, I want to hear all about how delicious this Victor of yours is." She shot me a wicked grin. "I expect details."

20

VICTOR

February 1951

A towering stack of contracts loomed on my desk, demanding my attention. I loosened my tie and leaned back in my leather chair, hoping a different perspective might make them seem less daunting. It was Thursday—easily the worst day in the office since Barbara only worked the first half of the week. Monday felt a lifetime away. She was sharp, meticulous, and would have made quick work of these contracts…if I hadn't kept her otherwise occupied.

I rubbed my temples and glanced at the clock. Its hands crept toward noon. Time always dragged when you wanted it to race ahead. Was it Monday yet?

My eyes drifted shut, pulling me into vivid recollections. Barbara had been perched on this very desk just yesterday, legs elegantly crossed, feigning professionalism while I let my hands roam—testing the limits of her self-control. Her breath hitched, her composure slipping with every calculated caress.

A soft knock shattered the memory. My eyes snapped open.

"Come in," I called.

The door swung open, and Mrs. Miller popped her head inside. Her sharp gaze darted around the office, as if making sure I was alone. "There's a Mr. Frank Evans here to see you," she said quietly. "He's most insistent."

A knot formed in my stomach, and I sat up. "Send him in," I said, straightening my tie, trying to sound casual.

Mrs. Miller withdrew, and a moment later, Frank Evans strode into my office. He was a tall man—a full head taller than me—in his mid-twenties with the square jaw of a comic book hero. I could see why women might find him attractive. His brown suit was clearly cheap, but he'd dressed it up with a loud tie and pocket square to compensate. He forced a smile, but the tension around his eyes gave him away.

"Victor," he said, extending a hand. I stood and shook it, noting the rough calluses of a man who had, at some point, done real work with his hands.

"Frank," I said evenly. "To what do I owe the pleasure?"

He took a seat without being asked. I sank back into my chair, studying him. He pulled a thick envelope from his inner jacket pocket and placed it on the desk between us.

"What's this?"

"That's the rest of the money I owe you."

I let the envelope sit unopened. "You pulled that together quickly."

Frank shrugged, but his eyes never left mine. "Seemed best to settle up sooner rather than later."

"Indeed." I pulled a cigarette from the silver case on my desk, lighting it with deliberate ease. I offered one to Frank, but he waved it off with a curt shake of his head. "So, we're square now." I exhaled a slow stream of smoke. "Is that all?"

He hesitated, and I knew in my gut that whatever he said next would be the real reason for his visit.

Frank leaned forward, his jaw set like a man bracing for a fight. "I need to talk to you about Barbara."

A dozen scenarios ran through my mind in the span of a

second. Had Barbara confessed? Was he here to threaten me? To beg?

"She's proving to be quite capable," I said smoothly. "You should be proud."

He snorted—a sharp, derisive sound that sent a prickle up the back of my neck. "Proud? Maybe if she were taking care of her family instead of gallivanting around like some…"

I took a long drag on my cigarette, letting the smoke fill my lungs and blur the room for a moment. "Like some what, Frank?"

He hesitated. "Like some career girl."

The tension in the room was thick enough to slice. I tapped the ash from my cigarette into a crystal tray and eyed the envelope of cash. "It's the fifties, Frank. Times are changing. Women can have careers these days."

"Careers," he muttered, almost spitting the word. "This isn't a career. It's a distraction. A dangerous one."

"So you think it's dangerous for her to work here?"

He folded his arms tight across his chest. "I think that she's gotten in over her head."

I studied Frank for a long moment, letting the silence do its work. He shifted uncomfortably in his chair but held my gaze.

"So, you want me to fire her?" I asked, sparing him the pretense.

Frank's eyes flickered—hope, perhaps for a second—before hardening again. "Yes. If she's not working, she'll come home. Things will go back to the way they were." He looked down at his lap. "The way they should be."

There it was. The real reason for his visit. I studied Frank's face—the tight lines around his mouth, the rigid set of his jaw. He wasn't a fool, but he wasn't as clever as he thought.

"Barbara is a grown woman, Frank. She can make her own decisions."

Frank uncrossed his arms and gripped the chair. "Can she?"

he challenged. "Because from where I'm standing, you're the one calling the shots."

I drummed my fingers on the envelope thick with cash. Frank's eyes flicked toward it, and his body tensed like he was sizing up a threat. I took another drag from my cigarette, savoring the acrid taste of tobacco, and let the smoke coil up from my lips in a slow, deliberate spiral.

"Are you accusing me of something, Frank?"

He was silent for a moment—the kind of silence weighed down by pent-up anger. Then he stood—slowly, deliberately.

"I'm not here to accuse," he said finally, though the heat in his voice suggested otherwise. "I'm here to get my wife back."

I exhaled slowly, letting the cigarette smoke curl between us like a lazy ghost. He leaned over the desk, his large hands splayed on the mahogany surface. The proximity was meant to intimidate, but it only confirmed how desperate he was. I recalled Barbara splayed out on the very same desk, breathless and undone, moaning and panting with pleasure—pleasure that Frank wouldn't recognize if it slapped him across the face.

The memory made me smile—a slow, deliberate curl of my lips. Frank stiffened. His jaw clenched, face flushing as he shoved the envelope across the desk at me.

"Take the money," he growled. "We're even, and she doesn't need this job anymore."

With casual disdain, I stubbed out my cigarette in the crystal tray and rose to meet his gaze. "Frank," I said, my tone almost gentle, "this isn't about the money."

His eyes narrowed, and for a moment, I thought he might take a swing at me. Part of me hoped he would. The physical release would be welcome, and it would give me an excuse to finish what I suspected he lacked the courage to start.

But Frank held himself in check. He straightened up, adjusted his cheap, gaudy tie, and stepped back from the desk. "You think you're some kind of big shot, don't you?"

I circled the desk, the air between us charged like a storm about to break.

"Careful, pal. Much more, and I'll start to take it personally."

We stood toe to toe, though he had the height advantage. Frank held his ground, his eyes drilling into mine with hatred and helplessness. I could almost hear his thoughts ricocheting in his skull, colliding like pool balls with nowhere to land. He was a man on the brink, and I suspected that one well-placed push might send him right over the edge.

"I don't want trouble," Frank said, his voice low, almost a growl. "I just want what's mine."

The way he said it—like she was a set of cufflinks he'd misplaced—made my blood run hot. It was no wonder she sought escape in her work. And in me.

For a moment—a flicker, a breath—he almost crumbled. His eyes wavered, and the hard lines of his face softened into something like sorrow. But just as quickly, he set his jaw and squared his shoulders.

"We're done here, Victor. And so is Barbara. She won't be back to work next week."

I plastered on an impassive mask. "And what does she think about that?"

"It doesn't matter what she thinks. She's my wife, and what I say goes." He turned toward the door. His shoulders were stiff, and his stride clipped.

Just as he reached for the handle, I spoke. "Frank."

He paused but didn't turn, his fingers curled tightly around the brass.

"Don't make the mistake of underestimating her." I let my voice drop low—so low he had to strain to hear it. "Or me."

Frank didn't say a word. He just turned the handle, opened the door, and closed it behind him—not a slam, not a bang. Just a quiet little click, like the snap of a trigger being cocked.

I stood alone in my office, the fading scent of Frank's cheap cologne mixing with the lingering smoke from my extinguished cigarette.

I lifted the envelope and tested its weight. The money meant nothing to me, but desperation was a currency all its own, and Frank was throwing it around like a gambler on his last chip. He was a man pushed to his limits, clutching at the last straws of a life he no longer controlled. A life that Barbara, in her restless ambition, had outgrown.

He was full of delusion—his belief that he could simply command Barbara back into the box he had constructed for her. It was almost pitiable. Almost. He still saw the world in terms of ownership and duty, unable to comprehend that the desires and dreams of others might take precedence over his own.

I walked to the window and looked out over the city. Los Angeles sprawled beneath me, a maze of possibilities. For a moment, I imagined what it would be like to walk away, to leave all of this behind and build something new. Something honest. The thought drifted like smoke—fleeting, weightless. And I dismissed it just as quickly.

Returning to my desk, I flipped open the silver case, pulled another cigarette, and lit it. The first drag filled my lungs with a familiar burn, temporarily blotting out the deeper pains.

Barbara was no fool. She could make her own choices. But choices had consequences, and she needed to understand what she was risking. Not just with Frank, but with her son, with her family. With me.

I picked up the phone and dialed Barbara's home number. After two rings, her angelic voice drifted through the receiver.

"Hello, gorgeous. Can I take you out to lunch today?"

21

BARBARA

"Lunch today?" I glanced at the clock on the front table. "Sounds divine, but I just got Frankie down for his nap." I hesitated. "And Frank has the car."

"Oh, angel, I know." Victor's voice was languid and smooth as velvet. "He paid me a visit."

I almost dropped the phone. "Come again?"

"He stopped by to chat," he said, like it was nothing.

My heart beat against my ribs, frantic as a caged bird trying to break free. What had Frank said? What did he know? My knuckles strained as I gripped the receiver tighter.

"Barbara? You still there?"

"Yes. I'm here." I forced myself to take a slow, deep breath. "What did he want?"

"Hmm, to size me up, I think."

I could almost see Victor—reclining in his leather chair, feet propped on his desk, phone cradled casually against his ear, a smug half-smile playing on his lips. He enjoyed this far too much.

I closed my eyes, pressure building behind them like an impending storm. "Victor, please tell me."

The silence on the other end stretched for an agonizing

moment. When he finally spoke, his voice was quiet. Serious. "He came to tell me you'd no longer be working for me."

A short burst of incredulous laughter bubbled from my lips. "Of course he did," I said, shaking my head in disbelief. "What did you say to him?"

"I told him the truth," Victor said. "That it's your decision, not his."

I leaned back against the wall. Relief and dread swirled together in my stomach like a volatile cocktail.

"Don't worry," he added. "He backed down. For now."

For now. The words hung in the air like a guillotine blade.

"Barbara," Victor said, his voice softer now, almost tender. "Say something, sweetheart."

I pressed the receiver against my temple as if I could pull Victor's warmth through the phone. "I'm just thinking." The silence on the line crackled.

"Think over lunch," Victor suggested. "You need to eat."

I bit my lip, glancing at the kitchen. The remains of a hastily made sandwich lay abandoned on the counter. "Victor." I hesitated. "Frankie is asleep. I can't leave him."

"When will he be up?"

"Around two," I said, winding the telephone cord around my index finger so tightly the skin turned purple.

"I'll come by and pick you both up," he offered, his voice like melted chocolate—rich, smooth, and irresistible.

My heart skipped.

"No," I said, perhaps too quickly. "The neighbors would talk."

Victor chuckled a low, knowing rumble. "Let them. But if it concerns you that much…" He trailed off, considering. "There's a small diner not far from you—Hanson's on Wilshire and Fairfax. You know it?"

I pictured the intersection in my mind—bustling streets lined with palm trees and sun-bleached storefront façades. "Hanson's —sure I know it."

"The owner is a friend of mine. He's got a discreet room in the back where we can meet privately. You could take the bus."

My heart warred against my better judgment. The risks were obvious, but so was the pull toward the life he represented. "I suppose that could work," I conceded. "But I'll have Frankie with me. I can't call my sister on such short notice."

"I'd love to meet the tyke. Let's say two-thirty?"

I let out a shaky breath and nodded. Realizing that he couldn't see me, I murmured, "Perfect. See you then."

"Wonderful," Victor said, warmth curling around his words. "Until then, my darling."

———

"The wheels on the bus go round and round." I took Frankie's hands in mine, guiding them in little circles in the air as we sang softly. His giggles bubbled up like a fountain, pulling a smile from me despite the tight knot in my stomach.

The bus jostled us as it turned a corner, and I held Frankie closer, kissing the top of his tousled hair. Outside the window, familiar streets passed by in a blur. We were getting closer, and my heart started to race.

Frankie pointed out the window. "Look, Mama! A big dog!"

Sure enough, a shaggy mutt trotted down the sidewalk, bushy tail wagging.

"Woof woof!" Frankie beamed, bouncing on my lap. Enthusiasm spread across his face and lit up his eyes.

I smoothed his hair. "That's right, sweetheart."

The intersection of Wilshire and Fairfax came into view, and I tugged the cord above the window. The bus began to slow, and the brakes hissed as we pulled up to the curb.

"Almost there, darling," I told Frankie, adjusting him on my hip as we stood and made our way to the front of the bus. The driver eased the door open, and we stepped out into the bright afternoon sun. I shaded my eyes and looked toward the diner.

"Mommy has to see a friend real quick," I said as I set Frankie down on his stout little legs and took his hand in mine. As we walked, I continued, "It won't take long. Then we'll get ice cream."

Frankie squealed with delight as he curled his fingers around mine. "Okay, Mama."

I took a deep breath, forcing my nerves into check, and led him toward the diner.

A bell tinkled overhead as I pushed open the door. The diner gleamed with chrome and turquoise vinyl, its long counter lined with swivel stools. A jukebox in the corner crackled out a scratchy rendition of "Bewitched," and the thick scent of bacon grease and griddled beef clung to the air. I scanned the room and saw no immediately familiar faces.

A stout man with a thick mustache approached, wiping his hands on a grease-streaked apron. "Can I help you, miss?"

I shifted Frankie closer, scanning the room again. "We're meeting someone."

The man gave a slight nod, his voice dropping to a near whisper. His breath reeked of garbage, and I fought the urge to lean away as his voice rattled like crumpled newspaper.

"If you're looking for Mr. Cardello, he's in the back. Follow me."

He led us past the counter, through a swinging door, and into a small room with a single booth. The walls were lined with framed photographs, their edges yellowed and curling from years of heat rolling off the kitchen. A rickety ceiling fan spun overhead, stirring the thick air into sluggish ripples.

Victor stood as we entered. His tall frame cast a long shadow over the booth, the soft glow of the overhead bulb catching on the sharp cut of his charcoal-gray suit. His dark hair was slicked to a perfect shine.

"Barbara," he greeted smoothly, stretching out an arm to take my hand. He kissed it lightly, sending an electric jolt skittering across my skin as he locked his intense eyes with mine. He bent down to Frankie. "And this must be Frank. Hello, young man."

I placed a hand on my son's shoulder. "Say hello, Frankie."

Frankie looked up at Victor with curious eyes. "Hello."

"He's got your eyes," Victor said, looking up at me. "A striking young lad."

I remained standing, glancing at the door behind me.

"Sit, please," Victor urged as he straightened up. "You make me nervous standing there like that."

I chuckled as I ushered Frankie into the booth. "I didn't think anything could make you nervous."

"Ah, then I hide it well. Inside, my heart's knocking like a salesman on payday." He placed a hand over his chest with a lopsided grin.

My shoulders relaxed, and a smile crept onto my lips. I slid into the booth beside Frankie, who was busy examining the menu, his little fingers tracing over the pictures. Victor sat across from us and leaned in, his presence commanding even in the cramped space.

"He's adorable," Victor said, his voice low, eyes flicking between me and Frankie. "I've ordered some milkshakes. I hope that's all right."

Frankie's face lit up, and he looked to me for approval. I nodded, though my mind was elsewhere—Victor, so close, his cologne cutting through the greasy air, was almost too much to bear. All I wanted to do was throw myself into his arms, consequences be damned.

"Thank you," I said, forcing the words through a tight throat. "That's very kind."

Victor leaned back, casually draping an arm over the top of the booth. "I'm so glad you came." His eyes almost twinkled as he smiled at me, the finest of lines spreading out from the creases of his eyelids.

"So, this isn't the part where you hand me a pink slip over a milkshake?" I deflected, arching a brow.

Victor's smile widened. "Fire you? Never. My days would be utterly unbearable without you in them."

Relief washed over me, cooling the feverish tension that had built during the bus ride. Victor's assurances were a balm, though doubt still lingered like a fresh bruise.

The swinging door squeaked open, and a young waitress appeared, balancing a tray laden with three tall glasses. Condensation dripped down the sides, pooling onto the chipped enamel surface as she set them down with a clatter. Frankie's eyes widened, round as saucers, at the sight of the whipped cream and cherry crowning the milkshake in front of him.

"Enjoy," the waitress chirped, her voice cutting through the hum of the ceiling fan.

Frankie lunged for his glass, but I intercepted his hands before he could send it toppling onto his lap.

"Easy, darling. Don't spill." I scooped up a spoonful of whipped cream and offered it to placate him. He accepted eagerly, his face lighting up in pure, unfiltered joy. I eyed Victor. "You do realize he'll be up half the night now with all this sugar."

Victor leaned back in his seat with a lazy shrug. "Let the boy live a little."

"When he's still bouncing off the walls at midnight, I'll remember the part you played."

"If I'm not keeping you up at midnight, I'm not doing my job right." He winked, his voice smooth as silk.

Heat flooded my cheeks. I took a long sip of my milkshake, hoping the thick, rich chocolate would cool the warmth creeping up my neck.

Victor's gaze settled on Frankie, who had a ring of whipped cream around his mouth like a clown's smile. His expression softened, though a flicker of something unreadable passed through his eyes.

"I never knew my Margaret at this age," he said wistfully.

"I'm sure she was a cherub."

Victor swirled his milkshake, watching the whipped cream disappear into the chocolate below. "Barbara," he started, then hesitated. "There's something you should know."

A thousand thoughts collided in my mind like billiard balls on a crowded table. I focused on Frankie, who sucked at his straw so hard that his milkshake burbled up over the rim, dribbling down the sides like a tiny chocolate volcano.

"Well?" I prompted, brushing a napkin over Frankie's sticky fingers. "Don't keep me in suspense."

Victor looked up from his glass. "It's Frank. And the other reason he came to see me today. I wasn't sure if I should tell you because up until now, it's been none of my business. But…"

My breath caught. "But?" My voice was thinner than I intended. "Does he know about us?"

Victor's lips curved slightly, but there was no humor in it. "Well, *that* would most definitely be my business." He swirled his glass. "And if he did, darling, I'd have had to scrape him off my office floor." He let out a short, dry chuckle. "But, no, I don't think so. He might suspect something, but if he knew for certain, I imagine he would've done something remarkably foolish."

Relief washed over me, loosening the knot in my chest—until Victor's expression told me it wouldn't last. "What then?"

"Did you know that I loaned Frank money several months ago?"

"I didn't." My tone was measured, my words deliberate.

"Didn't think so. Anyway, he paid off the loan in full today."

"How much money are we talking about?"

"Five thousand."

I choked on the air.

Frankie looked up, his innocent eyes confused by my reaction. "Mama?"

"I'm fine," I said, patting his head as I cleared my throat. "Just surprised is all." I coaxed him back to his milkshake and took a long sip of my own to soothe the sudden dryness in my throat. The sweet treat tasted like chalk. I turned my gaze to

Victor, studying his face, searching for his angle, his intent. "What on earth did he need that kind of money for?"

Victor leaned back in the booth, his posture relaxed, but his eyes sharp. "Gambling debts. He was in pretty deep at the track." He let that hang in the air a moment, watching my reaction.

I shook my head slowly. "I had no idea. He promised he'd stopped…"

Victor exhaled through his nose, the faintest trace of amusement in his expression. "Promises are easy to make. Harder to keep."

"So, you bailed him out. That was very…generous of you."

He looked up at me through his long lashes. "Not exactly. Frank pushed through the insurance payouts on a few properties for me. Made sure there were no delays, no complications. In return, I loaned him what he needed to clear his debts and have some breathing room."

The new information sank in like spilled red wine on white carpet.

"Mama, all done," Frankie declared, his milkshake reduced to a frothy residue at the bottom of the glass. He wiped his mouth with the back of his hand, smearing the cream further across his cheek.

"Hold still, sweetheart," I said, grabbing a napkin from the table. "Let me clean you up."

As I tended to Frankie, my eyes flicked back to Victor. He watched us with an intensity that made my skin prickle.

"So Frank is in the clear?" I asked, dabbing at Frankie's face. "No more debts hanging over him?"

"Not from me. But that doesn't mean he's in the clear." He paused, pressing his lips into a thin line. "There's no way he came up with that sum on his own."

"Then how…" I trailed off, not sure I wanted to know the answer.

He shrugged. "You know him better than I do."

"Do I?"

Victor didn't answer.

"Why are you telling me this?"

"Because you deserve to know what's going on with the people in your life." His voice was steady, but something lurked beneath the surface—something that made my chest tighten. He leaned in across the table, his intense eyes stripping away whatever flimsy defenses I had left. "I never want to be the one keeping you in the dark. Ever."

My heart pounded in my ears. The hum of the ceiling fan and the clatter of dishes from the kitchen blurred into a single, dissonant note.

"The way Frank talked about you had me seeing red, Barbara." Victor's voice was taut with restrained anger. "Like an ornament to be kept on a shelf. Like you're not capable of thinking for yourself. Maybe that would have flown in the last century, but not now." He shook his head vehemently. "No, not even then. It's maddening, and you deserve so much more."

Victor slid his hand across the table, fingers just barely brushing mine. The warmth of his touch seeped into my skin.

Frankie fidgeted in his seat and tugged at my sleeve. "Mama, go now?" he whined, and I saw the tiredness in his eyes—the kind that follows a brief, unsustainable sugar high.

"In a minute, sweetheart," I said, but my focus was locked on Victor. He had leaned back again, one arm draped over the booth, the picture of nonchalance—but his eyes told a different story. I fished a small wooden car out of my purse and handed it to Frankie.

"Vroom!" He ran the car along the edge of the table and around the empty milkshake glass.

Victor smiled. "He's a car man. Like me." The smile lingered as he watched Frankie, but when his eyes found mine again, his expression turned somber. "Barbara, I'm worried about you."

The booth's vinyl creaked as I shifted uncomfortably. "You're worried about me?"

"About your home life."

I started to protest, but Victor leaned in.

"Just hear me out." His words were gentle but firm, cutting through my defenses before I could mount them. "It's no secret that I hate the way he treats you. You deserve so much more. But Frank's in trouble, and that means you're in trouble too. The way he spoke to me today—it wasn't the voice of a man in control. He was desperate. I have no idea how he came up with the money to pay me off, but I promise you it wasn't from insurance commissions."

I swallowed hard, my pulse thrumming in my ears.

"My hands aren't clean, Barbara, and I'd never claim otherwise. But I'm not the most dangerous fellow out there. I don't know who owns Frank now, but..."

"But what?"

He reached across the table and took both my hands in his. "But when I owned him, you were never in danger. I can't say that anymore."

Victor's hands were warm and firm around mine. I stared at his fingers—strong, capable.

"Barbara," he said, his voice low and earnest. "You need to think about what you really want. Not just for now, but for the future. A future where you're happy, where you're safe, where you're free."

"Are you saying," I began slowly, "that you think I should leave Frank?"

Victor's eyes never wavered from mine. "I'm saying you should consider a future with someone who truly loves you, respects you, and has your best interests at heart."

"You mean with you."

Victor's gaze was unwavering. "Yes."

I pulled my hands away from his, and a rush of cool air filled the space between us. "A tryst is one thing, Victor. And don't misunderstand—I wouldn't give that up for anything." I lowered my voice to a hush. "But you're married too."

"I'm handling it."

I looked down at the chipped, worn enamel of the table and traced the cracks with my fingernail, avoiding Victor's piercing gaze. The silence between us was thick. I didn't trust myself to speak. My thoughts raced, colliding with each other in a chaotic tangle—Frank's debts, Victor's confession, the looming uncertainty.

"Say something, Barbara. Please."

I looked up and took a measured breath, letting the air slowly fill my lungs. "It's all a lot to take in, Victor."

"Don't you want a life with me?" His dark eyes bored into mine.

"More than anything." The words were out of my mouth like a bullet before I could stop them—before I could even think. I clapped a hand over my mouth.

Victor's eyes lit with a dangerous hope. My stomach twisted into a dozen sailors' knots. How had we ended up here so quickly? Just weeks ago, the idea of an affair had been unthinkable, and now we were talking about futures and feelings that ran deeper than the bed sheets.

"Then what are we waiting for?"

My breath caught. This was real. He was making it real.

"My lawyer has already been working on my divorce from Dotty. I'm meeting him this afternoon to see how far he's gotten." He leaned in closer, his presence enveloping me, and took my hand into his own. "So you see"—he pressed his lips to my palm—"I'm all in, angel."

"I don't even know how to get started."

Victor kissed my knuckles, lingering just long enough to send a shiver through me. "I'll set you up with my lawyer. He and I go way back. We served together in France, and I trust him with my life."

I blew out a shaky breath and nodded my assent.

"I'll go take care of the check," he said, standing tall with an air of determination. He paused before stepping away, locking eyes with me. "We can have it all, Barbara."

He walked toward the front of the diner, his movements effortless, the confident stride of a man accustomed to winning. I traced the broad line of his shoulders with my eyes, then shifted my gaze to Frankie, now half-asleep in the booth, wooden car clutched loosely in his small hand.

I gathered our things slowly, deliberately. The hum of the diner filtered back into my consciousness—the sizzle of the griddle, the muted murmur of voices in the main dining room, the tinny notes of the jukebox up front. Everything felt surreal— like waking from a vivid dream only to find yourself in another.

Victor returned and stood beside the booth. He looked down at me with dark, intense eyes. "Let me drive you home."

I went to protest, but it was clear that he wasn't asking. I nodded and turned to Frankie, gently coaxing him awake. Victor knelt so he was at eye level with my drowsy little boy.

"Would you like to ride in my car?"

Frankie's face brightened, his tired eyes sparking back to life. He enthusiastically nodded his head, his straw-blond hair bouncing with every move. "What color?" Frankie asked.

"Blue," Victor answered, looking up at me. "I drove the Jaguar today."

Frankie, fully awake now, latched on to Victor's hand and tugged him toward the swinging door. "Come on!"

Victor chuckled, a rare, unguarded smile spreading across his face as he followed, willingly strung along by an eager little boy who had already decided he was a friend.

22

VICTOR

"What on earth do you want?"

"Always nice to see you, Dotty." I removed my hat and ran my fingers along its woolen brim.

Dorothy folded her arms across her chest, popped her hip to the side, and raised an unimpressed eyebrow. "You didn't answer my question. What do you want, Victor?"

"May I come in?"

She hesitated before stepping aside. I walked into the front hall of what used to be our home. The scents of lavender and lemon polish lingered in the air, tugging at dead memories. She shut the door behind me and placed her hands firmly on her hips.

"A little notice would have been nice."

I set my hat on the polished mahogany side table. "Why? Need to run off a gentleman caller?" I removed my coat and hung it on the rack.

"Not this time."

I let out a humorless chuckle as I scanned the room, listening for noise from upstairs. "Where's Margaret?"

"Out riding her bike with her friends."

"I was hoping to see her…" I rocked back on my heels.

Dorothy's glare could have cut diamonds. "You know how I feel about that."

"She's still my daughter, Dotty."

"When it's convenient." She waved a hand to cut me off before I could offer a rebuttal. "What do you want, Victor? I won't ask again."

"Well, first I'd like a drink."

Dorothy rolled her eyes and turned toward the living room. "And?"

I followed behind her. "And…a divorce."

Dorothy stopped in her tracks, her back rigid. The lamplight slanted across the walls, casting elongated shapes in the quiet room. She turned slowly to face me, her expression smooth as glass.

"A divorce?" she repeated, as if testing the weight of the word on her tongue.

I watched her closely, waiting for the explosion, the sharp retort—something to shatter the fragile hush that had settled between us. Instead, she walked silently to the liquor cabinet, pulled out a crystal tumbler, and poured a generous measure of bourbon. She handed me the glass, and our fingers briefly touched.

"You're not surprised," I said. A statement, not a question.

Dorothy shrugged, then sank into a plush floral armchair, crossing her legs with casual elegance. "I'm not an idiot, Victor."

I swirled the bourbon in its glass, the aroma of oak and vanilla wafting up and mingling with the lavender that still lingered in the air. I sat on a hunter-green velvet sofa and took a slow, burning sip.

She exhaled sharply, smoothing an invisible wrinkle from her skirt. "But why now? What's the rush? We have a decent arrangement. You do what you want, and I do what I want. We're fine like this."

"Are we? Are we really, Dotty?"

She let out a short, brittle huff. "Who's the girl?"

I threw back my bourbon in one last swig, feeling the consuming warmth spread through my chest. "That's not what this is about."

Dorothy stood, walked to the liquor cabinet, and poured herself a drink. She didn't offer me another. "Of course it is. If you're going to blow up our lives, I have a right to know why."

"Fair enough." I set my glass down with a deliberate click. "Yes, I have met someone."

She swirled her glass, then took a long, measured sip. Her lipstick left a scarlet smudge on the rim as she set it down and leaned against the cabinet. "Do you love her?"

"Yes." The single word dropped like a hammer.

Dorothy took another drink, slower this time. "What makes this one different?"

I leaned forward, resting my elbows on my knees, and clasped my hands together. "I see a future with her, Dotty. A real one."

"A future." She scoffed before retraining her face into an impassive mask.

I stood, the alcohol fueling a restless energy within me. "We've been living a lie for years, you and I. This 'arrangement,' as you call it, is nothing more than a convenient fiction. We've been divorced in all but name. It's time we were honest with ourselves."

She drained her drink. "You're the last person with any right to talk about honesty." She motioned around the opulent room. "You think I don't know where all this money comes from? Every cent is dripping in blood, and I've always turned the other way." Her voice turned to steel. "Don't you dare lecture me about being honest."

Dorothy set her empty glass down with a delicate yet forceful clink, the crystal catching a flicker of light as it met the marble surface of the liquor cabinet. She stood silently for a moment, smoothing the fabric of her skirt. Her lips tightened into a thin line.

"How would it even work?" she asked, her voice measured, as if reading from a script. "The divorce."

I took in her poised stance and the lingering tension in her shoulders. "Lawrence will handle everything. He's in with several judges who are…forward-thinking. We just need to decide who files against whom and work out the details of our arrangement."

Dorothy walked to the sofa and ran a finger along the velvet, idly following the grain of the fabric. "You mean an arrangement that's best for you." She didn't sit.

"I mean what's fair," I said. "I gave you my word that I would take care of you and Margaret, and I will continue to do so. Have I ever let you down on that score?"

She exhaled sharply, shaking her head with the ghost of a humorless smile. "As husbands go, you've been a letdown from the beginning. But no, you've never gone back on your word."

The warmth of the bourbon began to ebb, replaced by a cold gnawing in my gut. I looked at Dorothy—really looked at her—searching for the woman I had once adored. Her dark hair was impeccably styled, her green eyes far harder than they used to be. She was only thirty-one, but all traces of the vivacious girl who had so eagerly said "yes" ten years ago were gone. I had done that—driven her away.

"I never wanted to hurt either of you," I said.

"Spare me whatever sentimental nonsense you're about to spew." She walked to the window and parted the heavy drapes just enough to peer outside. The last of the afternoon light had faded to a dusky purple, casting a melancholic hue over the manicured lawn.

I ran a finger along the rim of my glass, almost gently, as if it were made of spun sugar. "I'm trying to do this the right way."

The dim twilight cast her in a ghostly glow. She let the drapes fall back into place and turned to face me. "There is no right way, Victor. Just be a man and tell me how it's going to be."

I stepped closer, stopping at the edge of the Persian rug that anchored the room. "So you'll agree to it?"

She shrugged, a gesture so nonchalant it bordered on resigned. "What choice do I have?" Her words drifted off like smoke.

"I'll have Lawrence draw everything up," I said, testing her oddly calm demeanor. "I'll file, and in the meantime, nothing changes—you and Margaret will be maintained on the same terms as our current separation."

Dorothy's lips parted slightly, as if to speak, but she held back. The silence stretched, almost elastic, threatening to snap at any moment. She walked slowly around the perimeter of the room, her fingertips grazing the tops of furniture like a pianist playing an absentminded melody.

When she spoke, her voice was calculated and sterile, each word placed with surgical precision. "I will see my own lawyer. You'll cover his fee, of course. I will be the one to file. You'll take the blame in court. And we'll revisit the terms of our separation agreement for something more appropriate. You're going to make this worth my while."

"Dorothy—" I started, but she held up a hand to stop me.

"Those are my conditions. If I'm going to bear the stain of being a divorced woman, then it damn well better be worth it to me."

The words stung more than I expected. I nodded silently.

"You should go," she said, glancing back at the window. "Margaret will be home soon, and I don't want you here."

I opened my mouth to protest, but the glacial set of her eyes froze the words in my throat. She meant every bit of it—every condition, every accusation—and I knew there would be no negotiating this tonight.

The plush carpet muffled my steps as I walked to the foyer. I could almost hear Dorothy's breathing, each inhale and exhale a metronome to the growing tension. I reached for my coat, the familiar wool brushing against my fingers, grounding me. My hat sat on the small mahogany table by the door where I had left it.

I paused for a moment, hoping for something—a rebuttal, a concession, even a parting shot—but there was only silence, vast and suffocating. The soft tick of the wall clock marked time like a dripping faucet.

"I'll see myself out."

23

BARBARA

April 1951

Thursday, April 12, 1951
7:00 p.m.

My darling,

I'm at my desk at the office working late
tonight until about ten or so. I don't mind too much
anymore because it delays my going home to that
empty apartment and makes my evenings a little
more tolerable. I started to write you this morning,
but then at noon, I had such a marvelous surprise
that I thought I'd better start all over again. It
was really good hearing your voice so unexpectedly.
All morning, I sat looking at the phone, thinking
how easy it would be just to pick it up and dial

your number. It's an awful temptation, you know. I don't know if I can go through with this time apart! I miss you oh so very much already. It doesn't seem fair that two people in love such as we are should be kept apart! Knowing I'm not going to see you, hold you, touch you…leaves me with a horrible feeling of being all alone, like a whole portion of my being has been removed. You have become an integral part of my life, and your presence is essential to my peace of mind. I feel too that I've similarly affected you, which makes this all so difficult. And at times like now, sweetheart, the whole waiting for passing of time seems so senseless. But I do love you, and I do want you so very much. And time will pass…

I keep champing at the bit. I'm crazy to get started on our plans—specific plans for our house and everything. I'd like to sit down at the board or sprawl on the floor with you beside me and get something tangible down on paper. Start figuring out the little things—like where the bookcases go, what we will put in the dressing room, and what kind of pictures we will do for Frankie's room. I want to get going on any planning and dreaming that we can share—really share! I want to take care of you and love you truly—no more of this tomorrow or day after or later business, but NOW!

I have to give my written consent for Dorothy

to speak to my lawyer. I understand, and I'll take care of it after I finish my note to you. I want to get the divorce finalized as soon as possible so that you can finally file.

How goes the battle with you, sweetheart? Bet your days are long and lonely too, probably more so than mine because I have so many distractions all day long—work, I mean. I'm terribly sorry for the upheaval I've caused you. You've gone through so much on my account. I know you never would have done it if you didn't honestly love me and want me for your own. That's the only thing that makes it possible to go on waiting and hoping. Your devotion is the dearest thing in the world to me. Your love is the thing I count on when there is nothing else.

This is the last letter I can write this week. I'll send it by courier so that you get it tomorrow. I'll write again on Saturday, so you'll get another letter on Monday. I'll be working the next four Saturdays at least. If you need me for anything, I'll be here... As a matter of fact, I think I'll have a surprise for you. Maybe I'll get Phil to bring it by, or perhaps I'll mail it. We'll see, but since you're not the curious type, I won't even give you another hint!

Bet you're just as beautiful (and you are, you know) today as you were the last time I saw you—your long blonde hair, your fresh "just showered" *look… Everything I remember about you starts the fire all over again for me. You excite me and make me want to do wonderful things for you, my darling. You're all I've ever wanted, everything I've ever hoped for.*

Until later, dearest. Remember, you're mine, and I adore you.

Always,

—V

P.S: I wish I could have one of your extra special "kisses" right now…

I always thought those girls who gushed about butterflies in their stomachs were hopeless romantics. But Victor's words, his voice, and the feel of his hands on my skin—all of it sent a delicious flutter through me. Maybe those girls weren't just spouting vaporous nonsense after all.

I folded Victor's letter, replaced it in its envelope, and locked it away in the hand-carved wooden box he had brought me from his trip to Mexico. I traced my fingers over the intricate designs on the lid, lost in thoughts of Victor and what lay ahead for us.

The doorbell startled me from my reverie. I hurried out of my room, half expecting to see Phil with the surprise Victor mentioned in his letter. My heart quickened at the thought as I made my way to the door, smoothing my dress and checking my hair in the hall mirror.

When I opened the door, my excitement deflated like a punctured balloon.

"Mother," I said, unable to mask my disappointment. "I wasn't expecting you."

My mother, the redoubtable Agatha Montgomery, stood tall and imperious, her eyes taking in every detail of the entryway with their usual critical sharpness. She wore a navy-blue overcoat and clutched a small handbag, her lips set in a thin line.

"Well? Aren't you going to invite me in?"

I hesitated for a fraction of a second, wondering what she could want this time. I was never on her list of social calls.

"Of course," I said tentatively, stepping aside to let her through.

Agatha slowly, deliberately removed her overcoat, revealing a slate-gray dress with black piped trim along clean, sharp lines. Her low-heeled black leather pumps matched her handbag. She handed her coat to me as she strode through to the living room.

"I see you've...redecorated," she said as she surveyed the room down her nose.

"A little here and there. If you visited more often, it wouldn't seem so drastic. Shall we sit?"

Agatha let out a short huff as she perched on the edge of the sofa and crossed her legs at the ankles. "It's rather...austere."

"I prefer to call it modern. Would you like some tea?"

"I'm not staying long enough."

I settled into Frank's armchair. "All right then, to what do I owe the pleasure?"

Agatha's eyes flicked toward me, cool and assessing. She unclasped her handbag, then thought better of it and clasped it shut again. "I was relieved to hear from Frank that you've set aside your little secretarial position and resumed your proper place at home."

Of course Frank had run straight to Mother. The two of them had become thick as thieves. I braced myself for the lecture that was sure to follow.

"Left is not the same as quit," I corrected. "It's just a pause."

"Whatever you call it," Agatha said, sitting rigidly upright. "It's good for your family. They need you here."

"You've made your position abundantly clear, Mother. Surely you didn't drive all the way out here to tell me that."

Agatha tilted her head, lips pursed. "Frank tells me things between you are…strained."

I gripped the arms of the chair, the rough fabric like steel wool against my palms. "Frank has been rather chatty, it seems."

"He's concerned, Barbara." She paused, weighing her next words with uncharacteristic care. "As am I."

I opened my mouth to retort, but Mother held up her hand to stop me.

"Listen, Barbara."

I remained silent.

"Now it's no secret that I didn't approve of your marriage in the first place. You married beneath you when you could have done so much better. But what's done is done." She shifted her weight and recrossed her ankles. "And I will even go so far as to admit that Frank has proven himself to be a decent man, despite his less-than-stellar credentials."

"How magnanimous of you, Mother."

"What I'm saying is you chose him. You chose this life. So it's on you to make it work. Our kind of people are never unhappy in marriage. At least not publicly."

I studied her face, searching for some trace of the warmth other girls described when speaking of their mothers. Her features were as precise and unyielding as a marble statue— cheekbones carved high, nose straight as a ruler, lips a severe slash of red, gunmetal-gray hair scraped back into a tight bun— any trace of softness long sacrificed to dignity.

"Mother," I said slowly, choosing my words with the same caution she had employed earlier. "I appreciate your concern. Truly. But this is something Frank and I need to work out on our own."

Agatha studied her manicured fingernails, then me, then the

pictures on the walls. "I do hope you will work it out," she said, her tone softer but no less piercing. "But tell me, how can you, when you're spending so much time…elsewhere?"

My breath caught in my chest. I sat up straighter. "Say what you mean, Mother."

Mother picked up a studio portrait of Frankie from the side table, running her fingers along the embellished silver frame, then set it back down.

"Where is your son?"

"Your *grandson*? He's asleep in his room. And you're deflecting."

She pursed her lips for a moment before speaking again. "You were twelve when your father campaigned for state senate. You remember that, don't you?" she asked, looking at the photo of Frankie, not at me.

The change in subject threw me off balance. "Of course I remember."

"He spent nearly every weekend away, traveling the district, as politicians do." She turned to look at me, hands clasped primly in her lap. "It was a difficult time for our family."

I shifted uneasily in Frank's chair. "What are you saying?"

"By then, his campaign was already behind him. He'd bowed out of the race, if you recall." She shot me a pointed glance. "But he continued to stay out on the road."

Realization sunk in like a cold stone going straight to the bottom of a pond. I gripped the chair's arms tighter, my knuckles blanching.

"He was having an affair?" I asked, though I already knew the answer.

Agatha shrugged one shoulder, the movement almost nonchalant. "It wasn't the first and certainly not the last. Why do you think he's still in Hawaii?"

"He's there with the statehood commission," I answered dutifully, though the words felt flimsy as straw.

"He could have come back a dozen times over, but he

hasn't." She gave me a long, assessing look. "Men have their weaknesses. The important thing is he always comes back to us in the end. He fulfills his responsibilities and keeps up appearances."

"Why are you telling me this?" My voice was low and tight.

She shot me a sharp, knowing glare. "Men have their indulgences, Barbara. But women don't get that luxury."

I shot up from the chair, unable to sit still any longer under her scrutiny. "Times have changed, Mother. You act like we're still in corsets."

"Not where it matters." Mother's eyes bore into mine, unflinching. "You're treading on dangerous ground, Barbara. One wrong step, and everything your father and I built— *everything*—comes crumbling down. You aren't some nobody from a no-name family. What you do reflects on all of us. And for what?" Her voice dropped to a searing whisper. "A tumble in the sheets with your employer?"

My blood turned cold. "Get out."

Agatha rose with the measured grace of a ballerina, plucking her coat from where I'd draped it over the back of the sofa. She made no move to put it on, instead letting it dangle from her fingers as she made her way toward the door.

"Struck a nerve, did I?" she asked.

I opened the front door, letting the cool spring air rush in. "Thank you for your visit, Mother. Now, please leave."

She stepped onto the threshold and turned back, her posture as erect as a flagpole. "The family always comes first, Barbara," she said. "Never forget that."

I shut the door before she could say another word.

The silence of the house closed in around me like a heavy quilt. Outside, I heard the rhythmic click-clack of her heels on the walkway, then the soft, muted slam of a car door. The low growl of the engine roared to life before fading into the distance.

What I wouldn't give to be in Victor's arms.

This enforced separation was going to be hell.

24
VICTOR

I flashed my empty inner coat pockets at Lawrence. "Look, no cigarettes."

His forehead wrinkled as his eyebrows shot up. "Well, I'll be damned." He let out a low whistle. "Didn't think I'd see the day." He motioned to the empty pair of leather chairs in front of his desk. "What prompted that miracle?"

"They make Barbara wrinkle her nose."

Lawrence chuckled. "Your best pal hacks out his burnt lungs, and nothing. But your girl wrinkles her nose, and suddenly you're a model of clean living."

I smirked and sank into the chair. The leather groaned as I leaned back. Lawrence's office smelled of old books, paper, and polished mahogany—the scent of bureaucracy and long hours bending the law into the right shape. Sunlight slanted through the Venetian blinds, carving the cluttered desk into bands of light and shadow.

Lawrence adjusted his glasses, the gold rims glinting. "So, how are you holding up? I know waiting isn't your strong suit."

"We're managing," I said. "How much longer do you think?"

He opened a file and flipped through a few pages, and for a moment, there was only the rustle of paper. "I'm doing everything I can to push things along. I got the case filed in a district with a sympathetic judge who won't waste our time, but there's only so much I can do."

"How long until we get a court date?"

"Two months, give or take. That's if everything goes smoothly." He closed the file and steepled his fingers. "I met with Dorothy, and she agreed to our terms. For now. But Victor, don't get comfortable. I wouldn't carve it into stone just yet."

"She's angling for more, Larry. Always is."

"She wants to see you suffer," he said, his tone measured. "And that's why you have to be on your absolute best behavior. A veritable choir boy. You can't give her any ammunition with the judge." Lawrence rocked back in his chair, tapping a pen against his lips. The striped shadows from the blinds cut across his face, masking his expression in bands of light and dark. "You understand that means no contact with Barbara. Not even a phone call. You might have a tail, Victor. Hell, I'd put money on it. If the judge suspects any collusion or infidelity, he could throw out the case."

I shifted in my seat, my slacks sliding along the smooth leather. My jaw tightened at the thought of Barbara—waiting, hoping, trusting me to navigate this.

I nodded. "She's left my office. I haven't seen her since. We've talked on the phone, but we've been careful," I said. "Discreet."

"Discreet won't cut it," Lawrence said, turning back to me. The creases between his brows deepened as he spoke. "You need to be invisible."

I exhaled slowly. "She's out there on her own, Larry."

Lawrence removed his glasses and rubbed the bridge of his nose, the skin raw from years of pressure. "I know," he admitted, "but it's the only way. Especially considering who her family is."

I frowned. "What do you mean?"

"What do I mean?" His tone turned exasperated. "You do know who her father is, don't you?" His face twisted as he ruffled a hand through his thinning hair and tugged at it by the roots.

In all of our time together, Barbara and I had never once discussed her family.

"Victor!" he exclaimed, throwing his hands up in disbelief. "For Christ's sake—she's a Montgomery! How the hell didn't you know that?"

"She would have told me," I protested.

Lawrence huffed as he fished a file from one of the stacks on his desk and flipped it open. "Barbara Evans, born Barbara Montgomery—the youngest child of Milton and Agatha Montgomery. Milton Montgomery was the mayor of Los Angeles back in the twenties. From there, he served in the state legislature in the thirties and eventually in the US Congress during the war. Currently, he's on delegation to Hawaii as part of the statehood commission."

I let out a slow breath. "Oh, hell."

"Indeed." Lawrence shut the file with a soft thud. "She comes from serious stock, Victor. The kind of family that makes the society pages just for having Sunday dinner. You really didn't know any of this?"

I ran a hand through my hair, trying to process the new information. The mahogany-paneled walls seemed to close around me, the scent of aged paper and leather thickening like smoke. "No. She never mentioned her parents."

Lawrence shrugged. "Maybe she wanted you to like her for herself, not for her connections. Or maybe she thought you'd put two and two together."

I stood, unable to sit still any longer. The striped shadows from the blinds danced on the walls as I paced. "Why does it matter who her family is?"

"It matters because they're powerful, Victor. And power means scrutiny. Every move she makes is watched, and by extension, every move you make with her."

I stopped pacing and turned to face Lawrence. "Are you telling me to walk away?"

"I'm telling you to go through this with your eyes open." He leaned forward, resting his elbows on the desk. "You're not just dealing with a difficult wife and a slow legal system now. Which brings me to my next point…"

"There's more?"

"Afraid so. With the added scrutiny, particularly when Barbara files for divorce—which will make the papers, I can promise you—you'll need to distance yourself from your…less-than-reputable operations."

I stopped pacing. "Which operations?"

Lawrence sighed, long and deep, as if summoning the patience of a saint. "Victor, don't insult me. You know exactly what I'm talking about. If you've got a good lieutenant, now would be the time to start handing him the keys. Don't just distance yourself. Make a break as wide as the Grand Canyon. Your hands need to be clean enough to hold communion."

I walked toward the window, peering through the Venetian blinds. Outside, Los Angeles moved at its usual frenetic pace—cars honking, people shouting, life rushing by with urgency. My thoughts drifted to Barbara again—her soft golden curls and how she bit her lip when she was deep in thought. A Montgomery. It made sense now—her elegance, her composure, her drive. But how had I missed something so monumental? And why had she never told me?

Lawrence joined me by the window, his voice breaking through my inner turmoil. "This won't be easy, but it's necessary if you want things to go smoothly." He looked at me over the gold rims of his glasses. With a soft clap on my shoulder, he continued. "You came to me because you trust me. I'm giving it to you straight." He dropped his hand back to his side. "I can help you make this work, but it will require sacrifice and time. If this is truly what you want, I'll back you all the way."

I nodded. "Thank you, Larry."

He shrugged. "What are friends for? But next time, do me a favor and bring me a smaller mountain to climb. You really can pick 'em."

———

The phone line crackled. "Hello?" Barbara's voice was angelic.

"Hello, Barbara, my darling."

A soft sigh drifted through the line. "What a pleasant surprise!"

I pinned the receiver between my ear and shoulder as I rocked back in my desk chair and flipped open the paper to the society pages. A photograph of Mrs. Agatha Montgomery commanded the page. She stood matronly and poised even as she held a ceremonial pair of oversized scissors—absurdly large in her dainty, gloved hands—for the ribbon cutting of the new city library.

"Are you busy?" I asked.

"Not especially," she answered sweetly. "And my day is miles better now that I'm talking to you."

"Good," I said, closing the paper and setting it aside. "I wanted to talk to you about something important."

The pause on her end was almost tangible, like a held breath. "Yes?"

"Do you know the new library on Robertson? The one with the Frank Lloyd Wright design?"

"Yes, I think so," she said, her voice cautious.

"There's a lovely piece in today's paper about the grand opening."

"Oh?" Her tone shifted, curiosity overriding the tension. "I haven't seen it."

"There's a picture of your mother cutting the ribbon. It's quite something."

Silence flooded the line, heavy and awkward. I could almost hear her mind racing, piecing together my intentions. A deep breath rustled on her end, the static making it sound like dry leaves skittering across pavement.

"I didn't realize you read the society pages," she said, her tone now guarded.

"I don't," I replied. "But sometimes interesting things catch my eye." I let that hang for a moment. "Barbara, why didn't you tell me who your family was?"

"Because it doesn't matter."

"Barbara—" I started, but she cut me off.

"It doesn't, Victor. I wanted you to know me for who I am, not for who they are. I've lived in the Montgomery family shadow all my life. It was nice to be seen for myself for once." She was quiet for a fragile moment. "Does this change things?"

"Not in the slightest, darling." I let out a long sigh. "I just wish you had told me yourself." I rubbed my temples, the beginning of a headache creeping up my neck to settle behind my eyes. "I'm just trying to understand why you kept it a secret."

"It wasn't a secret," she said, exasperation threading through the static. "It just wasn't important. My family isn't me."

This conversation was slipping in the wrong direction. I loosened my tie, inhaling deeply, and searched for a way to pull us back from the edge. "Barbara, I'm not accusing you of anything. I just wish I'd known—"

"Why?" Her question punched through the line.

"Because it puts us under a magnifying glass." A beat. "And it might complicate the divorce."

Her voice was soft and vulnerable when she spoke again. "What do you mean? What does my family have to do with it at all?"

I switched the receiver to my other ear and sat up straighter in my chair. "Lawrence says that with your parents' influence, there will be more scrutiny. It's not just us anymore. There's no way to keep this out of the public eye. These things can get messy…"

The hush on the line stretched thin, taut as a wire.

"I just need to be prepared. That's all. Forewarned is forearmed, right?"

Her tone turned brittle. "Well, pardon me for making your life difficult."

"Aw, don't be like that."

Silence again. If not for the low hum of static, I might have thought she'd hung up on me.

"I need to see you, darling." My voice was softer, coaxing.

"We can't, Victor. Lawrence was crystal clear about that. No contact until your court date."

"I know, I know. But I need to hold you in my arms. Now more than ever."

The line crackled as she hesitated. "Victor, if we're seen—"

"We won't be," I assured her. "Give me some credit. I do know how to do things on the sly when I need to."

She sighed, and I could almost see her biting her bottom lip, weighing the risks against the pull of desire. "When and where?"

I grinned. "Tomorrow at noon. Do you have a pen?"

25

BARBARA

I glanced at the slip of paper in my hand—2375 Glendale Boulevard. A slight frown creased my forehead as I looked up and down the street. Bohemian boutiques and cafés dotted the block, tucked between stucco bungalows with rust-colored Spanish tile rooftops. This wasn't an area I frequented, even during my more artistic days. It was bohemian in a way that felt almost foreign—far from the polished refinement of Hancock Park or even the structured grandeur of downtown.

I checked the address once more. It matched.

The small whitewashed building sat like a forgotten relic among the riot of color, as if time had passed it by while the rest of the street moved on. Above the door, a faded wooden sign read "Rosemary's Art & Antiques" in delicate, hand-painted script. A string of tiny bells tinkled as I pushed the door open. Peeling white paint flaked off and fluttered to the ground.

A musty warmth enveloped me as I stepped inside. The scent of old wood and aging fabric mingled with a faint trace of lavender, wrapping around me like a moth-eaten shawl. The interior was cluttered but charming—an organized chaos of vintage furniture, framed paintings, and porcelain knickknacks jostling for space like overgrown plants in a hothouse.

I let the door close behind me, and the bells faded into a soft clatter. This wasn't Victor's style at all. Where was the sleek sophistication, the understated opulence? I hesitated, glancing once more at the slip of paper in my hand. 2375 Glendale Boulevard. It was right—but nothing about this place felt right. Had I written the address down wrong?

"Can I help you, dear?" A frail but sweet voice broke through the stillness. An elderly woman with wispy white hair and large, round glasses emerged from behind a beaded curtain, her hands as gnarled as ancient vines. She wore a lavender shawl draped over her shoulders, its fabric whispering with each step.

I hesitated. "I'm supposed to meet someone here," I said, slipping the paper back into my bag. "Perhaps I have the wrong address."

The old woman peered at me through her glasses, which were fogged from the steam trickling up from the cream-and-rose porcelain teacup in her skeletal fingers. She smiled, her lips thin as parchment. "No mistake, dearie. You're in the right place." Her voice carried the ghost of a Scottish accent softened by decades of distance.

I bit my lip, unconvinced, as I glanced around again. As far as I could tell, the shop was empty except for the two of us. "Do you know where I'm supposed to meet my…friend?"

She nodded slowly. "Come with me."

I followed her through the beaded curtain, the long strands clicking and clattering like a handful of glass marbles in a child's pocket. The back room was even more cluttered than the front, with stacks of yellowing books and boxes overflowing with lace doilies and tarnished silverware. It had the feel of a forgotten attic, a place where memories drowned in dust.

The old woman—I hadn't thought to ask her name—set her teacup down on a chipped enamel table and motioned toward a narrow staircase.

"He's waiting for you upstairs."

Upstairs? I opened my mouth to speak, but she had already

turned away, busy sorting through a heap of fabric swatches. I looked at the staircase. It seemed too flimsy to support even my slight frame, let alone a man of Victor's stature. Taking a deep breath, I gripped the wobbly handrail and started up, each step groaning like an old man rising from a chair.

A single door awaited me at the top, its paint cracked like sunbaked earth. I held my breath and knocked softly.

The door swung open, and Victor stood before me, his tall frame filling the doorway. His shirt sleeves were rolled to his elbows, and suspenders hugged his shoulders. The top two buttons of his shirt were undone, and his tie hung loose. A warm rush of relief washed over me.

"Barbara, my darling," he said, his voice a smooth caress. "Come in."

I stepped inside, and Victor closed the door behind me. The space was surprisingly cozy, with a low ceiling and slanted walls that gave it the feel of a ship's cabin. Sunlight filtered through gauzy curtains, casting a soft glow over a battered leather sofa and a wooden coffee table scarred from use. A hot plate and sink occupied one corner, and a patterned rug covered most of the hardwood floor.

Victor took my hands in his and pulled me close. "I was beginning to think you wouldn't come," he murmured as he kissed my forehead.

I leaned into his chest for a moment, savoring the spicy scent of his cologne. "This place…" I said, pulling back slightly. "It's not what I was expecting."

He smiled, a boyish curve to his lips that momentarily smoothed the tension from his face. "That's the point. No one would think to look for us here."

I glanced around the sparse room again. "Is it one of yours?"

He let go of my hands and walked to the window, looking down at the street below. "Not on paper. But yes."

I moved to stand beside him. "What does that mean?"

"In short, it means it can't be traced back to me."

"Why do you need such a place?"

He dismissed the question with a flick of his hand. "Never mind that. Let me look at you." He pulled back and caressed every inch of my body with his eyes. "My memory and imagination don't do you justice, angel."

Warmth rose from my chest to my cheeks.

"Sit," he said, gesturing to the sofa. "I have some news."

I perched on the worn leather, which sighed and sank beneath me. "Don't keep me in suspense."

He sat next to me, and our knees touched, sending little electric shocks up my legs.

"Dorothy agreed to the terms. We have a court date."

A flutter of hope took wing in my chest. "When is it?"

"June twenty-first."

I exhaled slowly—a feeble attempt at tempering my emotions. Two months felt like an eternity, but at least there was an end in sight now.

"That's wonderful," I said, though the words came out more measured than I intended.

Victor's eyes searched mine, and for a moment, I thought he might press me about my hesitation. Instead, he leaned in and kissed me, his lips soft but insistent. I yielded to him, letting the tension I was carrying melt away.

When he pulled back, he stroked my cheek with the back of his hand. "God, I've missed that."

I touched my fingers to my lips, still tingling from his kiss. "Me too," I said, knowing it wasn't enough but afraid to say more.

Victor took my hand again, his touch warm and reassuring. "You understand, don't you? I can't bear being away from you. But until the divorce is final, we have to be very careful. And Lawrence assures me that as soon as mine is settled, you're clear to file for divorce from Frank."

I nodded, though a knot formed in my stomach. "I know. It's

just…hard to wait. When all I want is to be with you, yet I have to keep pretending."

He squeezed my hand. "Barbara, we'll get through this. We just have to hold on a little longer. Stay with Frank for now and keep up appearances." He kissed the back of my hand. "You're an actress, right?"

I smiled at his recollection but quickly looked away, focusing on the delicate patterns of the curtains as they swayed in the breeze. "Victor…" I started. "Edith knows. She's the only one I've confided in, but I trust her completely."

His grip on my hand tightened, then relaxed. "Your sister… She's always been supportive of you, hasn't she?"

"Yes," I said, turning back to him. "She understands what I'm going through. She'd never betray me."

Victor sighed and ran a hand through his dark hair, mussing its usual razor-sharp lines. "All right. But no one else, Barbara. If this gets out…"

"I know," I said quickly. "I know what's at stake." The knot in my stomach tightened. "But my mother suspects. If she stirs up trouble—"

"She won't," he interrupted, though his voice lacked its usual certainty. "She's not so foolish as to air dirty laundry in public."

I pulled my hand away and crossed my arms, sinking back into the sofa. "You don't know her like I do. She'll do whatever it takes to protect the family. And in her mind, divorce is the devil, and a 'well-brought-up girl' should stick it out in a miserable, loveless marriage rather than try for happiness." I shook my head and let out a bitter laugh. "She's still stuck in the last century."

"Then all the more reason we give her nothing to go on, darling."

I nodded, letting out a shaky breath.

Victor studied me in silence, his dark eyes probing. "Speaking of being stuck in the last century…I've been wondering about something."

I uncrossed my arms and sat up straighter. "Oh?"

"The age difference between you and your siblings—it's quite pronounced, isn't it?"

I nodded. "I'm the baby of the family. There's an eleven-year gap between me and my brother, Bill. He's the next youngest. Why?"

Victor leaned back, his fingers idly drumming on his knee. "Your parents—they're older than I expected. Older than my own, even. And I've got ten years on you, darling."

"Yes, Mother was forty when she had me. Apparently, I was something of a surprise." I studied him. "Where are you going with this?"

"If you were the surprise baby—the 'change of life miracle,' if you will—I'd expect your parents to dote on you more. Indulge you, even."

A rueful smile dusted my lips. "My father does. When he's around, that is. When I was a kid, he treated me like a princess. I remember once, between meetings with very important bigwigs during his time as city mayor, he made time to come to a tea party with my dolls. I couldn't have been more than three." I sighed, the memory warm but distant. "He's always so sweet to me."

"But not your mother?"

I let out a quiet, humorless laugh. "No. Mother is all rules, manners, and propriety. Very no-nonsense. She'd have made a great general."

Victor chuckled, low and knowing. "I took orders from a few just like her during the war."

I loved Victor's face, the way his eyes crinkled at the corners when he laughed. This was a pleasant moment of levity, and I hesitated to disrupt it with what I needed to say.

"Victor," I began, my voice quieter. He turned his full attention to me. "I want Frankie to have every bit of love and attention I never got."

He tilted his head, listening intently.

"It's not just about me," I continued. "Or about us. When I leave Frank, it means taking Frankie away from his father."

Victor leaned back, one arm draped over the sofa's worn top rail. "Barbara, you're not taking him away forever. Fathers have rights. Or they should, anyway. Frank could still see him."

"But would he?" I asked, my voice rising with the swell of emotion I'd been holding back. "Frank barely makes time for him now when we're all under the same roof."

"Are you saying Frank doesn't love his son?"

"I'm saying that Frank loves the *idea* of having a son—the status symbol of having a boy with his name. But the reality of fatherhood is something else entirely. He never plays with him, never reads him a bedtime story, nothing. If Frank can't be bothered when it's easy, why would he make the effort once we've split?"

A heavy silence settled between us, thick as the dust motes dancing in the sunbeams.

Victor's expression softened, and he closed the distance between us with an easy slide across the worn leather sofa cushions. He took my shoulders gently in his hands and kissed my forehead.

"Barbara," he murmured, his voice steady and sure. "I can't predict what Frank will or won't do. But I can promise you this —Frankie will never want for a father under my roof. Not ever."

I looked into Victor's eyes, searching for the certainty I needed to see. The knot in my stomach loosened just a little.

"Come here," he said, opening his arms.

I happily slid into his embrace. He held me tightly, as if trying to fuse us together, to make us unbreakable. I closed my eyes and let myself disappear into him, wishing we could stay like this forever—caught in a moment outside of time, beyond the reach of complications and consequences.

"I love you," he whispered into my hair. "And I will love you and your boy as if my own blood ran through his veins."

Victor's words sent a rush of warmth through me, melting

the last of my reservations. I tilted my head and met his lips, first with a tentative brush, then a growing hunger. He deepened the kiss, urgent and demanding, and I responded in kind, threading my fingers through his hair and pulling him closer.

Victor's hands roamed down my back, tracing the curve of my spine before settling on my hips, and every touch sent sparks skittering across my skin. He pulled me onto his lap, and I straddled him, reveling in the hard press of his body against mine, the way the thin fabric of my dress offered little barrier to the heat radiating from his skin.

We kissed with the desperation of two souls stealing time from an unforgiving clock. I moved my hands to his shoulders, then slid them down his chest, admiring the firm lines of muscle beneath his shirt. He unbuttoned the top of my dress, grazing his fingers across my collar bones and sending shivers through me.

I broke the kiss and gasped for air, feverishly burning as I looked into his eyes. "Victor," I whispered, but whatever I meant to say was lost as he kissed my neck, then my shoulder, then my breast. His lips were fire on my skin, each kiss igniting a trail of molten desire. His hands were urgent and insistent as they roamed over my body, melting away the last of my resolve. We were a tangle of limbs and hurried breaths, desperately ridding each other of clothing.

He brushed his lips against the shell of my ear. "How about one of your extra special kisses?" he whispered.

I turned my head and pressed a soft, tender kiss to his lips.

He let out a low growl. "Tease." He took a fistful of my hair and pulled my head back—the perfect mix of firm and gentle— to meet his gaze. "You know that's not what I meant."

I kissed a path down his torso as he guided me to kneel between his legs.

"You're so gorgeous when you're on your knees for me."

Heat flushed through me as I leaned in and kissed his tip, tasting the first salty bead of his desire. I swirled my tongue around the head, taking my time, savoring the power I held in this moment. Victor's hands tightened in my hair, not forcing but guiding me deeper. I obliged, sliding him into my mouth with slow, deliberate strokes. I savored the saltiness of his skin and the way he throbbed against my tongue.

Each movement of my head sent waves of tension through his body. Each flick of my tongue drew guttural sounds from deep within his chest. I hollowed my cheeks and took him as far as I could, feeling him press against the back of my throat. My need grew almost unbearable as I worked him with a concert of lips, tongue, and hand.

Victor's breathing grew ragged, his chest rising and falling with increasing urgency. His grip on my hair tightened, then loosened, then tightened again as if he were fighting an internal battle.

"Barbara," he groaned, his voice thick from his impending release. "You are so perfect."

A surge of pride and desire coursed through me at his words. I redoubled my efforts, sliding him deeper, working him faster. His body tensed, every muscle coiling like a spring about to snap.

Just as he reached the edge, he pulled me away with a sharp intake of breath. "Wait," he commanded, his voice hoarse.

I looked up at him, my lips swollen and wet, my body heavy with unfulfilled need. He grazed my cheek with the back of his hand, then traced his fingers down my neck.

"I have something for you," he said, shifting me gently to the side as he stood, breathing deeply to regain control. He walked over to the countertop and picked up a small plain white box. My mind raced with curiosity and anticipation.

"Close your eyes," he commanded.

I obeyed, my heart pounding in my chest. I heard him move closer, felt the air shift as he knelt beside me.

"Trust me," he said softly, and then the cool satin of a blindfold slid across my eyes. He tied it securely at the back of my head.

My world went dark, but my other senses flared to life. The scent of Victor's cologne mingled with the leather of the sofa, creating an intoxicating blend. I could hear the rustle of the box opening, the soft thud of a hard object being carefully placed on the coffee table, and Victor moving toward the wall and then back to me.

His heat radiated behind me. He gathered my hair and draped it over one shoulder, then kissed the nape of my neck, sending a jolt of electricity down my spine. He placed firm hands on my shoulders and guided me to stand and face him.

"Sit back and spread those beautiful legs," he instructed. His voice held that perfect balance of authority and care that always sent shivers through me. The leather sofa cushion was slick and brisk on my bare buttocks. I hesitated for a moment before complying, slowly parting my thighs. The rush of cool air made me acutely aware of how exposed—and how…aroused—I was.

Victor's footsteps were slow and deliberate as he moved around me. My heart pounded in my chest, each beat echoing in my ears. I bit my lip, every nerve pulled taut, buzzing with anticipation.

"I want you to have something to remind you of me when we're apart," he said.

His fingers parted me, probing.

"Something to make you feel good when I can't be there with you." He nudged the inside of my knee with his elbow. "Wider, angel."

I opened my legs as far as my hips allowed. My groin ached from the stretch. Something cool, hard, and smooth replaced Victor's fingers. I gasped as a chill rippled through me.

"What is—"

He pressed a silencing finger to my lips as he moved the object in slow swipes, increasingly slippery as he glided it back and forth. I gasped when he ran it over my sweet spot in slow, deliberate circles.

"Don't make a sound," Victor commanded. "No matter how

much you want to scream. You know I love to hear you cry out, but we mustn't scandalize our poor hostess downstairs." His breath was hot, his voice a low, dangerous purr in my ear as he leaned in close. "And don't you dare pull back."

I bit down on my lower lip and slowly nodded. Every nerve was alert, and I trembled with anticipation and fear of the unknown.

There was a soft click, and the object in his hand shot to life with a low, rumbling hum. A jolt shot through me as the vibrations sent shockwaves to my nerves. I sucked in a breath, my chest tight as the sensation radiated outward, setting every inch of me alight. I bit down hard on my lip to stifle the cry that surged in my throat.

The realization hit me—a vibrator. I'd heard whispers, even seen less-than-discreet ads for "massagers." My sister, Edith, apparently had one in her dressing table that she affectionately called her "electrician," but I had never imagined using one myself.

Victor moved the vibrator in slow, teasing strokes, never lingering long enough for me to find release. I gripped the sofa's edge, knuckles straining as I fought to stay silent. Each pass over my sweet spot sent a current through me, like lightning striking a taut wire.

"You've never used one of these, have you?" His voice was a velvet caress, smug yet tender.

I shook my head, words failing me. The blindfold heightened every sensation—the cool air against my skin, the warm leather beneath me, the relentless buzz of the vibrator—as if my body were a tightly wound instrument, every nerve a plucked string.

Victor's free hand slid up my thigh, caressing the tender skin with the lightest of touches. My hips bucked involuntarily away from the vibrator, my nerves utterly overwhelmed.

"You pulled back," Victor chided, his tone a mix of disappointment and stern control. "I told you not to."

"I'm sor—" I started, but he cut me off.

"Keep those legs open for me," he commanded, nudging at my knees with his elbows.

I forced my trembling thighs wider, submitting to his will.

"That's it. You're doing so well, angel," he whispered. "I know you can take it."

The vibrator slowed to a torturous crawl, and I breathed a momentary sigh of relief—until I heard another soft click. The hum instantly turned louder, the pitch higher.

A strangled gasp escaped my lips as the new level of sensation crashed over me like a tidal wave. The vibrations were no longer teasing; they were an onslaught, a relentless barrage that left me no time to catch my breath. My hands flew to Victor's wrists, not to push him away but to anchor myself against the storm raging in my body. Unable to hold it in, my breaths turned to whimpers.

"Not a sound," Victor reminded me, his voice the only calm thing in the room. "And don't you dare close your legs."

I bit down on my lip so hard I tasted copper. The blindfold was wet where my tears had soaked through. Victor had forbidden me to cry out, so all I could do was cry—not from pain or sadness, but from rapture so intense without any other recourse for release.

I writhed against the unyielding force of the vibrator, desperate for relief yet unable to escape its torment. Each vibration sent ripples of pleasure and pain coursing through me, mingling in a dizzying cocktail that left me breathless.

My entire body tensed, every muscle a drawn bowstring ready to snap. I bucked and writhed, my hands clutching Victor's wrists with desperate need.

"Please," I whispered, my voice cracked and fragile. "Victor, please."

He didn't answer. Instead, he pressed the vibrator harder, its furious vibrations sending me over the edge with a violent, uncontrollable force.

My back arched, I dug my fingers into Victor's wrists, and a white-hot explosion tore through me. The first pulse rocked me to my core, a shockwave of ecstasy that left me momentarily paralyzed. It was followed by another, and another, each one building on the last in a relentless cascade of pleasure. Hot fluid gushed from me, running between my legs and pooling on the sofa.

My mouth opened in a silent scream, every muscle in my body contracting with unbearable intensity.

I couldn't see.

I couldn't speak.

I was lost in the maelstrom of my release—a puppet to the strings of sensation Victor had so expertly pulled.

He held me steady, his grip firm but gentle as he rode out the storm with me. The vibrator continued its merciless work, prolonging my climax into a series of explosive aftershocks that left me weak and gasping for air.

When I thought I would pass out from pleasure, Victor eased the vibrator away and switched it off. The sudden absence of its hum left a deafening silence, and my body collapsed like a rag doll. I lay splayed out, utterly spent, every inch of me tingling.

Victor leaned in and kissed my forehead through the blindfold. "You were perfect," he murmured, his voice tender and full of admiration. "So beautiful, so ravishing."

He untied the blindfold, and the dim light of the room seeped slowly back into my eyes. I blinked away the haze and looked up at him, his face a picture of serene satisfaction. He stroked my cheek with the back of his hand, then traced a fingertip along my jawline.

I tried to speak, but my throat was too dry, my voice too weak. All I could manage was a breathy shudder. Victor's lips curved into a smug, roguish smile. I looked at the abandoned vibrator on the coffee table. I wasn't sure what I had expected it to look like, but it was deceptively innocent. Corded, handheld, and metallic arsenic green in color, with sleek, modern lines and a black rounded knob at the tip. It looked almost like a kitchen appliance—something you'd use to beat eggs or mix pancake batter.

Victor followed my gaze to the vibrator. "Ingenious little device, isn't it?"

I could only nod, dazed from the intensity of what had just happened. My body felt foreign to me, as if it were no longer mine but an instrument Victor had played to perfection and then set aside, still humming with residual notes of pleasure.

He leaned down, his face inches from mine, his breath a warm breeze on my cheek as he spoke. "Take it home, and think of me every time you use it during our time apart." He chuckled to himself. "But I hope you don't grow too fond of it," he said, a playful glint in his dark eyes. "I'd hate to be replaced by a machine."

A weak laugh escaped my lips. "I don't think that's possible. Nothing could ever replace you."

"Mmm, I may need to remind you of that before you go."

Victor slid his hand behind my neck and pulled me into a deep, languorous kiss. My lips were still tender from biting down so hard, but the pain mingled with pleasure as his tongue explored my mouth.

He broke the kiss, his lips trailing over mine with a lingering softness that made my heart ache. "I need you, Barbara," he said, his voice a low growl that sent a shiver down my spine. He took my hand and guided it to palm his erection. "Feel how much I need you."

I wrapped my fingers around his length and gently squeezed. He was hot and rigid in my grasp, throbbing with pent-up desire. I stroked him slowly, sensually, and he closed his eyes, a flicker of raw need crossing his face.

In one fluid motion, Victor pulled me to my feet and spun me around so that he was standing flush behind me. He clamped his hands on my hips and pulled me tight against him, the solid wall of his body pressing into my spine.

Victor's hands slid up my torso, claiming my breasts with a

possessive squeeze that sent a fresh wave of arousal through me. He kneaded them firmly, his fingers pinching and rolling my nipples, coaxing them to harden under his touch. My head lolled back against his shoulder, and he scraped his teeth along my neck, biting just hard enough to make me gasp.

"I need to be inside you." His breath, hot and ragged in my ear, sent shivers cascading down my spine. The raw urgency in his voice stirred something deep and primal within me, awakening a fierce longing that had been momentarily sated but now roared back to life. His words were a spark to the smoldering coals of desire that still burned from my recent climax, setting me ablaze once more.

In a swift, fluid motion, Victor bent me over the arm of the sofa. The supple leather was cool against my flushed, feverish skin. I braced myself on the cushions, my fingers digging in as I looked over my shoulder at him. His eyes were dark and predatory—a hungry wolf's gaze as he palmed my buttocks and took in the view before him with unrestrained lust.

"You're dripping," he observed, his voice thick and heavy with desire. My breath hitched in my chest as he grazed the wetness between my thighs, sending a jolt of electricity through my already overcharged nerves. He parted me with the precision of a surgeon, and I gasped when a firm, cool finger slid inside me. "And boiling hot." He pumped his finger in and out, each stroke sending waves of pleasure rippling through me, before withdrawing it with agonizing slowness. "So ready for me."

I bit down on my lip, the anticipation almost too much to bear. My body ached for him, every nerve ending screaming for the release only he could provide. He'd commanded me to stay silent, but a whimper escaped my lips despite myself.

Victor positioned himself behind me, his hands possessively gripping my hips. His hard length pressed against me, teasing me with the promise of what was to come. He didn't push in. Instead, he rocked his hips slowly, letting his tip slide up and down, coating himself with my arousal. Each movement sent sparks flying, my body tensing and relaxing in a maddening cycle of expectation.

The blindfold lay discarded on the coffee table, and for a moment, I wished it were still on. The uncertainty, the heightened sensations, the complete surrender of control—it had all made the experience so much more intense. But now I could see every detail—the way Victor's muscles tensed and flexed, the sheen of sweat on his brow, the fierce concentration in his eyes. This visual overload was almost too much, but I drank it in hungrily.

"The gateway to my personal heaven is between your thighs, angel," Victor murmured, his voice taking on a reverent, almost worshipful tone. His free hand caressed the curve of my buttocks, then moved to my apex, rubbing in slow, torturous circles. My knees threatened to buckle, and I pushed back against him, desperate for more than just his teasing touch. "Let a poor devil in."

Before I could respond or even nod my head, he thrust his hips forward and drove into me. The force of his entry sent a shockwave through my body, mingling pain with pleasure in a dizzying rush. I cried out as he filled and stretched me. My fingers clawed at the sofa, my back arching as I worked desperately to accommodate him. He held himself deep inside me, unmoving, letting me feel every inch.

The room was thick with the smell of intimacy and perspiration, the air heavy and stifling. My breaths came in ragged gasps, each exhale a soft moan. Victor's chest heaved against my back, his hands roaming my body with a greedy, frantic need. He pulled almost all the way out, then drove back in with a force that blurred my vision.

His pace was brutal, each thrust harder and deeper than the last. My body moved with his, our motions a violent, passionate dance. The leather of the sofa creaked and groaned beneath us, and I wondered if the shopkeeper downstairs could hear. The thought of her knowing what we were doing, of her listening to our illicit activities, sent a thrill through me.

Victor's hands were everywhere—on my breasts, my hips, my neck—claiming me. He pulled my hair, yanking my head back, and bit down on my shoulder. The pain was sharp and immediate, but it only fueled my arousal. I was a maelstrom of conflicting sensations, each one amplifying the other.

My climax built swiftly, an unstoppable tide rising within me. I met each of Victor's thrusts with equal force, my body demanding its due. The tension in me reached a breaking point, and I exploded around him, contracting in violent spasms.

Victor groaned, a deep, guttural sound, and his rhythm faltered. He drove into me with short, desperate strokes, and he swelled and pulsed as he exploded inside me.

Waves of warmth radiated from our joined bodies, with Victor draped on top of me, his weight a comforting burden as we both struggled to catch our breath. Perspiration trickled off my back, and his heart pounded against my shoulder blade. The once-cool leather was now warm and sticky against my skin. Black-and-white specks danced in my periphery as my head spun.

Victor kissed my neck, my shoulder, my back, his lips soft and contrite after the mauling he had given me. He finally pulled out—slowly, deliberately—sending one final shudder through my exhausted body. I collapsed onto the sofa, limbs heavy and unresponsive, as he sank beside me. He pulled me into his arms, and I nestled against his chest. The warmth of his skin seeped into mine, and a drowsy contentment washed over me.

We lay in silence, our breathing gradually returning to normal. I traced lazy patterns on his chest with my fingertip, feeling the rise and fall of his ribcage, the softness of his skin overlying the hard contours of his muscles. He stroked my hair, then moved his hands to caress my back in long, soothing swipes.

"Will this be enough to last you?" I asked, my voice a whisper, hesitant to break the sweet tenderness that enveloped us. "For the next two months?"

Victor tilted my chin up so that I was looking into his eyes. They were softer, the fierce hunger temporarily sated. "Not in the least." His voice was tender, yet there was an underlying tension that made my heart tighten in my chest. "After that, I can't bear to be away from you for two minutes, let alone two months."

Victor trailed his fingers along my arm, leaving goosebumps in their wake. "Every inch of you is perfection," he murmured, his voice vibrating against my ear and down to my core. "A goddess walking the earth."

A flush of warmth spread across my cheeks and chest. I was too tired to move, but the embers of desire flickered back to life at his words. He kissed my forehead, then my nose—each peck laden with an affection that made me ache in a different way.

"I don't deserve you," I whispered, stilling the patterns I'd been drawing on his chest. Doubt gnawed at the edges of my satisfaction, threatening to consume it whole. "You know that, don't you?"

He stroked my hair, his touch as light as a summer breeze. "It's the other way around, angel. I'm just a poor sinner, and I'm not worthy to even be in the same room as you, much less have the pleasure of utterly consuming every bit of you." He nibbled at my ear, making me shudder, then pressed a worshipful kiss to my lips, silencing any response that may have been there. "You deserve every happiness," he whispered against my mouth. "And I'll spend the rest of my life proving it."

INTERLUDE

Frank Jr.
June 2012

The doorbell rang, its chime bouncing off the empty living room walls, startling me from my concentration. I set down the cut crystal vase I'd been wrapping in newsprint and wiped my hands on my jeans.

"Coming!" I called toward the door as I stood and stretched. My back throbbed from sitting too long. I waded through a sea of boxes and packing paper. My hips were stiff and ached with each step. *Damn.* Getting older was a pain. Literally.

A young man in a red polo shirt stood on the porch, beads of sweat trickling down his brow from beneath his backward-turned baseball cap.

"Dragon Wok?" he said, holding up a plastic bag filled with small white cardboard containers.

"Yeah, right here," I replied, fishing in my wallet for cash. I handed him a twenty. "Keep the change."

"Thanks, mister," he said, already halfway down the steps.

I closed the door and inhaled the piquant aroma of General Tso's chicken and pork fried rice. One nice thing about being back in Southern California—the food was so much better. Except for barbecue. My stomach growled in anticipation. I hadn't eaten since breakfast, too consumed with the task of dismantling my mother's life piece by piece.

In the dining room, I cleared a space on the cluttered table. Empty silver-plated photo frames and crumpled tissue paper formed a haphazard centerpiece. I opened one of the takeout containers and scooped up a bite with a pair of chopsticks, too hungry to bother with a plate.

The house felt cavernous and hollow without Mom's things in their rightful places. The walls, once adorned with paintings, photographs, and eclectic art pieces, now stood bare, like stripped-bark trees in winter. Each room echoed with an almost tangible silence.

I'd been at it for two weeks, and each day followed the same pattern. Mornings were spent sorting through Mom's belongings —deciding what to keep, what to sell, what to donate, and what to throw away. In the afternoons, I boxed everything up and labeled it. Evenings, I collapsed from exhaustion—too tired to think, too sore to sleep.

And then there were the nights.

When the house was finally still, I read.

The stack of letters from Victor to my mother was the last thing I had expected to find hidden away in her closet. I thought I'd known their whole story. Not even close.

Victor's words were almost lyrical—a quality I hadn't at all expected. He had been an artist without doubt—his photographs were stunning and could have filled galleries if he'd ever sold them—but I'd never pegged him as a poet.

My eyes wandered to a photograph on the sideboard— one of the few I hadn't packed away yet. It was of Victor, taken in the mid-to-late sixties, around when I graduated from high school. He was fifty or so in the photo, yet still every bit the dashing rogue he'd been in his youth—tall and broad-shouldered, dark hair slicked back with streaks of gray at the temples. He wore a charcoal suit and a slim burgundy tie, his trademark pencil mustache as precise as an artist's stroke.

Mom had placed that photo at her bedside the day Victor died back in 2006. He'd lived a full ninety years—fifty-four of them married to her.

I finished shoveling a mound of fried rice into my mouth and wiped my lips with a paper napkin. My mind drifted back to the letters, to Victor. In them, he was the same man I'd known all my life, yet more. More passionate, more vulnerable. The depth of his love for Mom was staggering, and reading his words had reopened a well of memories.

I remembered the first time Victor took me horseback riding on Laguna Beach. I couldn't have been more than five or six years old. The salty breeze tangled in my hair as we rode along the shoreline, the Pacific's cool mist kissing our faces. The early morning sun peeked through the marine haze, low and lazy, streaking the sky in pink and purple.

At first, I'd been terrified of the big chestnut mare Victor had set me atop. She seemed ten feet tall to my child's eyes, and her sheer size made me feel insignificant, fragile. I clung to the saddle horn for dear life, my knuckles white and my heart pounding. But Victor was patient. He walked beside me, holding the reins and gently encouraging me.

"You're doing great, Frankie," he said, his voice smooth and unhurried. "Just breathe. Let your body move with her. She knows what she's doing."

I swallowed hard and nodded. I trusted Victor, and if he said I could do this, then maybe I could. Within minutes, my fear melted into exhilaration as I imagined myself a dauntless cowboy. We spent hours that day riding up and down the beach, just the two of us.

I smiled at the memory. That day on the beach had been the beginning of many adventures with Victor. He taught me to ride a bike, stole me out of school to go to a Dodgers game, and hoisted me on his shoulders the day Disneyland opened in Anaheim.

Though not related by blood, Victor had been my dad in every way that mattered. He was the dad I needed—the one my own father had never been. He was the example I'd followed when it was my turn to raise a child.

I gathered the empty takeout containers and dropped them into the large black trash bag I had set up in the kitchen—an unfortunate necessity after I'd foolishly gotten rid of the trash can. Thankfully, I hadn't made the same mistake with the single-serve coffee maker. I rinsed my cup in the sink, popped a pod in the machine, and brewed a steaming cup of medium roast Colombian.

Coffee mug in hand, I returned to the dining room table and pulled out the letters I had planned to read that night. These were different from the ones I'd already read, and curiosity itched at the back of my mind. Each of these letters had been written during May and June of 1951, and Victor had noted a countdown in the top margin of each letter: 58 days to go, 52 days to go, 39 days to go…

Victor's letters read like a forbidden romance novel—the kind my daughter wrote. Except this was real life—Mom and Victor's. And, in many ways, the foundation for my life too.

I spied the fortune cookie from my dinner. Something urged me to open it.

I unwrapped it and cracked the shell with a swift twist of my wrists. The scent of stale, dusty almond rose up as a brittle shard of cookie skittered across the table. I fished out the small strip of paper and smoothed it with my fingers.

LOVE IS THE ONLY THING YOU CAN TAKE WITH YOU.

26

BARBARA

Tuesday, April 24, 1951
58 days to go...

My darling,

It's only been an hour since I told you goodbye, and I guess our waiting is truly underway. June 21st is the day... That's 58 days, sweetheart. But you're worth it, and I'd wait 1,000 days if I knew you were the prize at the end.

I'm awfully sorry for the emotional display, but when there is even a remote possibility of losing someone so very precious, it's impossible to keep all those fears bottled up. Just some of my Italian background popping out, I'm afraid... Hopefully, you can love me in spite of it.

On the drive out to Malibu after letting you go, I tried, with success but very little satisfaction, going over all the wonderful moments we've had together, especially since we've been in love. I don't know how I could pin down any one particular memory as being the best. Still, the one that keeps coming to mind—the most persistent mental picture—is our very first afternoon together at my downtown apartment. The day you first told me you were mine. Funny how those moments fly. At the time, you know that in just a while they'll be only memories, and you try so hard to hold each fleeting second tightly so as never to let it escape, and yet it does... And then it seems only to be a dream. We'll never recapture that moment again, darling, but we will have more—even better!

Perhaps this summer we can manage a week or two away. Your sister could keep Frankie, and we could get a place on Catalina Island—something on the water, second story with a balcony. We could get a sail in at sunset and have those marvelous star-studded evenings all to ourselves. Maybe a stroll along the boardwalk or nestle together on the beach watching the boats coming and going. But most of all, my darling, just being there with you, planning our future together, is all I want. To hold you close to me and know you are mine—mine alone—is my fondest dream!

I keep telling myself that eight weeks is really a very short time, that it will go quickly, and I pray it will, but as of this moment...

    I can't erase the picture of your beautiful, damning blue eyes. I can't forget the magical touch of your hand on mine or the tender touch of your lips, my darling. You can calm all my fears so easily. When we are together, I am yours—your subject, your lover, anything you want me to be. My darling, I do adore you so! I'm yours completely if you'll only have me!

    I want to thank you, honey, for every minute we've had together these past few months. It's probably the nearest thing I've ever known to complete happiness. The Hi-Fi is playing "Moonlight Becomes You" in the background, and I guess I'm getting carried away, but I don't care. It's you I'm in love with, and I want you to know just how much!

    Remember that you belong to me, sweetheart, and that I love you and you only. Always.

Good night, my love.

—V

"I don't know if I can keep this up, Edie."

Frankie charged ahead on his little pedal bike, legs pumping furiously as I guided him with the long handle. I let go, and he wobbled forward, the bell on his handlebars jingling with each unsteady turn.

Edith and I settled onto a weathered park bench beneath a sprawling jacaranda tree, its violet blossoms forming a fragrant canopy overhead. The late afternoon sun stretched long shadows across the grass, and a warm breeze carried the mixed scents of salt air and spring flowers.

"Of course you can keep it up," Edith said, patting my hand. "You've already come this far."

I sighed deeply, sinking into the slats of the bench. "It's just so hard, Edie. Reading his letters, hearing his voice in my head… It makes me miss him even more. I want to be with him *now*, not in some distant future."

Edith pulled a silver cigarette case from her handbag, tapped one loose, and nestled it between two fingers before striking a match. She inhaled deeply, the ember flaring, then exhaled a slow plume of smoke that curled in the breeze. "The future isn't that distant, Babs. Two months will fly by."

I watched Frankie loop around an enormous oak tree, his cheeks flushed with excitement. "And that's just the beginning. Then I have to leave Frank and start my own divorce."

"He still doesn't know?"

I shook my head, waving away the ribbon of smoke drifting toward me.

Edith took another languid drag and tilted her head back, contemplating the sky through blissful, almost-closed eyelids. "Why not just leave Frank now? Why wait if you're so sure?"

"Victor's lawyer says any hint of scandal could wreck his divorce case. It will make everything look like collusion," I said, my voice tinged with the frustration that had been building for weeks.

Edith raised an eyebrow, her hazel eyes piercing through the smoke. "So that's what worries you—Victor's divorce?"

I hesitated, watching Frankie attempt to navigate a small hill. His bike teetered dangerously before he put his feet down to steady himself. The park buzzed with life—children playing, birdsong, and the distant hum of afternoon traffic.

"It's all connected," I said finally. "If Victor can't get free, then..."

"Then you're stuck waiting even longer," Edith finished for me with a sigh.

Frankie pedaled back toward us, his little chest heaving with exertion and triumph. "Mommy, Auntie, did you see me? I goed so fast!"

I ruffled his sweat-dampened hair and kissed his forehead. "You were wonderful, sweetheart. Just like a real racer."

Edith handed Frankie a bottle of soda pop she'd been carrying in her handbag. He grabbed it like a prospector who'd just struck gold.

"Are you keeping him tonight?" I ribbed. "Seems fair since you're getting him hopped up on sugar."

Edith shrugged. "I'm more than happy to if you need the evening to take care of things." She was hedging, and I knew I wouldn't want to hear whatever was coming next.

I stretched my legs out in front of me, crossing them at the ankles, and leaned back into the bench, trying to prepare myself for whatever bombshell Edith was about to drop. The jacaranda blossoms above us rustled in the breeze, their perfume mingling with the acrid tinge of Edith's cigarette.

"Babs," she started, flicking the ash from her cigarette. "Have you thought about getting a Nevada divorce? You could bypass the California courts altogether."

I sat up straight, my muscles tensing. "A Nevada divorce? You mean running off to Reno like some starlet in a scandal?"

"It's not as dramatic as all that," Edith said, rolling her eyes. "People do it all the time. You'd only have to live there for six weeks to establish residency. It's quicker. Cleaner."

I shook my head. "No good. First off, Frank would have to agree—not likely. And second, even if by some miracle he agrees, we could never afford to take off for six weeks."

"Mother could cover it."

A nervous laugh escaped my lips. "She'd never. Not for me."

"You might be surprised. She recently floated Frank the money to pay off some massive debt he owed."

My jaw dropped. "She *what*?" I cleared the rasp from my throat. "Why would she do that for Frank?"

I sank back into the bench, my thoughts spinning like a whirlpool. The warm breeze that had seemed so soothing now pricked at my skin like tiny needles. The scent of blooming flowers turned cloying, almost suffocating.

"Victor wondered how he managed to pay it off so quickly," I murmured, half to myself.

Edith's eyes sharpened. "What does Victor have to do with it?"

"Frank borrowed a large sum from Victor a while back to pay off some gambling debts—before I knew Victor. When he had trouble making the payments late last year, Victor was understanding—more than he needed to be. Then, out of nowhere, Frank came up with the full amount a couple of months ago and paid Victor off in one go." I exhaled, shaking my head. "I think he did it to get me to quit working at Victor's firm, but..."

Edith crushed the remains of her cigarette against the bench's metal armrest, sparks flying before dying in the breeze. "And you didn't think to ask Frank where the money came from?"

"I didn't want him to know that I knew. Besides, Victor was concerned for our safety. He thought Frank had borrowed from some dangerous loan shark." I blew out a relieved sigh. "At least that's one mystery solved."

"The plot thickens." Before I could respond, Edith continued, "We can get into that drama another day. But my point is that Mother might be more willing to help than you think."

"After the tongue-lashing she gave me the other day? Not likely. And knowing that she gave Frank the money he needed to get me to quit working proves that she'd take Frank's side, not mine."

"Well, she's got to find out some time or other. Might as well be now. On your terms."

"On my terms," I repeated. The words tasted foreign.

Edith stood and smoothed her skirt, the fabric rustling like dry leaves. "Babs, you know I love you and will back you up one hundred percent." She paused, her gaze sharp enough to cut through me. "But you need to stop waiting for other people to determine your future. If you want to leave Frank, then leave him. If you want to be with Victor, then be with him. But decide for yourself."

I bit my lip, weighing her words. Edith had always been the bold one, the brash trailblazer, the queen of the Jazz Age. She'd made choices—some brilliant, some disastrous—but they were always hers. And she didn't give a fig about what people around her said. Could I really do the same?

"Mommy, look!" Frankie called. He'd dismounted his bike and was attempting to climb a low-hanging branch of the oak tree. I started to rise, but Edith put a hand on my shoulder.

"He'll be fine." She raised an eyebrow for emphasis. "With the other thing too."

My heart ached in my chest. "I hope to God you're right."

"Kids are more resilient than we give them credit for. He'll be just fine. Shoot, probably better than fine if Victor's even half the man you make him out to be."

Finally, an easy smile graced my lips. "I'd like you to meet him, Edie. When all this nonsense is over."

She bent down and kissed my forehead. "I thought you'd never ask."

27
VICTOR

May 1951

The damp, earthy scent of the basement seeped into my clothes as I descended the steps. The last time I was down here, Joey Rizzo was still breathing.

This was Phil's domain.

A single bare bulb swayed slightly, casting long, wavering shadows on the rough concrete walls, which gave the space an eerie, subterranean glow. Phil stood at his usual post—a makeshift workbench cluttered with ledgers, an overflowing ashtray, and an old adding machine. The faint scratch of his pencil was the only sound in the otherwise oppressive silence.

I cleared my throat, and Phil straightened. He had a towering frame, broad shoulders, thick hands, but a mind sharp as a straight razor. His eyes met mine—cool, calculating—but always carrying that spark of loyalty I had come to rely on.

"Victor." A nod. No more words were needed. He knew why I was here.

I walked over, my leather soles scuffing lightly against the concrete floor. I glanced at the ledger filled with meticulous columns of numbers, every figure carefully noted in Phil's steady script. Detail work bored me to tears, but it was essential for keeping the machine running.

"How's it looking?" I asked, though I already knew the answer. Phil was nothing if not thorough.

"Solid," he said. "The new establishments are paying out better than we expected."

I allowed myself a small smile. "Good. We'll need that cushion while I'm…away."

At my words, Phil's brows creased. He didn't press, but the pause in our conversation was weighty. The distant hum of the furnace and the occasional drip of water from the pipes above made the lull in our discussion feel like the calm before a storm.

"You understand why I need to step back for a while," I said finally. "Until my divorce is final, I need to be squeaky clean."

Phil's eyes never left mine. He didn't need to say anything.

I continued, "Private investigators, depositions… If they find any of this, it could get messy."

The bench groaned as Phil leaned on it, crossing his arms over his chest. "Say no more, Boss. You'll be clean as a whistle. One hundred percent aboveboard."

I nodded. "Thanks, Phil. There's no one I trust in this more than you. I trust you with my life."

Phil cracked the faintest of grins. "I've gotcha, Boss. You go walk the straight and narrow, and I'll hold down the fort."

The single bulb above us swayed again, making his face flicker in and out of shadow, like a statue coming to life in brief flashes.

"So," he said slowly, "exactly how much are you giving me?"

I met his gaze. "Lock, stock, and barrel."

———

I flipped on the foyer light of my penthouse apartment. The

warm glow illuminated a space of sharp angles and minimalist furniture, all in muted tones of gray and white.

I walked straight to the wet bar and poured myself a bourbon, neat.

Another night alone.

I made my way to the kitchen, drink in hand, where a tidy stack of sorted mail sat on the marble countertop. The first delicious swig of bourbon slithered down my throat as I leafed through the envelopes—bills, advertisements, more bills, a letter from my cousin. One letter caught my eye—handwritten with no return address. The handwriting was unmistakably Barbara's.

My stomach tightened. I took the envelope and my drink to the living room and set the glass down on the coffee table. I opened the envelope carefully, almost reverently, and pulled out a piece of thick paper. It was a sketch of a dress—sleek and modern with lines that screamed glamorous elegance.

I held it up, letting the light catch the faint pencil strokes. Barbara had real talent. It was easy to see why she felt so stifled in her life as it was. Who in their right mind would want to keep Barbara's brilliance bottled up? It was a crime.

This dress belonged on the silver screen, on a woman who turned heads when she entered a room. On Barbara.

I pictured it—her blonde waves cascading over one shoulder, those blue eyes sparkling with that beguiling mix of fiery ambition and tender vulnerability that had first drawn me to her.

Beneath the sketch was a folded piece of stationery. My pulse kicked up as I unfolded the page, bracing for bad news.

Wednesday, May 9, 1951

Victor,

I hope you like the design. It's one of my better

efforts, I think. I was thinking of you when I drew it. Maybe I'll sew it up and wear it with you for a jazzy night on the town.

I miss you. Every day seems longer than the last, and life feels so colorless without you. I miss our afternoons together, our talks, your touch... I miss everything about us.

Frank is more insufferable by the day, and I'm not sure how long I can keep up the act.

Victor, I'm so afraid that by the time we're both free, we'll be different people—that this waiting will change us in ways we can't predict. I need to believe that this pain is temporary, that it will all be worth it in the end. Please tell me you believe that too.

All my love,

Barbara

PS: Mother knows. Sorry...

I let the letter drop to my lap, staring blankly at my warped reflection on the surface of the glass coffee table.

Barbara's words clouded my mind like smoke. I tipped my glass, watching the bourbon catch the light in slow, amber ripples before draining it and returning the glass to the coffee table with more care than it deserved.

The room was quiet. Too quiet. The kind of silence that presses in on you and slowly suffocates. I picked up the letter again, reading Barbara's words once more, as if rereading them might change them. Might soften them. Might make them less desperate, less real.

Mother knows. Sorry...

"Damn it." The curse slipped out, low and rough. This complicated things. Barbara's mother was Los Angeles old money—back when that meant something. The kind of woman who hosted charity galas, sat on museum boards, and crushed men's careers with a single phone call. Worse, she was a moral crusader from another century. A woman who believed marriage was a life sentence, no matter how miserable the prisoner. If she had any sway over Barbara, we were in trouble.

I rose from the sofa and walked to the large windows that framed the city skyline. Los Angeles glittered below me, a sprawling sea of lights stretching to the horizon. A thick marine layer had rolled in from the Pacific, muting the stars and casting a spectral glow over the city. It was alive and vibrant—everything I longed to be.

I loosened my tie and undid the top button of my shirt, sighing as the constriction around my neck released. A million dark solutions flitted through my mind. It wouldn't be hard to get Barbara free. One call to Phil, and I'd be reading about the unfortunate event over breakfast.

I shook my head, banishing the idea. No, that wasn't the way. Barbara would never forgive me. And neither would the man I was trying to become. Barbara was my fresh start. This had to be done right. Clean. For both our sakes.

Damn, I was getting soft.

I picked up Barbara's sketch again. My fingers traced the elegant lines of the dress, imagining her hand as she drew them. I pictured Barbara's breasts filling the bodice, the dress hugging the beautiful curves of her hips, and the creamy skin of her long, slender leg peeking out through the thigh-high slit.

The ache in my chest deepened. Six weeks. Just six more weeks until my divorce was final. Then I could extricate her from her marriage, and we could start our life together properly.

An idea took root. It was risky—potentially disastrous if it went wrong—but it might just work. I reached for the phone on the side table and dialed a number I knew by heart.

"Phil? It's me. I need you to do some digging. Find out everything you can about Frank Evans's finances."

Phil's gravelly voice came through the receiver. "Can do, Boss. Didn't we already turn this guy inside out last year?"

"Yes, but I need you to go deeper this time. Find out everything, and I mean everything. Bank accounts, debts, investments, the works. I want to know if he has so much as a nickel hidden under his mattress. And put a tail on him."

"Sure thing, Boss. What are we looking for exactly?"

I let the silence linger a second longer. Then, softly, decisively—"Leverage."

28

BARBARA

Frank was sitting at the kitchen table when I walked in from outside. The sight of him stopped me cold.

"Goodness, Frank!" I gasped. "I didn't expect you home until after six."

His eyes were fixed on an unsealed envelope on the table. His voice was flat. "My meetings wrapped up early today, so I cut out and came home. I thought I'd surprise you, make an evening of it." He never looked up. "Where's Frank Junior?"

"At my sister's." I let out a long, controlled breath. "You know how he loves his Aunt Edith."

"That's probably for the best."

My stomach tightened. I pursed my lips.

"That way, he won't hear any of this." Frank slid the unsealed letter across the table toward me. It was addressed to me, and the handwriting belonged to my mother.

"You opened my letter?"

"I thought it was important. Why else would your mother write instead of picking up the telephone? Good grief! I thought someone had died!"

I stared down at the envelope in silence, my pulse thudding in my ears. The room felt stiflingly hot.

"What's she talking about, Barb?"

I picked up the envelope and removed the letter.

"*Who* is she talking about?"

I tossed the letter on the table and leaned against the countertop, arms folded tight. "Well, I guess now is as good a time as any."

Frank finally looked at me, eyes wide and terrified like a scolded puppy awaiting a rolled-up newspaper.

"Frank, it's over." There went the newspaper. "It's been over for a long time. It's high time we admitted it."

"No, no. This isn't how it's supposed to work. We have a life together, Barb. We have a son."

"I know, and that's what makes this so difficult. But we can't go on like this."

Frank shoved his chair back and stood so abruptly it crashed to the floor behind him. He gripped the edge of the table, eyes pleading. "What did I do, Barb? Tell me what I did, and I'll set it right."

"You didn't do anything." My voice wavered, but I forced myself to hold his gaze. "Damn it, I almost wish you had. It would make this easier."

"Then what?"

"We've just grown apart. We were so young when we met, and we didn't see each other very long before we whisked off and got married. You were just back from the war, and I was twenty-one. How could either of us have known what we truly wanted?"

Frank paused and studied me. "What are you saying, Barb?"

"I want a divorce."

His face crumpled like a starched shirt left out in the rain. "A divorce?"

"Yes, Frank. A divorce."

He stood motionless. Processing. Calculating. "On what grounds? What have I done?"

"We're just no good together."

The calculation was over. His eyes narrowed, and his voice turned sharp. "Who is he?"

"What?"

"*Who is he?*" he repeated, a bitter edge curling his lips. "A woman doesn't just walk away without a reason. And don't feed me that 'we grew apart' nonsense. You're a smart girl, Barb. I'm sure you've got it all figured out." He jabbed a finger at the letter from my mother. "Your mother seems to know all about it. So I know there's someone. Who is he?"

"Does it matter? It changes nothing."

"Of course it matters! I at least deserve to know who I'm being thrown over for!"

I hesitated for a fraction of a second. "Fine. I suppose you'd have found out anyway. It's Victor Cardello."

Frank inhaled sharply, like I'd knocked the wind from his lungs. He repeated the name, soft and venomous. "Victor Cardello." He curled his fingers into fists. For a moment, I thought he might lunge. Instead, he slammed a hand onto the table, rattling the salt and pepper shakers. "Damn it, Barb! *I knew it!* I never should have let you near him."

"He's not the reason, Frank. This was coming long before Victor."

"Oh, spare me!" His laugh was hollow. "You've had one foot out the door since you went to work for him. How long, huh? Since the beginning? How long did it take for you to—" He gripped his jaw, cutting himself off.

I stiffened. "You have no idea what you're talking about."

"I'm not blind, Barbara. And I'm not stupid."

"I never planned this, Frank. I swear to you, I never did."

"Oh, that makes it better?" His voice was all acid now.

My cheeks flushed hot with anger. I forced myself to meet his eyes. "No. But it's the truth." I paused. "I never wanted to hurt you, Frank," I said softly, almost tenderly.

"Well, you've done a bang-up job of that, haven't you?" His voice dripped with sarcasm. He paced the kitchen, raking a hand through his hair. "Victor Cardello? Christ, Barbara! Have you lost your mind?"

"I know exactly what I'm doing," I said, my voice steady. "Victor and I love each other."

Frank let out a harsh laugh, shaking his head. "Love? You think that's *love*? He's using you, Barb. Men like him don't fall in love. They take what they want and move on."

"You don't know him like I do," I shot back, my pulse hammering. "He's different with me."

"Oh, I'm sure he is." Frank sneered. "I bet he tells you you're special. That you're not like the others. That you're the one who'll change him. That's what men like him do."

His words struck like a slap. I swallowed against the tightness in my throat, forcing down the sting behind my eyes. I wouldn't let him see me cry.

"You don't know what you're talking about," I murmured.

The laugh he let loose was bitter, devoid of any real humor. "Oh, Barbara. Sweet, naïve Barbara. You really don't know, do you?"

A chill ran up my spine. My fingers dug into the counter's edge. "Know what?"

"Your precious Victor isn't just some big-shot businessman. He's a criminal, Barb. A mobster."

The room tilted. My breath caught. "No," I whispered, shaking my head. "That's not true. Victor's a real estate developer. He—"

"*Wake up!*" Frank roared, slamming his palm on the table.

The crash sent a jolt through me.

"His 'real estate developments' are just fronts," he said, seething. "He's running protection rackets, illegal gambling dens, and God knows what else."

My mind reeled as his words sank in. A wave of nausea rolled through me.

"You're lying," I whispered, more to myself than Frank. "Victor would never..."

His face twisted into a cruel sneer. "What's the matter, Barb? Your knight in shining armor's not so shiny after all?"

"You don't know what you're talking about. Victor is a good man."

"A good man?" Frank spat. "Is that what you tell yourself when you're spreading your legs for him like a cheap whore?"

The slap came before I even realized I'd moved. A sharp crack rang through the kitchen as my palm connected with his cheek. Frank stumbled back, stunned, one hand hovering at his face. A dull sting pulsed through my fingers, but I barely noticed it over the fury burning inside me.

"Frank, I—" I began, my voice faltering, but he cut me off with a raised hand—not to strike, but to silence.

"Don't," he said, his voice tight with fury. "Don't you dare."

A deep red mark bloomed on his cheek, stark against his pale skin. Guilt gnawed at me, but so did rage. The once-cheerful yellow kitchen suddenly felt like a pressure cooker, the heat and tension threatening to explode.

Frank straightened up slowly, adjusting his tie with stiff, trembling fingers. "You want to know how I know about Victor Cardello?" he asked, his voice eerily calm. He didn't wait for an answer. "Because I owed him money. A lot of money."

"I know."

His eyes narrowed, suspicion flickering. "How could you possibly know?"

"Victor told me"—I swallowed hard—"when you paid off the debt in one lump."

Frank let out a hollow, bitter laugh. "And you thought that was the whole truth, didn't you? Remember those 'business trips' last year?" Frank let out another humorless laugh. "I wasn't working. I was gambling. And losing. Big."

"I know that too."

His gaze drifted past me, unfocused. "I thought Victor was doing me a favor." His voice dropped, the words edged with shame. "I'd worked with Victor a few times, insuring some of his high-end properties. We got along. I thought maybe we even had a friendship. So when I was drowning, I went to him. I thought he was offering me a lifeline."

I could see where this was going, and I hated it.

"But kindness turned to something else. He started making demands. And then, when I couldn't keep up, he got his eyes on you."

A cold chill ran through me.

"Do you remember that dinner in December?"

I remembered it all too well—the way Victor had watched me, the casual yet intense interest in his eyes. At the time, I'd felt flattered. Admired. Completely unaware.

"That was when he decided," Frank said, his words heavy with resignation. "He wanted you, Barbara. And he knew the surest way to get you was to offer something I couldn't refuse."

I barely found my voice. "What do you mean?"

Frank's eyes were hard, his jaw clenched. "You were part of the deal."

The air in the room shifted.

"I couldn't keep up with the payments, and Victor offered a…solution. He said if you came to work for him, he'd consider it partial payment on my debt."

My mind reeled, trying to process this information. I thought back to that day when Victor had offered me the job—how excited I'd been, how it had felt like a lifeline thrown to a drowning woman. Had it all been a lie?

"No," I murmured, shaking my head. "That can't be true. Victor wouldn't—"

"Wouldn't what, Barb?" Frank cut in, his voice edged with contempt. "Wouldn't use you as a pawn? Wouldn't manipulate both of us for his own gain? Grow up."

I struggled to find something to say—some retort that would cut through Frank's accusations and make them less real, less devastating. But nothing came.

"He's playing the long game, Barb," Frank continued,

relentless. "You think he cares about you? That he loves you? He's just getting you in deeper and deeper. And the worst part is, you're letting him."

I bit my lip, the pain a slight distraction from the storm inside me. "I don't believe that, Frank," I said slowly. "Victor has always been honest with me."

Frank's laugh was a cold shard of ice in the stifling room. "Honest? You believe that? Then why didn't he tell you any of this?"

I had no answer. The silence stretched, heavy and oppressive.

"Barbara," Frank said, his voice softer, almost pleading. He reached for my hands, and before I could stop myself, I let him take them. His grip was warm, familiar. "We can still fix this. Think about our family. Our son."

I looked at him—really looked at him—my husband for almost four years. The father of my child. The first man I'd ever loved. The conflict within me surged, tearing me in two.

I closed my eyes, hearing Victor's voice. *"A divorce won't be simple, angel. Not in a town like this."*

I pulled my hands away.

"No. We can't. You wouldn't understand."

"Understand?" Frank's voice sharpened. "What's there to understand? You're leaving me for another man. It's as simple as that."

"I'm leaving because I'm unhappy, Frank. Because we're unhappy. Can't you see that? This isn't just about Victor. It's about me wanting something more, something different. Something I can't have with you."

Frank paced the kitchen, his hands clenching and unclenching at his sides. "So, what now? You just walk out on our family? On our son?"

"Of course not," I said, my voice softening. "Frankie will always be my priority. But he deserves parents who are happy, not just…coexisting."

Frank stopped pacing and leaned against the counter, his shoulders slumped. "And Victor makes you happy?"

I hesitated, knowing my answer would hurt him, but unable to lie. "Yes. He does."

His face hardened. "Well, I hope you two will be very happy together," he spat. "But don't think for a second that I'll make this easy for you. I'll fight you on everything—the house, the money, custody of Frank Junior. Everything."

My heart sank. I had hoped—foolishly perhaps—that we could handle this amicably. "Frank, please. Let's not make this uglier than it needs to be."

"If you think I'm going to let that thug anywhere near my son, you're out of your damn mind. And no judge in *his* right mind will leave Frank Junior with you."

My blood ran cold. "You wouldn't," I whispered, my voice shaking.

"Wouldn't I?" Frank's eyes were ice, his jaw set. "You're a two-bit whore, and you're leaving me for a goddamn gangster, Barbara. If that doesn't make you an unfit mother, I don't know what does."

I refused to let him see how deeply his words cut. "You don't know the first thing about caring for a child. You wouldn't last a week on your own."

Frank yanked his keys from his pocket and stormed to the door. He turned to me, his voice cold and soulless. "I need a drink. When I get back, maybe you'll have come to your senses."

He slammed the door behind him so hard, the kitchen windows rattled. A coffee cup fell from the counter and smashed on the linoleum floor.

I took a shaky breath and mechanically moved to clean up the broken pieces.

Mother's letter on the kitchen table caught my eye. I had to know what she had said to damn me.

Wednesday, May 16, 1951
Barbara,

Your news came as a shock. I should have written sooner, but to tell the truth, I didn't know what to say. I know little more now.

I do hope you know what you're doing. This is quite a decision for you to take. I was under the impression that this man was friends with your husband. What "friends" can do to a family... I should know.

You mean to tell me that Frank is doing nothing about this??

All I can say is be sure of everything, take plenty of time to decide, and don't be impulsive. But you seem to have everything worked out, down to the last detail.

I hate to see this happen.
You've really let me down.

Mother

29
VICTOR

A sharp rap at my front door pulled me from my haze. My heart quickened, anticipation and dread colliding in my veins. I checked the clock—9:45 p.m.

If someone was popping over unannounced at this hour, it couldn't be good.

Another knock. More urgent this time.

I sprang up, reaching for the revolver I always kept close. I checked the cylinder, pulled back the hammer, and moved swiftly to the entryway with soundless steps. I took a quick glance through the peephole.

Barbara.

She stood on the other side, arms wrapped around herself, fidgeting nervously.

With a relieved breath, I eased the hammer down and placed the revolver on the entry table before sliding back the deadbolt. The moment the door cracked open, I pulled Barbara inside, scanning the hallway to ensure no prying eyes had witnessed her arrival. The lock clicked shut behind us.

For a moment, we stood frozen, drinking in the sight of one another. It had been weeks since I'd last held her. The soft glow of the living room lamps cast a warm halo around her golden hair, but her eyes were in shadow, wide and unreadable. Without a word, I cupped her face, stroking her delicate cheekbones as I drew her into a desperate kiss.

At first, Barbara was rigid, her lips resisting, her body tense. But as I deepened the kiss, pouring all my longing into it, she gave in—with a shift, a soft sigh, the way her fingers curled into the lapels of my smoking jacket and pulled me closer. The familiar scent of her perfume—gardenias and jasmine—enveloped me. I broke away just enough to breathe her in.

"Barbara, what are you doing here?"

"I had to come. I know it's against the rules, but I had to." Her words came out in a tumble. "Frank said things. Horrible things. And I need to know if they're true."

My stomach dropped, a cold sweat prickling at the back of my neck. I kept my expression neutral, years of practice making it second nature. "What are you talking about, darling?" I reached for her hand.

Her eyes darted to the revolver on the table and fixed there. She froze.

Damn.

I slipped an arm around her shoulders and pulled her into the living room. "The Web" was playing on the television. I clicked off the set, and the picture shrank into a tiny pinhole before vanishing into darkness.

"Drink?"

She shook her head, wrapping her arms more tightly around herself.

"Sit, baby," I soothed, guiding her next to me on the sofa. "Tell me what's happened."

"Frank and I had a fight tonight. He knows about us, and everything hit the fan. I know I was supposed to keep up the act, but I guess I've blown it now."

My jaw tightened, a muscle ticking beneath my skin. My mind raced, weighing the fallout. My lawyer was going to have a coronary, but I'd deal with him later.

"It's fine, darling. We'll handle it," I said gently, my voice steady, smoothing over the cracks. "What else?"

Barbara twisted the fabric of her skirt. "He said...he said you're not who I think you are. That you're involved in... terrible things." Her voice cracked, and she dropped her gaze to her lap.

I leaned back, draping my arm across the back of the sofa. My fingers itched for a cigarette, but I resisted the urge. "Do you believe that?"

Her eyes searched mine, desperate, pleading. "I don't know. Maybe." She shook her head. "But that's not what has me bothered."

I waited, every second stretching like taffy. If she didn't believe Frank's accusations about my business, then what could have her so unstrung? Not knowing gnawed at me. I studied her face—the delicate angles, the soft curve of her cheek. Even in distress, she was radiant.

"Victor," she began, her voice fragile. "Frank told me everything. About his debt to you. About how you wanted me to come work for you as part of it." She paused, swallowing hard. "He said you've lusted after me from the beginning, that I'm just a piece in some long game you're playing." Her breath hitched. "That you hired me just to get me here—" The last word cracked in her throat as she gestured around the room, hand trembling. "To get me into your bed."

Barbara bit her lower lip, a habit she'd picked up when she was trying to hold back tears. Her eyes shimmered, glassy with the threat of a deluge. I reached out, but she recoiled, hugging herself tighter. The rejection stung, sharp and immediate, like a slap.

"Tell me, Victor, is any of it true?"

"Barbara," I began slowly, like a bomb technician choosing which wire to cut.

She sprang to her feet and pressed a hand to her lips. "Oh God...it is true."

"Darling, I have never lied to you. There are things I haven't told you, but I have never lied to you."

She stood, trembling, her silhouette stark in the subdued lamplight.

I rose slowly, not wanting to startle her, and stepped closer. "Barbara," I said softly. "You came here because you wanted to hear it from me. So let me tell you."

Her eyes locked on mine, a fiery blue storm of swirling hurt and hope.

"Yes," I said, each word a deliberate breath. "It's true that Frank was in deep with me. It's true that I saw an opportunity when I first met you, which was why I asked you to work for me. And it's true that I've wanted you from the start."

She flinched as if struck, but I pressed on.

"But it's also true that I love you. Desperately, Barbara. And that has changed absolutely everything."

She stood motionless, carved from ice.

"I've never lied to you, darling. If I wanted a conquest, I'd have made my move, had a good time, and been done with it. But I don't want a conquest. I want you. All of you. For always. And nothing else matters."

"Then why did you hide the truth from me?"

I nodded. "That was my mistake. But let me fix it, okay?" I put my hands on her shoulders. She didn't pull away this time, but she was still stiff beneath my touch. "Ask me, Barbara. Anything. I promise, I'll tell you whatever you want to know. No matter what."

Barbara narrowed her eyes and drew her lips into a thin line. She looked past me, toward the revolver on the table. "Why do you have a gun out?" she asked, her voice small but steady.

I followed her gaze to the revolver. "Protection."

She looked back at me, unconvinced. "From whom?"

"From the kind of men who don't settle disputes with words." I paused. "I have enemies."

"Enemies like Frank?"

A cold trickle of fear ran down my spine. How much did she know? How much did Frank know, for that matter? And how much had Frank told her in his desperate bid to save their doomed marriage?

"Frank has never been my enemy," I said gently. "He's just a man in a bad position." I watched her closely. "I'll admit I don't like him much, but that's because of how he treats you. He's never deserved you. But he's not an enemy. He doesn't have the courage to do any real harm."

Barbara studied me, searching for any flicker of deceit. With slow, deliberate movements, she sat beside me and folded her hands on her lap. "Then what kind of enemies? What are you involved in, truly?"

She didn't look away. And so, against my better judgment, I told her. I laid it all out—the protection schemes, the gambling rooms, the nightclubs, the smuggling, the loan-sharking, the strong-arming. Every sin, one by one, like cards on a table.

When I finally finished, the silence pressed in all around us. I waited for her to scream, to cry, to flee. Instead, she sank back into the sofa.

"Say something, darling."

She drew in a slow, calculating breath. "You're a mobster..."

I shrugged. "I'm a businessman. My business just isn't all legal."

"Why didn't you tell me from the beginning?"

I rubbed the back of my neck, feeling the prickle of sweat. "Because I didn't want you to look at me like you are right now."

She didn't blink.

"I hoped that if you got to know me first, it would matter less." My voice softened. "That you'd see beyond what I do and love me for who I am."

I reached for her hand and was surprised when she let me take it. Her skin was cool, her grip tentative. I kissed her palm softly, reverently. She didn't pull away, but she didn't respond either. The silence crackled like static inside my head.

"What happens now?" she asked at last.

I took a deep breath, knowing my next words could seal my fate. "Now," I said slowly, "I'm completely at your mercy."

She looked at me, uncomprehending.

"Barbara, you have enough to turn me into the police and put me away for the rest of my life." I wrapped her hands around my wrists like handcuffs. "If that's your choice, then so be it."

She stared at our hands, her eyes distant and troubled. The silence had a life of its own, pulsing, breathing between us. I could almost hear the ticking of her thoughts, each one a potential bomb waiting to explode.

"Why would you put yourself in this position?" she asked, her voice eerily measured as if she were reading a verdict in court. "You're not a fool, Victor."

"No," I said quietly, "I'm not. But I am a man in love, and that makes me vulnerable in ways I never expected." I searched her face for any sign of what she was thinking, what she was feeling, but her features were a marble mask, beautiful and unyielding.

"Barbara," I said, my voice breaking the fragile surface of the quiet. "I've never let anyone in like this. Not Dorothy, not my closest associates. No one." I took a deep breath, the air thick and heavy in my lungs. "I trust you enough to be completely honest, completely vulnerable. This is me, laid bare. All my sins, all my desires."

Her eyes flickered, and for a moment, I thought I saw the ice begin to melt. The tension between us stretched taut—one more breath, one more hesitation, and it would snap.

I stood and removed my jacket, then unfastened my shirt buttons one by one. Barbara watched in silence, her gaze steady, unblinking.

Slowly, deliberately, I dropped to my knees before her. Taking her hands, I placed them flat against my bare chest. "Feel that?"

My heart pounded, and my chest heaved against her palms. "This is what you do to me. You have the power, Barbara. You've always had the power. You can drive a dagger through my heart, or you can take it as your own."

She looked down at her hands on my chest, then back into my eyes. Her lips parted, but no words came. The conflict within her was palpable, tearing her between doubt and desire.

"Either way," I continued, "you're my queen. Everything I have, everything I am—it's yours."

The room seemed to hold its breath. My skin prickled with anticipation, every nerve ending on high alert. I searched her eyes for an answer, for forgiveness, for love.

Slowly, she traced a finger along the line of my sternum. A shiver rippled through me as her touch sent a shockwave through my body. I closed my eyes, bracing for whatever came next.

When I opened them, her face was closer, her breath warm on my lips. Then she kissed me—not a blade to my heart, but a whisper of salvation. I surged forward, my hands tangling in her hair as I kissed her back hungrily, desperately. Like a man reprieved from execution.

We broke apart, breathless. Her eyes had softened, the storm within them calming to a quiet tide.

"Victor," she whispered, "I can't lose you."

A wave of relief crashed over me, nearly knocking me off balance. I rose to sit beside her on the sofa, pulling her into my arms. She came willingly, resting her head on my shoulder.

"You won't lose me, darling," I said, stroking her hair. "Not unless you send me away. Probably not even then."

She sighed deeply, her breath syncing with mine. "This is a lot to take in—the danger, the secrets."

"I'll keep you safe," I promised. "And there will be no more secrets. Not between us."

We sat in silence for a long moment, but this was the kind of silence that healed rather than wounded.

I reluctantly broke the quiet. "How did you get here tonight?"

She shifted in my arms, pulling away just enough to look at me. "I took a cab."

A slow burn of anger coiled in my chest. "Where's Frank?"

"At the bar," she said, her tone flat. "He took the car after our fight."

I worked my jaw, biting back the string of curses waiting to spill. "And Frankie?"

"With Edith." She paused, studying my face. "They're fine, Victor. It's not the first time."

I exhaled, forcing myself to let it go—for the moment. What mattered was the here and now—the woman in my arms, the future we were fighting for.

"Do you want to move out? Now that he knows about us…"

Barbara's shoulders stiffened, and she pulled back, tucking her legs beneath her as she sat up straight. "I don't know," she said, fingering the hem of her dress. "Maybe. I suppose there's no point in keeping up the act now."

"No, but we've still got to be careful—get our divorces through."

"What do you suggest?"

"I can put you and Frankie up in your own place until we can be together. But first things first—I'm buying you a car."

30

BARBARA

June 1951

"A house in Long Beach, a new car, and some delicious frosting…" Edith motioned to my matching diamond solitaire earrings and pendant set. "You'd better be glad I love you so much, or I'd throw my hat in the ring. He really does spoil you, doesn't he?"

I shrugged, trying to downplay the opulence surrounding me. "Edie, you know I'm not doing this for the money."

She clapped me on the shoulder. "Relax, Babs. He's all yours." She huffed hot breath on her fingernails and buffed them on the front of her blouse. "Besides, he's too young for me anyway."

"Edie, you're only forty."

"Forty-one," she corrected.

"Oh my goodness, I missed your birthday. I'm so sorry!"

"Relax. You know I don't celebrate those anymore." Edith unpacked a cut crystal vase and placed it on a side table. "You've done good, kid," she quipped, gesturing around the living room.

The new house was swanky by most standards—nothing like

the mansion Edith and I grew up in, but still polished and modern. For me, though, even a shack on the beach would have done the trick. Anything to get away from Frank.

"Frankie loves it here," I said, changing the subject. "The beach, the new nursery school. He's already made a bunch of friends."

Edith sighed and plopped onto the overstuffed sofa. "I don't doubt it. But it's strange not having you just up the road."

I joined her on the sofa, resting my hand on hers. "This isn't forever, you know. It's just until things settle."

"Until things settle," she repeated, her tone dubious. "Babs, I'm just worried. You have a lot on your plate right now. The new place, Frankie starting in nursery school, the divorces…"

"Victor's court date is in two weeks," I said. "Once his divorce is finalized, everything will be simpler."

Edith raised an eyebrow. "What about *your* divorce?"

I sighed, knowing where this was heading. "We've been over this. The lawyer says I can't file until Victor's divorce is final. It's a perception thing."

"I think it's a horseshit thing, but I won't hash it out again." She sighed at my silence. "I just hate that you've got men controlling you every which way you turn. I want you to be free, Babs."

"I'll leave the femme fatale act to you, Edie. I never quite got the smolder down." I gave her a playful elbow to the ribs.

She smirked but didn't let the moment pass. "And Frank?" Edith's voice softened. "Is he playing nice yet?"

I hesitated before answering—not because I didn't know the answer, but because admitting it aloud made it all so stark and real. "He's been stoic and detached as always," I said finally. "He makes no effort to see Frankie or even talk to him." I paused, gathering my thoughts like scattered leaves in a storm. "Despite all his blustering about having me declared unfit and taking custody—"

"Blustering?" Edith raised an eyebrow.

"That's all it ever was. Just words. He's made no effort to actually be a father." I hesitated, then added, "Lately, he's gone quiet altogether. Not that I mind."

Edith leaned back against the sofa cushions and studied me with those keen hazel eyes that rarely missed anything important. "So you think he'll just let you go without a fuss? Let you take Frankie?"

"I don't know, Edie. But he's given me this much, and for now, it's enough."

Edith stood from the sofa and stretched her arms overhead. Her red-and-white checkered shirt came untucked from her dark blue jeans. She made pants look good—natural, even. I wasn't anywhere near brave enough to try it.

"I should get going. Let me take Frankie for the weekend."

I hesitated. "Edie, you don't have to—"

"I want to," she said, cutting me off. "I miss the little rascal. It'll be like old times. Besides, I imagine you need some time to catch up on sleep or"—she winked at me—"any other 'undercover' activities you might get up to." She pressed a finger to her lips with a devilish grin. "I know it's against the 'rules,' but your secret's safe with me. You're already breaking them, doll. So why not toss the whole damn rule book out the window?"

I smiled. "Thank you."

Edith walked to the door and put on her coat. "Don't thank me yet. I plan to spoil Frankie rotten and return him to you completely unmanageable."

I laughed and opened the door for her. "I wouldn't expect anything less."

31
VICTOR

A single fading crimson-and-purple swipe over the water was all that was left of the sunset. Gino pulled up to Barbara's new bungalow in Long Beach.

"You're sure we weren't tailed?" I asked.

Gino scoffed. "Positive. I took the long way, and the car is a loaner. No trace to you, Boss."

I glanced around the quiet street before opening my door. "Thanks, Gino. Pick me up tomorrow morning at eleven."

"Is that enough time, Boss?" he asked with a chuckle and a sideways glance.

"Hmm, make it noon." I grabbed my leather bag and slipped out of the car.

The sea air was cool and carried the scent of salt and kelp. I liked Barbara's new place—modest but charming, with ivy creeping up the stucco walls and a small garden out front that looked perpetually in bloom.

I knocked on her front door, smoothed my hair, and adjusted my tie—fidgeting like a schoolboy on his first date.

The door opened, and there Barbara stood, wearing the sleek black dress she'd drawn for me. The sketch had been lovely, but it came nowhere close to doing justice to the way she wore it.

The neckline dipped lower than any dress I'd seen her in, teasing soft, creamy skin that I ached to touch, to taste. Golden waves cascaded over her shoulders, framing the blue eyes that had undone me from the start. A glass of white wine in one hand, she beckoned me inside with the other.

"I was just trying on the new dress," she said, closing the door behind me. "But if you'd rather I take it off…" A wicked gleam lit her eyes.

"And here I was about to compliment the craftsmanship… But I suppose I'd need a closer inspection to truly appreciate it."

We moved to the living room, where soft jazz played from a phonograph in the corner. She handed me a glass of wine and leaned against the doorway, swaying gently to the music. The dress moved with her, a black silk shadow that clung to her curves. It was at that moment that I noticed the slit—high on her thigh, teasing me with every sway.

I took a slow sip, the crisp wine a poor distraction from the fire curling low in my stomach.

"Frankie's with your sister for the weekend?" I asked, though I already knew the answer.

"Oh yes, we're quite alone." She flashed me a knowing smile and batted her eyelashes before taking another sip of wine, then walked over and took my free hand. "Dance with me."

I set our glasses on a side table and took her in my arms. The warmth of her body seeped through the silk of her dress as I placed my hand on the small of her back. Her body melted into mine as we swayed to the lazy, dreamy notes of a trumpet.

Her breath was soft on my neck. "I've missed you," she whispered.

I pulled her closer, letting the music and her touch melt away the tension I'd carried all day. The soft, tantalizing scent of her perfume intoxicated me more than wine ever could.

"I've missed you too, darling. Desperately."

The music slid into silence, leaving only the soft crackle of the phonograph. I cupped her face, her skin warm beneath my palms. She closed her eyes and tilted her head up, lips parting just enough to draw me in.

I kissed her slowly, deeply, savoring the way she softened against me. Her lips were warm and sweet—like the first bite of a perfectly ripened peach.

Barbara pulled back just enough for our noses to brush. "Are you hungry?" she asked softly, her breath warm on my lips.

"Starving," I said in a low growl. "But not for food."

A playful spark lit in her eyes. She stepped back and retrieved her wine glass from the side table. With languid grace, she swirled the liquid, watching it slide against the glass before taking an unhurried sip.

"I thought you'd like this dress," she said, tracing one fingertip along the rim of her glass, then skimming it down her neckline, following the curve where silk met skin.

I loosened my tie with one hand, never breaking her gaze. "You look scrumptious enough to feast on."

Her soft laugh rang out as she moved around me in a slow, deliberate circle. The slit in her dress parted with each step, revealing flashes of smooth, toned leg—an elegant but tantalizing striptease crafted by nothing more than the sway of her hips.

"You have a real talent for design," I said, my voice thick with desire. "The fit is impeccable." I reached out, letting my fingers trace the seam from her hip to where the silk split at her thigh. The fabric was cool against my fingertips, but beneath it, her warmth was a low-burning flame. "It's exquisite work," I continued, my voice dipping lower. "But to truly judge its quality, I'd need to see the seams from the inside."

A sly smile curled at the corners of her lips. "And how do you propose to do that?" she asked, lifting an eyebrow in challenge.

I took a step closer—so close I could feel the static of her presence tingling on my skin. Her eyes were locked on mine, daring me to make the next move.

"Carefully. Meticulously. Thoroughly…" I let each word drip with intention.

My hands moved to her shoulders and down along her arms in a featherlight caress. She leaned into my touch, her breath hitching just enough to betray her desire. Her lips parted, but no words followed—only the softest exhale of breathy anticipation.

I slid my fingers under the delicate straps and dragged them slowly over her shoulders. The fabric resisted just for an instant before sliding down against her skin with a whispering sound, coming to rest half-mast across her arms. I traced my fingers along her neck and tangled them gently in her hair as I tilted her head back.

She was Aphrodite carved from living marble. Her throat stretched long and elegant before me. I kissed the hollow at its base, then worked my way up slowly, savoring each inch like forbidden fruit. She gasped when I reached that tender spot just below her ear. I nipped gently, earning a delicious shiver from her entire body.

I kissed down along her jawline, then traced a path with my lips over her collarbone and into the valley of her cleavage. The dress was precariously perched, threatening to fall at any moment, yet held in place by some fashion sorcery.

"You've designed this so perfectly," I murmured against her skin. "It shows off your beautiful breasts just enough to drive a man mad with desire."

Her breathing grew heavy, each rise and fall of her chest an invitation. "I'm glad you approve," she said, voice tinged with breathless excitement.

I moved my hands slowly down the curves of her sides until they rested on her hips, then pulled her closer so she could feel the exact effect she was having on me.

"It would take a very good man to leave such a masterpiece intact," I said softly as I kissed back up toward one exposed shoulder.

She laughed—a light, musical sound that dissolved into a

moan when I took her tender flesh between my teeth. "Are you a good man?"

I rounded behind her and eased down the zipper at her back. "No, I'm not."

The dress loosened and slid down her body, like honey trickling over porcelain. Her back was a long, supple line of muscle and bone. I kissed along her spine as it curved like a swan's neck, each vertebra a delicate pearl in an unbroken string.

She turned to face me, wearing nothing but her heels and a dress pooled at her feet.

"You didn't tell me you weren't wearing any silks."

"They mess up the lines." She stepped out of the pool of fabric. "You're certainly taking your time," she said with a teasing lilt. "I thought you were starving."

"Oh, I am," I replied, urgently shrugging off my jacket and unbuttoning my shirt collar. "Show me your new bedroom, and I promise you, darling, I'll devour you whole."

Barbara extended her hand, and I took it, the delicate bones of her fingers intertwining with mine. She led me down the narrow hallway, each glance over her shoulder a spark to tinder.

We reached the bedroom door, and she paused, turning to face me. Her eyes were a stormy blue, churning with emotion and desire. Without a word, she pulled me into a kiss, fierce and demanding. Her naked body pressed against my semi-clothed form, creating a delicious contradiction of textures and temperatures. I kissed her back with equal fervor, hands roving over the curves I had spent the last several weeks craving.

She broke the kiss abruptly and pushed the door open. The room was modest but cozy, with a large bed dominating the center. Soft moonlight filtered through sheer curtains, casting a silvery glow over the white linens and creating deep shadows in the corners.

Barbara walked to the edge of the bed and turned to face me. Her silhouette was art in motion, every curve etched in half-light. I stood in the doorway, momentarily transfixed.

Finally, I stalked over to her, pulling her close and reveling in the sensation of her hardened nipples pressing against my chest through the thin fabric of my shirt. She slid her hands around my back, then up to my shoulders, urgently gripping. I kissed her again, more hungrily this time, our lips and tongues clashing like a sudden summer storm.

Barbara broke the kiss and pushed me down onto the bed with unexpected force. I landed on my back, propping myself on my elbows to watch her. She stood over me, a goddess in nothing but heels, breathing heavily.

"I think you're the one who's starving, darling," I teased.

She put one knee on the bed, then the other, crawling towards me with the predatory grace of a panther. Her hands found my belt buckle and worked it free, then tugged at the waistband of my trousers. I lifted my hips to help her, and she slid them down, along with my shorts, in one swift pull.

She paused for a moment, taking in the sight of me, her eyes alight with lust and affection. Then she lowered herself, kissing a trail up my thigh, her breath hot against my skin.

"Freedom suits you, my dear," I mused.

She looked up at me through her thick lashes and licked her lips. "It would take a very good woman to resist you right now," she said, echoing my statement from earlier.

I smirked. "Are you a good woman?"

Her eyes glinted. "No, I'm not."

I grabbed her by the hips and swiftly rolled us over so that she lay beneath me. "You're wrong." I trailed my hand down her side, over the smoothness of her skin and the sharp jut of her hip bone. She arched her back, pressing herself closer to me. "You're an amazing woman, and you make me want to be a better man." Bending down, I took one of her nipples into my mouth, swirling my tongue around it before biting gently.

She gasped and tangled her fingers in my hair, pulling me tighter against her.

"You're perfection, and you give me something to strive for.

That's why I call you 'angel.' But…" I slid my hand between her legs and parted her with a single finger. She was already soaked. "Even angels fall. And even good girls can be so very naughty."

Barbara's breath caught in her throat as I slid a finger inside her—hot and tight, like a velvet glove. I pumped in and out of her, slowly, deliberately. Her back arched, and she let out a soft, helpless moan that sent a surge of heat through my entire body. Her face contorted with pleasure, every muscle tensing and releasing like waves crashing against the shore.

"Fall for me, my angel," I whispered into her ear as I added a second finger. She gripped me like a vise. "Fall to earth just for tonight."

Her eyes fluttered open, dazed with lust and need.

I kissed down the length of her body with measured slowness—grazing my lips over sternum, then ribcage, tracing circles with my tongue around the taut skin of her abdomen.

When I reached the mound between her beautiful legs, I paused long enough to breathe in deeply—to delight in the scent of arousal—before pressing her knees apart and gently parting her.

My mouth met flesh already engorged and throbbing. I flicked her with the lightest touch of my tongue. She cried out, her hands flying to my head, weaving her fingers through my hair and tugging with desperate need. I licked her slowly, from bottom to top, savoring the taste of her. She bucked her hips, seeking more, but I held her thighs firmly to keep her at my mercy.

I circled her swollen flesh with my tongue, sending shivers through her entire body. Her breathing was ragged—each inhale a struggle, each exhale a whimper. Soft thighs clenched around me, the promise of release coiling hot and close. But I wasn't ready to let her have it yet.

Pulling back just enough to speak, I said, "I do believe you missed me, angel."

Barbara's response was a strangled plea, her body writhing

in a dance of desperate need. "Victor, please," she begged, her voice breaking with the intensity of her desire.

I swirled and sucked a few more times before pulling away again. "Have you been using your vibrator like I asked you to?"

Barbara's eyes widened, a flicker of hesitation disrupting the stormy sea of her desire. "Yes," she said, her voice soft and uncertain.

I smiled down at her, running my fingers lightly over her inner thigh, just close enough to tease. "Where is it?"

She turned her head toward the nightstand, and I followed her gaze. "In the drawer," she said quietly.

I rose from the bed, my erection straining painfully as I walked to the nightstand. The vibrator was in the top drawer, concealed beneath a few fashion magazines.

Barbara propped herself up on her elbows, her body a long, sinuous line against the white linens. She tracked the vibrator in my hand, a mixture of trepidation and anticipation on her face.

I walked to the wall socket, plugged it in, switched it on, and handed it to her.

"Show me how you make yourself feel good, angel."

Barbara hesitated, her hand trembling slightly as she took the vibrator from me. The hum of the device filled the room with a low, electric tension. She bit her lower lip and glanced away, a flush creeping up her neck and cheeks. It was the first time I had ever seen her truly embarrassed, and the vulnerability made her even more alluring.

"Don't be shy," I said softly, my voice a caress. "You're beautiful when you blush."

She looked back at me, her eyes swimming with a thousand unspoken words. Slowly, she lay back on the pillows and spread her legs, knees bending to create an inviting curve. The vibrator in her hand hovered above its target as she teased herself with the anticipation of contact.

I stood at the foot of the bed, my eyes drinking in every detail —the way her chest heaved with each breath, the slight quiver in her thighs, the glistening sheen on her skin. My desire was a beast straining against its cage, but I held it in check, savoring the sight of her.

The tip of the vibrator finally touched down, and Barbara's entire body jolted as if struck by lightning. A gasp tore from her lips, and her back arched off the bed. She pressed the vibrator against tender flesh with a tentative hand, rolling her hips in slow, agonized circles. Her mouth hung open, eyes half-lidded and unfocused, lost in the immediate rush of sensation.

I stroked my length—hard as iron and aching—as I watched the woman I loved succumb to her own touch. "That's it, baby," I murmured. "God, you're gorgeous."

Barbara's hand grew more confident, more insistent. She traced wet lines with the vibrator, dipping lower to tease her entrance before sliding back up to her clit. Her breathing was quick—each inhalation sharp and desperate, each exhalation a trembling sigh.

"Keep going, angel," I said, my voice thick with lust. "Just like that."

She turned her head to the side, biting down on the corner of a pillow to stifle her moans. The hum of the vibrator mingled with the sounds of her increasing arousal, creating a symphony of erotic tension.

"Don't hide from me," I commanded.

She snapped her head back, eyes on me.

"I want to see how good you feel. I want to hear you cry out."

Her lips parted, and the pillow slipped from her grasp. Her first true moan burst forth, raw and unrestrained. It sent a shiver through me, igniting every nerve in my body. I moved my hand in time with hers as I stroked myself, imagining her gripping me tight.

Barbara writhed on the bed with growing urgency. She tilted her hips to meet the vibrator, her movements more frantic, more desperate with each passing second. Her skin glowed, and her hair spread out in a disheveled halo around her face. She was the very picture of carnal beauty—an angel in the throes of human desire.

"You're doing amazing," I told her, my voice a low growl. "I love watching you like this. So needy, so hungry."

Her eyes fluttered shut, then open again, locking on mine with an intensity that nearly undid me. "Victor," she breathed, the single word a plea, a confession, an invocation.

"Don't stop," I commanded. "I want to see you come undone."

Barbara worked the vibrator with feverish precision now, her body a taut bowstring ready to snap. Her legs began to shake, and her toes curled tightly. The sounds coming from her throat were a chorus of build and release, a prelude to the explosion I knew was imminent. Her hips thrust upwards in a final, desperate motion.

With a sudden, piercing cry, Barbara shattered. Her body convulsed in violent waves. Her head thrashed from side to side. The tension in her muscles released in a cascading torrent of pure, unfiltered pleasure. I watched in rapt fascination as her climax took its course, every second an eternity of exquisite agony for her.

"You're perfect," I said, not recognizing my own voice. It was ragged, almost broken. "So perfect."

Barbara slowly came to rest, like a leaf settling after a gale. Her breathing was deep and uneven, her skin flushed with the rosy hue of spent passion. She looked up at me with eyes that were simultaneously dazed and grateful.

I took the vibrator from her hand, clicked it off, and set it on the nightstand. She started to move her legs together, but I placed a firm hand on her knee.

"Stay just like that."

Her eyes questioned me, but she obeyed, her body still trembling. I climbed back onto the bed, positioned myself between her legs, and leaned down to kiss the skin of her stomach, hot and slick and salty.

"Victor," she whispered, her voice fragile as glass.

I kissed my way up to her breasts, nuzzling them gently before taking a nipple into my mouth. She let out a small whimper at the touch. I roamed my hands over her sides, her hips, her body, memorizing every curve and contour. I pressed her legs open as wide as they would go and admired her laid out before me like an offering.

"You're an absolute goddess," I murmured, brushing my lips against her collarbone. "I can't believe you're mine."

She tangled her fingers in my hair, weak but yearning. "Victor," she said, and in that single word, I heard all her longing, all her love.

"I need you, Barbara. I'm desperate to be inside you." I kissed her neck, inhaling the scent of her skin. "I don't have it in me to be gentle tonight."

A shiver ran through her at my words, and she spread herself wider, more inviting. "Then don't be."

I needed no more invitation than that. With one swift motion, I thrust deep inside her. A gasp tore from her lips as I filled her. Her heat enveloped me, and I had to fight against the urge to come undone right then. She was even tighter than usual, the echo of her recent release making every stroke an exquisite torture.

I pulled back slowly, savoring the drag of her walls against me, then plunged in again. Her body rocked with each thrust, and she clutched at the sheets as if they were the only thing keeping her anchored. Her sounds were a delicious mixture of pain and pleasure, each one driving me further into a frenzy.

"God, you feel incredible," I groaned, eyes locked on hers. "How on earth can you be so tight?"

Her body was a furnace, an inferno that threatened to consume me whole. Barbara moved in perfect sync with me, meeting each drive with her own fervent push. She raked her nails down my back, leaving trails of fire in their wake. The pain only spurred me on, intensifying my need to possess her completely.

I shifted my weight and grabbed her wrists, pinning them above her head. Her eyes flew open, wide and burning with desire. She loved it when I took control, when I asserted my dominance over her. With her hands restrained and her body laid bare, she was utterly at my mercy—and I at hers.

"Harder," she breathed, and I obliged without hesitation. I pistoned my hips with savage intensity, driving into her with a force that bordered on violent. Each collision sent shockwaves through her body, making her breasts bounce and her lips quiver.

She wrapped her legs around my waist, heels digging into my lower back as if to pull me even deeper. The bed frame groaned in protest, but we paid it no mind. The world outside could have crumbled, and we never would have noticed.

"Do you like that?" My voice was rough like gravel. "Do you like feeling me so deep inside you?"

She nodded frantically, eyes rolling back as another moan burst from her throat.

"I want to hear you."

"Yes...yes, Victor. God, yes!"

I smirked at her response, feeling a surge of primal satisfaction. I moved my hips faster, each thrust deliberate and forceful, designed to coax those delicious cries from her and push her further into ecstasy.

"That's it." I leaned down so our foreheads nearly touched. "Let me hear you. Let the whole damn city hear what I do to you."

She lolled her head back on the pillow, her eyes fluttering shut as she surrendered to the overwhelming sensations. "I love it... I love it so much," she gasped out. "Victor...oh God...please don't stop."

"Never," I vowed, driving into her with renewed intensity.

Barbara arched beneath me, pushing against every thrust with desperate hunger. Her breathing turned ragged, her chest rising and falling with the intensity of a storm-tossed sea. She was beginning to tighten around me, the first signs of another climax building in her core. Each stroke sent a jolt through her, like a current running along a frayed wire. She was close—so achingly close.

I didn't slow. I couldn't.

I was on the edge myself, teetering on the precipice of release. But I held back, determined to drive her over the cliff first, to watch her plummet into the abyss of pleasure. I wanted to see her shatter again, to feel her convulse around me.

"I'm going to make you explode again," I growled, my voice thick with lust. "I want to feel you squeeze me so hard it hurts."

Her only response was a whimper of pure need and helplessness. She was so close, teetering on the brink, just waiting for that final push.

I shifted my weight and ground my hips against hers, making small circles that rubbed against her most sensitive spot. Her head snapped back, and she let out a strangled cry. Her hands, still pinned above her head, clenched into tight fists.

"Do you feel that?"

Barbara's lips parted, but no sound came out. She was beyond words. Beyond thoughts. Every nerve in her body was a live wire, every touch adding to the overload.

I ground against her harder. The friction was maddening, a tease that brought me perilously close to losing control. Her walls fluttered around me, a prelude to the crushing tightness that would come with her release.

"Let go, Barbara," I commanded. "I want to feel every second of it. Don't you dare hold back."

Her body obeyed before her mind did, seizing around me, muscles contracting with a force that stole my breath. A wail tore from her throat, raw and primal, as wave after wave of release crashed through her. Each convulsion squeezed me brutally, and

I fought to hold on, to prolong the exquisite torture of her pleasure.

She screamed my name, the sound echoing off the walls like a gunshot. Her back arched, lifting her chest toward me as if offering herself up for more. I watched her face as she came undone—the contorted features, the closed eyes and furrowed brows, open mouth gasping for air. She was beautiful in her agony—an angel brought low by mortal desire.

"That's it," I murmured, my voice a rough whisper. "Take it all, Barbara. Take every bit of it."

She opened her eyes, glazed and unfocused. She was lost in it, drowning in the sensations. But there was thankfulness in her gaze—thankful that I had driven her to this point, that I had given her what she craved.

I was drowning in her.

I could hold back no longer. With a final, brutal thrust, I buried myself as deep as I could go and let the tidal wave of my release crash over me. A guttural roar tore from my chest as I exploded inside her, each spasm sending hot surges of ecstasy through my body. I emptied myself into her, the warmth spreading between us.

She milked me with every contraction, squeezing out every last drop with a relentless grip. The intensity of it was almost too much to bear. It bordered on painful. My vision blurred, and for a moment, the room spun around us, a kaleidoscope of sweat-slicked skin and disheveled sheets.

I collapsed onto her, my weight pressing her into the mattress. Her hands slipped from my grasp, and she wrapped her arms around my shoulders, holding me close as we both struggled to catch our breath.

"Damn, woman," I said, pressing soft kisses to her forehead, lips, neck, ear. "Where have you been all my life?"

32

BARBARA

We had never spent the night together before. I wasn't exactly sure what to expect, but the comfort and ease of sharing a bed with him was as natural as breathing. Victor lay on his side facing me, his broad shoulders rising and falling in a slow, steady rhythm. In sleep, the weight of the world had slipped from his face, leaving him unguarded, peaceful. I could have stayed like that for hours, just watching him, memorizing the rare softness in his features. But breakfast wasn't going to make itself.

I slipped out of bed, careful not to disturb him, and made my way to the en suite, where I quietly dressed and did my hair and makeup. I loved the man, but it was too soon to spoil the illusion.

I put a record on the phonograph and flitted around the kitchen, pulling out all the breakfast essentials: eggs, bacon, cantaloupe, and, of course, the makings for buttermilk pancakes. I considered myself a decent cook, but my pancakes were my *pièce de résistance*.

As I poured myself a steaming cup of coffee, Victor's gravelly voice broke the stillness behind me. "Good morning, beautiful." He wrapped his arms around my waist and rested his chin on my shoulder. Then he nuzzled my neck and crooned, *"Sugar in my coffee, honey on my toast. Guess I love you the most."*

I turned in his embrace and kissed him gently. His aftershave was rich and spicy. He was fully dressed, every detail of his suit in perfect order.

"You're dressed," I mused.

"So are you," he replied, pulling back to look me up and down. "Too bad. The idea of you dancing around the kitchen in nothing but an apron really gets my motor going."

I swatted him lightly on the shoulder before turning somber. "Where are you going?" I asked, a hint of disappointment creeping into my voice.

"I have something to take care of this afternoon," he said, running his fingers through my hair. "But I'll send Gino with the car to bring you to the beach house this evening."

I bit my lip. "Is that wise? What if I'm seen there? We're so close to your court date."

"That's why I'm sending Gino. No one keeps a low profile better than him." He leaned in, his voice dropping to that low, sultry murmur that sent a thrill down my spine. "Bring that dress from last night. I want to photograph you in it."

Heat rose to my cheeks, and I turned toward the counter and reached for a mug. "Coffee?" I poured the dark, steaming liquid into his cup.

He didn't let go of me immediately, his hands lingering on my hips before he stepped back. I handed him the cup.

"I made it extra strong," I said, watching as the tendrils of steam curled around his face.

"Just how I like it." He inhaled deeply, savoring the aroma before bringing the cup to his lips. Our eyes locked over the rim, the steam curling between us like a whisper. "You always know how to give me exactly what I crave."

I shrugged, playing it cool. "It's not that hard to remember how you take your coffee." His innuendo was not lost on me, but I felt delightfully coy.

He took a slow sip of his coffee. "No other secretary has ever paid as much attention to my preferences as you."

"And I hope no future secretary ever does."

Victor chuckled, a deep, warm sound that sent a pleasant shiver through me. "You know, I really do miss having you in the office."

"Oh?" I raised an eyebrow. "Is it the coffee you miss most?"

He set his cup on the counter and stepped closer, his hands sliding around my waist again. "The coffee is certainly a part of it," he said with a teasing lilt. "Myrtle does her best, but she wouldn't know strong coffee if it bit her in the ass." He kissed the tender spot behind my ear. "But you also make a stellar secretary. No one else keeps me in line the way you do."

"So it's my exceptional filing skills you miss?" I let the moment stretch before adding, "Or my ability to take dictation?"

He kissed down the column of my neck to my collarbone. "*Especially* your ability to take dictation." He pulled back and looked at me, desire smoldering in his dark eyes.

"Maybe you should hire me back," I suggested, running a finger along the lapel of his suit jacket.

"Tempting...but think of my poor lawyer. We've already pushed him to his limit by bending his rules. Hiring you back would send him straight into an early grave. And that would certainly throw a wrench in the divorce."

"Poor Larry. We can't do that to him. Not when he's gotten us this far."

"But..." He slid his hands down to rest firmly on my backside. "Do you know what I miss most about having you at the office?"

I pressed my hips into him. "Do tell."

He whispered in my ear. "Having you right where I want you—bent over my desk."

I pulled away—slowly, teasing. "It's a wonder you get anything done, Mr. Cardello."

Victor smiled. "What can I say? You inspire me." He chuckled but then turned serious.

"What is it?"

"Last night," he said, "was everything I needed. Everything *we* needed. It reminded me of what we're fighting for." He gestured around the kitchen. "This is going to be our life. You and me. And Frankie, of course. I'm so anxious to get started, and we're close, baby."

He produced a black leather box from his jacket pocket. It was small, about the size of a deck of playing cards, with gold braiding along the edges. My heart skipped. It wasn't the size of a typical jewelry box, and that only made the curiosity burn hotter.

"What's this?" I asked, taking the box from his outstretched hand.

"Open it."

The box creaked and snapped as I opened it. Inside, pinned atop a bed of cream-colored satin, lay a military medal. I looked up at him.

"You never told me you were awarded a Bronze Star in the war."

He scratched the back of his neck as he glanced down at it, almost sheepishly. "Twice, actually." He pointed to the tiny metal medallion at the top of the red and blue ribbon. "That stands for a second award."

"Victor, this is—"

"It's important that you understand what I'm giving you," he interrupted gently. "This isn't just a token. I can give you all the glittering jewels you'd ever want. But this is a piece of me. It's a promise. Until I can put a ring on your finger, I want you to have this."

Emotion swelled in my chest, hot and overwhelming. I closed the box slowly, almost reverently, and held it to my heart.

Victor's eyes softened as he took in the way I held the box, as if it were sacred. He reached out and stroked my cheek with the back of his fingers, tenderly, like he was afraid I might break. He kissed me, slow and deep, as if trying to pour all his feelings into me. I melted against him, forgetting, just for a moment, the danger, the looming court date, the whispers that threatened to unravel everything.

In his arms, I was safe.

In his arms, I was home.

33
VICTOR

"You're a goddamn goddess, Barbara," I said as I captured three more photographs. The sleek black dress fit her like a second skin, and it shimmered with an almost ethereal quality under the hot glare of my studio lights. It was a masterpiece—but next to her, it was an afterthought. "That dress belongs in a couture house." I lowered the camera to admire her directly. "But it doesn't hold a candle to you."

Barbara struck another pose, her movements fluid and instinctual—the ease of a professional who knew her body and the camera's eye. "Flattery won't get you anywhere, Victor," she teased, though the pleased smile on her lips told a different story.

I raised the camera again, framing her silhouette as she turned to offer a view of the dress's daringly low neckline. "It's not flattery if it's true," I countered. "You were born for this—commanding every eye in the room, captivating every lens."

She laughed softly, the sound like glass chimes in a warm breeze. "You make it sound so grand. It's just a dress."

"It's not just a dress." I lowered the camera and walked toward her. "It's your creation. Your talent. Your future." I stopped short of her but close enough to feel the warmth of her skin. "I want to send these photos to a few fashion houses, see if anything comes of it."

Her eyes widened, blue as a summer sky, a flicker of hope breaking through. "You're serious?"

"They'd be fools to say no," I said, tracing a finger along the delicate fabric of the dress. "You told me you dreamed of being a designer. Let's make it happen, sweet angel."

For a moment, she was silent. I could see the wheels turning, the familiar tug-of-war between risk and duty. Then, slowly, her lips parted. "If anyone can make it happen, it's you."

"No, my darling. It's you." I stepped back and picked up the camera again. "Now, let's get a few more shots."

She resumed her poses, each more daring and confident than the last. And I saw it—right there in the soft glow of my studio lights—Barbara wasn't just modeling. She was stepping into something bigger, something entirely her own.

After several more clicks of the shutter, I lowered the camera and slowly walked toward her. "Now these…" I said, my voice hushed to a near whisper. "These are for my eyes only."

Barbara held her breath, and for a moment, I thought she might protest. But then her shoulders softened. She knew what I meant. Knew what I wanted. And she was willing—no, eager—to give it to me.

I stepped behind her and eased down the hidden zipper. With a whisper of silk, the dress slid down her body and pooled at her feet. She stood before me in nothing but her skin—a goddess unrobed, her beauty almost too much to take in at once.

"Don't move," I commanded, raising the camera to my eye.

The first flash captured her in stark relief against the white backdrop, every line and curve of her body etched in light. She didn't flinch. She didn't cover herself. But she wouldn't meet the camera's eye either. A beautiful blush bloomed across her cheeks and down her chest—a painter's dream of soft color against pale skin.

"Beautiful," I murmured.

Each click of the shutter was a brushstroke on canvas, each flash a burst of inspiration. I circled her, capturing her from every angle—the elegant slope of her shoulders, the soft arc of her hip, the effortless sensuality in the way she shifted her weight and tousled her hair. Her nude form was art in its purest sense, and I was merely documenting what already existed in perfect harmony.

"I remember the last time I had you here in my studio—so prim and proper in that pale yellow dress."

"How could I forget?" she replied, her voice distant and dreamy. "You said you just wanted to take some 'innocent' pictures."

I laughed, the sound rougher than I intended. "Innocent, yes. You were a saint in my lair, where you had no business looking so pure. It took everything I had not to ravish you right then and there."

"But you didn't," she noted, her eyes finally meeting mine with a challenge.

"No," I admitted. "Because you weren't mine yet."

I lifted the camera one last time. The flash burst against her skin like moonlight on water.

"And now?" she asked, her voice tinged with the same blush that colored her cheeks. "What's stopping you now?"

I let the question hang between us, the air electric, crackling with anticipation. Then, deliberately, I set the camera down.

Two strides. That's all it took to close the distance.

"Nothing."

———

Waves crashed and receded on the dark beach below. The crisp night air was thick with salt. I lounged on a deck chair, a loose Hawaiian shirt draped casually over my shoulders with the first few buttons undone, and my linen trousers cuffed at the ankles. I didn't dress down often, but it seemed appropriate given the setting—and the woman who made me feel more at home than any place ever had.

I toyed with a glass of bourbon, its contents swirling lazily in the dim moonlight that filtered through the cloud canopy. My fingers itched for a cigarette.

A door slid open, drawing my attention, and I looked up to see Barbara step onto the deck. She wore a pair of cuffed jeans and one of my dress shirts, the oversized garment hanging loosely on her slender frame. Her hair was a tousled halo, and she moved with an easy, unhurried grace.

"You know," she said, pausing for effect, hands running over her hips, "this is the first time I've ever worn pants."

I raised an eyebrow, surprised but also amused. "Is that so?" I set my bourbon down on a nearby table. "They suit you."

She shrugged, though the way she shifted under my gaze told me she was pleased. "Edith gave them to me a while back, but they've been sitting in the box ever since. She loves wearing pants, but I wasn't sure I could pull it off."

"You can pull off anything," I said, letting my eyes trace the lines of her body. The denim hugged her curves in all the right places, giving her an air of casual confidence that was effortlessly sexy. "You look incredible."

She bit her lower lip, a gesture that was both modest and playfully coy. "It's different, that's all. I'm used to dresses and skirts. And I can hear Mother chiding me that they aren't ladylike." She rolled her eyes.

"Sometimes a change is good," I said, beckoning her with a slow curl of my fingers.

She hesitated for a moment, then walked over and slid onto the lounge chair with me, her body nestling against mine. The intoxicating scent of her perfume mixed with the ocean air and a lingering trace of our earlier passion.

I draped an arm around her shoulders and pulled her closer. "I like seeing this side of you," I murmured into her ear. "More relaxed, more…real."

"I've never seen you dressed casually before," she remarked, her fingers playing with the loose fabric of my shirt. "It's always a tailored suit or…nothing at all."

She turned her gaze toward the restless ocean, opening her mouth and then closing it again as if weighing whether to speak. She decided against it. A blush spread across her cheeks, warm and luminous in the soft glow of the deck lights.

I smiled, enjoying the rare moment of vulnerability from her. "What's on your mind, sweet angel?"

She bit her lip—soft, uncertain. "It's silly," she admitted after a long pause.

"Now you have to tell me."

Barbara took a deep breath, as if summoning the courage to dive into deep waters. "Do you remember when I first came to work for you? As your secretary?"

"Of course. You were terrified of me," I teased, though we both knew it wasn't true.

"I most certainly was not." She shot me a look but softened almost immediately. "I'll admit I was intimidated," she corrected. "But also…fascinated." She searched my face for something—permission, perhaps—for what she was about to reveal. "After my second day, I had a dream about you."

My lips curved into a sly smile. "Oh?"

"In the dream," she continued hesitantly, "you were at a beach house like this one. You wore a loose shirt and trousers— just like now. You looked…different. Softer."

I slid a hand around her waist, letting my fingers skim the fabric of my shirt she wore, tracing slow, deliberate patterns. "Dreaming about your employer? Tsk, tsk. And here I thought you were the picture of propriety." My voice was low, teasing, an edge of possession creeping in. "Tell me, darling—what exactly happened in this dream?"

She paused, savoring the moment. "You went to kiss me," she said, her tone almost wistful. "But just as your lips touched mine, I woke up. A blasted thunderstorm ruined it."

I chuckled softly, the sound blending with the distant roar of the surf. "A thwarted kiss. How tragic."

"Not so tragic. The next day," she continued, "you took me for a drive and brought me out here for the first time. So I got a real kiss from you instead. And that was a much better deal."

I smiled. "Prophetic."

"And now," she added, her voice growing softer, "it's like I'm living that dream. Except this time, the kiss isn't interrupted."

Her eyes held mine—uncertain, searching, hopeful. The vulnerability in them cut through me, more intimate than anything we'd ever shared.

Slowly, I tilted her chin up with my fingers, brushing my thumb along the curve of her jaw. A shiver coursed through her. The anticipation in her eyes sent a thrill through my veins—the kind that came just before closing a high-stakes deal, before claiming something meant to be mine.

I kissed her—tenderly at first, a lingering brush of lips. She sighed against me, melting into my touch. That sigh undid me. I deepened the kiss, our mouths fitting together like they had always been meant to. The world faded to nothing but her warmth, her taste, her surrender.

When we finally pulled away, we were both breathless. I kept my hands on her waist, unwilling to let her go.

"Barbara," I started, but she touched my lips to silence me.

"Don't spoil it," she whispered.

We sat in silence for a while, wrapped in each other, listening to the steady crash of waves on the beach below. The salt air was thick and cool, but I felt something different pressing between us —Barbara's tension, coiled tight in her muscles, her breath just a little too measured.

"What is it?" I asked.

She shook her head, letting out a quiet laugh, though there was no humor in it. "How do you do that?"

"Do what?"

"Know when I'm fighting myself about whether or not to say something."

I shrugged. "It's a gift."

She shifted in my arms, turning so she could see my face. Her expression was unreadable, but her eyes were clear, sharp. "What did you have to take care of this afternoon?"

I tensed, my grip on her waist tightening slightly before I forced myself to relax. The comforting warmth of the moment cooled like embers in a dying fire. "It's nothing you need to worry about."

"Victor," she said, her tone insistent. "You promised. No more secrets."

I sighed, running a hand through my hair. She started to pull away, but I held her firm. "Fine," I relented. "Let's take a walk."

The wooden stairs that led down to the beach were slick with evening dew, the planks damp beneath our feet. Barbara gripped the railing with one hand, the other clasped tightly in mine. The air was crisp, thick with brine, and the persistent crash of waves mixed with the occasional whistle of a distant ship. As we descended the last steps, the mist curled around us, softening the glow of the deck lights behind us. Ahead, the ocean stretched into the darkness.

"Do you remember our friend, Kowalski?" I asked when we reached the sand.

Her fingers tightened around mine, a reflexive shudder passing through her. "How could I forget?"

"Well, he's come out of the woodwork recently, and he's proving to be a real thorn in my side. Truthfully, he's got more stones than I gave him credit for." I pulled her along gently, our bare feet sinking into the cool, damp shore. A breeze teased Barbara's hair, lifting strands across her face.

She slowed her pace, forcing me to turn and face her. "What kind of trouble?" she asked, her voice quiet but laced with genuine concern.

I stopped, letting the sand shift underfoot as I considered

how much to tell her. "Kowalski got wind that I lifted his development designs for the new residential build in the Valley," I admitted. "He's making noise—talking to people he shouldn't, threatening to go to the authorities."

Her eyes widened. "Can he prove anything?"

"Doubtful," I said, though the certainty in my voice didn't quite match the knot in my gut. "But even rumors might be a problem right now. I need everything to stay quiet."

We continued along the shoreline, the wet sand compacting under each step. A skeletal stretch of driftwood lay rotting ahead, its splintered edges jutting out like ribs. The tide lapped at its edges, slowly pulling it apart, piece by piece.

Barbara broke the silence, her tone cautious but insistent. "So what did you have to take care of this afternoon?"

I exhaled slowly. "I met with Phil," I said, my voice carefully measured, "to discuss how to best handle him."

She stopped again, and I turned back to find her staring at me, a storm of emotions playing across her face—concern, fear… something else I couldn't quite place.

"Handle him?" she repeated. "Victor, you're not…you're not going to hurt him, are you?"

"We'll do what we have to do," I said evenly, leaving it deliberately vague.

She looked away, her gaze fixed on the horizon where the inky sky swallowed the water. The wind picked up, sending a chill through the thin fabric of my shirt. Barbara shivered.

"Darling," I said softly, but she didn't respond.

Her silence was heavy. I moved closer, attempting to take her hand, but she crossed her arms over her chest, hugging herself.

"If you didn't want to know…"

She shook her head. "No, no. I asked."

The waves lapped closer to our feet, their cold fingers stretching up the shore. I watched as a foam-tipped surge kissed Barbara's toes. She didn't flinch.

She blew out a quick breath and looked up at me. "Are you in danger? Are we?"

I took her by the shoulders and pulled her body hard against mine. "We're safe, Barbara. I have good people working for me. Trust me."

Her eyes searched mine, desperate for certainty. "You can't promise that," she whispered.

I stroked her hair, my fingers tangling in the windblown strands. "I can, and I do."

She swallowed, clearly not convinced.

"There's something else," I said, bracing for her reaction. "I bought you a gun to keep at the house. Just in case."

Her eyes flashed with anger, and her body went rigid. "Victor, no. Absolutely not."

"It's just a precaution. I'd feel better knowing you and Frankie are protected."

"Protected from what?" she demanded, stepping back from me. "You just said we're safe."

"You are," I insisted.

"No, Victor," she said, shaking her head vehemently. "I don't want a gun in my house. Frankie's just a child—it's too dangerous."

"Barbara," I started, but she was already turning away, heading back toward the stairs. I caught up and took her arm— gentle but resolute. "No one knows where you are, and they have no reason to come looking. But until this thing with Kowalski blows over, I need to know you're safe. That's all."

She hesitated, exhaling sharply. "Victor," she said, her voice calmer but still resistant. "I don't even know how to fire a gun."

"It's not that complicated. Point and shoot, like in the movies."

She turned to face me, searching my eyes for some reprieve, some concession. I gave none.

"I'll teach you how to use it," I said evenly. "Chances are you won't ever have to, and it'll just collect dust. But I need to know you have the means to protect yourself when I'm not there. This is nonnegotiable, Barbara."

She bit her lower lip as the wind tossed her hair into a wild halo. For a moment, I thought she might cry, but she was stronger than that. Stronger than even she knew.

"Fine," she said at last, her voice resigned. "But I'm only taking it because you insist."

"I do insist." I brushed my lips against hers. "And now I'll sleep at night knowing no one can take you from me."

34
BARBARA

Gino sped up and whipped by my house.

"What on earth, Gino? Take me home."

He shook his head. "There was another car in the driveway. Mr. Cardello was very clear. I'm only to drop you off if it's safe."

I twisted in my seat, craning my neck toward the house. "Yeah, but…" I squinted, but Gino had already turned the corner. "I'm pretty sure that was my sister's car."

He glanced at me in the rearview mirror from under the brim of his driving cap. "You're sure?"

"Not one hundred percent. I didn't get a good enough look, but I think so."

Gino slowed for a moment, then turned the block sharply. "Okay, I'll drive by again. If it's her and it's clear, I'll drop you off."

"You know this is all so unnecessary."

"Maybe, but orders are orders."

He coasted toward the curb, the engine idling low as we approached my house. Plain as day, Edith's sky-blue Cadillac sat in the driveway, its whitewall tires and chrome accents gleaming under the late afternoon sun. The car looked like it belonged there—unruffled, poised, as if it had nowhere better to be. I let out a relieved sigh.

"It's her," I said. "You can stop."

Gino pulled to the curb and parked. I reached for the door handle, but his voice stopped me.

"Mrs. Evans, let me walk you inside."

I turned to him, exasperation clear on my face. "Gino, really. This is my family."

He removed his cap and ran a hand through his dark hair. "I get that. But until Mr. Cardello says otherwise…"

I slumped back in my seat, defeated. "Fine."

Gino walked around the car and opened my door, offering a hand I reluctantly took. As we moved up the walkway, his head stayed on a constant swivel, his sharp eyes scanning every window, every car, and every shadow.

At the front porch, he stepped aside but stayed within arm's length, his presence a silent but solid wall between me and whatever danger he thought lurked nearby. I fished my keys from my handbag and unlocked the door.

"Barbara!" Edith's voice rang out before I even stepped inside. "Please tell me that's finally you."

"Yes, it's me." I turned back toward Gino to thank him, but he didn't move. He lingered at the threshold, stance still firm, as if waiting for an all-clear that hadn't been given.

"Where have you been?" Edith's voice cut through the air, sharp and frantic, as she stormed toward me. Frankie was perched on her hip. She was as striking as ever, but worry lines were carved into her forehead. "I've been calling for hours!" Edith's eyes flicked to Gino, assessing him in an instant before locking back onto me. "Who is this?" she asked, suspicion creeping into her voice.

"He's just leaving," I said, my tone measured. "Thank you, Gino."

He hesitated a moment longer before giving a short nod. He

turned and walked down the steps slowly, deliberately. I closed the door behind him.

Edith shifted Frankie to her other hip and looked at me expectantly. "Where have you been?" she repeated, her tone calmer now but still urgent.

I took a deep breath. "I was at Victor's," I said, bracing for the inevitable lecture. "It was all spur of the moment."

"Barbara," Edith started, then stopped. She set Frankie down gently and kissed his forehead. "Go play in your room, sweetheart."

Frankie toddled off, casting a curious glance back at us. His small footsteps disappeared down the hall.

I crossed my arms, already weary from what I knew was coming. "Why are you so bent out of shape?" My voice came out sharper than I intended. "You knew I was spending the weekend with Victor. You and I arranged it, for Pete's sake."

Edith rubbed her temples, closing her eyes for a moment. She inhaled deeply, then exhaled, slow and measured. When she finally opened her eyes, they weren't angry. They were soft. Sad.

"Barbara, it's not that. It's..." She let out a breath through pursed lips. "Something happened."

A prickle of unease ran up my spine. "What do you mean?"

Edith swallowed hard. "Mother had a heart attack early this morning."

A pause, thick and suffocating.

"She's gone."

———

The service was nicely done—all the right readings, songs, and prayers. My brother, Bill, delivered the eulogy. He spoke of a caring and compassionate mother who loved and nurtured and gave the best childhood a boy could ask for.

Maybe my siblings got the lion's share of her maternal compassion, but by the time I came around, she was all dried up.

The church was packed. All of Los Angeles society turned up to attend Agatha Montgomery's funeral. Notably absent, however, was Congressman Milton Montgomery—Daddy. The official excuse was his work on the statehood commission in Hawaii. The real reason, murmured in hushed voices between pews, was much less dignified.

After the funeral, I stood in the receiving line with Edith and Bill, mechanically expressing our gratitude to each person who filed past. "Thank you for coming," I said. "We appreciate your condolences." The words had become a chant, stripped of meaning through endless repetition.

Usually, Edith was the one to stand out from the crowd—to buck the norm, as it were. But this time, it was my turn. Edith and Bill both stood dressed in traditional, conservative funerary black. I wore a crisp white dress with a wide lapel and a red satin sash about the waist.

The procession dragged on, a parade of solemn faces blurred together, each offering the same rehearsed condolences. These were Mother's people—social climbers and hangers-on, the lot of them. Their faces were familiar but not friendly. I'd seen them all at various galas and fundraisers throughout the years, offering the same false smiles and whispering the same veiled gossip.

"Thank you for coming," I said to Mrs. Hargrove, our mother's oldest friend and the most insincere person I'd ever met. "It means so much to us."

"The world is a poorer place without Agatha," she declared, her lips pursed in brittle, well-practiced sorrow. Her gloved hand clamped over mine, squeezing too hard, as if grief could be transferred through sheer pressure. "Be strong, Barbara."

I nodded, polite but unmoved, resisting the urge to roll my eyes as she moved on to smother Edith. *Be strong.* As if fragility were my problem.

I glanced sideways at Edith, who dabbed at her damp eyes

with a neatly folded handkerchief. She had real tears, real sorrow. I envied her that.

Guilt gnawed at me like a persistent rat. How many daughters had stood where I stood now, gasping for breath beneath the weight of their loss? A bond so deep that its severing should leave me shattered. But I wasn't shattered. I wasn't even cracked. I waited for the sorrow to consume me. But all I could muster was a dull, emotional flatline.

Half an hour later, the crowd had thinned enough for me to see the exit. My mind drifted to the glass of wine I'd pour once I got home, to the hot bath that would wash this whole insincere mess away.

The last of the mourners shuffled past, and I allowed myself a brief moment of relief. But then I saw Frank, standing back from the line with his hands in his pockets. My heart skipped— not with joy or dread, but with pure surprise. I hadn't expected him to come.

He approached slowly, almost cautiously. "Hello, Barbara," Frank said, his voice cutting through the murmurs of lingering guests. He stood a few paces away, as if unsure of his welcome.

I straightened, my surprise morphing into a guarded curiosity. "Frank." My voice was polite but edged. "What are you doing here?"

He shifted on his feet, uncharacteristically uncertain. There was no arrogance, no sharp retorts or accusations. Just quiet, unassuming sincerity.

"I always liked your mother," he said simply. "I wanted to pay my respects."

The words landed softly. I hesitated, thrown off balance by the unexpected sentiment. "That's…kind of you." The response felt inadequate, but it was all I could offer. "Thank you."

We stood in uneasy silence for a moment. Edith and Bill had slipped away. Frank's curly blond hair had grown out a bit, less tightly wound than usual, and there was a softness in his eyes that disarmed me.

"How is our son?" Frank asked, breaking the silence. His eyes met mine, and for a moment, I thought I saw something deeper in them—concern, perhaps.

"He's fine," I said. "He's down in the church nursery. I thought a funeral would be a bit much for him."

"I agree," Frank said. He glanced around, searching for something to anchor his attention, then exhaled slowly and tucked his hands back into his pockets. "Funerals are hard enough on adults."

I nodded, not knowing what to say. The silence between us stretched, taut and fragile. In the past, Frank's presence had been predictable—sometimes comforting, sometimes suffocating—but now it felt like uncharted territory.

"Barbara," he started, then hesitated. "I'm sorry about your mother. I know you had a complicated relationship, but…she was still your mother."

The softness in his eyes made my chest tighten. This new, gentler Frank was unsettling, and I had no idea what to make of it.

"Is there something you want, Frank?" I asked, more sharply than I intended. The tension of the day had frayed my patience, and his newfound tenderness left me unbalanced.

He studied me, and I braced myself for whatever bombshell he might drop. "I've been thinking," he said slowly. "About us. About the future." He paused, letting the words hang in the air like dense fog. "I'm okay with moving forward now."

"Moving forward?"

"With the divorce," he clarified. "If that's still what you want."

I stared at him, searching for the true motive behind this sudden shift. Weeks ago, he was desperate to keep me. Now, he was handing me an exit. "Why the change of heart?"

Frank shrugged—not casual, not careless, but uneasy. Like a man trying to shake off something clinging to his skin. "I want you to be happy, Barbara. That's all. I'm not going to fight it anymore. I understand better now."

"Understand what?" I asked, folding my arms.

"Why you're unhappy," he said. "Why you need…something different."

My suspicion sharpened. This wasn't like Frank at all. "Frank," I said slowly, "what's really going on?"

Instead of answering, he gave me a small, almost wistful smile. "Come with me," he said, gesturing toward the church doors.

I hesitated, then followed as he walked ahead. He pushed one of the large wooden doors open, and sunlight poured into the dimly lit vestibule, flooding the marble floor with gold. A rush of warm California air greeted me.

Frank held the door open and nodded toward the curb. A sleek red convertible idled in front of the church. A young woman sat in the driver's seat, her dark waves pinned back in a loose, effortless style. She wore large sunglasses and a lipstick-red scarf around her neck. Even from this distance, I could tell she was strikingly gorgeous.

I knew before I even asked.

"Who's that?"

"Her name is Giselle," Frank said carefully. "She's…helping me with some things."

I turned to Frank, who looked like a boy caught stealing apples. So this was it. All his pleading, all his resistance, all the promises that we could fix things…and he had someone waiting in the wings.

"She's beautiful," I said, and I meant it. Pain didn't cut through me—only clarity. "So this is why you're suddenly ready to move forward?"

He took a deep breath and squared his shoulders as if summoning courage. "Barbara," he said slowly, measuring each word. "I've fallen in love with her. With Giselle. We want to be together."

There it was.

I studied his face. He expected anger, maybe even heartbreak. I felt neither.

"I see," I said simply, my mind catching up with this new reality. "That was…fast."

"We didn't plan for this," he added quickly, as if that might absolve him. "It just…happened. I'm sorry."

"Don't be," I said, and I meant that too. If anything, his honesty was a relief. "I'm glad you told me."

Frank glanced back at the convertible, where Giselle now toyed with a cigarette holder, the thin column of smoke curling from the end like a lazy ribbon in the late morning sun. "We were thinking…" he started, then trailed off. I could almost hear the gears in his head grinding to a halt.

"You were thinking what?" I prompted, though I already had an idea of where this was going.

He raked a hand through his curly hair, mussing it further. "We thought it might be easier—for everyone—if we got the divorce done quickly. In Mexico."

"Mexico?" I repeated, thrown for a loop.

"It's faster down there," he explained. "Cleaner. And it's just as legal as here. We wouldn't have to wait six months. We could both move on with our lives."

I stared at him. Frank—the man who did everything by the book—was suggesting this? This wasn't the Frank I knew. This was someone eager to cut the rope and let go.

"You're serious."

"It makes sense, doesn't it?" He looked at me with those softened eyes again, hopeful, as if I'd see this as the favor he thought it was. "Barbara, I just want what's best for you—and for me."

For a moment, I couldn't speak. Too much had happened in too short a time. Victor's ominous warning, Mother's death, the ghastly funeral, and now Frank—once my greatest obstacle— was practically ushering me out the door.

I looked over at Giselle in the convertible. She'd removed her sunglasses and was applying ruby-red lipstick in the rearview mirror. The confidence she exuded was like a heatwave coming off asphalt.

"I see you're in good hands," I said, letting my gaze linger on Giselle's delicate, practiced movements. "Frank, I mean it. I'm glad you've found someone. I wish you both well."

Frank blinked, startled, as if he'd braced for anger or reproach and didn't know what to do with my quiet acceptance. "Thank you," he said, and his relief was almost painful to watch. "Barbara, we'll make this as seamless as possible. My lawyer will be in touch soon."

"Of course," I said, my voice even and calm. Inside, a rush of conflicting emotions swirled—anger, relief, sadness, and an odd sense of freedom.

Giselle tapped the horn lightly, and Frank flinched. He turned toward the car, then back to me with an apologetic shrug. "I should go. But…take care of yourself. And our son."

"I will," I said.

With that, Frank walked toward the waiting car, his pace quickening as he neared Giselle. She leaned in, whispering something in his ear, her lips curving into an undeniably smug smile. Frank grinned—boyish, carefree, unburdened.

He glanced back at me one last time, but I turned away and walked back into the church.

35
VICTOR

"I don't know what man in the sky you pray to, Victor"—
Lawrence pushed a document across his desk to me—"but
whoever it is, they came through for you."

My name, right there in black and white. My freedom, sealed by
ink and bureaucracy.

I fingered the page like a crisp million-dollar bill.

"It's done," I said softly—partly a question, partly to make
myself believe it.

"It is. In all my years practicing law, I've never seen a divorce
go through the courts so fast. Who did you… You know what,
never mind. I don't want to know."

"Barbara is free to move forward with her divorce now, right?"

Lawrence leaned back in his chair, the leather creaking like
old bones. "Yes…" he answered tentatively.

"But…"

"But just because she can move forward doesn't mean it will be as smooth for her as it was for you. Victor, you had every advantage—a willing spouse, the best representation money can buy, and a very 'amenable' judge. Barbara's situation is different."

"Her husband had a change of heart. He's on board now."

Lawrence glared at me over the rim of his glasses. "Did he now?"

I shook my head. "No, no, nothing like that. Barbara says he's found himself a girlfriend, so he's willing to move forward with the divorce."

He let out a relieved sigh. "Oh good, I was afraid I'd have yet another pot of boiling water to save you from."

Lawrence had saved my skin more times than I could count. As much as I valued his counsel, I needed him to understand the urgency.

"I'm serious, Larry. I want to marry her as soon as humanly possible. What will it take?"

Lawrence studied me, his gray eyes sharp behind his gold-rimmed glasses. "Victor, you realize that even with Dorothy out of the picture, you're still looking at a waiting period before you can remarry. Twelve months is the law. And if it's Barbara you're set on marrying, that's twelve months from the date of *her* divorce." He exhaled, rubbing his thumb along the edge of the desk. "I'm sorry, friend, but there's nothing quick about this, and there's no favor I can call in to speed it along."

I started to protest, but the look on his face told me he wasn't finished. "There's something you're not telling me."

"That's the law in *California*," he reiterated with a knowing look.

I could play ball. "But not somewhere else. Like Mexico, for instance."

Lawrence sat forward, elbows on the desk, fingers steepled.

"Victor, be very careful here. I'm your lawyer, and I have to advise you within the bounds of the law."

I waved a hand dismissively. "Hypothetically speaking, of course."

"Hypothetically, if one were to seek a quicker resolution, they might look into how things are handled in other jurisdictions. But remember, whatever you hypothetically do outside of California may not hold up here."

I held up the divorce decree, letting it sway between my fingers. "This will hold up, though. It's legitimate."

"It's as legitimate as it gets," Lawrence confirmed.

I set the paper back on his desk with exaggerated care. "Frank suggested they get a Mexican divorce. Said it would be quicker for everyone involved."

"Frank sounds like a man who's done his research," he said dryly.

"So if they did that," I pressed, "would it count? Would the time start ticking here?"

Lawrence removed his glasses and pinched the bridge of his nose. "Victor, a Mexican divorce can be risky. Sometimes they're recognized here; sometimes they're not. It depends on how the documents are filed and whether they meet California's legal standards. Even then, it can be challenged."

"But it's possible," I insisted. "It's an option."

He put his glasses back on and met my gaze. "Yes, it's possible. But understand that it's also a gamble. If you want my honest advice—"

"I always do. You're one of the few men on this earth who actually tells me the truth."

"The safest course is to have Barbara file here in California and go through the proper channels. Then you wait out your twelve months and happily walk down the aisle. That way, everything is aboveboard, and there are no unwelcome surprises down the line."

I nodded. "I appreciate that, Larry. I do. But you and I both know I can't wait that long."

"What's the rush, Victor? Is there a bun in the oven I don't know about?"

I scoffed. "Nothing like that."

I turned to the window, the Los Angeles skyline shimmering in the afternoon sun. The glass panels of the high-rises looked like stacked gold bars, glittering in the heat. When I turned back to Lawrence, I was calmer but no less certain.

"I love her, Larry. And not in some storybook way. Before her, I'm not sure I even knew what love was. She fills a void in me. I'm a better man because of her. I want to spend every godforsaken moment I have left on this earth with her."

Lawrence leaned back again, the creaking leather now a familiar refrain. The stern edge to his face softened, his lined features settling into something more reflective.

"Victor," he began slowly.

I braced myself for the lecture—the one about patience and making wise choices. Instead, Lawrence surprised me.

"I understand more than you think," he said. "Do you remember when I came back from the war? How distant and cold I was?"

I nodded. "It was a rough time for you. We were all worried."

"It wasn't just rough," he continued. "It was hell. Coming home to Emily and the kids should have been the happiest moment of my life, but I felt like a stranger in my own house. I couldn't connect. I was lost." He paused, his jaw tightening. "The only thing that got me through was knowing they were waiting for me no matter what, that we would eventually find our way back to each other. And we did. Love is what sustained me, Victor. The kind of love you're talking about now. So believe me when I say, I get it." He blew out a slow breath, then continued slowly, choosing his words with care. "As your friend, I understand the urgency—the need to seize happiness while you can. Life is short and unpredictable. The war taught us that if nothing else."

I said nothing, letting him work through whatever internal conflict held him back.

"So here's what I think," he said at last. "If you're determined to take the quickest route, then yes—have Barbara and Frank get their divorce in Mexico. But for heaven's sake, make sure it's done properly." He drummed his fingers against the desk. "Yucatán or Juárez would be their best bet. The residency requirement is only one day. But they both have to go in person. No mail-order divorce quacks."

I nodded, absorbing every word.

"Then you and Barbara marry in Nevada. They'll honor a Mexican divorce, and there's no waiting period."

"And that'll hold up here?"

Lawrence shrugged, a slow, deliberate motion. "It should. California honors a Nevada marriage certificate. But like I said, it's still a gamble."

I stood and extended a hand across the desk. "Thank you, Larry. For everything."

Lawrence took it, his grip warm and steady. "Just be careful," he said, not letting go immediately. "And send me a wedding invitation. I think I've earned that much."

———

"Pour us something, and make it sparkling, darling." I greeted Barbara at her door with two dozen roses in one hand and freedom in the other.

She pressed her hand lightly against her chest, searching my face. "Does that mean what I think it does?"

"You are looking at a bona fide free man."

She took the roses and kissed me softly. "Well, you'd better come inside before some pretty girl snaps you up."

Barbara's house smelled of vanilla and fresh linen. She wore a periwinkle dress that swayed with her as she glided to the kitchen, shimmering like a morning lake. I followed and placed a silver gift box on the counter. She peeked inside, and her eyes sparkled.

"Crystal flutes? You think of everything."

She retrieved chilled champagne from the fridge, the bottle sweating in her delicate hands. With a practiced twist, she sent the cork flying, its pop ricocheting through the house like a joyous gunshot. Bubbles spilled over the rim as she poured.

I took my glass and held it aloft. "To freedom."

Her lips curved into a knowing yet wistful smile as she clinked her glass against mine, the crystalline note lingering in the air.

We sipped, and the champagne's effervescence played a symphony on my tongue—light, airy, with an undercurrent of apple and pear that breathed life into my veins.

"I'm so happy for you," Barbara said. Her voice was warm, but her eyes held something else—hesitation, maybe hope. "This means we're one step closer."

"Closer," I echoed, rolling the word over in my mouth with another sip of champagne. I thought of Lawrence's warnings, the road still ahead, and the possible complications lurking beneath the surface. "Speaking of which, any news?"

Barbara swirled the champagne in her glass, watching the bubbles rise like tiny desperate swimmers. "Frank still insists on Mexico. He says his lawyer is handling everything."

I let that sink in as I took another slow sip, the cool liquid settling the uneasy feeling in my gut. "That makes things easier, then," I said, offering optimism I wasn't sure I believed.

She shrugged and moved to the sink to fill a vase with water. The rushing tap and the quiet clink of rose stems against glass cut through the room's fragile silence. "Easier, maybe. Quicker, definitely..." She turned back to me, one hand brushing a loose strand of hair behind her ear. She started to speak but hesitated, lips parting, then pressing together again.

I set my glass on the counter with a muted thud against the Formica. "What's on your mind, sweetheart?"

She shook her head. "Honestly, I'm just waiting for the shoe to drop. For him to change his mind, back out, or…"

"Or what?"

She glanced at the refrigerator, where a bright tangle of crayon strokes on manila paper clung to the door with a single magnet. "I'm worried about custody arrangements if we handle it out of the country."

I pulled her close and held her head against my chest. "You need your own representation," I said gently, pressing a slow kiss into her hair. "I don't trust Frank's lawyer to handle this fairly. Let me set you up with Lawrence. He's sharp, and I trust him with my life."

She nodded, curling her fingers into the fabric of my jacket.

"Don't you worry, my darling. We'll make everything right."

I expected her posture to soften, but it didn't. Barbara's eyes flicked to the side. I followed her gaze to an unopened letter on the counter—crisp, white, official. The return address belonged to a prominent Los Angeles law firm. She caught my gaze.

"It's from my mother's estate attorney," she said, her voice flat. "I don't want to open it."

"Why not?"

Barbara bit her lip. "Because I'm afraid of what it will say. Mother and I weren't on the best terms. I imagine she cut me out. But I still don't want to read it."

I released her and picked up the letter, weighing it in my hand. It was light—probably no more than a page or two. "Would it help if I opened it?"

She hesitated, her eyes locked on the letter as if it were poison. After a long beat, she nodded.

I slid a finger under the flap and tore it with deliberate care. The paper inside was thick and expensive—the kind rich people used for weddings and funerals. I unfolded it and scanned the first few lines.

"It's not what you think," I said, reading further.

"What do you mean?"

I exhaled slowly. "This isn't a legal document. It's a personal note from Agatha."

Barbara's hand went to her mouth. "From Mother? But how…"

"To be delivered upon her death," I said, my eyes tracing the precise, practiced handwriting.

Barbara took a step back and folded her arms tightly across her chest. "What does it say?"

I scanned down the letter, my eyes moving faster than my mind could process. A knot coiled in my stomach as I reached the bottom. I set the letter in front of Barbara, but she kept her eyes fixed on me.

"Read it," she said, her voice brittle. "I don't care how bad it is—I just can't."

"Barbara, maybe you should—"

"No." She shook her head, sharp and final. "Just tell me. Please."

I took a deep breath and picked up the letter, the expensive paper rustling in my hands. The words swam before me, and for a moment, I hoped they would dissolve like sugar in hot tea and take their meaning with them. I closed my eyes, then opened them slowly, bracing myself.

"Dear Barbara," I read, trying to capture the cold formality of Agatha's voice. "If you are reading this, then you know I have left this world behind. There are things I wished to say to you while I was still alive, but time and circumstance never deemed it appropriate."

I glanced at Barbara. Her face was a mask, unreadable.

"I know you always believed that I did not understand you— that I was unsupportive and unfeeling. The truth is, I did understand, perhaps more than you ever realized. I had the same desires and ambitions when I was your age."

I checked Barbara's face for any sign of emotion—anger,

sorrow, relief—but she remained a statue, her eyes unblinking and distant.

"None of this is easy for me to admit," I continued to read, "but you need to know the truth. Unfortunately, I was never able to be the warm, nurturing presence that you needed. The kind of motherly love you deserved was something beyond my reach."

The words hung in the air like lingering smoke. Barbara gripped the edge of the counter so tightly that her knuckles turned white. Still, she gave no other outward reaction to the words I read.

"I am sorry for that, truly. And for all the rest, though I imagine that comes as a small consolation at this late hour. There are certain truths that I promised to take to my grave, and rest assured, I've kept those promises. But just because I'm gone does not mean you're left without answers."

I shifted my weight, uneasy with what came next.

"Speak to Edith," I read slowly, each word a deliberate, slow drag of a scalpel. "She can tell you what I never could." A beat of silence. "Signed, Mother."

36

BARBARA

Edith's hands trembled as she read Mother's letter.

Silence filled the room like a dense fog—the suffocating, blinding fog over the water that swallows up the pier. She didn't speak, didn't move. A long breath hitched in her throat. Then with a sudden exhale, she tossed the letter on the coffee table and stalked toward the bar.

She pulled out two lowball glasses and set them on the jade bar top with an echoing clatter. Bourbon glugged generously into the glasses, filling them nearly to the brim.

Edith pressed her lips together as she brought the glasses back to the sofa and wordlessly offered me one. I shook my head, but she set it in front of me anyway.

She picked up her glass and swirled the bourbon, letting its aroma rise to her nose. She took a deep, unsteady breath and sipped—careful at first, then a long swallow. Color drained from her face, leaving her pale as porcelain.

I tapped my fingers against the letter on the coffee table. "It's not what I expected," I said. "More honest than I ever thought she'd be."

Edith stared at the letter as if it were a ghost come to haunt her. "Don't be naïve, Barbara. You know how Mother was." Her voice was distant and hollow. "Only honest when it suited her."

I stared at the sharply creased paper. "She said you have answers. Is it true?"

Edith drained her bourbon in one long, unladylike gulp. "It's true that I know things you don't," she said. "Whether you want to hear them is another matter."

I leaned forward, elbows on my knees. "I need to understand, Edith. I've gone my whole life not knowing why she treated me like an unwanted guest in my own family. I have no idea what I did or didn't do. I followed every rule, crossed every T, dotted every I, wore the right clothes, attended the right events, got into the right school, smiled for the camera, smiled when I was dying inside. And for what?" My voice cracked, then climbed to an angry crescendo. "The love of a mother that never came, no matter how perfect I was?"

Edith studied me with her piercing hazel eyes that always saw more than they let on. "Barbara, some secrets are buried for a reason. Are you sure you want to open this Pandora's box?"

I sat back and crossed my arms. "What choice do I have? Edith, if you don't tell me, I'll never understand why she was so cold. I'll never understand why she treated me like…like a bad smell that wouldn't go away."

Edith's gaze softened, and for a moment, I thought she might take me in her arms as she had so many times before when I was inconsolable. Instead, she reached for the untouched glass in front of me and downed its contents in a single, desperate pull.

"Fine," she said, her voice rough from the bourbon. "But don't say I didn't warn you."

My heart pounded.

"Mother treated you like an unwanted guest because to her… that's exactly what you were." Edith spoke without apology. "She took you in out of obligation, not out of love."

A chill ran through me. "Took me in? What the hell does that mean?"

Edith's eyes shot wide open. I rarely swore, and the rogue expletive must have caught her off guard. But I didn't care. Not now.

When she didn't answer, my mind raced through possibilities. "What, like a foundling?" My thoughts settled on my father—more absent than present, but always warm when he was around. "Was I Daddy's lovechild that Mother had to raise?"

A tight, humorless chuckle bounced off her lips.

"Jesus, Edith. Just tell me!"

She inhaled sharply. "You are *my* daughter, Barbara. Not Agatha's." The words struck like a hammer. "I am your real mother."

The room tilted as Edith's confession hit me, and for a moment, I thought I might slide off the sofa and onto the floor. I gripped the armrest to steady myself.

"You're my…*what*?"

"Mother and Daddy thought it best to cover the whole thing up," she continued. "I was only sixteen and, of course, unmarried. Forget doing what's right—they couldn't have the scandal. They said they were doing it for my benefit—to give me a chance in life. But I didn't buy that for a minute. The scandal would have ruined the family, or worse—Daddy's political career. I had no say in the matter. They sent me away, and when you were born, they took you from me and raised you as their own. They told everyone you were Agatha's change-of-life baby."

I stared at her, speechless. This was absurd. This was fiction.

"Do you understand now?" Edith pressed. "The coldness you felt from Agatha—it wasn't because she didn't love you. It was because she *couldn't* love you the way a real mother would. She played her part as best she could, but in the end, that's all it ever was—a part."

Every memory I had twisted and warped in my mind.

I could taste the bourbon in the air, hot and acrid. Edith rose unsteadily and walked back to the bar. She fumbled with the bottle, her hands less sure than before. I remembered them as steady as a surgeon's when she taught me to sew, to bake, to drive. All the things a mother teaches a daughter.

She poured herself another glass, not bothering to ask if I wanted one this time. She knew I wouldn't take it. She knew everything, it seemed.

"Why didn't you tell me?" I asked, my voice smaller now, like a child's.

Edith turned slowly, glass in hand, but didn't move from the bar. "How could I? That was the arrangement. If I told you the truth, it would have destroyed everything." She took a long sip of her third bourbon. "They hoped you'd never question it. That you'd never have to."

I couldn't breathe. The air in the room was stifled with half-truths and unshed tears. My skin prickled with the heat of anger and the cold of realization.

"So now what?" I asked, the words bitter on my tongue. "Do I start calling you Mom?"

Edith rolled her eyes. "Don't be ridiculous. We're still the same people with the same lives. Yes, you know the truth now. But it doesn't change a damn thing."

I stood, the room swaying around me like a ship in a storm. "I need to go."

"Barbara, sit. We're not finished."

I paused, one hand on the back of the sofa, the other clutching my purse like a life preserver.

"Please," Edith said. The word was soft, almost pleading.

I let go of my purse and sat back down, though my body remained rigid, ready to spring.

Edith set her glass on the bar—unfinished—and walked slowly back to me. She didn't sit, rather stood over me like a looming question mark.

"I know this is a lot to take in," she said. "But you need to understand that we did what we thought was best for you."

"We?" I asked. "So you agreed with all of this?"

She hesitated. "Not at first, no. But in time, I came to accept it." She sat down beside me and placed a hand on my knee. "Think back, Barbara. I was there for every important moment. All those scraped knees? I was the one who patched you up. When your cat died, who held you until you stopped crying? When Johnny O'Dell broke your heart in the tenth grade, who sat up with you all night? I watched you cross that graduation stage, cheered you on at every movie premiere, and when you walked down the aisle, I was right there." She stared at me, long and hard, tears tracing slow paths down her cheeks. "I *never* abandoned you."

37
VICTOR

"Phil! If it's such a goddamn emergency," I hollered as I headed down the basement steps, "you could at least pick up the phone."

Silence.

"Phil?"

I smelled him before I saw him. That ripe, unmistakable stink. I tasted the copper in the back of my throat. Blood. A lot of it.

I drew my revolver, thumbed back the hammer, and took another tentative step down.

"Phil?" I didn't expect an answer.

I took the remaining steps carefully, each one echoing in the oppressive silence. The flickering fluorescent light overhead stuttered, throwing jagged shadows against the concrete floor.

Phil dangled from a meat hook in the ceiling. The chain groaned. His flesh was flayed in strips, raw and glistening. His massive frame swayed gently, like a grotesque piñata. What was left of him looked more like a side of beef than a man. Except for his face. That part they left untouched, his dead eyes locked straight ahead. A slick red pool stretched out beneath him, the blood soaking into the cracks in the concrete like veins in stone.

"Jesus Christ."

I swept the room with my revolver, each shadow and corner getting its due attention. When I was sure I was alone, I lowered my weapon and turned back to Phil.

"Who the hell did you piss off?" I muttered.

Blood and mildew—two smells that never belonged together. But here they were, clinging to my sinuses like cheap cologne. I wiped at my nose with the back of my hand and took a slow breath through my mouth. The atmosphere was soupy. Breathing felt like sucking air through a wet rag.

I moved closer to Phil's body, careful to keep my shoes out of the blood. It glistened under the flickering light, still wet, still warm. Recent. Too recent. I followed the cuts, the places where his skin used to be. Stripped clean, down to the bone in some places, hanging like tattered rags. The precision was surgical. This wasn't some back-alley hack job. This was the work of a pro. A pro with a message.

I fought the urge to pull Phil down. There was nothing I could do for him now, and touching the body would only leave evidence. Not that the cops would bother—they stayed well clear of my affairs—but it was good practice to be careful.

I scanned the room again, this time looking for something more specific—a note, an object, some kind of calling card. Pros liked to leave their mark, a signature to let the right people know who wielded the knife. But there was nothing. Just Phil's papers and ledger strewn about the desk and the dripping silence of this makeshift slaughterhouse.

My gut tightened. Whoever did this wanted me off balance. They wanted me looking over my shoulder, second-guessing my next move. And damn if it wasn't working.

Phil swore he had Kowalski under control. So what the hell happened? Did he screw it up that bad, or did Kowalski bring in fresh blood—someone with this kind of skill?

"Damn it, Phil. You were smarter than this."

Kowalski was a hothead and a loudmouth, but he'd never

had the stones to come at me outright. If he was making moves like this now, we were in deeper trouble than I thought. Or maybe Phil got to him first and this was retribution. Either way, I was running out of time to figure it out.

My gut burned. It wasn't just the sight of Phil—or what was left of him. It was the audacity. The goddamn nerve to walk into my house and do this.

Phil wasn't just an employee. He was family. The kind of loyalty he gave me was rare, and now it was gone for good. I curled my fists, my nails biting into my palms, then forced myself to turn away.

A floorboard groaned at the top of the stairs.

I spun, revolver up, finger tight on the trigger. A shadow stretched down the stairwell, growing with each step.

"Boss, it's me!" The voice floated down, hushed but urgent. "Christ, don't shoot!"

I didn't lower the gun. "Gino?"

He stepped into the dim light, hands up, face pale. "I was worried when you didn't come back to the car." His gaze snapped to Phil, and the color drained from his face like someone had pulled the plug.

I motioned him down with a flick of the barrel. He hesitated, then took each step like it might be his last. I kept the gun trained on him the whole way. Trust wasn't something I handed out anymore—not even to my own men.

"Holy mother of—"

"Save it," I cut him off. "Won't change a damn thing."

He swallowed hard. His voice wavered. "Who…who did this?"

I holstered my weapon—not out of relief, just resignation. I didn't answer him. "Gino, get the car ready."

I crossed to the desk and picked up the telephone. The clicks of the rotary grated on my frayed nerves.

Gino stayed put, eyes fixed on Phil. His mouth worked, but nothing came out. I shot him a glare. He flinched, then hurried up the stairs. I liked that he was scared. Fear made men predictable. It kept them careful. Kept them breathing.

The line crackled to life. "Yeah?"

"It's Victor. Get a crew to Phil's butcher shop. Fast. Some meat got left hanging, and it's starting to stink."

A pause. "Got it, Boss."

I hung up and wiped down the receiver with a rag from the desk. I scanned the room one last time. The fluorescent light washed everything in a sickly green, like an old silver plate photograph gone bad.

I flipped through the ledger. Every deal, every payoff, every debt—Phil kept it all neat as a banker. Coded, sure, but it was all there. Everything else in this basement could burn. But not this.

I shoved the ledger and papers inside my coat, their uncomfortable bulk pressing against my ribs. I started up the stairs, each step heavier than the last—like dragging myself out of a grave. Phil's grave.

Then it hit me.

Barbara.

If someone could get to Phil, they could get to her. To Frankie. My gut twisted. I ran through a dozen scenarios, each blacker than the last. They were more vulnerable than any of us, more exposed. And she was the one person I couldn't afford to lose.

A jolt of fear punched me square in the chest, hard and mean. Not the slow-burn kind I could manage—this was raw, primal, out of control. I bolted up the stairs into the shop where Gino hovered near the door, wringing his hands like a schoolboy caught cheating.

"Boss—"

"Why the hell aren't you in the car?" I grabbed his collar and hauled him outside, shoving him toward the curb. "We need to go. Now!"

Gino scrambled, flinging the door open for me before diving behind the wheel. The engine roared to life, spitting smoke and fury. For half a second, I almost believed we'd make it.

"Where to, Boss?" Gino asked, voice still shaking.

"Barbara's. And step on it."

The car lurched forward, tires squealing against concrete. Los Angeles streaked past in a smear of neon and asphalt, the night burning bright and cold around us. Gino tore through traffic like a man with nothing to lose. Horns blared and voices cursed, the city's hum thick with heat and anger.

Gino took a sharp left, slamming me into the door. I gritted my teeth and shot him a look that should've killed, but I kept my mouth shut. He looked like a haunted man, and maybe he was. Fear spreads like an infection.

Phil should've seen this coming. Hell, I should've seen it. We were slipping. We got soft. No—*I* got soft.

My thoughts raced ahead of us, already at Barbara's doorstep. Would they be waiting for me? Using her and Frankie as bait? How had it all gone to hell so fast?

God, if you're up there—and if you give a damn—let me get to her in time. Don't take her from me. Please...

38

BARBARA

"He's already sound asleep, Babs. Best to let him stay here for the night." Edith covered Frankie with an extra blanket. "Wake him now, and he'll be cranky as a bear. You'll never get him back down."

I nodded. "I suppose I could use some time alone with my thoughts."

"I'll take him to school in the morning. Or maybe I'll keep him here and spoil him. I haven't decided yet."

"Take him for the week if you like," I said, only half kidding. "Thank you, Edie. For everything."

Edith walked me to the door and kissed my cheek. "You know I'm always here for you, Babs. Always. Call me when you get home."

I stepped out into the night. The sky was a murky, starless void, and the streetlights threw long shadows across Edith's well-manicured lawn. Crickets chirped in an unsteady chorus, their rhythm broken by the occasional bark of a distant dog.

I slid into my new DeSoto and started the engine. The dashboard cast a faint ghostly glow as the engine rumbled to life.

Leaving Frankie was never easy, but tonight, I felt a guilty relief. I needed the space to sort through the bombshell Edith had dropped—that she was my real mother, that our "parents" had adopted me to save her from scandal. It made a twisted kind of sense—why she'd always favored me, watched over me like a hawk, treated me more like a daughter than a kid sister. But knowing the truth was something different altogether. It changed everything, and yet nothing.

I made the drive from Edith's on autopilot. It was a miracle I got home because I had no recollection of the drive—I was too absorbed in my thoughts. Maybe I ran a red light. Maybe I didn't. Either way, I made it.

I exited my car into the thick night air, heavy as a wool coat in the rain. As I ambled to the front door, my keys jingled softly in my hand, the sound oddly loud in the hush that had settled over the street.

Something made me pause—an instinctual twinge at the base of my skull. I glanced around the front yard, then over to the neighbor's house across the street. All was still, yet a prickle of unease ran down my spine. I shrugged it off and turned the key in the lock.

The door swung open with a soft creak, and I stepped into the foyer. I set my purse down on the hall table and closed the door behind me. The oppressive night stayed on the other side, but it still felt like something had followed me in. I flicked on the foyer light, its soft glow bleeding into the adjacent living room.

A scent hit me. Cologne—thick, intrusive, clinging to the air like oil. Not Victor's.

"Evening, doll face."

My heart seized.

A hulking figure was sprawled in the armchair, one leg slung over the other like he owned the place. The heavy-lidded eyes, thick neck, receding hairline, and coarse features were unmistakable, even in the low light. I knew that grin, and it sent a cold spike of fear through my core.

"Mr. Kowalski." My voice was steady and composed, though my pulse pounded in my throat.

"Flattered you remember me, doll. Thought maybe you weren't coming home."

Every muscle in my body tensed, ready to bolt. But where? "What are you doing here?" I asked carefully. The snub-nose pistol Victor had given me was hidden on top of the liquor cabinet in the living room. But Kowalski was planted right there, eyes locked on me.

"Social call," he said, his voice slick with false charm. "Wanted to catch up with an old friend."

A cold ripple of panic spread through me, but I steadied my breath. I needed to stay calm and composed. I was alone in this —no Superman to swoop in and save the day.

"I don't recall us being friends," I said, moving cautiously toward the living room. The plush carpet muted my steps, but my heart pounded loudly enough to fill the silence. I switched on the lamp. "You still haven't answered my question. What do you want?"

Kowalski grinned wider, flashing teeth stained by years of cigars and cheap whiskey. "Straight to the point. I like that." He uncrossed his legs and leaned forward, resting his elbows on his knees. "It's simple, doll face. I want to know where your man is."

"Which man would that be?" Each word felt like walking barefoot over broken glass.

"The dago," he said, his tone tight.

I stiffened, appalled by the slur but careful not to show it. "I'm sure I don't know who you mean. And kindly leave words like that outside my home."

I glanced toward the liquor cabinet, calculating the distance. Even if I made it there, what then?

He lifted his hands in a lazy shrug. "Didn't mean to ruffle your delicate feathers." He dropped his hands and his grin. "Where's Cardello?"

"Mr. Cardello?" I repeated, feigning confusion. "I haven't worked for him in months. Why on earth would I know where he is?"

Kowalski stood, rolling his thick neck with a slow crack. He took a few slow but deliberate steps toward me, and I instinctively backed away. "You're cute when you play dumb," he said. "But we both know you're not that stupid."

"I'm not playing," I said, my voice smaller than I intended.

He stopped just close enough for his shadow to swallow mine, his smirk curling at the edges. This close, his cologne was overpowering, like he had bathed in it. He was all chest and shoulders, his belly pressing against his belt like an afterthought. Even though he was slightly shorter than me, he could overpower me in an instant if he wanted to.

"Try again, doll face." His voice grated like gravel underfoot.

I swallowed against the dryness in my throat, the tang of fear sharp on my tongue. "You have to believe me," I said, desperation creeping into my tone. "I don't know where he is. He doesn't tell me anything."

"Call him," Kowalski said, low and firm. "Tell him to come see you."

I shook my head. "If I don't know where he is, how can I—"

"Humor me," he growled.

Slowly, I started toward the phone in the foyer. My mind raced ahead of me, grasping for any plan that might save me—save us all. Could I scream? The neighbors were elderly—their hearing weak, their steps slower. Even if they called the police, would help arrive in time?

The plush carpet melted into polished hardwood as I reached the telephone table. I coiled the cord in my grip like a waiting snake.

"Go on," Kowalski said. He had drifted closer, standing at the threshold between the living room and foyer. His hands rested in his pockets, but his posture was anything but relaxed.

I lifted the receiver to my ear, hesitated, then dialed Victor's downtown apartment. The line rang. No answer. A cool wave of relief swept through me, dampening the feverish panic clawing at my mind. If Victor didn't answer, he was safe—for now. But a hollow ache followed quickly on its heels. I needed Victor's strength, his certainty. I needed him to tell me what to do.

I set the receiver back in its cradle and turned to Kowalski. "There's no answer. He's not home."

Kowalski's eyes narrowed, and he took a deliberate step forward. The hardwood groaned beneath his weight, the sound slicing through the stillness of the house. "Try again," he said, his voice sharp as a blade. "And call every place he might be."

My hand hovered over the phone, fingers itching with the impulse to grab the receiver and hurl it at him. A childish, futile instinct. I was trapped in my own home by a man with nothing to lose.

I dialed the office. No answer. My pulse thrummed in my throat as I tried the Malibu house. Nothing. Only the hollow, ringing silence of unanswered calls.

Kowalski shrugged. "No rush. I'm more than happy to wait him out. He'll turn up sooner or later." He cocked his head, watching me like a cat toying with a wounded bird. "In the meantime, why don't you get me that cup of coffee you stiffed me on when we first met?"

My mind flashed back to that encounter in Victor's office. The filth—moral or otherwise—rolling off him was just as pungent now as it had been then. "If it's coffee you're after, there's a perfectly good diner down the street," I said, hoping against hope that he'd take the hint and leave.

"Cute," he drawled, stepping closer. "But I think I'll stay put. Nice place you've got here. All alone…?"

A slow chill coiled in my stomach. There was no way out. I had to play along, buy time. "I'll put on a pot," I said, turning toward the kitchen.

Kowalski didn't follow, but his presence pressed against me like a shadow. Every move took a calculated effort not to rush—anything to mask the sheer terror clawing at my ribs.

I switched on the kitchen light. The percolator sat waiting on the stove, as unbothered as ever. I pried open a tin of coffee, inhaling the rich, earthy aroma. For a fleeting moment, it almost felt like any other evening—until reality slithered back in.

The slow thud of footsteps on hardwood made me freeze. Kowalski lounged in the doorway, one shoulder pressed against the frame. "Funny," he mused, "I always wondered what a classy dame like you saw in a thug like Cardello."

I measured out the coffee, forcing my hands to stay steady. "It's just a job," I said. "Or it was."

He chuckled, low and thick, like he had gravel in his throat. "Sure. Just a job." He let the silence spool out, long enough to make my skin prickle.

I filled the percolator with water and set it back on the stove. "It'll take a few minutes," I said, gaze fixed on the burner— anywhere but him.

"So tell me, sweetheart, how much stuff did he have to buy you before you warmed his bed? Or is that how you got promoted from the steno pool?"

I gripped the edge of the counter, imagining it was his thick neck. My chest constricted. "You have a vivid imagination," I said, my voice taut as a piano wire.

Kowalski pushed off the doorframe and prowled into the kitchen. "It's not imagination, sweetheart. Just the way things work. Guys like Cardello, they take what they want. And girls like you—"

"Get out," I said, cutting him off. "Get out now before I call the police."

He barked a short laugh. "Ah, don't be like that, doll face." He took a step toward me, leading with his belly, his eyes predatory. "We're just getting to know each other." He reached out a hand to cup my cheek.

I sidestepped out of his reach and moved to the other side of the kitchen, wiping at imaginary spills on the spotless counter, feigning distraction.

"Mmm, feisty. I like that in a broad."

My gaze swept the kitchen, cataloging possibilities—the cast-iron skillet hanging over the island, the butcher knives resting in their wooden block near the sink, the weighty glass jars of flour and sugar, the percolator bubbling with scalding coffee. I focused on the percolator's glass knob as if it were a crystal ball, as if it might hold an omen—a glimpse of whether I'd survive this night.

It burbled and hissed, and the rich scent of coffee curled through the kitchen. I watched the steam rise, willing it to burn away the suffocating weight in the air. My hands were steadier now, my mind settling into the cold reality that I had no choice but to serve this brute before me.

I pulled a ceramic mug from the cabinet and poured the coffee into it in an unhurried stream. Turning, I set the mug on the counter in front of Kowalski. He didn't touch it. Didn't even look at it. His eyes stayed on me, his smirk curling at the edges like a bad habit.

"Where's yours?" he asked.

"I don't drink coffee at night," I said. "It keeps me awake."

Kowalski's smirk darkened into something more sinister. "You think I'm stupid? Poison is a woman's trick. I'm not that easy to put down."

My pulse stuttered. Did he really think I'd try to kill him? The idea was laughable—I hadn't even worked up the nerve to reach for a skillet, let alone lace his coffee like some femme fatale in a dime-store novel.

The telephone in the foyer shrilled—a sudden, jarring slash through the tension-filled silence. I flinched, my pulse spiking.

Kowalski's gaze flicked toward the foyer, then back to me, unreadable. "Better get that."

I let it ring twice, my eyes locked with Kowalski's, neither of us moving. On the third ring, I turned toward the foyer, each step deliberate, my mind a riot of hope and fear. My hand hesitated on the receiver before I lifted it and cleared my throat.

"Hello?"

"Babs? It's Edith." Relief flickered, but it was fleeting. "You didn't call when you got home. I was starting to worry."

"Edie," I said, smoothing the unease from my voice. "I just got in. It's been…a long evening."

I risked a glance at Kowalski. He had drifted to the edge of the living room, one thick hand hovering near a framed photograph of Frankie. My stomach turned cold.

"Barbara," Edith's voice sharpened. "Something's wrong. I can hear it."

"I just got caught up with a few things in the kitchen," I said, forcing lightness into my tone. "I'm sorry I forgot to call."

Kowalski gestured for me to wrap it up.

"Just stay on the line a moment," Edith insisted.

"Look, I have to go. I'll call you in the morning."

"Babs, wait—"

I set the receiver down, cutting off whatever protest Edith had poised on her lips. The ache in my chest was sharp, desperate. I wanted to tell her, to let her know the danger I was in. But I couldn't. She would try to intervene, and that would only make things worse. I needed her to stay safe. To keep my son safe.

Kowalski sprawled in my favorite armchair, legs splayed wide, owning the space like he'd paid for it.

"Who was that?"

"My…sister."

He examined his fingernails, bored. "She sounds nice. The kind of gal who'd do anything for family."

A chill curled through me. "Nice enough."

The low growl of an engine made us both turn toward the front of the house. Headlights slashed across the walls, casting long, jagged shadows. My heart slammed against my ribs.

The engine cut. A car door slammed, cracking through the silence like a gunshot.

I lunged for the window, but Kowalski was quicker than he

looked. He clamped thick fingers around my wrist and yanked me back as he pulled a revolver from his waistband.

"Sit tight," he growled, jerking the gun toward the chair beside the telephone table. My legs folded before my mind caught up.

Kowalski moved to the window, peeking through the drawn curtains. "Looks like your white knight is here," he said, his voice tinged with something like glee. He turned to me, the gun now pointed squarely at my chest. "Don't get any crackpot ideas, or you're both finished."

Kowalski moved to the hinged side of the door, pressing himself into the shadows where he'd be invisible until it was too late. The revolver in his hand looked absurdly small against his meaty paw, but I knew it was lethal enough. My breath turned shallow as I imagined Victor stepping blindly into the lion's den.

The sound of a key entering the lock sent my heart into a frenzy. The door creaked open, and the sticky night air rushed into the foyer. Victor stood silhouetted by the porch light, revolver in hand. He scanned the room, and his eyes locked with mine. Relief washed over his features, but it shattered the instant he took in my rigid posture and the fear etched on my face.

"Barbara," he breathed, starting toward me.

"Victor—" I began, but it was too late.

Kowalski lunged from his hiding spot, swinging the revolver at Victor's head. Victor ducked and twisted just in time to dodge the blow, but Kowalski's momentum carried him forward, sending both men crashing into the wall. The force of their collision rocked the entire house. Plaster cracked and rained down like snow.

Victor recovered first, spinning on his heel, revolver trained on Kowalski. A deafening crack split the air as Victor squeezed the trigger, too quickly to be sure. A bullet buried itself in the wall, inches from Kowalski's head.

I screamed, hands flying to my mouth as the shot's

reverberations rang in my ears and sent my head spinning with terror and adrenaline.

Kowalski roared and swatted Victor's hand, knocking the gun from his grip and sending it skittering across the hardwood floor and into the living room. He swung a thick, meaty fist at Victor's jaw, but Victor sidestepped, fluid and calculated, delivering a sharp elbow to Kowalski's ribs. The brute grunted in pain but didn't buckle.

"You think you're tough, Cardello?" Kowalski spat through clenched teeth, his face beet red, eyes bulging with fury. He grabbed Victor by the lapels of his suit and slammed him against the wall again, the impact leaving a man-shaped dent in the plaster. Victor's head lolled for a moment, dazed, as his body hung limp.

"Victor!" I cried out, voice raw with panic. I jumped to my feet, hands trembling as I searched for anything to help.

"Shut up!" Kowalski snarled, his beady eyes flicking toward me for a split second. The menacing grin on his face widened, grotesque and gleeful. He was enjoying this.

Kowalski jammed the barrel of his revolver under Victor's chin. The cold steel bit into his skin, and Victor's neck tensed as he tried to hold himself still, swallowing harshly. My heart seized, the shifting, precarious balance of power beyond overwhelming. The room fell deathly quiet—the kind of silence that hovers just before a storm breaks.

I had to do something.

If I stayed frozen—if I obeyed—we were finished. My eyes darted to Victor's gun on the floor—just a few feet away from where I stood. It might as well have been a mile.

Still, with every ounce of backbone I had, I took a slow, measured step toward the gun. Then another. Kowalski, too absorbed in taunting Victor, failed to notice—until he did.

"Barbara, no!" Victor shouted as Kowalski dropped him and lunged at me.

His thick arm caught me across the chest, sending me

sprawling backward. Pain exploded in my shoulder as I collided with the doorframe. He snatched up Victor's gun from the floor and wheeled around, a grotesque grin splitting his coarse features. He held two guns now, one in each of his beefy hands, and both barrels were aimed with deadly intent—one at Victor, who staggered to his feet, clutching his neck, and the other at me, where I pressed myself against the wall.

"Sit tight, doll face," Kowalski sneered. "Wouldn't want you to catch a stray."

Terror surged through me like ice water in my veins. This was it.

Victor wiped a smear of blood from his lips, his eyes never leaving the twin barrels Kowalski wielded.

"I'm the one you want, Kowalski," Victor said, his voice rough but measured. "This is between you and me. Let her go."

"No, I don't think I will," Kowalski said, his grin widening to a deranged crescent—dangerous and feral. "Where's the fun in that? I'm in the business of having fun tonight. Your pal Phil and I already had a grand old time. But I think you know that. Or, at least, I hope you do."

Victor's eyes flickered—a subtle shift, but I caught it. He was calculating. "Phil had it coming," he said, his tone dismissive. "He was a thief and a rat." Victor shrugged and took a casual step forward. "You actually did me a favor."

Kowalski's laugh was a guttural bark, like a dog with a bone lodged in its throat. "Is that right? Maybe I'll do you another favor, Cardello, and take care of your little lady here next." He jerked his chin in my direction, swinging the gun barrel with it. "Gals like that make a man weak, and she looks like a real liability."

The threat hit me like a jolt of cold electricity. I tried to make myself smaller—to fold into the wall and disappear—but my eyes stayed locked on Victor. He had to have a plan. He always had a plan.

Victor's jaw tightened, his voice cold and measured. "Leave

her out of this." He took a cautious step forward. "I clearly misjudged you." Another step. His gaze flicked briefly to me, then darted to the telephone table beside me. "I thought you were a bigger man." Another step. Victor's lips curled into a half-smile, steel in his gaze. "I didn't realize you needed to hide behind a broad."

Kowalski's jowls quivered, eyes burning with rage. Like an arrow, Victor lunged at him. I dove under the telephone table and instinctively covered my head with my hands. Bodies crashed together as the two men grappled like titans.

I peeked out from my makeshift shelter. Fear gripped me, but I couldn't look away. The two men rolled and heaved, grunting and straining, each struggling for dominance. Kowalski pinned Victor with his massive frame, but Victor's wiry strength and agility gave him the upper hand. He twisted free and delivered a sharp knee to Kowalski's stomach, knocking the wind out of him.

Victor wrenched one gun free and twisted Kowalski's arm, using the leverage to disarm him of the second. Both weapons clattered to the floor, and for a heartbeat, time froze.

Then, with a swift kick, Victor sent one of the revolvers skidding across the floor toward me. I scrambled out from under the table and seized it with surprisingly steady hands. The cold metal was heavy, solid, powerful. I stood and pointed it at Kowalski as his chest heaved like a bellows.

Victor leveled the remaining revolver at Kowalski's head. His command cut like an unforgiving blade. "On your knees."

Kowalski hesitated, his eyes darting between Victor and me. His nostrils flared, breath coming short. Then, with a reluctant exhale, he sank to the ground. His face contorted with rage, but his bottom lip trembled—an unconscious betrayal of the fear he was desperately trying to swallow. The balance of power had shifted again, but it was unsteady—a glass teetering on the edge of a table.

"Barbara," Victor said, his eyes never leaving Kowalski, "you don't want to see this."

I didn't move.

"Angel," he pleaded. "Please go into the other room."

It was like a bad car crash on the highway—I couldn't pry my eyes away.

Kowalski spat on the floor, his lips curling into a sneer. "You've gone soft, Cardello. The old you would have put a bullet in me already and been done with it."

Victor's grip tightened on the revolver, the veins in his arm rising like angry rivers.

A shadow crossed the room.

Gino stood in the open doorway, pistol by his side.

"Everything okay, Boss?"

Relief crossed Victor's face. "Yeah, we're good."

Gino stepped into the foyer and locked eyes with me. "Why don't you come with me?" he asked, his voice gentler than I expected.

Victor nodded to me, and I reluctantly lowered the gun. I exhaled shakily. The adrenaline was wearing off.

Gino approached me slowly, his steps measured and calm. I flinched as he reached for the gun, but his touch was gentle when he took it from my hands. He turned it over, inspecting it briefly, before he uncocked the hammer and tucked it into his belt. Relief washed over me, cooling the fevered fear gripping my chest.

"Come on," he said, motioning toward the door.

I hesitated, looking back at Victor and Kowalski. Victor's eyes were hard and unreadable, but he gave me a reassuring nod.

Gino slipped an arm around my waist, and I moved with him. The tension in my shoulders finally began to ease. I let out a shaky breath.

He tightened his grip.

The barrel of his pistol pressed against my temple—ice-cold and unyielding.

39
VICTOR

"Gino?"

My voice cut the silence like a blade, but the moment I heard myself speak his name, I knew. Barbara's eyes were wide, her body stiff as stone. Gino's arm was locked around her waist, his pistol pressed to her head.

"Sorry, Mr. Cardello," Gino said, his voice dry as dust. "You know how it is."

Betrayal has a distinct taste—bitter, like scalded coffee.

Kowalski pushed himself up, rubbing his wrists and rolling his shoulders. A sick grin stretched across his face as he cracked his neck. He glanced at the revolver in my hand, bored, like a man eyeing yesterday's newspaper.

"Thanks for getting me out of that scrape, Gino," he said as he shot me a knowing look. "You're *always* so helpful."

My gut twisted. My mind raced, connecting dots I should have seen long before now. The leaked plans. Our compromised safe houses. Phil's murder. And now, Barbara's house.

"How's about you hand over that gun," Kowalski said, taking a casual step toward me. "And we chat man-to-man."

I shifted my stance, weighing my options. None of them were good. "So what now, Gino?" I asked, my voice calm despite the fire burning in my chest. "You think Kowalski will take care of you like I do?"

Gino tightened his grip on Barbara, and she let out a small whimper. My jaw clenched.

"Don't take it personally," Kowalski said, grinning as he grabbed my revolver by the barrel. I let it go. "Business is business. Now, let's talk terms."

"I thought you wanted me dead," I said, stalling for time, gauging my options. They were few and grim.

"Oh, I do," Kowalski said with a lazy shrug. "And you will be. But a dead man can't sign papers."

"Papers?"

He jabbed my chest with the barrel of my own damn revolver. "Yeah, papers. You bled me dry, Cardello. Robbed me blind, and you're going to fix it."

I stole a glance at Barbara. Her fire had dulled, her gaze glassy and distant. She was pulling inward, shutting down. I couldn't let them take her like they had taken Phil. Like they would take me. Or worse…

"Fine." The word tasted like bile. "I'll sign whatever you want. Just let her go."

Kowalski let out a laugh, thick and wet, rattling in his throat like a clogged drain. "You really have gone soft, huh? Pathetic." He turned to Gino. "Hold on to the broad for now. We'll see how cooperative he really is."

Gino dragged Barbara toward the living room, his pistol never wavering from its mark. She walked like a marionette, her limbs moving in mechanical compliance. My gut churned as I watched them disappear around the corner.

"And you"—Kowalski gestured toward the dining room with the revolver—"have business to take care of." His grin stretched the seams of his face, like a mask about to split.

I moved slowly and deliberately, desperately buying time I didn't have. The stiff leather soles of my shoes scuffed the floor with every shuffled step. My eyes flicked to the living room where Barbara sat perched on the edge of the sofa. Poised. Composed—regal, even. A Los Angeles aristocrat to her core, even now. Gino hovered over her, pistol in his sweaty grip.

Bastard.

Papers were neatly fanned out on the dining room table, a fountain pen resting in front like an executioner's blade. Kowalski slid one of the documents toward me, the rustle of paper against wood absurdly gentle given the current situation.

"These are nice and legal. My boys worked real hard making sure everything's in order."

I scanned the page, my eyes catching key phrases—"transfer of ownership," "intellectual property," "full rights." It was worse than I thought. He wasn't just reclaiming the stolen project—he was seizing control of my entire operation.

"You can't be serious," I said with an incredulous scoff.

"As a bullet in the brain." Kowalski shifted his gaze to Barbara, then back to me. He leaned against the wall, chest puffed up like a prizefighter who already knew he'd won. He twirled the revolver in his hand, then pointed it lazily in my direction. "Here's your shot to make things right. You sign these, and maybe I let your lady friend walk away."

I stared at the papers. "What guarantee do I have?"

"Scout's honor."

I sneered. "That's rich, even for you."

Kowalski's grin widened. "Believe what you want, but this deal ain't getting any sweeter." He flicked his wrist back and forth, the revolver making an easy arc through the air like a metronome. "Clock's ticking, Cardello."

My mind scrambled for a way out. A bluff, a stall—anything. Nothing came. I lifted the pen. It was heavy and ice-cold.

I glanced toward the living room. Barbara's eyes locked on mine—hollow, desperate. She shook her head ever so slightly, pleading for me not to give in. But what choice did I have?

"Vic-tor," Kowalski singsonged, drawing out each syllable, his tone dangerously patient. "We're waiting."

I put the pen to the paper and paused, letting the moment stretch like taffy. "I didn't realize we were on first-name terms, *Henry*."

Kowalski's jaw twitched, just a flicker, but enough to know I'd struck a nerve. "You're about to be on dead-man terms if you don't sign the damn papers already."

A deep indigo inkblot bloomed where the pen's nib connected with the page. I squeezed the pen tighter, its weight crushing my hand with the burden of what I was about to do.

"If I sign these, it means nothing without a notary. They're just pieces of paper."

"That ain't your problem, sweetheart. I've got people for the formalities." He leaned in, his breath a mix of cigar smoke and rancid meat. "Less talking, more signing." He tilted the revolver toward Barbara. "Before I lose my patience."

I scrawled the first letters of my name—Victor Car—then hesitated. Just long enough to make them watch. Then, I deliberately botched the rest, twisting the ink into a jagged mess of lines that spelled "Cardeyo." I signed each document with the same subtle error, banking on the slim chance that Kowalski wouldn't notice. I set the pen down gently, like it was a loaded weapon.

"There, it's done."

Kowalski snatched the papers, eyes gleaming like a kid with his first nickel at the candy counter. "See? That wasn't so hard." He stacked them together, tapping the edges straight against the table. "Maybe you are smarter than you look."

I exhaled and slumped in my seat in feigned defeat, masking my relief. The documents were worthless as they stood, but Kowalski's ego was too big for him to suspect a trick. He thought he'd already won. We weren't safe, not by a long shot, but I'd bought some time.

"Hey, doll face," Kowalski called to Barbara. "Make yourself useful and fix us a drink. We've got some celebrating to do."

I tensed, waiting for Barbara to resist, to say something that would set him off. Instead, she rose slowly and walked to the liquor cabinet, her movements fluid but subdued, like a cat conserving its energy.

Kowalski turned back to me, smirking. "Don't get comfortable. You're still a dead man." His voice dripped with condescension. "But since you were so cooperative, I'll let you choose how it goes down."

"Let her go, Kowalski. She's got nothing to do with this."

He shrugged, light as a card trick. "Wish I could. But she's a witness now. You get it." His grin stretched, lazy and cruel. "Now, what's your poison? A bullet? Cement shoes? Or maybe you'd rather swing like a Christmas ornament—just like your pal."

Ice water poured down my spine as my mind shot back to Phil—hooked like butcher's meat, his skin in ribbons.

Kowalski snapped his head toward Barbara. "Where's my drink?" he barked.

Gino nudged Barbara with his elbow. She reluctantly reached up to the top shelf of the liquor cabinet for a glass. My heart pounded in my ears, drowning out rational thought.

"Let her go, and I'll come quietly." My voice cracked. "I'm begging you."

Kowalski let out a dry chuckle. "Begging doesn't suit you, Victor. I'm starting to lose respect."

I forced a nervous laugh. "Respect is the least of my worries." I was out of options and out of time.

Barbara's hand flicked up to the top of the liquor cabinet. For a split second, it looked like she was reaching for another glass. Then her fingers closed around the snub-nose pistol I'd stashed there. My mind screamed at her to stop, to wait—but it was too late. In a single, fluid motion, she wheeled around and fired.

The pistol cracked, splitting the air like lightning.

Gino staggered back, clutching his shoulder, his face a mask of shock and pain. Blood bloomed through his fingers, dark and spreading—like the ink I'd let bleed on the page.

That's my girl.

"Jesus Christ!" Kowalski spun, his eyes wide, disbelief plastered across his face.

He barely had time to process before I slammed into him, clawing for the revolver. He staggered back, his body a dense, unyielding mass. But I didn't stop.

"You son of a bitch!" he roared, voice cracking with fury and fear. He swung at my head, wild and desperate. His stout fist clipped my cheekbone—a white-hot jolt to my skull—but I held on.

With a desperate twist, I wrenched the revolver from his grip. It burned hot in my hand, alive with the tension of the moment. Kowalski's eyes locked on mine, surprise and realization dawning in their beady depths.

I leveled the revolver, dragging the barrel up from his chest to his face—slow, surgical.

"Any last words?" I spat, breathing hard.

Kowalski opened his mouth to speak.

"You know what? I don't care."

The trigger pull was slick and smooth. The gunshot struck like a gavel.

Kowalski's head snapped back, and a crimson bloom unfurled between his eyes. He swayed for a few beats. Then he dropped—boneless, gone.

I stood frozen, the revolver still aimed at the empty space where his head had been. The room was eerily silent, as if the very air were holding its breath. Slowly, reality sank in, cold and heavy. It was over.

"Barbara," I breathed, turning toward her. She still held the pistol in her hand, her eyes fixed on Gino's struggling form. He was still alive. Pain rolled off him in waves as he labored for breath.

I rushed to her and pulled her into my arms. She was stiff as a board, her body unyielding against mine. Her pistol hit the carpet with a soft thump.

"It's all right now," I whispered, running a hand through her silky golden hair. "It's over. You're safe."

She didn't move. Didn't speak. The shock coming off her was a cold front that threatened to freeze us both. I held her tighter, trying to will some warmth into her.

"You were so brave," I murmured, my voice cracking. "I'm sorry, Barbara. For everything. This is all my fault. My stupidity brought this to your door."

Realization hit me like a sucker-punch.

"Where's Frankie?" I asked, panic rising in my throat.

"At Edith's," she answered mechanically.

"Oh, thank God." I let out a shaky breath.

A whimper. Gino. I'd almost forgotten he was still in the land of the living.

I pressed Barbara's head firmly against my chest, shielding her eyes, covering her ears. Like that could keep my world from staining her forever.

Without hesitation, without a word, I raised the revolver and fired.

The bullet struck Gino in the chest with an irrevocable thud. Dead center. His body crumpled like wet paper.

The room deflated, the tension hissing out like a punctured balloon. I holstered my weapon, scooped Barbara to me, and held her tight enough to melt her into me if I could. My knees went weak. My head swam.

"Thank God," I whispered into her hair, savoring the scent of her. "Thank God you're all right."

She was silent, her body still and rigid. Something was off—maybe it was the shock, maybe it was something deeper—but I didn't care. She was here. She was safe. She was mine.

"Pack a bag," I said softly into her ear. "Do you want to go downtown or to Malibu for the night?"

She pulled back just enough for our eyes to meet. But she wasn't seeing me. Just the space behind me, hollow and endless. "Victor, I—"

"You were amazing," I cut her off, not wanting to hear whatever doubt she was about to voice. "So strong, so brave." I stroked her cheek with the back of my hand, then leaned in to kiss her. She didn't resist, but she didn't melt into me either.

"Victor," she started again when I broke the kiss. "We need to—"

"We need to get out of here," I said, taking her by the shoulders. "Barbara, listen. You've been through hell tonight. You need rest. We'll figure everything out tomorrow."

She opened her mouth, but no words came. Whatever she wanted to say was lost, buried somewhere deep. She pressed her lips into a thin line and nodded.

Her eyes were as vacant as a ghost town.

40

BARBARA

August 1951

"Well, that didn't take long," Edith chirped as she slid the newspaper across the table, already folded open to the community announcements.

Evans–Marceau Nuptials Announced

Mr. and Mrs. Claude Marceau of Los Angeles are pleased to announce the marriage of their daughter, Giselle Louise Marceau, to Mr. Frank William Evans, son of Mr. and Mrs. George Evans, also of Los Angeles. The couple exchanged vows in a quiet ceremony on August 22, 1951, in Las Vegas, Nevada, with close family in attendance.

The bride, a recent graduate of St. Catherine's Women's College, was active in the school's French Club and student government. Mr. Evans, a Navy veteran

who served honorably during World War
II, is currently employed as a
successful insurance agent in Los
Angeles.

Following their wedding, the couple
departed for a honeymoon in Hawaii. They
will make their home in Glendale.

Edith plucked a honeydew melon from the fruit basket and sliced it clean through, the blade thudding against the cutting board.

"It's been a week since you got back from Mexico."

"Yes," I answered absently.

"You're a free woman."

"Yes."

"Geez." She waved the knife. "It's easier to find water in the Gobi Desert than to get more than a word out of you."

I shook my head to clear the fog. "Sorry, Edie." I closed the newspaper and set it aside. "At least he was decent enough to wait two whole days before rushing to the altar."

"How gallant." She gathered the melon cubes into a glass bowl and sprinkled sugar on top. "Have you talked to Victor?"

"Nope."

"Are you going to?"

"No...I don't know."

Edith set the bowl in front of me, pulled out a chair, and dropped into it with a sigh. She studied me with that perfect mix of concern and curiosity she'd honed over the years.

"I'll figure it out," I said, though even I didn't believe myself. I stared at the closed newspaper, imagining the words bleeding through like an oil stain—quiet ceremony, successful insurance agent, honeymoon in Hawaii. It all sounded so tidy, so planned. Unlike my life at the moment.

Edith nudged the bowl of sugared melon toward me. I

picked up a melon cube, syrup slick on my fingers. It melted like cotton candy on my tongue, but I tasted nothing.

"You've got a clean slate, you and Frankie," Edith said. "You can make whatever you want of it. Make your life whatever you want it to be. But whatever you do"—she placed her hand on mine—"do it for you."

"What do you mean?"

"You've lived your whole life trying to meet everyone else's expectations. It's time to live on your own terms. Take care of Barbara first."

I pulled my hand away and stood, pacing to the sink. Outside, Edith's garden bloomed, an explosion of color against the green backdrop.

"Edie, I don't even know what my terms are," I admitted, turning back to her. "My whole life has been mapped out by someone else. First Mother and Daddy, then Frank. Now…"

"Now the pen's in your hand," she said, rising and crossing the room. "You can write your own story."

"I appreciate you letting me stay here," I said, shifting the subject. "Just until I figure out where to go."

"You can stay as long as you need," she said with a soft smile. "You know that."

"I don't want to be a burden."

"You? A burden?" She snorted, squeezing my shoulder. "A pain in the ass, sure. But never a burden."

For the first time in weeks, I laughed.

41
VICTOR

"You look like shit, Victor."

Lawrence filled the doorway of my downtown apartment, a silhouette against the dim light from the hallway. He shut the door behind him and took in the wreckage —empty liquor bottles littering the coffee table, overflowing ashtrays, takeout containers stacked like a goddamn monument to bad decisions. The curtains were drawn tight, shutting out the world and casting the room into perpetual twilight.

I slumped deeper into the sofa, nursing a glass of something amber and mean. I'd lost track of what I was drinking. Bourbon, I think. Maybe whiskey. My eyes burned like sandpaper, my head a dead weight on a brittle neck.

"Nice to see you too, Larry," I muttered, gulping more liquor. It stung going down, but I barely noticed. I liked the burn.

He walked over, picked up an empty bottle, and turned it in his hand like he expected it to explain something.

"This isn't like you. Drinking yourself stupid? Letting the place rot?"

I shrugged and stared into what little was left in my glass, hoping it might offer some form of absolution.

Lawrence took a seat across from me, unbuttoning his suit

jacket with the slow, deliberate movements of someone who knew he had work to do. "Victor," he said, softer now but in command. "You won't get her back like this."

I tried to focus on him, my vision swimming in the alcohol haze. "What the hell do you know?" I snapped, but there was no fire behind it. Just a child throwing punches in the dark.

"I know enough." He adjusted his gold-rimmed glasses. "I've seen men go through worse and come out the other side. But they didn't do it by drowning themselves in booze."

I let his words hang in the air—too tired to argue, too broken to care. He was right, of course. Lawrence was always right. That's why I kept him around.

"She won't have me," I said finally, my voice cracking like dry wood. "She's…gone." I closed my eyes and sank back into the sofa cushions. The fabric scratched against my neck like an old dog's paw. "I never thought it would hurt this much," I admitted.

Lawrence leaned back in his chair, crossing his legs with the composure of a man who had all the time in the world. "Love is a funny thing, isn't it?"

His words swirled in my head like whiskey in a glass.

"It can build you up higher than a skyscraper or crush you like a tin can. But it's never an excuse to stop living."

He stood, wandered into the kitchen, and sifted through the wreckage until he found a clean glass. He poured himself a drink from one of the less-empty bottles, letting its aroma rise.

"You need to make a decision," he said, returning to the sofa but not yet sitting. "Are you going to fight for her, or will you let her go?"

I sat up slowly, my body protesting with a chorus of aches and stiff joints. "It's not that simple."

"It never is." He took a measured sip, then carefully set the glass down on the coffee table—too gently for this wreck of a room. "But wallowing in this purgatory won't make it any easier." He raised an eyebrow. "When was the last time you shaved?" He sniffed the air and scrunched his face. "Or showered?"

I rubbed my cheek, the coarse bristle of a week's worth of neglect scratching against my palm. My skin was gritty, and the stink wafting off me was starting to cut through even the numbing fog of alcohol.

Lawrence sat back down, his movements slow and deliberate as he studied me from behind his glasses. "What will it take to get her back, Victor? If that's truly what you want."

"I can't put her in danger again." My voice was hollow, carved out like dead wood. "Or Frankie. I can't let my darkness touch them. I can't live with that."

"That's a tall order, given your chosen line of work."

I finished the last of my drink, letting the empty glass dangle between my fingers. "Maybe it's time to cash out. Cut loose. Start fresh somewhere else." I set the glass down on the coffee table with a definitive click. "Aboveboard and clean."

Lawrence's expression softened—just a fraction. He understood the complexities and weight of a life like mine. "That's music to my ears, Victor. I won't pretend it's not. But you're talking about leaving everything behind. Are you prepared for that?"

"For her? For them? And for my daughter, if I'm ever allowed to see her again?" I met his gaze. "Yes. Yes, I am."

Lawrence swirled his drink, the liquid catching in the lamplight and casting slow, lazy reflections on the walls. "If that's truly your decision, then I'll help you with the legal and business details. We can make it a clean break."

A strange sensation prickled at my chest—hope? Fear? Maybe both. "Thank you, Larry." My voice came out softer than I'd heard in years. "I mean it. You've come to my rescue more times than I can count."

He waved a hand dismissively, but a small smile crept onto his lips. "You pulled me out of the trenches back in France, Victor. It's the least I can do."

The war came rushing back—the mud, the shelling, the faces of men we'd served with. Some living. Most dead. And there we were—two survivors who had forged a brotherhood out of that inferno.

And every other inferno since.

42

BARBARA

Frankie sat on my lap, flipping the pages of a picture book. The full skirt of my favorite blue-and-yellow checkered dress fanned between us like a picnic spread. We sat together atop an old quilt against the trunk of an oak tree in Edith's front yard, soaking in the afternoon sun. The sky stretched out in an endless crystal blue, and the temperature hovered at a perfect seventy-five degrees—a beautiful southern California summer day. A lazy breeze rustled the leaves above, sending playful shadows dancing across Frankie's book.

"Where's the dog?" I asked, tapping the page.

Frankie pointed enthusiastically.

"Good job, my sweet boy! And where's the house?"

His little finger darted to the illustrated home.

"Lovely! What color is the house?"

"Red!"

I kissed the top of his head, inhaling the soft scent of baby shampoo and sunshine. "You're so smart, my darling."

For a moment, I let myself sink into the simplicity of the present—a mother and son, tucked away in a peaceful corner of the world, caught in a moment that should be captured in a photograph and pinned to a memory board. Yet a quiet restlessness nibbled at the edges of my contentment, threatening to unravel it. I pushed the thought away, determined to savor this fleeting peace.

The sharp chime of a bicycle bell shattered the idyllic scene. A teenage boy in a navy-blue courier's uniform was walking his bike up the sidewalk.

"Can I help you?" I called out, shading my eyes with one hand.

"Oh, yes, ma'am." He pulled a letter from his canvas satchel. "I'm looking for a Ms. Barbara Evans."

I scooted Frankie off my lap and stood, smoothing my skirt and patting my hair into place. "That's me."

He handed me the letter. "Here you are, ma'am. Have a nice day."

I held the envelope like a live wire, afraid the wrong touch might set it off. It had no return address, but the only person who sent me letters by private courier was Victor.

The hinge on the front door creaked. I glanced over to see Edith in the doorway, hands in her blue jean pockets.

"Who was that?"

I held up the letter.

"Is it from him?"

"Probably." I ran a finger along the edge of the envelope, half expecting it to cut me. Inside, I imagined words like sparks—a fire that could either warm me or burn me to ash.

Edith stepped onto the porch, her bare feet making soft thuds on the wooden planks. She moved with the easy grace of a woman at home in her own skin. "Are you going to read it?"

I hesitated. "Should I?"

"Oh, no. You're making that decision on your own."

"I'm just not sure I can handle whatever he has to say. An apology, a plea, an explanation—it'll require a response. And I honestly don't know what mine will be."

I turned my attention back to Frankie. He'd lost interest in the picture book in favor of a set of wooden blocks, trying to build a tower on the uneven surface of the quilt. I wanted to join him—to lose myself in something as simple and tactile as stacking blocks. But this letter... I shifted my gaze back to the envelope in my hands, turning it over, looking for answers. It gave me none. I looked helplessly to Edith.

She shrugged, but there was a knowing softness in her eyes. "You don't have to decide anything right this second. That's the beauty of your situation, Barbara." She hardly ever used my full given name. "You can do—or not do—whatever you want. But..."

"But what?"

"You need information to make a decision." She glanced up at the porch awning and recited, "'It's all that's left unsaid upon which tragedies are built.'"

"That's oddly poetic for you."

She chuckled. "I read it somewhere. But it fits." She nodded to the letter. "See what he has to say. You don't have to do anything about it, but at least read it. Unless..."

"Unless what?"

She folded her arms and cocked a hip. "Unless you're scared of what it will make you feel."

I stared at the envelope, its white surface glaring in the sunlight.

"I'm not scared," I said, though even I could hear the thinness of my voice.

"Sure you're not," Edith jabbed, but not unkindly.

A clatter grabbed my attention. Frankie's tower of blocks had toppled, and he was busily reconstructing it with the determination only a toddler could muster. I slipped a finger under the envelope's flap and tore it open, savoring the sound of ripping paper like a match striking, catching, burning.

Sunday, August 26, 1951
11:00 a.m.

Hello, my darling,

I really shouldn't be writing you, but my heart is so heavy this morning, I just can't help myself. There are so many things I want to say to you, and this is the only way.

I'd like to report that getting by on my own is a smashing success, but, darling, I'm afraid it isn't. I've never felt so alone, so entirely out of place. I've given you a part of me that no one else will ever know. Never have I wanted or needed anyone as I need you. I keep reflecting on all the adventures we've had together—all the quiet moments, too—and it seems impossible that it could all be over. I keep hoping something will happen to bring you back to me. I honestly believe we belong together.

I keep wondering what you're doing at this very moment. I can't help but remember our Sunday mornings together, and although they may have seemed rather dull at the time, they feel wonderful now. What I wouldn't give for your homemade pancakes or reading the "funnies" in bed.

Well, at any rate, Frank is out of the picture now, and you're free. I hope it's everything you dreamed it would be. Of one thing I am sure, my dearest—I love you sincerely and desperately, now and always. Just the slightest indication that you want me back will bring me running so quickly you won't know what happened. I belong to you completely, and if you want me, I'll be here... waiting.

Regardless of what's happened, I know we still share a love that will not die, and I promise I'll be here when you find it. You've taken a place in my heart no one can fill. Oh, darling, don't you know how dear you are to me?

These days apart have been a nightmare. As cliché as it sounds, I can neither eat nor sleep for missing you. If all the rest are as bad as these, I don't know what I'll do with myself. It breaks my heart to know that you're alone too. But if that's what you want, sweetheart, I hope it brings you peace.

In the meantime, please let me hear from you and see you once in a while. I need to know how you're doing. This is terribly important for us both! I'm sorry I'm so persistent, but you're still everything to me. If we could have only been a family—night and day—to share everything together... I know it would have worked!

I'm a damn fool for saying it, even more for writing it, but I've decided to sell up and start anew. No more funny business. Living an honest life and making a secure home for you and Frankie *is all that matters now. If you ever need the evidence, there it is… I know you'd never use it against me, but I want you to know that I'm honest in wanting you!!*

I love you, my darling, so much I fear you will never truly know. But I can do no more to prove it to you.

All my love, dearest, always,

−V

PS: I enclosed a letter I received the other day. You might be interested in the offer.

I stared at the letter, Victor's words blurring into a white-hot smear as I blinked back tears. A breeze stirred, rustling the hem of my dress. I closed my eyes and took a deep, sanctifying breath.

"Well?" Edith's voice cut through my daze. I opened my eyes to see her studying me—half curious, half concerned.

"It's…intense," I said, folding the letter slowly, deliberately, as if rushing might cause it to explode. I slipped it back into the envelope, which felt lighter than it should in my trembling hands.

I pulled out the second page, and my breath caught in my throat. It was printed on thick, cream-colored stationery with an elegant letterhead: The Ameline Studio, Dallas, Texas. My eyes skimmed over the typewritten lines, disbelief twisting into shock as I took in the words.

Dear Ms. Evans:

We recently had the pleasure of reviewing the dress design Mr. Victor Cardello submitted on your behalf. We are very impressed with your work and believe it has great potential in the current market. Your design's simplicity and elegance align seamlessly with our brand's aesthetic.

We would love to discuss the possibility of producing your design as part of our upcoming collection. Please contact us at your earliest convenience to arrange a meeting.

Sincerely,

Vivian DuBois
    Creative Director, The Ameline Studio

My hands went numb, and the letter fluttered from my grip as I dropped onto the porch steps. Edith hurried toward me, eyes wide with alarm.

"Babs?" Her voice seemed miles away. "What is it?"

I couldn't speak. I picked up the letter and handed it to her, my fingers reluctant to let go. She snatched it and read quickly. Her lips formed a silent "O" before breaking into a triumphant smile.

"Can you believe this?" She waved the letter like a winning lottery ticket. "This is amazing! You have to go!"

I stared at the wooden planks beneath my feet, tracing their grain with my eyes. A thousand thoughts collided in my head, tangled and spinning like carnival bumper cars.

Could I really go to Dallas? I'd never been that far away from Frankie. And the money—how would I afford the trip? Would they even take me seriously? Victor had submitted my design, and his name carried weight. Not mine. At least, not my married name. Victor had always believed in me more than I believed in myself. But this—this was something else. This was a future I'd never even dared to dream.

Edith plopped down beside me, her exuberance tempered by my silence. "Babs, this is your big break. Don't tell me you're not over the moon."

"I'm…I don't know." Excitement stirred beneath the surface, but I was terrified to acknowledge it. Don't ask me why. "It's just so sudden. So unexpected."

"Opportunity knocks when you least expect it." Then, softer, "You deserve this."

Deserve. The word lodged in my mind like a splinter. Did I really deserve any of it? The success, the recognition, the love that Victor still held for me despite everything?

I thought about the night of Kowalski's ambush—the raw fear in Victor's eyes, the cold realization that I might lose him. That fear had crystallized something in me—something I wasn't ready to face then. Something I maybe still wasn't ready to face now.

A shadow fell across the porch. I looked up at a tall figure walking toward me. My heart knew before my eyes did. Victor moved with his usual swagger, though there was a heaviness in the set of his shoulders. He carried something in his hand, wrapped in brown paper and tied with string.

"Mama!" Frankie shouted, startling me. "It's Mister Victor!" He abandoned his blocks and tore across the yard with the unfettered joy only a child can summon. I bit my lip and glanced at Edith. She raised an eyebrow but said nothing.

Victor paused and knelt to meet Frankie, ruffling his sandy hair. "Hey there, champ," he said, his voice warm but subdued. "I brought you something."

Frankie's eyes widened as Victor looked up at me. For a moment, we held each other's gaze, and a thousand unspoken things passed between us. He waited for my nod. I gave it, and Victor handed over the parcel. Frankie ripped into the brown paper, revealing a gleaming red firetruck, complete with a brass bell and ladder. His face lit up as if it had been plugged into an electric socket.

"A firetruck!" he crowed, bouncing on his heels. "Just like the real ones!"

"Only smaller," Victor said with a tired smile. He stood slowly, his movements deliberate, as if he were conserving energy. I wondered how much sleep he'd been getting.

"What do you say, Frankie?" I prompted.

"Thank you, Mister Victor," Frankie called over his shoulder, already dashing toward the house to show off his new prize to no one in particular. I watched him go, my heart swelling and breaking all at once.

"Victor—" I began, but he held up a hand.

"It's nothing," he said. "I just saw it in a shop window and thought of the boy."

His tie was loose, his collar unbuttoned—minor signs of disarray that, on anyone else, might not mean much. On Victor, they screamed trouble.

"Where's your car?" I asked, only now noticing its absence. Victor's cars were as much a part of him as his mustache and tailored suits.

He shrugged lightly. "Didn't want to disturb you. I left the car down by the park."

Edith stood, swiping at the knees of her blue jeans like there was something to brush away. "I should check on Frankie," she said, casting me a meaningful glance. "And I think I left the kettle on." She lingered for a beat, then slipped inside the house.

I looked at Victor, then away, settling my gaze on the azaleas blooming in the yard. Their vivid pinks and purples seemed almost gaudy in the soft afternoon light. We stood in a silence so thick it muffled the world. The distant hum of a lawnmower, the chirping of birds in the oak trees lining the street—all of it felt muted, like we were underwater.

He took a step closer. Close enough for me to feel the heat of his body, smell the faint mix of cigarette smoke and cologne that clung to him. My pulse quickened despite myself. If he was smoking again, it had to be bad.

Victor broke the silence first. "I wanted to congratulate you," he said, his voice low and rough-edged. "That fashion house offer—it's a big deal."

I studied his face, searching for something—sincerity, perhaps, or hidden motives. His dark eyes were unreadable, but they had an intensity that prickled my skin.

Victor started to speak, but I didn't let him. "Did you mean it?"

He paused, eyes narrowing slightly. "Mean what?"

"In your letter." My voice was tight. "You said you wanted to start over. To live an honest life. Did you mean it?"

Understanding dawned in his eyes. He took a deep breath. "Every word. I want—"

"I need to know," I interrupted again, more forcefully this time. "I love you. God, I love you so much. But the fear...the not knowing if you're going to come home in one piece... I can't go through more nights of terror and bloodshed. Not even one."

The air crackled with tension. A sparrow dipped down from the porch railing, pecked at something on the walkway, and flew off in a burst of flapping wings.

I stepped close to him and lowered my voice to a hushed, urgent whisper. "Victor, I killed a man..."

"No, you didn't." He took my hands into his and peppered my fingertips with soft kisses. "I did. Your hands are clean, angel."

His lips on my fingertips sent a shiver through me, a cruel reminder of how much I craved his touch.

"You saved my life. For that, and for too many reasons to count, I owe you mine."

"Victor…" I pulled my hands away, though it pained me. "I can't live like this. I can't live in fear." I glanced back at the house. "I can't put Frankie in danger."

The hurt in his eyes was almost more than I could bear. "I know," he said softly. "And even if you won't be with me, please know that I still meant what I said. Lawrence is already working on selling everything. And I mean everything."

Victor's words lingered, heavy as gathering storm clouds. I studied his face—the worry carved around his eyes, the way he held himself taut as a drawn bow. He believed what he was saying. Or at least, he needed me to believe it.

"I have more than enough put aside," he continued, his voice gaining a steadiness that bordered on fervent. "I can invest, start something new. Whatever we want."

The scent of azaleas tangled with the lingering traces of Victor's cologne, dizzying and inescapable. A warm breeze brushed my cheek, tugging at loose strands of my hair. I closed my eyes, trying to ground myself against the rush of it all.

"Barbara." His voice was closer now. I opened my eyes to find him watching me, his dark gaze burning into mine. "Throw a dart at the map, and we'll go there. Wherever you want."

I looked down at Victor's hands—strong, capable hands that had built an empire and now promised to tear it down for love. Hands that had held me tenderly one moment and wielded lethal violence the next. I imagined those hands holding a newborn baby, caressing my hair, building a future that wasn't stained with blood. Could it really be possible?

His eyes flicked to the envelope sitting on the porch steps.

"You want to go to Dallas? Let's do it." His voice was infused with a new, fiery energy. "You've made my dreams come true. Let me help you make yours."

My breath caught in my throat. He was winning me over, and he knew it.

"Victor—" I began, but he wasn't done.

"Remember when we dreamed out loud? When the future felt like something we could shape with our own hands?" He took another step closer, and I was almost sure his heartbeat synced with mine. "This is our chance, Barbara. A real chance." He reached out and touched my cheek, featherlight. "Take that chance with me. Please."

The warmth of his hand on my cheek spread through me like a glass of brandy. I placed my hand over his, holding him there, savoring the moment. A thousand reasons to say no battled in my mind, but they were growing weaker, more distant by the second. The thought of a life without him—without this passion, this fire—was a gray, colorless thing.

"Yes," I whispered, so softly I wasn't sure he'd heard me.

He froze, and for a moment, the entire world seemed to hold its breath. "Yes?" His voice was hushed, laced with cautious hope.

I met his gaze. "Let's take the chance."

A radiant smile broke across his face, banishing the shadows that had taken up residence there. Before I could brace myself, he pulled me into his arms and swung me around in dizzying circles. The world blurred into a whirl of color—the bright sky, the gaudy azaleas, the soft greens of the lawn. Laughter bubbled up from somewhere deep within me, light and unburdened.

He slowed and set me gently on my feet but kept his arms around my waist. My head swam, but I didn't care. Victor leaned in and kissed me, his lips soft and passionate against mine. Heat surged through me, pooling deep, turning my knees to silk.

I pulled back, breathless. "The neighbors will see."

"Forget the neighbors." He kissed me again. "Pack a bag. I'm taking you to Vegas."

I stared at him, dazed, as his words sank in. Vegas. The sheer enormity of it all made my heart race. He was serious. It was clear in the way his eyes sparkled with boyish excitement, a restless eagerness that was infectious.

"Victor—" I gasped, but his kiss silenced me—soft at first, then deep and urgent. With that kiss, he spoke of longing, of promises, of a future he was desperate to seize.

"Don't think." His eyes blazed with determination. "Just say yes."

I wrapped my arms around his neck, fingers threading through his hair. "Yes."

43
VICTOR

"Dance with me, Mrs. Cardello." I extended my hand to her, and she took it with the poise of a goddess.

She wore a simple, elegant dress—cream-colored satin that accentuated every delicious curve and shimmered with every step. My heart swelled as the light glinted off the gold band on her finger.

"Blue Velvet" played on the phonograph, low and sultry, as I pulled her onto the balcony. She melted into me, soft and warm. In my arms, she was a perfect fit—pure elegance, pure grace, and purely mine.

Outside, on the penthouse balcony of the Golden Oasis Hotel, the warm desert breeze teased the hem of Barbara's dress. We danced together beneath the canopy of stars. The Las Vegas strip hummed with life, its neon glow casting a soft, colorful wash over her skin, turning her into something ethereal, otherworldly.

"I still can't believe it," she murmured, her voice a soft hum against my chest.

"Believe what?" I dipped my head to catch her gaze.

"That we're here. That we did it." She held up her left hand, admiring her new wedding band. "It all feels like a dream."

I kissed her forehead, breathing in the delicate fragrance of her skin. "If it's a dream, please don't ever wake me up."

The music wove a sultry spell around us as we swayed, lost in each other. Her warmth seeped into me, a soothing balm for the countless wounds and scars I carried—the ones on my body and the ones on my soul.

The record spun to a close, leaving only the soft crackle of the needle on vinyl. We stood in silence, just holding each other, letting the night soak into our bones.

"I love you," I said, and I meant it with every fiber of my being. "You've made me the happiest man alive."

She smiled, sharing that radiant joy that could chase away the darkest shadows.

We walked back inside the suite, and I poured two glasses of champagne. The room was opulent, dripping with the kind of gaudy luxury only Vegas could pull off—crystal chandeliers, plush velvet furniture, gold-trimmed everything.

We met in the center of the room, and I handed Barbara a glass. She lifted hers high, and the chandelier's glow danced through the crystal, scattering light like diamonds.

"To our future," she said, her voice a soft, melodious lilt.

"To us." I clinked my glass gently against hers.

The champagne was crisp and effervescent. Barbara closed her eyes as she took a long, savoring sip. She opened them again, and they were half-lidded and sultry, fixed intently on me.

"What are you thinking?"

"I'm thinking"—she set her glass down on the table and stepped closer, sliding her hands under the lapels of my jacket—"that we have far too many clothes on."

She tugged at my jacket, and I let it slide off my shoulders, catching it in one fluid motion before tossing it onto a nearby chair. Her fingers skimmed my chest through my shirt, sending electric sparks skittering across my skin. Heat radiated from her body as she leaned in, her breath warm against my neck.

I kissed her, our lips crushing with an urgency that had been building all night. I drifted my hands to the small of her back, pulling her closer, eliminating the space between us. She moved with me in a slow, deliberate rhythm, each motion promising what was to come.

With a swift, graceful turn, she spun out of my grasp and strolled toward the bed, her hips swaying with seductive confidence. She looked over her shoulder, her blue eyes blazing with invitation.

I loosened my tie and started after her, unbuttoning my shirt as I went. Perched on the edge of the bed, she played with the straps of her dress, teasing me. I quickened my pace, but just as I reached her, she dashed to the other side of the bed, laughing softly.

I loved this playful side of her—mischief laced with desire. It was a promise that our passion would never fade, that fire and laughter could live side by side. I circled the bed slowly, like a predator stalking its prey. She backed away, eyes alight with a tantalizing mix of apprehension and eagerness.

"Come here," I commanded, my voice low and rough.

"Make me," she challenged, biting her lower lip.

In two swift strides, I was upon her. She tried to dodge, but I caught her wrist and pulled her hard against my chest. Her breath came in quick, shallow bursts as I held her firm, immobilizing her. I kissed her ear, then her neck, tracing a line with my lips that made her shiver.

"Got you," I whispered.

Her resistance melted as she leaned into me. I kissed her with a fierce hunger, devouring her as my hands roamed over her supple curves. The searing heat of her skin bled through the cool fabric of her satin dress. I found the zipper at the back and pulled it down slowly, savoring the sound of cloth giving way. The dress loosened, and I peeled it from her body with reverence, like unwrapping a Christmas present.

She stood before me in nothing but delicate lace. I paused for a moment to drink in the sight of her—her flushed cheeks, her parted lips, the curve of her collarbone, the swell of her breasts. She was a vision of pure desire.

I stripped off my shirt and tie, then unfastened my pants, letting them fall to the floor. My heart pounded in my ears, blood rushing like a river in spring. I stepped closer, the heat between us rising as I unhooked her bra and let it fall away. Her breasts were soft and delicate in my hands, nipples hardened against my palms. The moan that fell from her lips was smooth, enticing.

I lowered my hands to her hips and knelt before her, my breath hot against her stomach. Kissing a trail down her abdomen, I pulled at the waistband of her panties with my teeth, then with my hands, letting them glide down her legs. She stepped out of them, and I rose to kiss her again, fiercely crushing her lips against mine.

In one swift motion, I scooped her up in my arms. She let out a surprised but delighted gasp as I carried her to the bed. With a playful toss, I sent her sprawling onto the plush black-and-gold covers. She laughed, a musical, carefree sound that quickly dissolved into breathless anticipation as I pounced on top of her, pinning her wrists above her head. I was desperate to be inside her. The feel of her naked body beneath mine, the way she writhed in anticipation—it drove me to the brink of madness.

I usually took my time—savoring each kiss, each touch—but tonight was different.

Tonight, I couldn't wait. And neither could she.

I spread her legs with a commanding yet gentle press, my hands sliding down the silken skin of her thighs. Her heat beckoned me, a fiery core that promised to consume us both. I could feel her wetness even before I pressed against her, and it sent a jolt of electric need through my entire body.

"Victor," she breathed, her voice cracking with longing.

With a swift, urgent motion, I thrust into her. A gasp tore from her lips, echoed by a guttural moan from my own throat. She clenched around me, hot and slick, pulling me deeper with each pulse. The sensation was overwhelming, like plunging into molten glass—intense, searing, and exquisitely painful in its pleasure.

I drove into her again and again, each stroke more desperate than the last. She raked her nails down my back, leaving trails of burning fire on my skin, and arched her body to meet my every thrust. Her breath came in ragged, needy gasps. The bed creaked and groaned under our combined weight and force, our colliding bodies filling the opulent suite with a primal symphony.

I gripped her hips and rolled, pulling her on top of me. She straddled my waist, hands resting on my chest as she ground her pelvis against mine, her eyes half-closed in bliss.

She rode me with a frantic fervor, her pace quickening with each passing second. I reached up and cupped her breasts, kneading them gently at first, then harder as her moans climbed the walls.

"Victor," she cried out, her voice high and strained. "I'm—"

Before she could finish, I sat up and wrapped my arms around her, crushing her body against mine. She pressed her lips to my neck, biting and kissing with a desperate hunger.

I held her tight, whispering into her ear, "Ride me, angel. Grind against me until you see stars."

A shiver ran through her, and she pulled back just enough for me to see the fervent gleam in her sapphire eyes. There was no hesitation as she shifted her weight and moved her hips in slow, deliberate circles, each motion sending a wave of burning pleasure coursing through my body. My hands gripped her waist, fingers digging into her flesh as I fought to contain the surge building within me.

She threw her head back, her hair cascading like a golden waterfall, eyes closed in rapture. Her breasts bounced and heaved with each thrust. The sight of her lost in ecstasy was heaven.

I was aware of every inch of her as she took me in deeper

with each roll of her hips. She tightened and pulsed around me in a sinful rhythm that threatened to undo me.

"Victor," she breathed, her voice thready and fragile. Her body tensed like a drawn bow. Each movement of her hips grew sharper, more urgent. I could see it in her face—the way her mouth formed a silent "O," the way her eyes squeezed shut as if to contain the explosion building within her.

A strangled cry tore from her throat as she climaxed, her entire body convulsing with sheer power. She dug her nails into my shoulders, leaving crescent moons of pain that only fueled my desire. She clenched and spasmed around me, pulling me deeper into her with each wave of her release.

I seized her and flipped her onto her back, not giving her a single moment to recover. Her eyes were wide and dazed with pleasure as I spread her legs wide and drove into her with a single, punishing thrust. A high, keening wail burst from her lips, mixing overwhelm and lingering ecstasy.

"That's it," I growled, my voice raw. "Scream for me, baby."

"Yes!" she cried out as I thrust deep, grinding my hips to press every inch inside her. "Oh, God, yes!"

"Louder," I commanded. "I want the whole damn city to hear you."

Her hands gripped the sheets, knuckles white against the black-and-gold fabric. Her breasts swayed with each stroke. Her flushed skin glistened. She craned her neck, tendons standing out like cords, as she gave herself over to the moment.

"Victor!"

Her cry was my undoing. I thrust into her one final time, as deep as I could go, and held her there as my release tore through me like a bullet. My vision blurred, my muscles locked in torturous pleasure. Hot waves of ecstasy surged from my core, shooting out to every nerve ending, leaving me trembling and weak.

I collapsed onto her, my chest heaving against her breasts, my face buried in the crook of her neck. Her skin was warm and soft beneath me, her breathing slow and deep. I rolled to the side, careful not to crush her, but kept an arm draped around her waist.

She was mine. Truly mine.

She turned to face me, eyes glowing with a sated tenderness. For a long moment, we just stared at each other. I traced a finger along the curve of her hip and then up to her ribs, feeling the delicate rise and fall of her breath. She bit her lower lip and closed her eyes, a warm smile blooming at my touch.

"Is it real?" she asked softly. "No more hiding? No more pretending?"

"It's real," I replied, my voice a gentle rumble. "You're mine. I've wanted you to be mine from the first moment I laid eyes on you. So I'm afraid you're stuck with me."

"And now we can have the life we dreamed of." She sighed wistfully. "You saved me, Victor."

I shook my head. "No, angel. You saved yourself. I just held up a mirror so you could see what a strong, amazing woman you are."

"Do you really believe that?"

"I wouldn't say it if I didn't. But you"—I pressed a long kiss to her forehead—"have saved me a thousand times over." I peppered her hair with kisses. "Thank you, my darling, for giving me a fresh start. For believing in me."

She looked up at me, her blue eyes catching the light like sun on the sea.

"Guys like me aren't supposed to end up with girls like you." I exhaled, letting the words settle. "The hero always gets the girl in the movies, and I'm no hero. Not by a long shot. I've never heard a story where the villain gets the girl, but maybe we're writing one right now."

Her lips curved into a soft, mischievous smile. "Heroes are boring." She gently kissed me. "Give me the villain any day."

EPILOGUE

Frank Jr.
July 2012

"I'm so glad you're home, Frank."

My wife, Donna, ambushed me in the entryway before I could even set down my suitcase, wrapping her arms around my waist with an iron grip. Damn, the woman could give a hug.

I pulled Donna close, breathing her in—Giorgio Red perfume and the faint trace of the tobacco she still thought I didn't notice. Being away from her had stretched time unbearably, each day dragging out like an ache. Now, back in the warm cocoon of our home, relief hit me in a crashing wave.

"I'm glad to be home too," I murmured, kissing the top of her auburn head. "It was a long month."

She loosened her grip and looked up at me, her green eyes searching my face. "How are you holding up?"

"Better now," I said, though we both knew that *better* was a relative term. Losing Mom had knocked the stuffing out of me.

Somehow, I always thought she'd outlive us all—she was too stubborn not to.

"Come sit down," Donna said, taking my hand. "You must be exhausted from the flight."

As we walked toward the living room, I asked, "Is Savannah here? I noticed her car out front."

"She's in the kitchen," Donna said, glancing toward the doorway. "She's deep in editing her latest book. So she came over for a change of scenery."

I went back to my abandoned suitcase, unzipped it, and pulled out the wooden box of Mom's mementos.

Donna's eyes narrowed. "What's that?"

I ran a hand over the intricate carvings on the lid. "Something she might be interested in."

I headed to the kitchen, the box cradled in my elbow like a football.

Savannah sat at the table, headphones on, completely absorbed in her laptop screen. Her hair was pulled up in a messy ponytail, and she wore one of those oversized collegiate hooded sweatshirts she loved.

I paused in the doorway, watching her work. She had Mom's delicate features and our family's signature blue eyes. Seeing Savannah was like looking into the past and the future all at once. It gave me a sense of continuity, of life moving forward despite my recent loss.

I cleared my throat softly, not wanting to startle her. She looked up, then yanked off her headphones.

"Dad!" she exclaimed, a broad smile breaking across her face. She popped up and rushed over to me, wrapping me in a tight hug. "I missed you."

"I missed you too, sweetheart." I held her close for a moment before pulling back. "How's the editing going?"

She scrunched her nose—half grimace, half shrug. "Slowly. I've been at it for ages, but I feel like I haven't made a dent."

"You'll get it done," I assured her. "You always do."

We broke from our embrace, and I held up the wooden box. "I thought you might want to see this."

Her eyes widened with curiosity. "What is it?"

"Some of Grandma's old things." I set the box on the table. "Photos, trinkets, keepsakes. Some of them go all the way back to the forties."

Savannah peeked inside, her expression wonderstruck. "Wow. It's like a time capsule." She looked up at me, and for a moment, I saw the little girl who used to hang on every one of her grandmother's stories, the young woman who devoured books with an insatiable hunger.

"Have you started writing your next book yet?" I asked.

She shook her head. "Not yet. I haven't found the right inspiration."

I reached into the box and pulled out the stack of letters from my stepfather, neatly tied with a faded red ribbon. Savannah tracked my hands, her eyes growing wider when she saw what I held.

"These are from your grandfather," I said, handing them to her carefully, as if they were made of glass. "Love letters from their early days."

She took them slowly, almost reverently. "I had no idea these existed."

"Neither did I," I said. "They're...something else. A little 'spicy,' I think you'd call it."

She brushed her fingers over the stack of letters. "Are you sure it's okay if I read them? I don't want to invade their privacy."

I nodded my head. "It's a story worth reading. Truly. I thought you might find some inspiration."

"For what?" she asked, though I was sure she already understood the weight of what she held.

"Your next book."

END NOTES

Frank Jr.

I've always loved the part at the end of the movie where you get a glimpse of where everyone ends up after the curtain falls. I didn't know Mom and Victor's story the way I do now—probably more than I ever wanted to. But I do know what came after.

After eloping in Las Vegas, Victor moved Mom and me to Dallas. We left behind the familiar chaos of Los Angeles for the sunbaked sprawl of North Texas. It turns out that when they eloped, Mom was already pregnant, though neither of them knew at the time (or so I assume). My little brother, Jacob, joined us on Valentine's Day 1952.

Mom flourished, designing couture dresses for Ameline Studio—finally bringing her girlhood dream to life. Victor threw himself into Dallas's real estate scene, investing in up-and-coming areas like Highland Park. His eye for lucrative opportunities paid off handsomely, and he made out extremely well. And he stayed true to his word and kept every bit of his business clean and aboveboard.

Despite their success, they both longed for the familiarity of home—for the palm trees and ocean breezes of Southern California. So, after a few short years, we packed up and returned to Los Angeles, where they planned to spend the rest of their lives. And so they did.

In their empty-nest years, Mom and Victor turned house-flipping into a shared passion. What started as a casual interest quickly became an obsession. They traveled the world, Victor documenting every destination with his camera. Their home became a living gallery—framed snapshots of their adventures, photos of us boys, and, of course, entire walls devoted to Mom. You could hardly see the wallpaper.

They were happily married for fifty-four—almost fifty-five—years until Victor's death at age ninety. Even then, Mom spoke of him as if he were simply on another trip—gone, but never truly absent. She survived him by six years, passing at eighty-six.

Aunt Edith never let go of her wild, flapper, Jazz Age youth. She and Mom remained close, their bond all the stronger for knowing the truth of their kinship. Mom always saw Edith as her big sister, confidante, and best friend—truth be damned. Edith never remarried, always preferring the freedom of the single life. "Men are like buses," she'd say. "There'll be another one along in ten minutes." She lived to the impressive age of ninety-six and was wild right to the very end.

Lawrence—or "Uncle Larry," as I knew him, even though we weren't related—remained Victor's closest friend. Bonded in wartime and true friends for life, they were as close as brothers. Lawrence was a constant presence at our family dinners, offering his dry wit and sage advice. He died in 1968 of lung cancer, which the doctors said was likely a sequelae of gas exposure from the war.

I don't recall ever meeting Victor's ex-wife, Dorothy. But I know she was true to her word and kept Victor's daughter, Margaret, from him. When Margaret came of age, Victor tried to develop a relationship with her, but it never got off the ground. He regretted it for the rest of his life.

My father married his wife, Giselle, before the ink was dry on the divorce from my mother. She was a force to be reckoned with and ran their household like a dictator. And though my father wasn't henpecked per se, it was crystal clear that Giselle wore the pants in that family. She had him at her beck and call, but as far as I could tell, they were happy enough.

Growing up, I spent time with my father—obligatory family functions, birthdays, and the like—but our relationship was always strained. Things got better later in life, but not as much as I'd have liked. He never quite knew how to talk to me, or perhaps he didn't want to. I understand why he resented my mother, but I felt his resentment trickled down to me as well. I'd ask him why, but he died just before Mom did. So I suppose I'll never understand.

Victor was my dad—in every way that mattered.

And as for me?

After college, life and love led me back to Texas—Houston, this time. I met my wife, Donna, on a blind date gone sideways, and a year later, we ran off to the courthouse and made it official. By all logic, we should have been doomed from the start.

But if there was one thing I ever learned from Mom and Victor, it's that love chooses you. It rarely makes sense, and I'm not sure it should.

Donna and I are coming up on our thirty-fifth wedding anniversary, and she is everything to me. Our daughter, Savannah, is my pride and joy, as cliché as that sounds. Even as a child, she was wildly imaginative, and as soon as she could write, she was penning stories. At seven, she wrote her first "book"—a story about two elephants caring for their friends in need. I still have it. She graduated from Rice University with a Master's in Fine Arts a few years back and is now a thriving author. I couldn't be prouder.

When I look at her, I see Mom's creativity, passion, and dazzle. That's why I know she'll understand Mom's story better than anyone else could. That's why the cache of Victor's love letters is safe in her hands. She's got a far better way with words than I ever will, so I know she'll do justice to the tremendous love story that ultimately made us all who we are today.

Will she write it?

I believe she will. She's one of us, after all.

And when she does, I hope you'll read it.

Because some stories are worth getting lost in.

And this story is far from over…

STILL BURNING FOR MORE LETTERS FROM VICTOR?

Some words were too tender.

Too brazen.

Too dangerous to say aloud...

So he wrote them to her.

Victor's letters to Barbara were meant for her eyes only—raw declarations penned in secret, steeped in longing, laced with temptation. But not all of them made it into the book.

Now you can read the ones that didn't.

The bonus collection includes never-before-published letters—more passion, more devotion... and one secret that threatens to upend everything you thought you knew.

Unlock the letters at:

www.NadineTheiss.com/bonusletters

GRATEFUL BEYOND WORDS!

Thank you—*truly*—for joining me on this journey.

Letters From Victor has been a passion project from the very beginning, and I hope you fell for these characters as deeply as I did. Barbara and Victor's story has stayed with me in the best—and most haunting—ways, and I'm honored you chose to spend your time with them.

If you enjoyed the book, I'd be incredibly grateful if you left a review on the site where you purchased it. Reviews help stories like this reach new readers—and they mean the world to authors like me.

Thank you again for reading.

The next adventure? If you enjoy forbidden sparks and dangerously smart leading men... class is about to be in session. But that's all the tea I'll spill for now...

I hope you join me again!

With love and fire,
Nadine

ACKNOWLEDGMENTS

First and foremost—to my husband—you are my rock, my anchor, and my greatest champion (as I endeavor to be yours). Thank you for helping me work through scenes, tighten character arcs, and shape Victor's point of view. (There's a reason Victor notices Barbara's…"curves" as much as he does.) And for all your noir film knowledge and romantic soul (hidden beneath a tough exterior, but you're not fooling anyone)—this story is stronger because of you.

Also, next time you jokingly offer "inspiration" for the acknowledgments section… don't test me. You know I will call you on it. (Love you.)

To Amanda—this book might still be gathering dust if it weren't for you. In one of my random ramblings, I mentioned a cache of old love letters and a long-abandoned manuscript, and you didn't miss a beat: "I'd totally read that," you said. So I finished it. Thank you for that spark.

To Shirley—my dear friend and erstwhile English teacher— you're the one who introduced me to the beauty of a frame story and encouraged me (way back when) to pursue writing seriously. I raise my glass to you for seeing something in me long before I did.

To my brilliant editorial and design teams—thank you for breathing life into this project and turning my chaos into something cohesive and beautiful. And specifically to my editors at HEA Author Services—thank you for indulging my comma feelings, tolerating my adverb phases, gently nudging me when I repeated my favorite words sixty-seven times, and somehow keeping track of what day it was in 1951.

To my incredible beta readers and content reviewers—thank you for your sharp eyes, your thoughtful insights, and your unwavering honesty. You caught the stumbles I didn't see, asked the hard questions, and pushed me to dig deeper. Your feedback helped shape this book into something far more layered, authentic, and emotionally resonant than it could have been alone. And thank you, too, for letting me ramble endlessly—giddy as a schoolgirl—about every scene, subplot, and sultry smirk. I couldn't have done this without you.

To the readers who've joined me on this journey—whether you're new here or have been with me since the beginning—every email, every DM, every word of encouragement means the world. Thank you for reading, for caring, and for letting these stories live on in your hearts.

To the fabulous folks at Grey's Promotions and their stellar ARC team—thank you for enthusiastically supporting me and getting this book out into the world. If you're reading this and you're not in my immediate network, it's likely because of this wonderful team. Thanks for taking a chance on me.

To my friends and family—thank you for the love, support, and laughter that carry me through the wild ride of writing and publishing. Whether you offered caffeine, childcare, unsolicited plot ideas, or just let me ramble about imaginary people as if they were real, you helped keep me grounded and going. I wouldn't be here without you—truly.

To my parents—no longer with us, but still with me every day. You would have been my loudest cheerleaders. Dad would have blushed through the steamy scenes, all while building a killer business plan and perfecting my supply chain. And Mom? She would have proudly handed this book to everyone she met, spice and all—then handed me her notes. I miss you both more than words can say, but somehow, I still feel you beside me.

To my grandfather—PawPaw—thank you for answering all

my random 1950s questions with patience, detail, and humor. Google has nothing on you. Whether it's sage advice, sharp wit, or packaged noodles—your steady presence in my life is a gift I treasure.

And finally—to *J* and *D*—the real-life couple whose love inspired this story—

Thank you for daring to love against the odds.
Thank you for proving that passion can echo across decades.
Thank you for trusting me to carry your fire forward.

THIRSTY FOR MORE?

Check out Nadine's other books!

STARCROSSED NOCTURNE

An ancient vampire running from her tortured past.

A human mystic who sees the light within her.

A forbidden love could destroy them both…

———

UNNAMED

(Written as N. Theiss)

I have no name. No freedom. No escape.

A brutally dark survival story.

———

For the most up-to-date listing of works by Nadine Theiss, visit:

www.nadinetheiss.com/books

ABOUT THE AUTHOR

Nadine Theiss is a U.S. Navy veteran with a sharp pen and a taste for the unexpected. She's been writing since she was twelve —long before she had any idea just how far stories could go. With degrees in Modern Language and Psychology and a passport that's seen some things, she blends rich cultural detail with emotional depth and just the right amount of bite.

Whether she's crafting fierce heroines, bending genre lines, or burning down outdated expectations, Nadine writes with fearless intensity and without apology. She draws inspiration from *The Great Gatsby*, *Memoirs of a Geisha*, and the deep lore of *Star Trek*, *Star Wars*, and *Harry Potter*.

She lives in Charleston, South Carolina, where she's fueled by coffee, chaos, and the occasional trivia night—always chasing the next story that refuses to behave.

———

CONNECT WITH NADINE!

Join the Fan Club for first looks, cover reveals, behind-the-scenes peeks, upcoming events, and first dibs on books and promos.

www.nadinetheiss.com

FOLLOW NADINE ON SOCIAL!

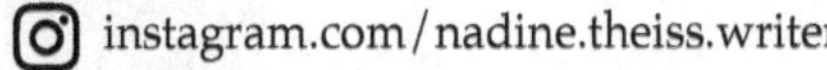 facebook.com/nadine.theiss.writer
instagram.com/nadine.theiss.writer